"Anyone who loves romance must read Sabrina Jeffries!"

—*New York Times* bestselling author Lisa Kleypas

HELLIONS OF HALSTEAD HALL

"Another sparkling series with winning potential"
(*Library Journal*)

from *New York Times* and *USA Today* bestselling author

SABRINA JEFFRIES

Praise for

THE TRUTH ABOUT LORD STONEVILLE

"Jeffries pulls out all the stops with a story combining her hallmark humor, poignancy and sensuality to perfection."

—*Romantic Times*

"The first in a captivating new Regency-set series by the always entertaining Jeffries, this tale has all of the author's signature elements: delectably witty dialogue, subtly named characters, and scorching sexual chemistry between two perfectly matched protagonists."

—*Booklist*

"Lively repartee, fast action, luscious sensuality, and an abundance of humor make the first installment of the Hellions of Halstead Hall essential for libraries."

—*Library Journal*

This title is also available as an eBook

"*The Truth About Lord Stoneville* has the special brand of wit and passion for which Sabrina Jeffries is recognized, where each enthralling scene will thoroughly capture your imagination."

—singletitles.com

"Sabrina Jeffries excels in the historical romance genre, and *The Truth About Lord Stoneville* is no exception. . . . Starts another excellent series of books which will alternatively have you laughing, crying, and running the gamut of emotions. . . . Enjoy Oliver's transformation from unreformed rake to devoted husband, and I guarantee you will have a tear in your eye."

—Romance Reviews Today

More acclaim for Sabrina Jeffries and the "warm, wickedly witty" (*Romantic Times*) novels in her national bestselling series *The School for Heiresses*

WED HIM BEFORE YOU BED HIM

"Includes all the sweet, sexy charm and lively action readers have come to expect, and true love triumphs over all obstacles. . . . Bravo to Jeffries."

—*Library Journal*

"An enchanting story brimming with touchingly sincere emotions and compelling scenarios. . . . An outstanding love story of emotional discoveries and soaring passions, with a delightful touch of humor plus suspense."

—singletitles.com

DON'T BARGAIN WITH THE DEVIL

"The sexual tension crackles across the pages of this witty, deliciously sensual, secret-laden story. . . . Teases readers with hints of the long-awaited final chapter, *Wed Him Before You Bed Him*."

—*Library Journal*

LET SLEEPING ROGUES LIE

"Consummate storyteller Jeffries pens another title in the School for Heiresses series that is destined to captivate readers with its sensuality and wonderfully enchanting plot."

—*Romantic Times* (4 ½ stars)

"Scandal, gossip, greed, and old enmities spice up the pot in this fast-paced sexy romp that bubbles over with Jeffries's trademark humor and spirit. . . . Sparkling dialogue, stirring sexual chemistry, and an engrossing story."

—*Library Journal*

BEWARE A SCOT'S REVENGE

"Irresistible. . . . Larger-than-life characters, sprightly dialogue, and a steamy romance will draw you into this delicious captive/captor tale."

—*Romantic Times* (Top Pick)

"Exceptionally entertaining and splendidly sexy."

—*Booklist*

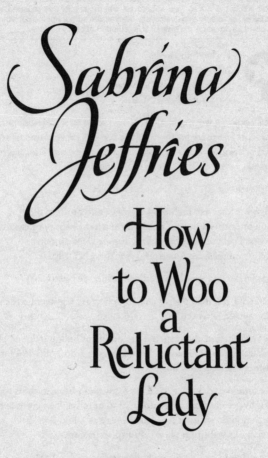

Sabrina Jeffries

How to Woo a Reluctant Lady

POCKET STAR BOOKS

New York   London   Toronto   Sydney

Pocket Star Books
A Division of Simon & Schuster, Inc.
1230 Avenue of the Americas
New York, NY 10020

This book is a work of fiction. Names, characters, places, and incidents either are products of the author's imagination or are used fictitiously. Any resemblance to actual events or locales or persons, living or dead, is entirely coincidental.

First Pocket Star Books paperback edition February 2011

POCKET STAR BOOKS and colophon are registered trademarks of Simon & Schuster, Inc.

For information about special discounts for bulk purchases, please contact Simon & Schuster Special Sales at 1-866-506-1949 or business@simonandschuster.com.

The Simon & Schuster Speakers Bureau can bring authors to your live event. For more information or to book an event contact the Simon & Schuster Speakers Bureau at 1-866-248-3049 or visit our website at www.simonspeakers.com.

Cover design by Lisa Litwack; illustration by Jon Paul; handlettering by Iskra Johnson

Manufactured in the United States of America

10   9   8   7   6

ISBN 978-1-4391-6755-7
ISBN 978-1-4391-6758-8 (ebook)

To the wonderful people who help take care of my autistic son when he's not in school, enabling me to write my books: my wonderful husband, Rene; our longsuffering caregivers Mary, Ben, and Wendell; our wise caseworker, Greta; and our always helpful agency liaison, Melissa. Thanks so much, all of you, for what you do!

Dear Readers,

I do not mean to complain, but I have reached the end of my tether with my eldest granddaughter, Minerva. She insists upon writing her gothic novels under her real name! She does it just to shock, without caring one whit that she is also shocking all her potential suitors.

Oh, I know that she *says* she does not wish to marry, but that is pure poppycock. I see how enviously she watches her newly married brothers when they are not looking. Although she is a trifle opinionated, she would still make some gentleman a good wife . . . and life would never be boring with Minerva.

But does she encourage this? No. Instead she writes about blood and villains and death. Perhaps I should find some dastardly spy to carry her off to a moldering castle. That might actually appeal to the chit, though it could give Gabe and Celia the wrong ideas about marriage.

Minerva's latest scheme is to interview gentlemen as potential husbands, for which purpose she *advertised in a ladies' magazine*! Clearly she only did that to try my hand, but she is in for a surprise. I am not budging in my resolve, no matter how many suitors find their way to our door.

I *am* a bit alarmed, however, that Mr. Giles Masters answered her advertisement. He seems bent on having her . . . and he is the only man I have ever seen her respond to with anything more than indifference. A pity that he is such a rascal, as her brothers have told me countless times.

Then again, my grandsons were thorough rascals until they married. Is it possible that Mr. Masters is cut of the same cloth? I do hope so for Minerva's sake, because she certainly seems fascinated by him. I wonder if he has a moldering castle somewhere. That might just do the trick!

I shall have to monitor this situation very closely, but one way or the other, I mean to see my granddaughter happily married. Even if it ends up being to a rascal!

Yours truly,
Hetty

Prologue

Halstead Hall, Ealing
1806

*T*here were bugs on the boxwood leaves. Mama would be cross with the gardener.

Then tears flooded nine-year-old Minerva's eyes. No, Mama *couldn't* be cross. She was in that horrible casket in the chapel. Next to the one with Papa in it.

Huddled inside the maze, Minerva fought hard not to cry. Someone might hear her, and she couldn't let anyone find her.

A voice drifted through the hedges. "How could the girl disappear so quickly?"

That was Desmond Plumtree, Mama's first cousin.

"This funeral is a travesty," his wife, Bertha, complained from very near her hiding place. "Not that I blame Prudence for shooting the whoring fellow. But to kill herself? Your Aunt Hetty should be grateful that the jury found Pru *non compos mentis.* Otherwise the Crown would be carting off the family's assets this very minute."

Shrinking beneath the hedge, Minerva prayed they didn't come around the corner and see her.

"Well, they couldn't find her anything else," Desmond said. "She clearly *wasn't* in her right mind."

Minerva practically bit her tongue in half to keep from protesting. It had been an accident—an awful accident. Gran had said so.

"I suppose that's why your aunt wants the children at the service," Cousin Bertha said, "to show people she doesn't care what they say about her daughter."

Cousin Desmond snorted. "Actually, Aunt Hetty has some notion that the brats should say good-bye in person. Cursed woman never has a problem with flouting society when it suits her, no matter what it means for the rest of . . ."

As the voices moved away, Minerva scooted out of her hiding place to flee in the opposite direction. Unfortunately, when she darted around the corner of the maze, she ran right into a gentleman. She tried to scurry away, but the man caught her.

"Hold on now, moppet," he cried as he struggled to restrain her. "I'm not going to hurt you. Be still, I say!"

She was on the verge of biting him when she caught sight of who it was—her brothers' eighteen-year-old friend Giles Masters, who'd come for the funeral with his family. Cousin Desmond had wanted to keep the gathering small, on account of the scandal, but Gran had said that the children needed their friends at a time like this.

Perhaps since he wasn't family, Minerva could convince him to help her. "Please let me go!" she begged. "And don't tell anyone I'm here!"

"But everyone is waiting on you so they can start the service."

She dropped her eyes, embarrassed by her cowardice. "I can't go in there. I read what the paper said about . . . about . . . you know." *Mama shooting Papa and then herself.* Her voice rose into hysteria. "I can't bear to see Mama with a hole in her chest and Papa with . . . with . . ." *No face.* The very thought made her tremble again.

"Ah." He squatted down. "You think they'll be lying in the casket exactly as they were found."

She bobbed her head.

"You needn't worry about that, dear girl," he said gently. "Your father's casket is closed, and they've made your mother look pretty again. You won't see the hole in her chest, I swear. There's nothing to fear."

She chewed on her lower lip, not sure if she should believe him. Sometimes her older brothers tried to trick her to get her to behave. And Gran always said Mr. Masters was a devilish scoundrel. "I don't know, Mr. Masters—"

"Giles. We're friends, aren't we?"

"I-I suppose."

"How about this?" he went on. "If you come with me into the chapel, I'll hold your hand for the service. Whenever you get frightened, you can squeeze mine as hard as you like."

Gathering her courage, she gazed into his face. He had kind eyes the color of forget-me-nots. Honest eyes, like Gran's.

She swallowed. "You promise that Mama and Papa won't look like . . . how the paper said?"

"I swear it." He made an *X* over his chest with appropriate solemnity. "Cross my heart and hope to die." Rising, he offered her his hand. "Will you come with me?"

Though her heart pounded in her chest, she let him take her hand. And when he led her into the chapel, she found he hadn't lied. Papa's casket was closed. Though she knew what must lay inside, she pretended that Papa was as he'd always been.

It helped that Mama looked like a sleeping, dressed-up version of herself. But what helped the most was Giles keeping hold of her hand. He clasped it throughout the service, even when Cousin Desmond's bratty son, Ned, snickered. Every time she got scared or sad, she squeezed Giles's hand, and he squeezed back to show that she wasn't alone. Somehow that made everything tolerable. He didn't release her hand until the caskets were in the ground and everyone was walking away.

That was the day she fell in love with Giles Masters.

London
1816

BY HER NINETEENTH birthday, Minerva was still in love. She knew everything about Giles. He hadn't married, hadn't even courted anyone seriously. Like her brothers, he lived a rogue's life. But unlike her brothers, he had a profession—he'd been called to the bar just last year. So surely if he was to rise as a barrister, his rogue's life would have to end soon. Then he'd need a wife.

Why shouldn't it be her? She was pretty enough—everyone said so. She was clever, too, which a man like him would surely appreciate. And he wouldn't snub her for her family's scandalous behavior, like the narrow-minded gentlemen she met in society now that she'd had her come-out. He'd been dealing with a scandal of his own ever since four months ago, when his father had killed himself. She and Giles had that in common.

But as she gazed about at her birthday party guests—none of whom were Giles, though he'd been invited—she felt a stab of disappointment. How could she get him to see her as anything but the younger sister of his friends, when she never saw him?

After the party was over, she went to the garden to soothe

her lowered spirits and overheard her brothers talking as they smoked cigars in the mews.

"The lads told me that the party at Newmarsh's house starts at ten," Oliver said. "I'll meet you two out here around then. It's close enough to walk, thank God, so we won't have to mention it to the servants. You know how they are—they tell Gran everything, and she'll lecture us about going off somewhere on Minerva's birthday."

"Gran's bound to notice us slipping out wearing costumes," Jarret said.

"We'll come out one at a time to stash them in the garden until we can leave. Just be careful not to let Minerva see. No point in hurting her feelings."

She was on the verge of giving them a piece of her mind for going to a party without her on her birthday, when it dawned on her. If they were attending a party with "the lads," then Giles would be there! And since it was a masquerade, she could attend without anyone being the wiser. She knew exactly what to wear, too. She and her younger sister Celia had once come across a stash of Gran's clothes from over thirty years ago—that would be perfect.

At nine, she slipped into the garden shed with fourteen-year-old Celia, who'd promised to help, in exchange for a full account of what Minerva saw at the ball. They fitted her into one of the old-style corsets and two modest panniers. Then she donned the elaborate gown of gold satin that Gran had worn to their parents' wedding.

Giggling the whole time, they stuffed her light brown hair under a powdered wig piled high in white curls. Then they covered her face with a mask and attached a patch to one cheek. The final touch was an old-fashioned blue cameo of Gran's.

"Do I look like Marie Antoinette?" Minerva asked, careful to keep her voice low. Her brothers hadn't made an appearance in the garden yet, but she was taking no chances.

"You look *splendid*," Celia whispered. "And very exotic."

Exotic was Celia's new favorite word, though Minerva suspected that it actually meant "seductive." The bodice *was* cut shamelessly low.

Then again, she *did* want to entice Giles. "Go on now," she said to Celia. "Before they come down."

Celia hurried out. Minerva then had to wait until after her brothers dressed in the gardens and headed off down the mews before she could follow them.

Fortunately lots of people were going the same way, so she merged with the crowd on the street once her brothers had entered the house. Though she didn't have an invitation, it proved oddly easy to get inside. Finding Giles might be difficult, since she had to avoid her brothers, so she bribed the butler to tell her what costume her quarry was wearing.

"Mr. Masters isn't here, love," the servant said with shocking familiarity. "He declined the invitation on account of having to be in the country, seeing to his mother."

She didn't know whether to be glad that he'd not come to her party because of his other engagement, or disappointed that she wouldn't get her chance with him.

"But if you're seeking a protector," the butler went on helpfully, "you ought to aim a bit higher. Mr. Masters is only a second son."

A protector? Why on earth would she be seeking a protector?

That's when she took a closer look at the assembly. In an instant, she realized this was no ordinary masquerade. Her "exotic" costume looked downright angelic compared to those of the other women.

Grecian gowns and Roman togas abounded, with slits in indecent places. There was a milkmaid with a gown cut lower than any real milkmaid would wear, and a woman who wore only feathers in strategic positions. Across the room, her brother Jarret danced with a Maid Marian who was no maid, his hand slipping down her back to rest on her—

Minerva turned away, blood heating her cheeks. Good Lord. This was a Cyprian's Ball. She'd heard of such affairs, where women came to find protectors and men came to enjoy . . . the women. If anyone found her here, it would be disaster!

Before she could escape, a fellow dressed as a French courtier clasped her about the waist and hauled her up against him. "Well, if it isn't the Queen of Queans!"

He laughed at his little jest, and she gaped at him. Had he just called her a *whore*?

To her disgust, he pressed his mouth to her ear and thrust his tongue inside. "Why don't you come upstairs, sweet, so we can play our roles in private?"

Before she could stomp on his foot, she was jerked from him by another fellow, who said, "Bugger off, Lansing. I saw her first." A knight in shining cloth draped an arm about her shoulders with a lascivious grin.

Lansing? Could that be the *Earl* of Lansing? Why, she knew his wife—a sweet young thing, though a trifle plump. He attended the same church as Gran, for pity's sake!

"Come now, Hartley, give over," Lansing said peevishly. "I'm dressed the part."

Hartley must be the highly esteemed Viscount Hartley, whose own wife had a frosty beauty only matched by her frosty manner. Hartley and Lansing were grand friends. And Minerva had always assumed they were decent fellows, too . . . until now.

She was still reeling from the realization of their true characters when Lansing grabbed her arm.

"We could share her," he said without an ounce of conscience. "Done it before."

Share her! As if she would go off willingly to a room with two drunken buffoons.

She wriggled free. "I beg your pardon, but I already have an assignation with Lord Stoneville." Oliver outranked them both, so perhaps that would put them off.

But Hartley just chuckled and flicked his finger toward the far corner of the room. "Stoneville's busy right now, dearie."

Minerva glanced over to find her brother sprawled in a chair, watching a woman dressed as Cleopatra dancing to entice him. He was as bad as Jarret, for pity's sake . . . as bad as these profligate lords.

Very well, she would teach him a lesson—and rid herself of these fools in the process. Planting her hands on her hips, she flashed him an exasperated look. "How dare that little weasel flirt with another woman after giving *me* the pox?"

That did it. Hartley and Lansing couldn't flee her fast enough.

Freed of her pesky admirers, she threaded her way through the crowd, heading for the door. A wicked smile crossed her lips. She hoped word got around about Marie Antoinette's "affliction" and who'd given it to her. It would serve Oliver right for consorting with such awful men.

The other guests were just as dreadful. As she went past kings and paupers, she heard things no maiden should ever hear, spoken in the familiar voices of men she knew. Some were young rascals like her brothers, sowing their wild oats, but several were married men. Good Lord, did all men have Papa's roving eye?

No, not all men. Not Giles. The very fact that he'd chosen to comfort his mother rather than come here proved that he was already mending his rogue's ways.

She finally pushed her way out of the room, then paused in the dark hall to gain her bearings. She didn't want to stumble into any more trouble than she already had.

Suddenly a door at the end of the hall opened and a man dressed as a priest came toward her, carrying a candle. Blood pounding, she melted behind some curtains and prayed he hadn't spotted her. The curtains weren't thick—she could see him too plainly for comfort—but she didn't think he could see her with the candle in his hand.

He paused nearby and cocked his head, as if listening. The light fell full on his profile . . . and on the mole below his ear.

She swallowed a gasp. She knew that profile only too well; she'd memorized every line of it. Giles *was* here. But what was he doing sneaking down the hall?

When he hurried into a nearby room, it came to her. He must be having an assignation with a tart! Curse him to hell, how could he? He was as bad as her brothers!

Unless she'd been mistaken. After all, the butler had *said* he wasn't in attendance.

She slid out from behind the curtains. How could she leave without knowing for sure if Giles was here consorting with some doxy? Oh, she couldn't bear it if he was, but she had to know.

Creeping down the hall, she came to the door he'd disappeared through, gathered her courage, and slipped inside. The man she'd followed was half-turned away from the door, too intent on rifling the desk to notice her silent entrance. Frozen, she watched as he methodically searched each drawer. If this was Giles, what on earth was he doing?

It certainly *looked* like Giles. He moved with the same subtle grace, the same leashed control, and his hair was the same wavy, walnut brown, from what she could see of it under his wide-brimmed hat. He pulled out a file, opened it, then held its contents closer to the candle. Cursing, he removed his mask to examine the papers better.

Her heart hammered in her chest. It *was* Giles. What was he up to? And why?

After thumbing through everything in the file, he shoved the entire thing under his priest's robes, then quickly turned, and spotted her. Without missing a beat, he pasted a charming smile to his lips and casually slid his mask back into place. "I believe you're lost, madam. The party is in the ballroom."

She should have played dumb, but she just couldn't. "If I'm lost, so are you, Giles Masters."

He sucked in a breath. In a flash he was across the room, lifting the mask from her face. "Minerva? What the hell—"

"I'm the one who ought to be asking questions. What are you stealing? Why are you here? I thought you were in the country with your mother."

His eyes glittered beneath the mask. "As far as anyone is concerned, I am." He scanned her with a critical eye. "And how did you get an invitation to a party thrown by the likes of Newmarsh, anyway?"

When she fumbled for an explanation, he shook his head. "You snuck in, didn't you? And it was just my rotten luck that you found *me.*"

That really hurt. "I wasn't trying to find you," she lied. "I merely came here on a lark after I heard my brothers talking about it. I happened to see you, and—"

"Your curiosity got the better of your good sense." He gripped both her arms, as if to shake her. "Bloody little fool—

what if I'd been some unscrupulous fellow who might stick a knife between your ribs for your meddling?"

"How do I know you aren't?" she snapped, annoyed at being called a fool. "You still haven't said why you're stealing."

"It's none of your concern, Miss Nosy Britches."

"Oh, for goodness sake, don't treat me like a child. I'm not nine anymore."

"Could have fooled me," he muttered as he tugged her mask back into place and propelled her toward the door. "I would leave you to the tender mercies of your brothers, but no one must know I'm here. And I daresay you don't want anyone to know *you're* here, either. So I'm taking you home before you get into more trouble."

She would have given him a blistering retort, except that they were now in the hallway, too near the ballroom to risk it. Besides, at the moment they had the same goal—to escape without being unmasked. But once he got her out of here, she would give him a piece of her mind. Miss Nosy Britches, indeed. And he hadn't even noticed her costume! Was he always going to see her as a little girl?

He led her through a dizzying warren of rooms and halls, which made her realize he'd been here before, probably for one of these parties. Unless he made a habit of stealing things? No, there must be a good explanation for that.

But he gave her no chance to ask. As soon as he got them outside and into the mews where they wouldn't be seen, he tore off his mask. "Who the hell are you supposed to be, anyway?"

"Marie Antoinette."

"Good God. Do you realize what could have happened if anyone had recognized you?" With purposeful steps, he hurried her down the lane toward Gran's town house. "It would have been the end of your future. After being discovered at one of Newmarsh's affairs, the scandal would have destroyed your reputation for good. No decent man would marry—"

"What decent man will marry me anyway?" As irritated as he, she jerked off her mask. "My family is mired in scandal, and the only men who've been sniffing around me during my season are fortune hunters and wastrels."

Besides, I want only you.

He shot her a sidelong glance. "If that's true, then you shouldn't be so eager to heap more scandal upon yourself. We both know how society repays those who flout its rules. You should be trying to redeem your family name."

Coming from him, that was infuriating. "Like my brothers are doing?" she said bitterly. "Like you are?" They'd reached the back garden of the Plumtree town house, so she had to get the truth out of him *now.* "Why were you stealing those papers, Giles? What are they for?"

A muscle worked in his jaw as he faced her. "You shouldn't have seen that. And I hope you'll have the good sense to keep quiet about it."

"And what if I don't? What will you do to me?" Her tone thickened with sarcasm. "Stick a knife between my ribs?"

"Very amusing." His eyes turned calculating in the faint moonlight. "But if you tell anyone about my being there, you'll have to reveal that *you* were there, and I daresay that's not something you wish to do. Especially when you're dressed like . . . like . . ."

When his voice trailed off and his eyes dropped to the cameo resting right in the center of her partially bared bosom, she caught her breath. At last he was seeing her as a woman. "Like what?" she asked, her voice as low and seductive as she knew to make it.

His gaze snapped back to hers. "Like some blowsy tart," he said tersely. "You don't want to be caught dressed like that *here.*"

A tart! He thought she looked like a tart? And a blowsy one, at that. "Why not? Because it might destroy my reputation? I doubt it's even possible to make my situation any worse."

"You have a dowry—"

"Which only ensures that the wrong sort of men seek me out." She tipped up her chin. "Besides, you wouldn't ruin my reputation for spite. I know you wouldn't. You're too much a gentleman for that."

He lifted one eyebrow. "And you wouldn't watch me hang for stealing. I know you wouldn't. You're too much a friend for that."

If he was trying to soften her up, he was doing a good job. "Ah, but I could mention it to your brother, the viscount," she pointed out. "I doubt he would approve."

That seemed to give Giles pause. "And I could mention your little adventure to *your* brothers. I know for a fact that they wouldn't approve."

"Go ahead," she bluffed. "I don't care what they think." She crossed her arms over her chest. "So you see, you have only one choice, and that's to tell me the truth."

"I have a better idea." He stepped closer and lowered his voice. "Name your price, Minerva. I don't earn much as a barrister yet, but I can afford to buy your silence."

"Don't be ridiculous." When his lips curved up in a sly smile, she realized he'd only been goading her with his talk of money and prices. "So you absolutely refuse to tell me what you were doing and why."

He shrugged. "I prefer to keep my secrets."

And he knew she would keep them, too, drat him, if he

asked it. But that didn't mean she had to roll over and play dead. "Very well, here's my price. A kiss."

That clearly startled him. "A what?"

"A kiss." Her tone turned sarcastic. "You know, like the ones you and my brothers bestow willy-nilly on every taproom maid, doxy, and opera dancer in your acquaintance. One kiss. To buy my silence." Perhaps *then* he would see her as a woman he could trust, could court . . . could love.

He raked her body with a long, slow glance, rousing warm feelings in places she'd never felt warm before and setting her pulse racing. "I don't think that's a good idea."

"Whyever not?"

"For one thing," he said drily, "your brothers would skin me alive if they heard of it."

"Then let's not tell them." When he just stood there, she added, "It's my nineteenth birthday, and I just had a loathsome experience at a scandalous party where two gentlemen discussed sharing me between them."

At the stormy look that came over his face, she added hastily, "Although I escaped their disgusting advances before they could do anything, I need something nice to help me forget I nearly became a rogue sandwich. And I'm asking you to provide it."

"What makes you think that a kiss from me would be *nice*?" he asked in a rough murmur that sent delicious shivers skittering down her spine.

She fought to sound as worldly as he. "It had better be, if you want me to keep your secrets."

To her surprise, he laughed. "Fine, you infernal minx. I'll meet your price."

He bent forward and pressed his lips to hers in a kiss that was as brief and disappointing as it was chaste.

When he drew back, she scowled. "Perhaps I should have clarified. By 'nice,' I meant 'satisfying.' I didn't mean the sort of kiss you give your grandmother."

He stared at her. Then an unholy light gleamed in his eyes, and without warning, he cupped her head in his hands and took her mouth again. Except this time his kiss was hard, unforgiving, overpowering. He parted her lips with his tongue, then delved inside her mouth over and over, until her head spun and her knees turned to mush.

In one fell swoop, he shattered her girlishly romantic dreams, replacing them with a wild, seething wanting unlike anything she'd ever known.

It shocked her.

It intoxicated her.

Without thinking, she lifted her arms to twine about his neck. He muttered some curse against her lips, then dragged her flush against him so his mouth could explore hers more thoroughly.

His stubbled chin scraped her cheek, and he smelled of candle smoke and brandy, the combination oddly enticing. This was everything she'd dreamed of. And when his hands then swept up her ribs, he made her yearn for more . . . more caresses, more kisses . . . more of *him*.

It was several moments before he drew back to say in a choked voice, "Does that suit your notion of a nice kiss?"

Still reeling from the wonder of his mouth on hers, she gazed up into his handsome face with a dreamy smile. "It was absolutely perfect, Giles."

He blinked. Then a look of pure alarm crossed his face, and he set her roughly from him. "So I've met my obligation?"

Too stunned by that response to do more than nod, she gaped at him, hoping for something to soften the cold word *obligation*.

"Good."

As she watched dumbfounded, he turned to walk away. Then he paused to glance back at her, his eyes now as lazy as his tone was careless. "Do be careful, my dear, next time you decide to act like a doxy. Some men don't take kindly to blackmail. You might find yourself on your back in an alley. And I doubt you'd enjoy playing the tart in truth."

The crude words slapped at her pride. He'd seen their kiss as her playing a doxy? Hadn't he felt the passion sparking between them, the thrill of two souls joining as one? Had he felt *nothing* from the kiss that had changed her forever from a girl into a woman?

Apparently not. He'd thrust his knife deeply enough to pierce her heart.

Somehow she held herself together as he sauntered off down the mews. But once he was out of sight, she burst into tears.

That was the night she fell out of love with Giles Masters.

Chapter One

London
1825

Shortly after dawn, Giles watched from the trees as the Viscount Ravenswood, undersecretary to the Home Office, entered the boathouse on the Serpentine River in Hyde Park. When fifteen minutes had passed and no one else had come along, Giles crossed to the boathouse himself and went inside.

After he and Ravenswood exchanged the usual pleasantries, the viscount said, "I hear you're being considered for a King's Counsel."

Giles tensed. He should have known Ravenswood would find that out. The man had eyes in the back of his head. "So they tell me."

"I suppose that if you're selected, you won't be able to continue your efforts for me."

"King's Counsel is a demanding position," Giles said warily. He hadn't expected to have this conversation quite so soon.

"And a very prestigious one for a barrister. Not to mention highly political. So pretending to be a scapegrace while you gather information for me won't be very convenient anymore."

"Exactly." He searched Ravenswood's face, unable to read his stoic expression. "To be honest, whether they choose me as King's Counsel or not, I've decided to stop my work for you. Things are quieter now, and I doubt I would be—"

"No need to explain, Masters. I'm surprised you continued with it this long. You've served your country well, with little benefit and even less pay, when you could have focused on your more lucrative position as a barrister. I don't blame you for thinking that it's time you consider your own career. You're what, thirty-seven now? Certainly you're old enough to want more out of life than doing this. And I'll support your decision as much as possible."

Giles released a long breath. He'd been dreading this conversation. But he should have known that Ravenswood would remain his friend no matter what.

He and the viscount had first met at Eton. Though the other man was three years older than Giles, they'd forged an unusual friendship, considering that Ravenswood had been sober and industrious and Giles wild and adventurous.

So it was Ravenswood, already being groomed for politics, whom Giles had turned to nine years ago when he'd burned to see justice done. Ravenswood had taken the documents Giles had stolen from Newmarsh and made good use of them. Thus had begun Giles's covert association with the Home Office and its role as keeper of the peace.

It had proved fruitful for them both. From time to time, Giles had passed information on to the undersecretary that the man wouldn't have learned any other way. Men in the stews let all sorts of juicy details slip out around the profligate Giles Masters. After the war, the Home Office had been swamped with cases of fraud, forgery, and even treason, and with different parts of the country on the verge of revolution, it had needed all the help it could get.

Occasionally Giles had actively sought out information, even from fellow noblemen. In return, Ravenswood had given him a reason for living after his father's suicide. A way to make up for the sins of his youth. But he'd been paying for those sins quite a while now.

"I suppose I don't need to tell you that your activities must be kept secret even after you've . . . er . . . retired," Ravenswood cautioned him. "You can never discuss it with anyone, never reveal—"

"I know my duty," Giles broke in.

That was the trouble. It was hard to have a real life when he kept secrets from everyone he knew. He was tired of keeping secrets. Tired of playing the role of hard-living rogue that had suited him once, but didn't anymore. If he stopped his work for the government now, no one would ever be the wiser, and he could start being more himself. People would assume he'd finally grown up. He could put these days of being an informant for the government behind him.

"This will be my last report," Giles said. "Will that leave you in any kind of difficulty?"

"As you might imagine, we'll regret the loss of you. But we'll manage. And as you say, things are quieter now."

"Which is why I don't have much to report." Giles told him of a magistrate he suspected of taking bribes and of a problem he feared was brewing with investments in South American mining companies.

Ravenswood scribbled notes, asking questions where it was pertinent. When Giles paused, he asked, "Is that all?"

"Almost. There's that favor I asked of you last month," Giles said.

"Ah, yes, the one for your friend Jarret Sharpe." Ravenswood thrust his notebook in his coat pocket. "Thus far, none of my other informants have the sort of knowledge concerning Desmond Plumtree that you're looking for. Is it possible that your friend is mistaken in his suspicions?"

Ever since Jarret and Oliver had married, they'd been looking into the deaths of their parents. Jarret had asked Giles for legal advice concerning the matter, and the situation had piqued Giles's interest.

"As far as I can ascertain from Mrs. Plumtree's will," Giles admitted, "Desmond Plumtree had nothing to gain by killing them."

"Yet that answer doesn't satisfy you."

"I can't explain it, but Plumtree has always rubbed me wrong. If I could suspect anyone of murdering the Sharpes, it would be him." And Giles hadn't risen as far as he had in his career as a barrister without paying heed to his instincts.

"Well, I'll let you know if anyone comes across anything pertinent. Sorry I can't be of more help than that." With a sudden twinkle in his eye, Ravenswood reached into his coat and pulled out a newspaper. "On a lighter note, with all your recent interest in the Sharpe family, I couldn't resist bringing you this."

Giles took the paper from him, then cast his friend a quizzical glance. *"The Ladies Magazine?"*

"It's my wife's. Just came out yesterday. She read something to me from it that I thought you'd find amusing. Look at the bottom of page twenty-six."

He flipped through, then sucked in a breath as he realized that it was the first chapter of Minerva's latest gothic novel. He hadn't known it was going to be serialized. "Can I keep this?"

"Certainly. Abby's already done with it." Ravenswood eyed him closely. "Have you ever read her novels?"

Giles went on the alert. "Have *you*?"

"I read what's in there. It was very interesting. There's a character in her book who rather reminds me of you."

"Is there?" he said, trying to sound bored. Damn it all to hell. If even Ravenswood noticed . . .

As soon as he got home, he'd have to read every word.

Unbidden, an image from nine years ago rose in his mind—of the pretty young woman wearing a Marie Antoinette costume with such sweetness, it made his teeth ache to remember it. By the age of nineteen, she'd grown into a classic beauty—bow-shaped lips, thick lashes, high cheekbones. But beyond her looks, there'd been nothing classic about Minerva.

He still couldn't believe the saucy wench had plagued him about what he was doing at Newmarsh's and then had blackmailed him into kissing her. He still couldn't believe what had happened when he'd given her the kind of kiss meant to teach her a lesson about the dangers of tempting a rogue.

Somehow he'd forgotten she was his best friend's sister. That he was a dissipated second son at the beginning of a shaky career, in no condition to take on a sweetheart, much less a wife. Somehow the kiss had become bigger, more dangerous . . . more intoxicating. She'd made him want and yearn and think the unthinkable.

She still did.

A pity that she hated him now. She'd made that perfectly clear in her books, laying him out on the pages in the guise of fiction, skewering him even as she circled ever nearer to his secrets.

He'd first been alerted to the problem at the Valentine's Ball they'd both attended a few months ago. Until then, he'd never read her novels. He'd had enough trouble putting their kiss behind him without having her voice in his head.

But the dance they'd shared had stoked the fire anew. They'd danced around each other in their conversation, layering innuendo upon innuendo until his blood ran hot and her remarks grew sharper, and he'd feared he might be reckless enough to do something foolish. Like whisk her out onto a balcony and kiss her senseless.

After it was over, he'd been left aroused, angry, and confused. Until that night he'd assumed that she'd forgotten about him, that his callous remarks when they'd kissed had squelched anything she might have felt. Discovering that they hadn't had sent him to her books. And that's when he'd discovered what Minerva was up to.

He'd put off doing something about it, hoping that her grandmother's recent demands might keep her too occupied to write anymore.

But here was a new installment. He could no longer ignore the problem of Minerva. What if she started including allusions to his activities that night at Newmarsh's town house? Anyone in the judicial system who connected him to the theft would realize he'd been the one to inform upon Newmarsh and his partner, Sir John Sully. Then it wouldn't take much to connect him to other cases for the Home Office, and those he'd informed upon would set out to ruin him. They'd start by ending his chance of becoming King's Counsel.

"You haven't even reached the pertinent part yet," Ravenswood said, jolting him from his thoughts. "Go to the page I told you."

Giles found it and immediately noticed the two paragraphs in a different font at the bottom. The first was about Lady Minerva's connection to the Sharpe family, something that only she would have the audacity to include. The bloody woman refused to take a pseudonym—it was a bone of contention between her and her grandmother.

But it was the next paragraph that left him staring in shock:

> Dear Readers,
>
> If you wish to read future installments of this book, you must help me with a troublesome domestic situation that has arisen in my life. I suddenly find myself in dire need of a husband, preferably one who possesses a tolerance for authoresses of gothic fiction. To that end, I ask that you send any of your unmarried brothers, cousins, or acquaintances to Halstead Hall on June 20, where I will be conducting interviews for the position of husband. I thank you for your support.
>
> Regards,
>
> Lady Minerva Sharpe

The twentieth of June? That was today, damn it!

"Amusing, isn't it?" Ravenswood said. "My wife laughed for a full ten minutes. What a clever joke."

"Not a joke," Giles retorted. "Her grandmother laid down an ultimatum earlier this year—the Sharpe siblings must all marry or they all lose their inheritance. Knowing Lady Minerva, this is her way of irritating her grandmother."

Ravenswood gaped at him. "You mean the woman is seriously interviewing husbands?"

"I don't know how serious she is, but the interviewing is undoubtedly real."

The chit was mad if she thought this would gain her anything. He could only imagine how Oliver and Jarret would react, not to mention Mrs. Plumtree. The old woman had a spine of steel—she wouldn't tolerate Minerva's nonsense for one moment. She certainly wouldn't change her mind about her plans.

He tucked the magazine under his arm. "I have to go."

"Planning to show up for the interview, are you?" Ravenswood joked.

"It's a thought," he said tersely.

"You and Lady Minerva? That's interesting."

"You have no idea."

An hour later, after he'd read Minerva's first chapter, he was furious. Damn her to hell. She'd gone too far this time.

So she wanted to interview men for a husband, did she? Fine. She was about to have one hell of an interview.

MINERVA PACED THE Chinese drawing room at Halstead Hall, her spirits falling lower by the moment. How was she to get Gran to rescind her ultimatum if no one showed up?

She'd envisioned scores of young fools and fortune hunters clamoring for her attention, overrunning Halstead Hall and making such a to-do in the press that Gran would *have* to give up. Or cut her off completely. And since Minerva refused to believe that Gran would make her siblings suffer for one grandchild's indiscretions, that was the outcome she was hoping for. Then she could find a small cottage somewhere and write what she pleased, free of any husband.

Hard to believe that she'd once considered marriage a good idea. Her parents' marriage had been disastrous. And through the years, she'd seen that men had no respect for the institution.

There'd been the publishers she'd approached to sell her book who'd made colorful suggestions about what she could do to gain their "favor." And the legions of fortune hunters who were never far from her door. Respectable gentlemen wouldn't have her, since she wrote novels under her own name.

Not that she wanted a respectable gentleman anymore—they were the worst. She'd had a few as suitors and she'd even kissed a couple. But as soon as they'd learned what she was really like, they'd run as far and as fast as they could. Men didn't particularly like women who spoke their minds.

Even her brothers were no great endorsement of respectable gentlemen, with their wild living and autocratic behavior toward their sisters. Perhaps Oliver and Jarret had been domesticated a bit, now that they were married, but would it last? And what if it didn't? Their wives would be trapped.

Women were always trapped. Minerva would never forgive Gran for trapping her with the cursed demand that they all marry. And Oliver and Jarret—how dare they betray their siblings by going over to Gran's side? Six months ago, they would have been leading the charge. Now, if they realized what she was up to and why, they would scuttle her plans at once.

Her eyes narrowed on the door. Was that why no gentlemen had shown up? Had her brothers—or Gran—found out that she was being outrageous again?

No, how could they? She'd purposely put her advertisement in *The Ladies Magazine* because it was delivered in the evening and no one in the family read it. Celia was too much a tomboy for such things, Gran only read the *Times,* her brothers wouldn't be caught dead even opening the thing, and—

Their wives. Drat it all. They had wives now. And while Jarret's wife, Annabel, didn't seem the sort to read a lady's magazine, Oliver's wife, Maria, was an avid supporter of

Minerva's books. She wouldn't have missed the first installment of the latest one.

Minerva cursed under her breath as she headed for the door. How could she have forgotten about Maria? So help her, if Maria had done something to—

A man entered the room. But he wasn't one of her brothers, and he certainly wasn't anyone who'd come to be interviewed.

He was the last, but not the least, of her reasons for not marrying. Giles Masters, her weakness . . . and the focus of a most unhealthy obsession. What a pity that she still found him more devastatingly attractive than any other man, even after all these years. And far more interesting.

Not that she would ever let *him* know it. "Good morning, Mr. Masters," she said in her frostiest voice.

"Same to you, my lady." He dragged his gaze down her person in a roguish glance. "You're looking well today."

So was he, unfortunately. Giles had always known how to dress. Today he was resplendent in a well-tailored riding coat of cobalt superfine, a figured waistcoat of sky blue marcella, white doeskin trousers, and highly polished black Hessians. He looked perfectly at home amid the Ming vases and gilt dragons meant to intimidate her would-be suitors and keep them in line.

Somehow she knew they wouldn't intimidate *him*. And no one ever kept Giles in line unless he wanted to be there.

She strove to appear nonchalant. "If you're here to see Jarret—"

"I'm here to see you." He tossed something onto the golden silk chair nearest her. "I've come to be interviewed."

When she saw *The Ladies Magazine* lying open, a pounding began in her chest. How much had he read? Just the advertisement? Or the chapter of her book, too? "You subscribe to *The Ladies Magazine*?" she asked with what she hoped was just the right dollop of condescension. "How droll."

"Apparently I'm not the only one, judging from the horde on your lawn."

She blinked at him. "What horde?"

"You didn't know?" He let out a sharp laugh. "But of course you didn't. You would have been out there railing at Gabe and Oliver by now if you'd known they were turning gentlemen away as fast as they arrive."

"Why, those arrogant, meddling— What about Jarret? Isn't he out there, too?"

"Apparently he'd already left for the brewery by the time they mustered the troops. But they've sent for him, so I'm sure he'll join the fray as soon as he gets here." Giles leaned against the doorway with a smirk. "I don't think you'll be interviewing any other gentlemen today."

She glared at him. "Yet they let *you* in."

"They think I'm here to visit Jarret. I chose not to disabuse them of the notion. I'm supposedly cooling my heels in the study while I wait for his return."

She headed for the door. "Well, you can cool your heels in here if you like, but I'm going to give my brothers—"

"Not so fast, my dear." He pushed off from the doorway to block her path. "You and I have some unfinished business." Without taking his eyes from her, he shut the door behind him.

An uneasiness rose in her that she fought to hide. "You know perfectly well it's improper for you to be alone with me with the door closed."

"Since when do you care about propriety, Minerva?" he drawled.

"And I haven't given you leave to call me by my Christian name, either."

His cold smile gave her pause. "I haven't given you leave to use me in your books, but that hasn't stopped you."

Oh, Lord. *Steady, Minerva. He might just be fishing for information.* "Are you saying that you've read my novels?"

"Is that so hard to believe?"

"Frankly, yes. Even my brothers don't bother."

"Your brothers haven't been vilified in them."

Though her unease exploded into alarm, she forced a smile. "If you're insinuating that—"

"I'm not insinuating anything—I'm stating it flat out." He circled her like a shark seeking to intimidate his prey. "You've made me into your favorite villain: the Marquess of Rockton."

Drat it all. He really had read her novels.

She tried to brazen it out. "You're confused. Everyone knows that Rockton is based on Oliver."

"Right. That's why Rockton has blue eyes and dark brown hair."

"I couldn't make him be exactly like Oliver, for goodness sake. I had to change a few details."

"Is that why Rockton has a father rather than a mother who committed suicide?" he went on, those blue eyes gleaming. "How clever of you to anticipate that people would assume you changed *that* detail, too. Your little personal joke."

She colored. Never in a million years had she thought he would read her books. "You're making absurd assumptions."

"Really? What about the lines in *The Stranger of the Lake* where the hapless Lady Victoria falls in love with Rockton and throws herself at him?" He stopped in front of her. "What was it he says? Ah, yes. 'Do be careful, my dear, next time you decide to act like a doxy. Some men don't take kindly to blackmail.' Sound familiar?"

That one she really couldn't get around.

"But the passage that settles it is the one I read this morning." With a blatant confidence that rubbed her raw, he strolled over to where he'd left *The Ladies Magazine* and picked it up to read aloud:

> "Lady Anne pushed her way through the crowds at the masquerade, praying that her Marie Antoinette costume was innocuous enough to keep her from being noticed by Lord Rockton's loathsome friends. As she burst into the study, relieved to have escaped unscathed, she realized she was not alone. Rockton himself stood by the fireplace in his priest costume."

He tossed the magazine back onto the chair. "The chapter ends there. What comes next? Rockton helping himself to the files in the study?"

She made a dismissive gesture with her hand. "All right, so I used some of our . . . encounter at Lord Newmarsh's party in my novels. I don't see how—"

"You swore to keep quiet about that night." He strode up until he stood so close that she could smell the spicy scent of Guard's Bouquet on him. "You exacted a price for it, as I recall, and I paid your damned price."

"I did keep quiet—about your stealing, at least. You ought to be glad that I have, considering that a brief explanation from you might have prevented my being interested in the first place."

"Or enticed you to write about it all the more. You'd probably even embellish the incident to make it worse. You made Rockton a spy for the French, for God's sake! Why would you put *that* in there?"

"Because I'm a writer. I invent things. It's called fiction."

He narrowed his eyes on her. "Not when you use real people as characters."

"You're missing the point. First of all, Rockton isn't you or Oliver or anyone. Just because I took a bit of what happened between us and—"

"A *bit*?" His gaze bore into her. "You put our kiss in the very first novel where Rockton appears. Rockton accosts the heroine in the mews and forces a kiss on her. She slaps him for not being 'nice,' and he says, 'What made you think that a kiss from me would be *nice*?'" His gaze dropped to her mouth. "You know perfectly well where you got that line."

"You read that book, too?" she squeaked. "How many of my novels have you read, anyway?"

"Since I found out that you're putting me in them? All ten. Imagine my surprise to discover that you've been flaying me alive in your 'fiction' for the last three."

He was right, though she'd never admit it to him. His rejection that night had stung her pride and wounded her heart, so she'd taken her anger out on him in her novels. But she'd honestly never believed he would read a word of it. Or that anyone would recognize him in it.

She had certainly never believed he'd be angry about it. Giles didn't get angry. He didn't seem to feel deep emotion of any kind. He joked and gambled and flirted his way through life without a care in the world. It surprised her to see him showing *this* much passion.

"I don't understand why you're so annoyed," she said. "No one knows that Rockton is . . . partly you. No one has even guessed."

"Only because you haven't given them enough hints," he bit out. "It's very clever of you to use *me*. Anybody else would sue you for libel, but you know I won't because I don't want people looking too closely into my secrets. So you think you can put whatever you want about me in your books with impunity."

"You're making a mountain out of a molehill, Mr. Masters."

"Am I? When were you planning to put the theft into your books? The next chapter, perhaps?"

"I promised to keep silent about that, and I will."

"Why should I believe you? You haven't kept silent about any of the rest of it."

She glared up at him. "What do you want from me?"

There was a subtle change in his manner, from anger to something far more disturbing. Awareness of her as a woman, one he could seduce. It was just like that night at the Valentine's Ball when they'd danced, when his flirtations had heated her blood while leaving him unmoved. Curse him for that.

He cast her a veiled glance. "What I want is to know *why*. Why you decided to put me in your books as the villain. Why you decided to make me a central character in your most recent novels."

"That . . . just happened. When Rockton first appeared, readers wrote me several letters about him, wanting to see more of him."

"Because you draw him in such loving detail. But why does he capture your imagination so? And why do you keep attributing to him things that *I* said and did? Were you so very angry at me over how I treated you that night?"

"It has nothing to do with you personally—"

"Liar." He bent close to press his mouth to her ear. "Admit it—you put me in your books because you can't forget me."

She jerked back. "Don't flatter yourself."

"And God knows, I can't forget you."

For a moment, she actually believed him, and her heart faltered.

Then she cursed it for its fickleness. The last thing she needed right now was her own private version of Rockton mucking with her determined spinsterhood. Especially when he didn't mean any of his smooth words. According to her brothers, his casual treatment of women was legendary.

Slipping past him, she went to stand at the window that looked out onto the courtyard. "Why are you here? If it's to berate me for putting you in my books, you've accomplished your aim, so you might as well leave. You're certainly not here for any interview—"

"Actually, you're wrong."

She whirled on him.

Seeming to enjoy her look of confusion, he sauntered toward her with a smile. "Here's the situation, Minerva. It's obvious to me that you're going to plague your grandmother with increasingly reckless behavior until you get what you want from her. And what would be more outrageous than to expose me as Rockton, so you can create a scandal like the one Lady Caroline Lamb did with her novel about Lord Byron?"

She bristled. "I would never—"

"So I can't really trust you not to keep writing about me. I'm not sure I can even trust you to keep quiet about who Rockton is. That leaves me with two choices, if I want to keep my secrets safe. I can murder you to keep you silent. Not a good choice at all. No matter how you treat it in your novels, murder is messy. Not to mention illegal."

A shiver swept her. "And the other choice?"

The sudden glitter in his eyes did nothing to quell the pounding in her chest. "I can marry you."

Chapter Two

To Giles's great surprise, Minerva burst into laughter. "You? As my husband? Are you mad?"

He hadn't expected wild enthusiasm, but incredulity wasn't what he'd been aiming for, either. "Quite possibly."

He'd spent the journey over here rehearsing what to say, how to approach Minerva, how to intimidate her into stopping this nonsense of putting him in her books. But as he'd neared the gates of Halstead and seen the crowds, it had dawned on him that the best solution was the simplest.

Make her his wife. That way he could control her and her "fiction." She was too practical to damage her husband's future. And she had to marry anyway if she and her siblings were to gain their inheritance.

A few years ago the idea might have thrown him into a bachelor panic, but with the upturn in his career, he would have to settle down with a wife soon. Especially if he became a King's Counsel.

And if he must have a wife, it might as well be one he desired. Minerva certainly qualified, no matter how she tried to hide her allure with her attire. Today she wore a fashionable morning gown of printed green muslin with a number of fussy flounces about the hem, those hideous puffy sleeves that had become so popular, and a bodice that ran right up to her chin.

Every feminine curve had been buried beneath furbelows and padded sleeves and lace edgings, and it didn't matter one whit. He already knew that her figure was lushly feminine. Thanks to the many evening gowns he'd seen her in, he could imagine it as clearly as if she were naked. And just the thought of taking her to bed made his blood quicken and his good sense vanish. Truth was, seeing her always did something extraordinary to him.

But God help him if she ever guessed it. Reading her books had offered him a peek inside her fathomless brain, so he knew she was clever enough to wrap him entirely about her finger if he allowed it.

"As if I would marry a scoundrel like you," she informed him with a minxish look that grated on his nerves. "Are you daft?"

"I believe we've already established that I'm halfway to being a bedlamite. But humor me anyway." Apparently she wasn't clever enough to see that marriage to him was her only viable choice. He would have to correct that. "You ought to leap at the chance to marry a scoundrel, given how much you enjoy writing about them."

She eyed him as if he really were a bedlamite. "It's not the same. You make an excellent villain precisely because you would make a wretched husband. You don't fit any of my criteria for a suitable spouse."

"Criteria? Ah yes, the interviewing. You must have drummed up some questions for your prospective spouses." He glanced about the room and spotted a stack of paper atop a red lacquered table. As he strode over, he asked, "Is this them?"

When he picked up the sheaf of paper, she hurried over. "Give me that!"

He held her off with one hand while he scanned the first page. "Let me see . . . Question one: 'Have you ever been married before?' That one's easy. No."

"Because no woman would have you," she muttered.

"That probably had something to do with it. Question two: 'Describe your ideal wife.'" He let his gaze trail leisurely over Minerva. "About five foot seven, golden brown hair, green eyes, with a bosom that would make a man weep and a bottom that—"

"Giles!" Hot color filled her cheeks as she crossed her arms over that bosom.

He grinned. "Suffice it to say, she's quite beautiful."

The brief satisfaction in her eyes told him that Minerva wasn't as immune to compliments as she pretended. "I wasn't speaking of physical appearances, as I'm sure you know. I wanted a description of their ideal wife's *character*."

"I see. Well then, my ideal wife is an unpredictable hellion, with a penchant for getting into trouble and speaking her mind."

"Sounds dangerous." Her lips twitched. "And utterly unsuitable for a man who keeps secrets."

"Good point." Except that her unsuitability was precisely the thing that intrigued him. She was wrong for him in every way. And that only made him want her more.

Besides, he could handle Minerva. He was probably the only man in England who could.

He tore his gaze from hers to read on. "'Question three: 'What domestic duties will you expect your wife to perform?'" He laughed. "What sort of answer are you looking for? Some indication of the frequency with which your applicant would wish you to share his bed? Or a description of the acts he would wish you to 'perform'?"

She blushed prettily. "That is *not* the sort of duties I meant, and you know it."

"It's the only sort of duty that matters to those louts out there," he said coldly. "Since they intend to hire plenty of servants with your fortune, they need only focus on the essentials of having a wife. For them, those essentials are obvious."

"But not for you? You haven't answered the question, after all."

"Whatever your 'domestic duties,' I'm sure you can handle them."

She glared at him. "It's whether I *want* to that's in question."

Leaving that alone for the moment, he turned back to her list. "Question four: 'How do you feel about having your wife write novels?'" He snorted. "Did you honestly expect anyone to answer this truthfully with you breathing down their necks?"

"Not everyone is as devious as you."

"Forgive me, I didn't realize you were expecting a progression of saints this morning."

She rolled her eyes. "Just for amusement's sake, what would be *your* honest answer?"

He shrugged. "I have no objection to my wife writing novels as long as they're not about *me*."

"You say that now," she said with quiet seriousness. "But you'll feel otherwise when you come home to find that your dinner isn't on the table because your wife was so swept up in her story that she forgot the time. Or when you discover her sitting in her dressing gown scribbling madly while your house goes to rack and ruin about your ears."

"I can afford servants," he countered.

"It's not just that." She gestured to the list. "Read the next question."

He glanced down at the paper. "'What sort of wife do you require?'"

"Any respectable man requires a wife who lives an irreproachable life. Why do you think I haven't married? Because I can't give up writing my novels." She flashed him a sad smile. "And you in particular will require an irreproachable wife if you're to succeed as a barrister."

She had a point, but not one he dared argue at present. "I've already succeeded as a barrister. In any case, I haven't lived an irreproachable life, so why should I expect my wife to do so?"

Her gaze turned cynical. "Come now, we both know that men can spend their evenings in the stews and their mornings cropsick, and other men just clap them on the back and call them fine fellows. But their wives aren't allowed to have even a hint of scandal tarnish their good names. They certainly can't write books." She gave a dramatic shudder. "Why, that smacks of being in trade. Horrors!"

"I already told you—"

"Did you know that my mother was a writer, too?"

Now she'd surprised him. "What did she write?"

"Poetry for children. She used to read her verses to me, asking my opinion." A heavy sigh escaped her. "But she stopped after she and Papa argued over her wish to have them published. He said that marchionesses didn't publish books. It wasn't done." Her voice hardened. "It was fine for him to toss up the skirts of any female who took his fancy, but God forbid Mama should publish a book."

He tensed. "I'm not your father, Minerva."

"You differ from him only in the fact that you're unmarried. Safer to keep it that way, don't you think?"

Damn it, sometimes his role as a scoundrel slapped him right in the face. It chafed him raw that she couldn't see past it any better than the rest of the world. "Or a man could change."

"For a woman? Really? In fiction, perhaps, but rarely in life."

"Says the woman who buries herself in her books," he snapped. "Your idea of venturing out into life is to surround yourself with your siblings and hold off every eligible gentleman who might come near you."

Her eyes flashed fire. "Oh, that is so like a man to say such a thing. I'm not jumping to marry you, so I must be a spinster pining away alone in her room writing. I tried venturing out into it today, didn't I? But my brothers wouldn't let me."

"That was merely a ploy, and you know it. You were never serious about interviewing gentlemen as husbands. You just wanted to provoke your grandmother into giving up her demands."

He knew he'd hit on the truth when she paled. "What makes you say that?"

"You advertised it in *The Ladies Magazine,* a public forum, when you could as easily have managed it privately with more discretion. And you just explained to me how no respectable man wants a woman who writes novels, yet you say you don't want *me* because I'm a scoundrel. If you don't want a scoundrel and you don't think you can have a respectable gentleman—"

"All right, drat you." She tipped up her chin. "I have no intention of marrying you or anyone else. Can you blame me?"

"No," he said sincerely. When she blinked, he added, "But your grandmother has made it perfectly clear that you must take a husband, so you have no choice. As long as you *have* to marry to inherit, why not marry me?"

"So *that's* what this is about." Her tone grew bitter. "You've found an easy way to plump up your pockets. Why not marry a shrewish spinster with no chance at a decent husband? Then at least you'd have a fortune to make up for your having to marry an 'unpredictable hellion.'"

He fought to keep his temper. "If you mean to insult me, try another tack. No amount of money would convince me to marry a woman I didn't want."

"I doubt that. You're a second son. They're all looking for an easy fortune."

"I'm also a barrister who is widely sought after for his legal advice and who charges exorbitant fees. Trust me, I can afford to keep you in gowns and jewels perfectly well without your grandmother's money."

"That very statement shows how little you know me. I don't care about gowns and jewels—"

"But you care about your siblings and their families," he said softly. "They'll be left destitute if you don't marry. Jarret had me look over your grandmother's terms for any legal way out of her demands. There is none."

A troubled expression knit her brow. "I'm working on a plan to change that."

"This interview idea?" he said with a mocking smile. "First of all, your brothers are nipping that in the bud as we speak. They're not about to let their sister marry some stranger off the street. They're not even going to let you be *exposed* to such men. Secondly, you know perfectly well that Mrs. Plumtree won't let your antics sway her from her purpose. You'll only delay the inevitable."

"Jarret was able to sway her from her purpose," Minerva retorted.

"Because he had something to bargain with. You don't."

She turned on her heel. "Feel free to leave at any time, Mr. Masters."

"You know what I don't see in this list of bloody questions?"

Giles bit out, determined to provoke her into dealing with him. "I don't see any mention of the intimate side of marriage. No questions about what your future husband would expect from you in the bedchamber. Or what *you* could expect from *him.*"

She whirled on him. "That would be vulgar."

"And interviewing gentlemen for the position of husband isn't? The trouble with you, my dear, is you've looked at marriage from every angle except the one that matters." Tossing her list onto the table, he approached her with determined steps. "How you feel about a man. What he does to you whenever he comes near. Whether he makes your heart race and your body heat. And in that one area, I am the perfect husband for you."

"Really?" she said, her voice deceptively sweet. "Is this the part where you sweep me into your arms and prove how you alone make my heart race and my body heat?"

"If you insist," he said and caught her to him.

She didn't resist when he covered her mouth with his. She even let him deepen the kiss. Though she didn't throw her arms about him or melt into him as she had that night long ago, she participated actively in the kiss, letting him drive his tongue into her mouth with slowly deepening strokes. She even twined hers with his, raising his pulse to a feverish pitch and his cock high enough to be uncomfortable.

Then she jerked back with a siren's smile that made his confidence falter. "Well." She tapped her chin. "That was a decent kiss, all things being equal." She pressed her hand to her chest. "My heart is, if not quite *racing,* then heading into a quick walk. But I need a thermometer to determine if and how high my body heated. I shall just go—"

"Don't you dare." He caught her by the arm as she was on

the verge of fleeing. "You know bloody well that you responded to that kiss."

With a suspicious glee in her eyes, she tugged her arm from his grip. "I'm not saying I didn't respond—just that I didn't respond to any overwhelming degree. But it was a good kiss, I suppose. Better than some, not as good as others."

"What the hell do you mean? How many chaps have you kissed in the last nine years, anyway?"

"No more than you've kissed women, I should imagine."

"My God."

"But don't worry—I don't think the average woman would complain about your kissing. You're perfectly competent."

Competent? Bloody insolent chit. Even knowing that she was trying to provoke him didn't ease his wounded pride. "Perhaps we should try it again."

She darted back from him. "I think not. You really ought to go, Giles—my brothers will be none too pleased to find you here alone with me. They don't approve of you for me at all."

That was true. Jarret had warned him away from Minerva only a few weeks ago.

"And Gran positively despises you," she went on. "She thinks you're a bad influence on Gabe. Last week, she said that the next time she saw you—"

She halted as if struck dumb, her gaze wandering to the sheaf of papers.

"Yes? The next time she sees me . . ."

"Oh my word, that's brilliant." Her gaze swung back to him. "You're brilliant, Giles!"

"That's what I've been trying to tell you for the past half hour," he grumbled.

"I mean it. This is the perfect solution to all my problems with Gran."

His eyes narrowed. "What is?"

"You! And me! We'll tell Gran that I've accepted your marriage proposal." Minerva began to pace, her face flushed with excitement. "She'll never approve. Seriously, she thinks you're a 'conscienceless scapegrace who would as soon sell his mother as behave honorably.'"

He scowled. "I knew she wasn't fond of me, but that's a bit harsh. I'll have you know I treat my mother damned well, considering that she spends all her time trying to marry me off to women half my age. And your entire family seems to overlook the fact that I am a well-respected barrister with a practice that is—"

"Yes, yes, you're a pillar of virtue." She rolled her eyes. "You're missing the point. Gran will never let me marry you. She's always regretted letting Mama marry Papa, and you're practically *him*."

"For God's sake," he said irritably, "are we back to that again?"

"It's the perfect plan. You pretend to be betrothed to me, and once she realizes I'm serious, she'll stop this nonsense."

He liked this plan of hers less and less the more he heard of it. "It didn't work for Oliver. He took Miss Butterfield as his pretend fiancée and look what happened. Not only did your grandmother hold fast to her plans, but he's now married to the chit."

Minerva shot him an exasperated glance. "Gran liked Maria from the very beginning. She just pretended not to, which is why his plan didn't work. Besides, it's not the same for my brothers as it is for me and Celia. They can take care of themselves, and Gran knows it. Men have all the power in marriage—they can legally beat their wives, take their money, and force them into anything they please."

"I hope you're not saying that *I* would—"

"I'm just saying that's why Gran wasn't worried about whom Oliver or Jarret married. But she worries a great deal about whom Celia and I marry, because our future husbands will take us out of her control. Anything could happen." A devilish gleam lit her eyes. "And *you* will send her into fits."

This was becoming annoying. "You underestimate your grandmother, my dear."

"Trust me, I know her too well to do that. But this will push her over the edge—I'm sure of it. The longer we're betrothed, the more alarmed she'll get." She rounded on him with a little cry of delight. "And if she doesn't, Jarret and Oliver will make sure she does! They definitely won't approve of you as my husband. They'll work on her to get her to relent, especially if they think I really mean to marry you."

She clapped her hands together. "Eventually I'll have her exactly where I want her, and she'll be forced to rescind her ultimatum. What a brilliant plan!"

"Only if I agree to it. And I don't."

That took the wind out of her sails. "Why not? All you have to do is court me."

"I don't want to court you—I want to marry you. Tomorrow, if possible, although I suppose we could push it off a few days—"

"I am *not* going to marry you, Giles!" She planted her hands on her hips. "Can't you get that through your thick head?"

He arched an eyebrow. "Then why should I help you with your plan? What advantage is there to it for me?"

That finally got through to her. She uttered a low curse that was decidedly unladylike. Then she began to pace again, this time with her pretty brow knit in a frown. "You do have a point. You have every reason to expect something in return."

"Exactly."

"I mean, you'll have to make it a proper courtship, squiring me to balls and parties, giving me little gifts—"

"I thought you said you didn't like gifts," Giles pointed out.

"You have to make it convincing."

"Then I definitely expect compensation." *You in my bed would be good.*

But she'd never agree to that.

"Compensation . . . compensation . . ." Suddenly she faced him, her face bright. "What if I kill off Rockton? Then you won't have to worry about my books anymore."

He eyed her skeptically. "You're not going to murder your most popular character."

"I can kill off whomever I please. And if I wish to do away with Rockton, I will."

"You don't have to say it with such enthusiasm," he grumbled, not sure he liked the fact that she could dispense with his character as easily as she might throw out an old gown. "Besides, aren't you worried that killing Rockton will damage your future as an authoress? What if your readers stop buying your books as a result?"

"If I have to marry some officious lord to please Gran, I won't be able to *write* any books." When he opened his mouth, she said, "And no, I didn't mean you. If I married *you,* you'd make sure I never wrote about Rockton again, so either way, he's got to go."

He closed his mouth. It was unnerving how she sometimes read his mind.

"So how about it?" she said brightly. "Will you agree to be my pretend fiancé if I agree to kill off Rockton?"

He could point out that killing off Rockton wouldn't prevent her from starting over with another character based on

him. He could reiterate that her plan was doomed to failure—
that her grandmother was no fool and would never let her
granddaughter pull the strings. He could argue yet again that
Minerva ought to just marry *him.* But that argument wasn't
working so far, and as long as her wall of misconceptions about
him remained, it never would.

He wished he could tell her the truth—about why he'd
stolen the papers, what he'd been doing since, why she had to
keep silent about their encounter. But he couldn't.

For one thing, he didn't trust her. Writers were magpies—
they took bits of things and wove them together to make
their stories. She had no reason to protect his interests . . .
or those of his superiors. For God's sake, she'd already made
him into a spy—that was skirting far too close to the truth
for his comfort. If anyone recognized the bits from her
novels and his theft was unveiled, he wouldn't be the only
one to suffer.

Ravenswood would be forced to explain why the government
had countenanced a theft from a well-known lord's home,
performed by a private citizen. Newmarsh would almost
certainly want vengeance for it, considering that he'd been
exiled from England for his part in the fraud. And everyone in
Giles's sphere who'd found himself in trouble with the Home
Office would assume it was Giles who'd put them there. That
couldn't possibly help his career.

He simply couldn't risk telling her the truth about that
night. Minerva was too unpredictable to trust with his future.

Besides, if he could skate past this issue until they were
married, it wouldn't matter. He wouldn't be working for
Ravenswood anymore; she'd have no reason to suspect him of
anything. In time she'd lose interest in that one theft, and his
secrets would fade into the past where they belonged.

If he married her. And he fully intended to. Agreeing to her plan wasn't a bad idea, actually. He could court her and let her get to know him. They would be in each other's pockets for weeks, possibly months, and if he couldn't convince her to marry him in that amount of time, he deserved to lose her.

A sudden bellow from somewhere in Halstead Hall's 356 rooms broke the stillness. "Minerva! Damn it, Minerva, where are you?"

Minerva jumped. "Oh, Lord, that's Oliver. He's probably coming to lecture me about this whole interviewing business. What do you say, Giles? I need your answer *now*."

"First, I want another kiss," he said, stepping toward her. "To help me make up my mind."

She colored. "Absolutely not. And don't think that this pretend courtship will include kissing, because it won't."

He eyed her askance. "Why not, if you find my kissing so uninspiring? Why should you care if from time to time I give you one of my merely 'competent' kisses?"

"Drat it, Giles, we don't have time for this!"

"Kissing is part of it, or no deal," he said firmly.

"Minerva!" roared Oliver from much closer.

She hurried to the door and opened it, then came back to him with a frustrated expression. "All right. From time to time you may kiss me, I suppose."

"Then I agree to your terms." He stepped nearer. "So let's seal our bargain with a kiss." He was going to get another crack at it if it killed him.

"Are you mad? If Oliver sees us kissing, you won't get the chance to court me—it'll be duels at dawn."

"How do you know it won't be duels at dawn when you tell him you've accepted my proposal of marriage?"

"Don't be ridiculous. He's not *that* hotheaded. Though I

daresay he may try to . . . er . . . knock some sense into you. He and Jarret. And possibly Gabe."

"Our bargain is looking better and better all the time," he said drily. "I get to fight the Sharpe men while you stand around pretending to care." He came close enough to whisper, "I will definitely require a few kisses of you if *that* comes to pass, minx."

"Step back!" she hissed just as the door swung fully open.

"Damn it, Minerva," Oliver began, "come out and tell these idiots—"

He broke off, the scowl on his dark brow deepening. "What the deuce is going on here? Masters, I thought you were in the study, waiting for Jarret."

Minerva faced her brother with a forced smile. "Actually, he came to be interviewed."

That was Giles's cue. "Sorry for the subterfuge, old chap, but I thought you'd forgive it in this case." He slipped his hand into the small of her back. "You see, your sister has made me the happiest of men. Minerva has finally agreed to be my wife."

Chapter Three

"Over my dead body!"

Hetty heard Oliver's roar from two halls over and hurried toward it as fast as her cane could take her. He must have found Minerva. Damned girl. Why couldn't she just marry some decent fellow and be done with it? Why did she have to drum up this nonsense about interviewing fools she solicited in the papers like a common whore?

Well, Oliver would put an end to that—he wouldn't want Minerva marrying some stranger either, thank God.

She followed the sound of heated voices into the Chinese drawing room, then stopped short. Oliver was squared off against that rogue Giles Masters—God only knew when *he* had snuck in. And Minerva stood with her hand tucked in the crook of Giles's elbow.

"What has happened?" Hetty demanded.

Oliver shot her an angry glance. "Masters has some idiotic idea that he's going to marry Minerva."

Hetty dragged in a breath. Masters? With her granddaughter? Never.

"Of course," Oliver went on, "I've just informed him that it's impossible."

"You don't get to decide that," Minerva said stoutly. "I'm

the only one who decides whom I marry. Besides, you've been pressing me to marry just as much as Gran. So why should you care who I choose?"

"Because it's *Masters*," Oliver said, "and he's—"

"A gentleman," Minerva said.

"You have no idea what he is," Oliver bit out. "Give me five minutes, and I can tell you stories that would blister your ears."

"I'm sure you could," Minerva said. "You're probably in every one of them. Don't you think it's hypocritical of you to malign his character when it's no worse than your own has been?"

"Are you just going to let her go off with this scoundrel?" Oliver asked Hetty.

Minerva shot Hetty a sly glance. "You gave no rules for *whom* we could marry, Gran, just *when* we had to marry."

"I don't give a damn about Gran's rules," Oliver snapped. "You can't marry Masters. As head of this household, I forbid it. He's unworthy of you."

"I'll grant you that," Masters said mildly. "But she doesn't seem to agree, and that's all that matters."

Oliver's fingers curled into fists at his side. "Angling after her inheritance, are you?"

Masters bristled. "Careful, Stoneville. We've been friends a long time, so just this once, I'll excuse your insult to my honor. I have no designs on Minerva's inheritance or her dowry. She can keep it all if she wishes. You can put that in the settlement."

Hetty watched Minerva to see what response that got. The start the girl gave when the word *settlement* was spoken gave Hetty pause.

"So you mean to support her on a barrister's pay?" Oliver snapped.

A dark flush rose in Masters's face. "I can afford to keep a wife well enough, if that's your concern."

Could that be true? Masters *was* well known for his competence as a barrister, but many a man of the law spent his evenings in whorehouses and gaming hells, where his money drifted away like desert sands. By all reports, Masters was one of them.

Just then Jarret and Gabe came in. "We got rid of most of those fools," Jarret said, "but some are— Masters? I thought you were in the study waiting for me."

"No," Oliver ground out. "He's in here, coaxing Minerva into marrying him."

"The hell he is!" Jarret growled at the same time that Gabe cried, "We'll just see about that!"

The men began to close in on Masters, who stood there with an odd glitter of defiance in his eyes.

"That's enough!" Hetty said sharply. "All of you, out. I wish to speak to Mr. Masters alone."

"Let us handle this, Gran," Jarret said.

"I will not have you brawling in your mother's favorite drawing room." She made a shooing gesture. "Go on, out with the lot of you. You too, Minerva. The only person who gets to decide if Mr. Masters is an acceptable suitor is me."

The others hesitated, then moved reluctantly toward the door. All except Oliver. He came up close to Hetty to murmur, "I'm the one who should make this decision. I'm the head of this household."

"Who has spent the past few hours trying to undo the damage that your sister's latest shenanigan has wrought." Hetty glanced past him to where Minerva was lingering, trying to hear what they were saying.

Hetty lowered her voice. "You cannot control the girl any more than I. She is long past the age of consent, and she will do as she pleases. I daresay she is hoping I will cut her off so she can molder in a cottage somewhere writing her books. She will keep getting into trouble until I give in or you and your brothers fight duels with half the county. It is time for another tack."

"Involving *Masters,* of all men?"

"I don't like it any better than you. But before we decide anything, let me talk to him."

"Fine. As long as I get my shot at him after." Oliver threw Masters a foul glance on his way out the door.

Masters returned it with a cool nod.

Once they were alone, Gran hobbled over to the brandy decanter atop a chinoiserie chest. "Something to drink, Mr. Masters?"

"None for me, thank you."

With a sly glance at him, she poured herself a glass. "Come now, I know you are no green lad."

"With all due respect, Mrs. Plumtree, I prefer to keep my wits about me in the presence of a master of manipulation like yourself."

A chuckle escaped her. "You always were forthright." She sipped her brandy. "So why not continue to be forthright, and tell me what this is really about?"

He eyed her warily. "I don't know what you mean."

She snorted. "My granddaughter has fought the idea of marriage for nine years now. There is no chance in hell that she decided to marry you just because you happened to show up to visit Jarret today."

"Actually, I came here purposely to interview for the position of her husband."

That took Hetty by surprise. "You read of it in *The Ladies Magazine?*"

"Exactly."

This got more interesting by the moment. "And you decided you were going to put aside your scapegrace ways and trot over here to make her your wife. For no other reason than you heard she was interviewing men to find a husband."

He smiled faintly. "No other reason."

"You do realize she is just using you to annoy me."

A moment passed while he searched her face. "I know."

Hetty went on a hunch. "She is hoping I will be so outraged by her choice that I will give up on asking her to marry."

"Asking?" he said, a sudden glitter in his eyes. "Is that what you call it?"

She sipped some brandy. "You do not approve of my methods."

"No. But that won't stop me from taking advantage of them to get close to Minerva."

"Why?"

"Because she's the only woman I've ever seriously considered marrying. I wasn't about to let some other fellow snag her."

She would swear that he was telling the truth—which was rather astonishing. "Come now, we both know she had no intention of marrying some stranger. She just wanted to rile me."

"Did it work?"

She rolled her eyes. "I'm not the fool my granddaughter takes me for. This nonsense with you is just another attempt to force my hand."

He gave her a considering glance. "Let's put our cards on the table, shall we? As you've already guessed, Minerva doesn't really want to marry me. What she wants is for me to pretend to be her fiancé until you grow so alarmed by the betrothal that you rescind your ultimatum."

"And you agreed to this scheme because . . ."

"I genuinely want to marry her."

"Again, I must ask you why."

"Have you ever read Minerva's novels?"

That threw her off guard. "What has that got to do with anything?"

"Minerva puts her whole self into her books. I should know—I've read them all. When she's with people she hides behind her clever quips and her cynical views, but you can see the real Minerva in her novels. And I like that Minerva."

So did Hetty. Still, she'd never told Minerva that she read her novels. Granted, they were rather good fun—full of twists and surprises and intriguing characters. But Hetty had never wanted to encourage her granddaughter in such a bluestocking profession.

Bluestockings didn't get married, they didn't provide their grandmothers with great-grandchildren, and they created scandal willy-nilly for the remaining great-grandchildren to endure. Just look at that fool Mary Shelley, who'd stolen a woman's husband and been ostracized for it. Hetty wanted better for her granddaughter. The Sharpes had quite enough scandal for one family already, thank you very much.

But sometimes when she was reading the girl's books, she felt as if she were brushing up against a part of her granddaughter she never saw. The part that missed her parents. The part that wanted a family of her own.

The part she hid from the world. How extraordinary that a man like Masters had seen it, too.

"Do you love her?" she asked bluntly.

His expression grew shuttered. "I admire and respect her."

"And want her in your bed."

He started, then flushed a dull red. "I would imagine most men want their wives in their beds."

"But you don't love her."

Something hard flickered in his eyes. "Love is for fools and dreamers. I am neither."

That didn't mean Masters was wrong for Minerva. It also didn't mean he was right. It was good that he hadn't lied about his feelings, but the fact that he didn't trust in love was a bit worrisome.

Still, he sounded just like Oliver and Jarret before they'd met their wives. And probably Gabe, too, if the rapscallion had ever taken the time to think about it. Oliver and Jarret had found love. And why? Because most men *were* fools and dreamers. They just didn't want to admit it to themselves.

"I do not wish to see Minerva hurt," Hetty said softly. "I did not come up with this scheme to punish her, no matter what she thinks. I did it to nudge my grandchildren out of the nest. To force them to face life instead of running from it. But that does not mean I will stand idly by while some blackguard steals her heart and tramples on it. Men like you tend to spend their nights with their mistresses and whores—"

"I mean to be faithful to Minerva," he said firmly. "I would make her a good husband, I swear. My profession is quite lucrative."

"And you gamble it away regularly, from what I understand."

"Don't believe everything you hear. All I ask is that you give me the chance to win her. I need time, and you need to give her some rope to hang herself. Let me court her. In the meantime, you can inquire about my business affairs if that will set your mind at ease."

"Don't worry, I will. And I assume that means you have no problem with Pinter sniffing into your life."

Jackson Pinter was the Bow Street Runner whom Oliver had hired to examine the backgrounds of any prospective spouses for Hetty's grandchildren.

That seemed to give Masters pause, but after a moment's reflection, he conceded with a terse nod. "If you hear anything that alarms you, then withdraw your approval, and I'll abide by your decision."

"Even at the risk of angering Minerva?"

He flashed her a lopsided smile. "I'm not an idiot, Mrs. Plumtree. I recognize who *really* runs this family. If you're not on my side, then I'll never have a chance with Minerva, and we both know it."

"Finally, a man who appreciates me." She liked Mr. Masters more by the moment, although she would still reserve judgment until she had a better sense of his prospects.

"Is it a bargain, then?" he asked.

She hesitated. But nothing else had worked with Minerva. Why not give Masters the chance to shake her up? "Very well."

"Thank you." He let out a long breath. "I believe I'll have that drink now."

With a smile, she poured him some brandy and handed him the glass. "You'll need it. My grandsons are preparing to beat you to a bloody pulp. And I'm going to let them."

He sipped the brandy. "So am I." He met her gaze steadily. "She's worth it."

"Are you sure about that? She will lead you a merry dance these next few weeks, I can promise you."

"I can handle Minerva."

She laughed. "Better men than you have tried and failed." She drank some brandy. "But you've got ballocks, boy. I'll give you that. That might just be enough."

He held up his glass with a devilish grin. "To my future wife."

Hetty eyed him askance but clinked his glass all the same. "We shall see."

Chapter Four

Minerva waited for Giles and Gran to come out, still shocked that he'd proposed marriage. Granted, he'd only done it to get her to stop writing about him, but still . . .

She tamped down the little thrill that coursed through her every time she remembered his saying that he couldn't forget her. It was the sort of thing all scoundrels said to women. He didn't mean it. He couldn't mean it. Could he?

No. After she'd given him what he'd wanted, he'd been only too eager to fall in with her plan for a pretend courtship. Undoubtedly he was relieved that he wouldn't have to sacrifice himself on the altar of respectability for his secrets, whatever they were.

"You can't really intend to marry him, sis," Jarret said for the third time.

"I thought you were his friend," Minerva shot back.

"I *am*. That's why I know he's not right for you."

"You don't know a thing about him." She turned her gaze toward her other brothers. "None of you do."

They all began to talk at once, babbling about this escapade or another.

"Quiet! I shan't listen to another bad word about him. I

know what he's done in the past, and I've made my choice. You three have naught to say about it."

They were sweet to be so concerned, but she was tired of their viewing her as some innocent who had to be protected from men at all costs. They didn't treat her like that in any other arena.

"Very well," Oliver shot back. "I'm sure Gran will have plenty to say."

Minerva certainly hoped so. Still, she grew more uneasy the longer Gran took with Giles. Whatever were they discussing? No doubt Giles was trying his patented charm on her.

Well, he might get around other women, but not Gran. Minerva had heard enough from the servants about her brothers' exploits—all of which had included Giles—to know that he was more familiar with brothels and debauchery than most of London's rakehells. Gran would never countenance his suit. Then Minerva would be free of her ultimatum at last.

As they stood in the hall waiting, Freddy, the cousin of Oliver's new wife, walked up. He and his own wife had been visiting since their return from America.

He made straight for a dish of lemon drops on a side table. "What's going on?"

Oliver's expression softened slightly. "Nothing that concerns you, lad."

"Minerva wants to marry a scoundrel," Gabe bit out. "Gran is giving the fellow what for."

"Is that why a group of men are pouring into the Crimson Courtyard?" Freddy asked. "Are they friends of his?"

Her brothers gaped at him, then bolted down the hall.

Minerva smiled. Freddy might be obtuse, but he had his uses. "How many men would you say there were?"

With a shrug, Freddy popped two lemon drops in his mouth. "Twenty, maybe?"

That should keep her brothers out of the way for a bit.

"At first I thought the fellows might be here for the race," Freddy went on. "Then I remembered that the race is tomorrow."

Minerva narrowed her gaze. "What race?"

Freddy looked at her, then blinked. "Dash it all, I forgot I wasn't supposed to say anything to you ladies."

"The race involves Gabe, I take it?"

"How did you guess?" he said, alarmed.

She eyed him askance.

"Oh. Right. He's the only one around here who races."

"He's a complete and utter fool, is what he is," Minerva grumbled. "Even after breaking his arm racing a few months ago, he's driven his phaeton in three more. Gran chides him every time, but it seems to make no difference."

Freddy sucked calmly on the lemon drop. "I think that's why we're not supposed to tell her about it."

"I daresay you're right." And that's why the only ones in the family who'd seen him race were her brothers, since the private affairs generally involved Gabe's rather fast set. Women weren't supposed to attend them because of all the drinking, gambling, and soiled doves.

Hmm. Perhaps there was a way she could use this in her fight with Gran. "Are Jarret and Oliver going?"

"They said they were." He gave a heavy sigh. "I wanted to go myself, but Jane wants me to take her and Maria shopping in town tomorrow. I hate shopping. There's never anything to eat. Just gowns, gowns, and more gowns. Why do you ladies need so many gowns, anyway? You can only wear one at a time."

"We have to have something to fill up the closet, or the mice move in and build nests," she joked.

"Really?" he said with perfect sincerity. "I had no idea."

Sadly, he probably didn't. "What time is this race?"

He looked uncertain. "I don't know if I should say."

"If you tell me, I'll tell you where Cook puts the kidney pies to cool."

His eyes lit up. Freddy was remarkably easy to bribe. "It's at ten in the morning."

"And where is it taking place?"

"Not quite sure. Near some inn in Turnham. That's all I know."

The door to the drawing room opened and Giles and Gran came out, looking suspiciously convivial. Minerva tensed. That wasn't a good sign.

Gran started. "Where did the lads go?"

"Apparently, the gentlemen who've come to be interviewed are overrunning the house," Minerva said with some satisfaction. "Freddy tells me they're filling the Crimson Courtyard."

"God help us all," Gran muttered. "I suppose I shall have to go marshal more servants."

When she headed down the hall, Minerva called out, "Wait! What about me and Giles?"

"I gave him permission to court you," Gran said with a dismissive gesture. "At least *he* is a legitimate suitor and not some riffraff who answered an advertisement." She shot Freddy a dark glance. "Keep an eye on those two, will you, lad?"

Minerva was still gaping at her when Gran hurried off. Drat the woman. Minerva should have known that Gran wouldn't give in so easily.

"What does she mean, 'keep an eye' on you?" Freddy asked.

"I believe she wants you to chaperone," Giles said drily.

"Oh, God," Freddy said with a hint of panic. "Don't know a thing about chaperoning."

Mischief glinted in Giles's eyes. "Don't worry. We'll just chaperone ourselves."

"That's like asking a dragon to guard the virgin," Minerva mumbled under her breath. She smiled brightly at Freddy. "There's no need for you to chaperone anyway. Our guest was just leaving." Though she meant to get some questions answered privately before he did. "I'll see him out and be back in a flash."

Freddy looked nervous. "Should I go with you?"

"Don't be silly," she said lightly. "What could possibly happen between here and the door?" Leaving a place as large as Halstead Hall required navigating several corridors and at least two courtyards, but with any luck Freddy wouldn't think of that. "I'm sure Mr. Masters can be a gentleman for *that* long."

"Masters," Freddy said, his brow furrowed. "I've heard that name before." He brightened. "Wait, did you bet Lord Jarret that you could drink ten tankards of ale in an hour and still pleasure a wo—" He broke off with a look of chagrin.

"Yes, Giles, are you *that* Masters?" Minerva asked sweetly.

"Absolutely not." Giles tucked her hand in the crook of his arm, then started down the hall.

As soon as they were out of Freddy's earshot, she said, "Liar."

"Not at all," he said grimly. "It was only five tankards."

He seemed embarrassed. That wasn't like Giles, from what she knew. Like her brothers, he'd always acted the carefree rogue with no apparent shame.

"And did you win?" she asked with an arch glance. She hated how much it bothered her that he'd made a wager that involved pleasuring *any* woman, even a lady of ill repute.

"Does it matter?"

"You're the one who said I should ask questions about what I could expect from my future husband in the bedchamber.

I figure that if you won the bet, that shows you have enough stamina to keep me happy."

Giles steadied a piercing blue gaze on her. "If you're trying to shock me, it won't work. I've read your books, remember?"

Yes, that was the trouble.

A niggling suspicion entered her mind. "You didn't tell Gran that I don't really mean to marry you, did you?"

His expression turned unreadable. "You promised to kill off Rockton. Why would I jeopardize that by scheming with your grandmother?"

"Good point." But she still didn't trust him. "So what *did* you say to Gran? How did you convince her to allow a courtship between us?"

"I told her I wanted to marry you. That I admired and respected you. That I could support you. Why? What did you *want* me to tell her?"

"I don't know. Something alarming."

"Like 'Please let me marry your granddaughter, Mrs. Plumtree, so I can beat her every morning and chain her to the bed every night'?"

She struggled not to laugh. "Something like that."

"You're too immersed in your gothic novels, minx. If I told her such a whopping lie, she'd smell a rat. Or she'd refuse to let me court you, kick me out of the house, and that would be the end of your plan. She has to see me as a problem, and how can I be a problem if I let her dispense of me too easily?"

"True. So how exactly do you mean to be a problem?"

He tugged her through the nearest open doorway, which led into the deserted breakfast room. Then he hauled her into his arms and covered her mouth with his.

He gave her no chance to think or marshal her defenses, as she had earlier. He just kissed her with a boldness that melted her to her toes. Her pulse jumped into a martial beat, and her head began to spin. He swamped her with the sheer, visceral power of seduction and turned her resolve to mush. Along with her brain, her knees, and a few other body parts.

Silky warmth stole through her body when the kiss turned blatantly wicked. Even knowing he was just behaving true to form for a scoundrel didn't keep her from responding. She'd spent nine years remembering their one toe-curling kiss, and she wanted another one too badly. She'd curbed her desires earlier; she couldn't curb them now.

Especially when his hands began to roam her body with decided possessiveness. He swept them up and down her ribs, making her ache to feel them in more intimate places. Would he dare touch her where he shouldn't? Did she dare let him?

Then the kiss was over, leaving her shaking with unmet urges she'd never thought to feel again.

He nuzzled her cheek. "Does that answer your question?" he asked in a husky murmur that resonated throughout her traitorous body.

She struggled to regain control of it. And to remember what he was talking about. Ah yes. How he meant to become a problem for Gran. "Your kissing me cannot possibly help this situation."

"If your grandmother sees us, she'll realize I'm more of a scoundrel than a suitor and she'll grow alarmed."

Minerva drew back to glare at him. "If she sees us, she'll proclaim me compromised and make me marry you."

"And that would work?" he said skeptically. "I got the idea that your grandmother couldn't *make* you do anything."

"I don't particularly want to test that theory." She pushed at his chest. "Besides, I've got a less dangerous way to make you into a prob—"

"God help me," muttered a voice from the doorway.

Minerva's heart sank as she turned to see Freddy, his eyes round at the sight of Giles's hands still clasping her waist. And Giles certainly took his sweet time about releasing her.

"What are you doing here, Freddy?" Minerva asked, irritated at them both.

"I thought there might be some muffins left from breakfast." His gaze turned accusing. "You said you were just showing him out." Freddy ran his fingers through his hair as he darted a glance in the direction of the Crimson Courtyard, named for its bright red paving tiles. "Dash it all, your grandmother will skin me alive. And your brothers will hold me down while she does it. I was supposed to chaperone." His voice rose with his hysteria. "You said nothing could happen between the drawing room and the door—"

"Nothing *did* happen," Minerva said firmly.

Freddy's gaze flew from her to Giles. "But Masters there had his hands—"

"It's fine, Freddy. He was just . . . steadying me. I almost fell."

The young man's eyes narrowed. "I'm not a complete idiot, you know."

She sighed. "Of course not. But honestly, there's no reason for anybody to hear about it. I won't say anything if you don't. Why should we bother Gran with this?" She cast him a sly look. "I would hate to see you get into trouble."

"That would be very bad," he muttered. "Jane would never forgive me. She likes your family. She wouldn't want us sent home with a cloud over our heads."

"Exactly," she said, feeling a small twinge of guilt at playing on his unreasonable panic. Especially since she could feel Giles's gaze boring into her. "We'll just keep this between us, all right?"

"All right. Although maybe I should go with you to see Mr. Masters out."

"Good idea," Giles drawled as he offered Minerva his arm.

She took it, her heart beating faster when he laid his hand on hers. He wore gloves, as did she, yet she swore she could feel the heat of his flesh through both layers of leather.

As they headed for the door, she said, "Let's avoid the courtyard, shall we? No point in reminding my brothers that they want to thrash Mr. Masters."

Giles shot her a half-smile. "Concerned for my welfare, are you?"

"Not a bit," she lied. "I just hate the sight of bloodshed."

"I would never have guessed," he said as they headed toward the back entrance to Halstead Hall, Freddy falling into step behind them. "Your books are full of it."

"That's precisely the trouble with you. You keep confusing fiction with real life."

He lowered his voice. "Only because you keep turning real life into fiction."

Shooting a glance to where Freddy lagged some steps behind them, she dropped her voice to a murmur. "And I'll continue to do so if you ever kiss me like that again in a place where my family might see. That will void our agreement, do you understand? I will keep writing about Rockton until I *die.*"

He searched her face, as if trying to determine her sincerity, then gave her a cool nod. "You drive a hard bargain, my dear."

"Don't you forget it."

They walked together a few moments in silence.

As they neared the back entrance, he asked, "May I call on you again tomorrow? I don't have to be in court until Wednesday."

"Actually," she said, "why don't you take me for a drive in the morning, say, nine o'clock? That sounds enjoyable." Though he wasn't going to like *where* she planned for him to drive her.

He eyed her with clear suspicion. "It sounds early."

"Too early for you? Or do you just not wish to go?"

"I didn't say that. It's an outing with you. Why would I pass that up?"

She snorted. "Save your false charm for a woman who doesn't know you as well as I do."

He sobered, his eyes gazing solemnly into hers. "You'd be surprised how little you know me, Minerva."

She wrenched her gaze from his. She wished that were true. She wished he were something other than a rogue like her father and her brothers. But there'd been nothing to indicate that in all their encounters. Certainly there'd been nothing to indicate it in the stories her brothers told about him.

"Here we are," she said blithely as they reached the entrance. She released his arm, but before she could move away he caught her hand and lifted it to his lips, pressing a kiss upon it.

His gaze burned into hers. *"Au revoir, mon petit mignon,"* he said, the roughly spoken endearment sending a frisson of anticipation along her spine.

It was only after he left that she realized why he'd called her his "little wanton" in French. Because that was what Rockton had called Victoria in *The Stranger of the Lake.* And the fact that Giles had remembered such a small detail from her book moved her more than anything else he'd done today.

Drat him. She could see that this faux engagement was going to be more complicated than she'd anticipated. If she weren't careful, she'd find herself back in the same place she'd been nine years ago when he'd broken her heart. And she simply couldn't allow that.

Chapter Five

Giles didn't even look up from his newspaper that evening when the Sharpe brothers showed up at Brook's, the club where they were all members. "I've been expecting you for hours."

"Get up," Stoneville gritted out.

Setting his paper aside, Giles rose. "I assume you wish to do this outside."

Jarret's eyes narrowed. "You do realize we've come to beat the living daylights out of you."

"Yes. So let's get it over with, shall we?" He'd had his fill of the meddling Sharpe brothers. Bad enough that he'd had to agree to letting Pinter dig around in his affairs. He felt fairly certain that his secret life would withstand the man's scrutiny, but it did make him nervous. This nonsense with Minerva's pesky siblings just made him angry, though he'd be damned if he'd show it.

Gabe blinked. "You're not going to argue? Try to get out of it?"

"What would be the point?" Giles said with a shrug. "You're out for blood. I doubt anything I say will change that."

"Is this some trick?" Jarret asked. "You're hoping we'll feel sorry for you?"

"No trick." Giles gazed steadily into the face of the man he'd long considered his closest friend, a man he had hoped knew his real character at least a little. Apparently he'd been wrong—and that hurt. "I know what you want. I'm going to let you have it. Then we can put it behind us."

"But surely you're going to defend yourself," Gabe persisted.

"Why should I? You think I deserve the thrashing, and who am I to say otherwise?"

"You damned well *do* deserve it," Stoneville growled.

"If not for this, then for something else, I'm sure," Giles retorted.

Like the kiss he'd shared earlier with Minerva. She might have pretended not to care about his first one, but he was certain she'd felt differently about the second. God knew *he'd* felt differently. The very scent of her had catapulted him back to that night in the mews nine years ago. The night he'd first wanted her. The night he'd realized he couldn't have her if he were to focus his energies on gaining justice for his family.

Jarret stared at him now as if through new eyes. "Why Minerva? Why not some other woman?"

"I need a wife. She needs a husband if she's to inherit. It's as simple as that."

"It's as I told you," Stoneville said. "He wants her inheritance."

"*She* wants her inheritance," Giles corrected him coldly. "I want *her*."

The brothers exchanged glances.

"If I'd wanted her for her inheritance," Giles went on, "I would have shown up at your door the day after I heard about your grandmother's ultimatum."

"Still, you have to admit that your timing is suspicious," Jarret said. "You've known her for years. And suddenly you just up and decide to marry her?"

"I couldn't very well let her throw herself away on some fool she met through her advertisement, could I?" When Jarret looked skeptical, he added, "There's more between me and Minerva than meets the eye, old chap. You know that or you wouldn't have warned me away from her two months ago."

"For all the good it did," Jarret muttered.

"What kind of 'more'?" Stoneville put in, a stormy frown darkening his face. "If you've laid a hand on her—"

"I haven't dishonored your sister, if that's what you're implying." Though they would probably define *dishonored* differently than he would. Giles drew in a heavy breath. "And if you want to know what lies between us, ask *her.* I won't betray her confidence."

Besides, he knew bloody well she would never reveal to her brothers the truth about what she'd been putting in her books. They wouldn't approve.

"Are we going outside or not?" Giles prodded. "I'd like to get this over with, since I'm calling on your sister in the morning."

"*Tomorrow* morning?" Jarret asked with a glance at Gabe.

Gabe shot his brother a mute communication that put Giles on alert.

"Why not tomorrow morning?" Giles asked.

"Because we'll be gone," Gabe said smoothly. Too smoothly. "Oliver and Jarret are going with me to Tattersall's to pick out a horse."

"Ah. And you think I should refrain from calling on her if you three can't be there to glare at me."

Stoneville shot him a mirthless smile. "Don't worry. We plan to make sure that you're in no condition to call on her anyway."

"Then let's get on with it.'" Giles headed for the door.

"Wait!" Gabe said.

Giles paused.

"Oliver, we can't beat him up if he won't fight back," Gabe said. "It wouldn't be gentlemanly."

"I don't give a damn about gentlemanly," Stoneville retorted.

"Well, *I* do." Jarret held Giles's gaze. "I owe him for keeping me from getting the hell beat out of me at Eton."

"*I* don't owe him a damned thing," Stoneville said. "And his older brother has said enough about some of his escapades for me to know we don't want him near Minerva."

Giles could well imagine what David had told Stoneville. Until their father's suicide, Giles had lived his life with a reckless disregard for anyone but himself. There were things he still regretted about that period of his life. Like the part he'd unwittingly played in keeping his brother and sister-in-law apart for so many years.

But that didn't change his plans for Minerva.

He met Stoneville's gaze steadily. "If it makes it easier for your brothers to get on with this, I'll defend myself. But it won't stop me from courting your sister."

"I imagine that depends on how badly we trounce you," Stoneville said. "We could lay you up for weeks."

"You could *try*." Giles smiled coolly. "But if you force me to defend myself, I'll do my damnedest to win."

Gabe laughed. "It's three to one, Masters. You *can't* win."

"He's just trying to provoke us into fighting him, Gabe," Jarret said. "He knows he can't win. He just doesn't care." Jarret searched Giles's face. "The question is why."

Giles thought about telling them the same things he'd told Mrs. Plumtree. He thought about arguing for his right to marry Minerva.

But why should he, damn it? They were going to trounce him either way, and he refused to beg off.

"Make up your minds," he clipped out. "Are we going to fight or not?"

"Not," Jarret said with a glance at his older brother. Though Stoneville stiffened, after a moment he nodded his assent. Jarret swung his gaze back to Giles. "For now, that is. I don't know what your game is, Masters, but before I take you on, I want to hear what Minerva has to say about this 'more' between you. I like to have all the facts."

Jarret smiled grimly. "But if I hear even a hint that you've harmed my sister, I won't rest until I've made it impossible for you ever to hurt her again."

"Fair enough."

"What's going on?" came a new voice behind them.

Giles turned to see that his older brother, David, the Viscount Kirkwood, had approached. David and Stoneville had been friends ever since Eton, even though David was thirty-eight, three years older than Stoneville.

David glanced from Giles to Stoneville. "What could my brother possibly have to do with your sister?"

When Stoneville lifted an eyebrow at Giles, Giles said, "I proposed marriage to Lady Minerva today."

"What? That's wonderful! Mother will be ecstatic." David glanced at the solemn faces of the Sharpe brothers. "Assuming that Lady Minerva accepted your proposal, that is."

"She did," Giles said. "But apparently her brothers aren't too pleased by the idea of having me in the family."

"Damn it, Giles," Jarret put in, "you know that's not it. We just don't want to see Minerva hurt."

When David bristled, clearly on the verge of defending his younger brother, Giles said hastily, "Neither do I." He gestured to the footman to bring his hat and coat. "Now if you'll excuse me, gentlemen, I'll take my leave. I promised my brother that

I'd join him and his lovely wife for dinner this evening. Come on, David."

David hesitated, probably trying to gauge what exactly was in the wind, but after a second he followed him out.

Giles could feel the Sharpe brothers watching them leave. He had a sneaking suspicion he'd only delayed the inevitable. Because if he was to secure Minerva he'd have to do more than squire her about town in the presence of chaperones. And his tactics would *not* meet with their approval.

"What the devil was that all about?" David asked as soon as they were on the street and walking toward the town house.

"The Sharpe men seem to think that I want to marry Minerva for her fortune."

"Do you?"

Giles shot him a dark look. "You, too?"

"You've never shown any interest in marriage before. And this is the first I'm hearing of your interest in Lady Minerva."

Tamping down his irritation, Giles strode ahead. "That doesn't mean I didn't have one."

David sighed. "Look here, Giles, I of all people know that marrying a woman for her money is tempting . . ."

"I am not marrying Minerva for her money, damn it! And yes, I did learn well from your example."

David's first wife, Sarah, had been an heiress. Her money had saved the Masters family after their father's bad investments had crippled their finances, but the woman herself had nearly destroyed David. Of course, Minerva wasn't Sarah, thank God.

They walked together in silence a while. Giles wished he could tell his brother everything, but he couldn't. Aside from the warning Ravenswood had given him about keeping it quiet, Giles didn't want to involve his family in his business for the Home Office. Not that David couldn't be discreet, but the less he knew, the less potential for him to let something slip. And the less possibility that he could be hurt by what some would perceive as Giles's informing on his peers.

"Hold up, will you?" David called out.

Absorbed in his thoughts, Giles had been walking so fast that he hadn't realized how far David had fallen behind. He stopped to wait as his brother caught up, walking with stiff steps.

"Is your leg paining you again?" Giles asked.

David nodded. "I went riding today. It always gives me trouble afterward."

Last year David had been stabbed while trying to save his second wife from a kidnapper. Remembering how close David had come to death still unsettled Giles. It was yet one more example of why it was best for a man not to let foolish emotions cloud his judgment. If David hadn't raced off to save Charlotte, had let the police handle it instead, he might not have been hurt.

For that matter, if he hadn't taken up with Charlotte again in the first place . . .

No, he couldn't blame his brother for that. David had clearly been in love. But that was precisely the problem. Love had led him to do some damned dangerous things.

Giles would never be such a fool. Too many of his court cases consisted of men who'd killed their wives' lovers in a passion or had started robbing to pay for nice things for some woman or had become drunks because of losing some "true love." Then there were the operatives who were betrayed by some woman they'd "fallen in love" with.

He snorted. It was fine for a man to marry, but fall in love?

Any man who did that was just handing his ballocks over to a woman. And Giles would shoot himself before he ever did *that*.

WHEN GILES ARRIVED at Halstead Hall the next morning, he was surprised to see that there were *still* gentlemen showing up to be interviewed. The servants were refusing them admittance as fast as they arrived, but the very sight of them galled him. He wasn't sure why. *He* at least had a chance with her. None of these chaps did.

Still, if she swallowed her pride and behaved like a woman of her rank was expected to, she could probably snag a decent husband. She had some notion that only fortune hunters would court her, but he'd seen how gentlemen in society looked at her. He'd even heard crude speculations about how she would be in bed. None of those men dared make inappropriate advances toward her, knowing that her brothers would call them out. So they would have to marry her to have her.

Granted, many of them would balk at marrying a wife with such a notorious family. Some, however, would weigh the benefits of having access to the Plumtree fortune—and to a beautiful woman's body—against the Sharpe family scandal and would decide that Lady Minerva would make a good wife indeed, even at twenty-eight. He could think of several who would do so.

He scowled. Not if he had anything to say about it.

As he approached the massive gateway into the first courtyard, he wondered if her brothers had ordered that he be barred from entering. He wouldn't put it past them. They'd said they would talk to her—what might she have told them? Probably not the truth, but she could say a great deal to hurt his case without revealing all. And Minerva was perfectly capable of changing her mind about their bargain after their kiss yesterday.

Not that he regretted their kiss. He didn't. And he hoped to kiss her again soon. Judging from how cordially the butler showed him into the Blue Parlor, that might not be too long. Apparently their bargain was still on—Minerva was waiting for him, wearing a wide-brimmed bonnet trimmed with numerous green silk bows and flowers to match her pelisse-robe of emerald silk.

But she looked agitated as she paced the Persian rug. He couldn't imagine why. Her grandmother sat in a chair by the fire, seemingly content to watch Giles take her granddaughter off for a drive.

He bowed to them both. "Good morning, ladies."

Minerva glared at him. "This isn't a good beginning at all, Mr. Masters. I said nine o'clock. It's a quarter past."

"Don't be rude, Minerva," her grandmother chided.

"Well, it *is*. And punctuality is important in a husband."

How odd that she would care about his being a few minutes late for a drive in the country. "Forgive me, I had some work to attend to."

"Oh, don't mind her," Mrs. Plumtree said. "Her brothers interrogated her about you last night, and she's been cranky ever since." Her gaze sharpened on Giles. "They seem to think you two have been friendly for some time."

"They said they got the idea from *you*," Minerva said, with a telling lift of her brow. "I can't imagine why you would imply such a thing. I told them that we danced together once, nothing more, but they already knew that."

"So you didn't tell them about our secret trysts through the years?" he said lightly. "The castle I carried you off to in

Inverness so that I could have my wicked way with you? The nights in Venice? Our elopement to Spain?"

"Very amusing, Mr. Masters," Mrs. Plumtree put in, suspicion fading from her face. "I daresay my grandsons didn't guess that your connection was through her books."

Minerva gaped at her grandmother. "How did you guess that those incidents were in my novels, Gran?"

Mrs. Plumtree sniffed. "I do know how to read, girl. And apparently so does Mr. Masters, even if your brothers don't seem to." She glanced around. "Speaking of your brothers, I'm rather surprised they went off to Tattersall's instead of staying around to protest this outing."

Minerva blinked, then said, "Yes, so am I." Taking Giles's arm, she gave it an unsubtle tug. "Which is why we should go, before they *do* show up to protest."

"I'll see you out," her grandmother said.

That was odd. Had Mrs. Plumtree heard from Freddy about what had happened yesterday? Surely not, or she wouldn't be allowing him to go off alone with Minerva in the first place.

Once they reached the drive, however, it became apparent why Mrs. Plumtree had followed them. "That's a very nice curricle, Mr. Masters," she said, running her keen gaze over the glossy black paint of his two-wheeled equipage. "And a nice pair of matched horses, eh? Must have cost you a pretty penny."

Her mercenary remark made him smile. "You assume that I bought it. How do you know I didn't win it at cards?"

"Because from what my grandsons tell me, you rarely win."

There was a reason for that: losers became privy to far more secrets than winners. They got to drown their sorrows in ale and hear other losers spill their stories. Since England was in a fight for its future, it needed lots of stories to find those unhappy citizens who did *not* want to play by the rules. Like the villains who'd spawned the Cato Conspiracy and plotted to murder the cabinet a few years back, before he'd alerted Ravenswood to their existence.

"Yet here I am, driving a nice rig," he said mildly. "So either I can afford it from my earnings or I don't lose as often as your grandsons contend."

"Or you're a spy for the French," Minerva said with a sharp-edged smile.

Mrs. Plumtree laughed. "Never had a spy in the family. Although as I recall, your father said there was a spy who came to visit—Sir Francis Walsingham, who did all sorts of treachery for Queen Elizabeth." She frowned. "Oh, dear, I may be confusing him with that vice admiral who stayed at Halstead Hall while fleeing Cromwell. His name was Main-something . . . Or am I thinking of that famous general? What was his name?"

"Gran!"

"Oh, forgive me. Don't mean to keep you from your drive." She flicked her hand toward the rig. "Go on then. Enjoy yourselves."

"We will," Minerva said and pointedly placed her foot on the step.

Giles hastened to hand her up. She was falling all over herself in her eagerness to get away with him. He'd be flattered, if not for her calculating expression. She was up to something, and it was undoubtedly something he wouldn't like. She looked far too much like the cat who ate the canary.

She patted the seat beside her. "Well, are we going or not?"

Leaping up into the seat, Giles took the reins from his tiger, waited until the young groom was settled on the back perch, then set the horses off. Mrs. Plumtree waved to them, then hobbled back through the archway.

As they headed down the drive, he stole a glance at Minerva. Her choice of attire seemed designed to drive him mad with lust. All those little frog fastenings—he itched to unfasten them one by one. And her bodice was just snug enough to make him wonder what it would be like to delve beneath the corset that barely constrained its ample treasures.

One honey dark curl fell across her cheek, and he felt a sudden impulse to sweep it back into place. Or tug off her bonnet to set her hair free to cascade down her slender back in a glorious display of wanton tresses—

Good God, wanton tresses indeed—he must be mad. How did she manage to do this to him every time he saw her?

As they reached the road he started to turn to the left, but she put her hand on his. "No, let's go the other way, shall we?"

His eyes narrowed on her. "It's not as pretty a drive."

"It's pretty enough," she said with a coy look that put him on the alert. She knew exactly what she did to him. The teasing seductress reveled in it, probably even meant to take advantage of it.

"Is there somewhere in particular you wanted to go, Minerva?"

"Certainly not. I just . . . prefer the other way."

He didn't believe her, but he'd let it go. For now. Until he figured out her game.

He turned his rig to the right.

With satisfaction on her face, she sat back in her seat. "So tell me, Giles, what *did* you say to my brothers to make them question me last night?"

"That there was more between us than they realized."

Glancing back at the tiger, she lowered her voice. "Aren't you worried that I'll reveal the truth about that night at the masquerade?"

"No."

"Why not?"

He shrugged. "It wouldn't serve your purpose. And you're nothing if not practical."

"Practical! If you're trying to flatter me, that's not the way to go about it."

He kept his voice low. With the noise from the horses, he doubted his tiger could hear, but no point in taking any chances. "You told me this was a pretend courtship. You said nothing about my having to exert myself to flatter you."

She laughed. "And would that really be such a chore?"

"Of course." He tooled the curricle around a sharp curve. "You're a writer—you'll expect the best in pretty compliments. And between dealing with your family yesterday, and rising at dawn to get some work done for an upcoming trial so I could be at your beck and call this morning, I've scarcely had time to prepare."

Her eyes scanned the road ahead, as if looking for something. "I thought you barristers had a natural bent for speechifying."

"Very well." He cleared his throat. "Lady Minerva, you are charged with attempting to disturb the peace of an esteemed barrister. How do you plead?"

She eyed him askance. "That is hardly a speech."

"It's the only kind of speechifying we barristers know. How do you plead?"

"Not guilty."

"I have a vast amount of evidence that says otherwise. For one thing, you're writing books about me."

"That evidence isn't pertinent to your case, sir. I didn't write them to disturb your peace, since I never thought you'd read them. I wrote only to satisfy my own whim. So there goes your evidence." She leaned forward. "Can't this curricle go any faster?"

He did nothing to increase his speed. If she wanted something from him, she'd have to ask for it. "I have more evidence. You're using me to fight your grandmother."

"But I'm not doing it to disturb your peace." Her eyes twinkled at him. "That just happens to be a happy side benefit. Without proving intent to commit a crime, you will lose your case against me very quickly."

"I see that you know the law a bit yourself. But you should know that I wouldn't take a case without being able to prove intent." He dipped his head toward her and dropped his voice to a seductive murmur. "My first piece of evidence is that you dressed to entice me this morning, in a gown that shows your fetching figure to best advantage. You're wearing rouge on your cheeks, which you never do. Nor do you ever wear jewelry, yet your ears are adorned with pearl earrings that accentuate your creamy skin, and gold bracelets that draw the eye to your slender wrists. All of it is quite weighty evidence that you deliberately set out to disturb my peace."

A blush brightened her cheeks. "You are very observant."

"I always have been." The talent had served him well as an informant for the government. And it was going to serve him very well in dealing with the sly Minerva. "That's why I've noticed that you're clearly bent on going somewhere in particular, probably somewhere you know I won't want to go. Are we far enough away from Halstead Hall for you to feel comfortable springing our new destination on me? Or must I wait until we drive halfway to London?"

He had the distinct satisfaction of seeing her start. Did she think him an idiot?

She stared at him a long moment, as if weighing her choices. Then she said, "Actually, I'm sure you'll be delighted to hear our destination. Gabe is racing this morning at ten o'clock. I want to watch the race. Undoubtedly you do, too."

That caught him off guard. How had he missed that bit of news? Ah, but he knew how. He'd been busy trying to corral a certain skittish female yesterday. "To be honest, I had no idea he was racing today."

She snorted. "Stop bamming me."

"I'm telling you the God's honest truth. In closing ranks around you, your brothers have clearly decided not to trust me with their secrets."

Her lips tightened into a line. "It doesn't matter. I know where they're racing. And I want you to take me there."

"It's no place for a woman."

"Exactly. When Gran hears that you took me to one of Gabe's private races and exposed me to the unsavory sorts who run in his fast set, she'll be appalled at the very idea of your marrying me and adding more scandal to the family name."

God, he hoped not. "If you say so."

"So hurry it up, will you? I don't have to arrive for the very beginning, but my brothers must at least see me there for this to work."

Damn. "You're determined to watch them thrash me, aren't you?"

"Don't be silly. I wouldn't let them thrash you. What use would you be to me then?"

He gritted his teeth. What use indeed? He began to think Minerva was enjoying her new game. Apparently she was tired of using him for a whipping boy in her books and had decided to use him as one in real life.

"Where exactly is this race?"

"You really don't know?"

"Would I be asking if I did?" he bit out.

"You don't have to be so snippy." She settled herself into the seat. "According to Freddy, it's near some inn in Turnham."

A cold chill went down his spine. "Gabe is threading the needle again?"

"Well, I can't see how he'd be threading a needle and racing at the same—"

"Not *a* needle, Minerva. *The* needle. That's the only reason he'd be racing near Turnham." Giles reined in the horses to stare at her. "Did Freddy say whom he was racing?"

"No. And why are you stopping?"

"Because I'm taking you home."

As he began to turn the rig, she jumped down. "You are *not*! I want to see Gabe race!"

He halted the horses to jump down, too, but motioned to his tiger to stay put. "You don't want to see *this* race, my dear. The last time Gabe threaded the needle, he broke his arm. This time, God only knows . . ."

The blood drained from Minerva's face. "Oh, Lord."

The course ran between two boulders on the outskirts of Turnham. The sporting set called the dangerous course "threading the needle" because the path between was too narrow for two rigs to run abreast, so one carriage had to fall behind to allow the other to pass through. Whoever reined in first generally lost the race; it was nearly impossible to make up lost ground between the boulders and the finish line.

Some of Turnham's townspeople had proposed blocking the track, but the local publicans and innkeepers made too much money off the private races run by reckless young blades to stand for that. Even the one death that had occurred hadn't dampened anyone's enthusiasm. Indeed, for the young men racing, it only lent more appeal to the course.

"There'd been talk about a rematch between Gabe and Chetwin because Gabe's accident kept them from finishing the race," Giles said grimly, "but I never thought your brothers would let Gabe go through with it."

Minerva's eyes turned cold. "You don't know Gabe very well if you think he'll listen to *them*. Not when it comes to Chetwin and that course. We have to stop him." Hitching up her skirts, she climbed back into the rig. "Come on!"

"Damn it, Minerva, you cannot—"

She took up the reins and flicked them to get the horses moving. "I'm going with you or without you."

As his tiger looked back at him in a panic, he sprinted to catch up with the rig, then leaped into it. Jerking the reins from her, he sent the horses into a run.

"If your brothers can't stop him," he clipped out, "what makes you think you can?"

"I have to try, don't you see?" Her face looked bleak now. "Do you know how difficult it has been for Gabe all these years since Roger Waverly died? All that nasty talk about Gabe being the Angel of Death . . ."

She bit her lower lip. "It wasn't *his* fault Mr. Waverly hit the boulders. If Mr. Waverly had just reined in when he saw he couldn't make it… But no, the man *had* to beat Gabe. He could never stand Gabe doing anything better than him. And Gabe hasn't been the same since. He acts like a happy-go-lucky fellow, but I've seen his face whenever Mr. Waverly is mentioned. I've seen how Gabe suffers."

"A good deal less than the Waverlys suffer, I imagine," Giles said tightly.

He could feel her gaze on him. "What's that supposed to mean?"

"His grandfather lost his only grandson, and Waverly's sister lost her only brother. Gabe knew what he was getting into when he ran that course. He should never have agreed."

"He was nineteen, for goodness sake! Did you do nothing foolish at nineteen?"

Thinking of the night when he'd unwittingly ruined his brother's prospective betrothal, Giles winced. "Gabe isn't nineteen now," he persisted.

"Yes, but he sees this as a matter of family honor. Chetwin insulted Mama."

Giles hadn't known that. He hadn't witnessed the incident that provoked Chetwin's initial challenge a few months ago— he'd been off in Bath, checking on something for Ravenswood. "Bloody hell."

"My sentiments exactly," she said.

Giles took a turn faster than he liked, throwing her against him. "Did you hear exactly how Gabe broke his arm?"

"Oliver said that the back of his rig hit one of the boulders as he came through ahead of Chetwin, and it sent his rig into a roll that tore it to pieces and threw Gabe from the carriage."

"That's right. And he could easily have broken his neck instead of his arm. I don't know if you can bear to watch—"

"I'm not going to watch. I'm going to stop him." Her voice thickened. "I refuse to see him die the same horrible death as Mr. Waverly."

"What time is the race scheduled for?" he asked.

"Ten o'clock."

"Check my watch. It's in my left coat pocket."

She did as he bade and let out a groan. "It's nearly ten already."

"We won't make it."

She dropped his watch back into his coat. "But I can see Turnham just ahead, and judging from the crowd, the course is on this side of town."

"Yes, but look at how many people are lining the course. We can't get through."

The sound of a pistol shot rang in the air, and they both knew what that meant.

"Oh, Giles!" she cried, grabbing his arm. "We're too late!"

"He'll be fine." He maneuvered his curricle off the road to skirt the crowd, trying to get closer to the makeshift track. "Your brother has a knack for escaping death."

That didn't seem to reassure her. She clung to his arm as he'd never seen her do with any other man.

Reining in, he leaped from the curricle and reached up to help her down. Then he left the curricle to his tiger and headed through the crowd with Minerva at his side. It took them several minutes to push their way through. They reached the front just in time to see Gabe enter the boulders just ahead of Chetwin.

"Good Lord . . ." She breathed, gripping his arm, her face pale.

An odd protectiveness surged through him. He covered her hand with his and squeezed. How he wished he could spare her this.

How he wished Gabriel Sharpe had less family honor and more good sense.

They held their breaths until Gabe shot free of the boulders.

"Thank the good Lord," Minerva whispered, her fingers a manacle about his arm.

Then they caught their breaths again until Chetwin had passed between the boulders safely, too. Once he was out he tried to make up the time, but Gabe had the clear lead to the finish line. The crowd surged toward the two posts marked with red ribbons.

"Lord Gabriel is winning!" cried a voice near them, and others took up the cry.

"He always wins, damn his eyes," grumbled a man with his back to them. "They all do."

When the man turned and headed down the road to Turnham, Giles got a good look at his profile and gave a start.

"Minerva," he said in a low voice. "What the hell is your mother's cousin doing here?"

Chapter Six

$\mathcal{M}$inerva missed Giles's remark in the cheers that followed as Gabe shot over the finish line. Relieved that he'd survived the race intact, she turned to Giles with a smile on her face. "What did you say?"

"Desmond Plumtree is here. Does he usually watch Gabe's races?"

She followed Giles's gaze to where a man in his fifties strolled down the road to Turnham. It was her cousin, all right. She'd recognize his discolored beaver hat with its narrow brim anywhere. Beside him was his twenty-six-year-old son, Ned.

"I can't imagine why Desmond would come for this," she said. "He's always been too priggish to approve of our 'outrageous ways,' as he calls them. And they live in Rochester where their mill is, half a day's journey away at least. What business could he and Ned possibly have here?"

"That's what I'm wondering," Giles said tersely. "It's not the first time he's been in Turnham."

A chill went through her. "Oh, Lord, you're right."

His gaze shot to her. "You know?"

"About Jarret's suspicions concerning Desmond and his possible involvement in our parents' deaths? Of course I know. Nothing is ever a secret in our house."

He eyed her askance. "Jarret wouldn't have told you."

"Well, no." She gave him a sheepish smile. "But I overheard him discussing it with Oliver. Jarret said Desmond stayed in Turnham on the day of our parents' deaths, and the groom who cared for his horse claimed that Desmond had blood on his stirrup when he returned to the inn from wherever he'd been."

Taking her arm, Giles started back toward his curricle.

"What are you doing?" she asked.

"I'm leaving you with my tiger while I follow the Plumtrees and find out why they're here. It's odd that Desmond should be in Turnham again, for no apparent reason. It might shed light on why he was here the night of your parents' deaths."

She snatched her arm from his hand. "If *you* follow him, so will I." She set off toward the road, along with those leaving the race, and headed toward Turnham. "It's my *family* we're talking about, you know."

Shooting her an exasperated look, he fell into step beside her. "Didn't you say you wanted to be seen by your brothers at the race?"

"This is far more important." It *was* odd that Desmond had come here. What did it mean? "And two of us have a better chance of uncovering the truth."

"All right. But follow my lead. We don't want him to see us. It could be dangerous if he realizes that we suspect him."

"Now you really *do* sound like a spy," she teased.

"Only because you think of everyone in terms of how they might fit into your fictional landscape," he countered with a thin smile.

"Fictional landscape." She chuckled. "I like that. I'll have to use it in a book. I may even give the line to Rockton."

"You're not going to write about Rockton anymore, remember?" His gaze sharpened at a point ahead of them. "They're entering the Black Bull."

"That's where Desmond stayed when he came to Turnham nineteen years ago." She kept her voice low because of the men around them who were also surging toward the Black Bull.

"I wouldn't make too much of that; it's the only inn in Turnham. And they might just be availing themselves of the taproom, as these other gentlemen plan to do, I suspect."

"There's an easy way to find out if they're guests," she said. "We could see if Desmond's rig is in the stables."

"Good thinking, my dear," he said, taking a sudden turn toward the stables. "No wonder you plot your books so cleverly."

The compliment warmed her more than all his earlier remarks about her "fetching figure" and "creamy skin."

He led them past the stables at a quick walk. "Would you recognize his rig if you saw it?"

"Certainly. His favorite equipage is a gig that's painted the most god-awful blue." She glanced casually into the stables. "It's there, Giles. He's staying in the inn. Why?"

They kept walking. "I don't know, but clearly he didn't just pop over here to watch Gabe race." He stopped at the other end of the stables to stare back at the inn. "If we could at least learn . . ." He groaned. "Uh-oh. He's coming back out."

Swiftly, he tugged her around the side of the stables. As they watched furtively, Desmond and Ned strode across the inn yard. After Desmond spoke to the ostler, they climbed into the gig and drove off toward Ealing.

Giles's gaze narrowed and he turned to Minerva. "I have an idea for how we can find out what he's doing here. Come on."

Taking her arm, he headed to the inn. As they walked, he removed his gloves and tucked them into his coat pocket, then fished a ring out of his other coat pocket and put it on his left ring finger. "Play along, Minerva."

When he covered her hand with his, she glanced down at the ring, then started. It was a signet ring of the kind titled gentlemen wore.

Before she could ask where he'd acquired it, he walked inside bold as brass and headed straight for the innkeeper, who was busily directing servants to accommodate the sudden crowd of thirsty gentlemen.

"Ah, my good man," he called to the innkeeper, "do you by any chance have rooms available? Or has this crowd rented them all?"

The innkeeper took their measure in one quick glance, then smiled broadly. "No, sir. They've only come to drink after the race. They'll be gone by evening. Did you need a room for the night?"

"Several nights, actually." When Minerva started, Giles squeezed her hand, as if to caution her. Then he added with the perfect amount of condescension, "I am Lord Manderley of Durham, and this is my wife."

The innkeeper's eyes lit up. Clearly he had no trouble believing Giles, and who wouldn't? As always, Giles was dressed as well as any titled lord—his coat and trousers of dark brown superfine were exquisitely tailored to show off his broad shoulders and muscular calves, his waistcoat was of the finest figured silk, and his Wellington boots were perfectly polished.

And he had the haughty manner down pat. "Your inn seems to be adequate for our purposes," he went on. "We are in the area looking at properties to purchase. We plan to spend the week at least, but we do have one question before we decide if your establishment will suit us."

"Ask anything you wish, my lord," the innkeeper said with great enthusiasm.

Minerva could practically see him calculating the amount of money to be made from a rich lord who would require a week's worth of lodgings and expensive meals, not to mention stabling for a team of horses.

"As we were approaching the inn," Giles said, "we saw a gentleman we thought we knew. A Mr. Desmond Plumtree?"

"Yes, my lord. Mr. Plumtree is indeed staying here with his son."

Giles turned to her with a frown. "I told you it was him, my dear. I cannot tolerate the sight of that man day after day, knowing what he did to my poor brother."

Catching on to his game, Minerva said soothingly, "Oh, I'm sure it will be fine, darling." She smiled at the innkeeper. "He's not staying long, is he?"

"Oh no, my lady, just one more night," the innkeeper said hastily. "And he's not even here at the moment. He's gone off on his wanderings."

"Wanderings!" Giles cried. "So he's in the neighborhood a great deal, is he?"

"No, my lord, certainly not! He hasn't been here in nigh on twenty years . . . until a few months ago."

"But he'll be here tonight." With a heavy sigh, Giles glanced at her. "We should find another inn closer to Ealing. Honestly, sweetiekins, there are more properties in that vicinity to suit our needs than in this one."

Sweetiekins? She stifled her smile. "But I'm so tired. Can't we just stay here?"

"I don't know. If we should happen to come across Mr. Plumtree, I'm not sure I can contain myself."

"My lord," the innkeeper interjected, "I swear that your

paths won't cross. I'll make sure that you're put in an entirely different part of the inn."

"I suppose he has taken the best room in the house already," Giles complained.

"Oh no, my lord. The best room is in the back, and his is in the front, overlooking the inn yard. So you see, it wouldn't be a problem."

"Come, my dove, I'm sure we can avoid him for just the one night," Minerva wheedled.

Giles gave the innkeeper a pouting look. "If you can assure us . . ."

"I swear you won't have to endure Mr. Plumtree's presence for one moment. I'll show you the room. I'm sure it will please you."

The innkeeper hurried up the stairs, his other guests forgotten.

As Minerva and Giles followed, she whispered, "This had better not be a ploy to get me alone."

"Now, sweetiekins, would I do that?" he teased.

"I wouldn't put it past you, my dove."

As they approached the room, Giles said, "And where exactly did you say his room was?"

"I'll show you, my lord." The innkeeper brought them to the end of the hall and pointed down another. "It's that last room on the left. He won't come back till late, and I'm sure you will have retired by then."

Giles sighed. "Very well, since my dear wife is so set upon it, we'll take it." He dropped some gold into the innkeeper's hand.

The man's eyes widened. "Yes, my lord, certainly." He led them back to their room and opened it. "Shall I have someone fetch your bags?"

"My man is coming behind with them in another rig. Do let me know when he arrives, will you?"

"Of course." He handed the key to Giles. "If you need anything else . . ."

"We'll be fine for now. My dear lady wants to rest."

"Certainly, my lord."

As soon as the man was gone, Minerva said, "You lie just a jot too convincingly for my taste, sir."

"I could say the same about you, sweetiekins." He grinned.

"Call me that again and you'll find yourself missing an essential part of your anatomy."

"What a spoilsport you are." He went out into the hall and looked both ways. No one was around. "Come on," he said and headed for Desmond's room.

She followed him, curious to see what he was up to.

Giles reached the door and tried it. It was locked. "Give me one of your hairpins."

She removed one and handed it to him. "What are you planning to do?"

He went to work on the lock. "Take a look at his room, what else?"

"Giles Masters, how on earth did you learn—"

"I work with criminals, remember? They've taught me a trick or two. Comes in useful when I stumble home drunk to find I've misplaced my key."

She eyed him skeptically. That was the flimsiest excuse she'd ever heard for a talent that was decidedly suspicious.

It took him mere moments to pick the lock. Then he led her inside and closed the door. He headed straight for the open trunk in one corner.

Minerva scanned the room. It was actually quite fine by coaching inn standards, with a chest of drawers, large bed, fancy dressing screen, and a lovely washbasin and pitcher of blue speckled china. "What are we looking for?"

"Anything that will tell us why he and his son are here."

"Well, it's not for their health," she said, taking note of the empty wine bottles piled up on the oak table and the pair of muddy boots sitting near the bed. "Someone's been tramping in the damp outdoors. Hunting, perhaps?"

"It's not hunting season," Giles said as he searched the trunk with great care.

"Nineteen years ago, he told the groom at this inn that the blood on his stirrup came from hunting."

"I know. It wasn't hunting season then, either."

"Depends on what you're hunting," Minerva said coldly. "Or *whom*."

Giles straightened and held something out to her with a grim expression. "Indeed it does."

She looked close to find that he held a crude, hand-drawn map. After one glance, she felt goose bumps rise on her flesh. "I think that's our estate."

"I agree it resembles it, but it's hard to tell with nothing but fields, forests, and hills delineated on it. And some of the landmarks look wrong." He examined it carefully. "If it *is* a map of the estate, what does Plumtree want with it?"

"I don't know. Giles, you don't think he really could have killed them, do you?"

"We don't have enough information yet to be sure. But if he did, what was his reason? And why is he returning so many years later . . . if that really is where he's going?" Heading back to the trunk, he said, "Look in those drawers over there. See if you can find a journal or letters or anything more than this."

A sudden sound in the hall made them both start.

"I can't believe you left it here, you blithering fool," said Desmond's voice. "We can't get anywhere without the map."

Casting her a warning glance, Giles tossed the map into the trunk and nodded her toward the dressing screen. She and Giles slid behind it just seconds before the door opened.

Thankfully, there was a chair there. He sat down and pulled her onto his lap so their heads couldn't be seen above the screen. Her pulse was racing, but he seemed surprisingly calm. He didn't even jump when Desmond's voice sounded again very near them. *She* nearly leaped out of her skin.

"I swear to God, Ned," Desmond grumbled, "how can you be such an imbecile? You left the door unlocked, too."

"I didn't! Why are you always blaming *me*?"

Giles wrapped his arms about her waist, and she leaned into him, half afraid that Desmond might hear the thundering of her heart. If he found them here, what would he do? Considering what he might have done to Mama and Papa—

No, that was absurd. Even if he *had* been involved in her parents' deaths, he wouldn't be fool enough to harm her and Giles in a public inn, with his son present. Besides, if Giles could talk his way in here, he could certainly talk his way out.

"I blame you because whenever things go wrong, it's usually your fault," Desmond complained to Ned. "You're the one who left the map here."

"At least now you can change your boots," Ned said. "You don't want to ruin your best pair."

"I suppose. Ah, and here's the map, at the very top of the trunk. You'd think you'd have seen it there."

"I swear it wasn't there when we left."

"Of course it was," Desmond snapped. The bed creaked, as if he'd sat down on it. "You never look for anything. I don't know why I even brought you along this time."

"Because I'm handy with a blade, that's why."

A chill ran through Minerva. Good Lord. When had her second cousin picked up *that* little talent?

"For all the good *that* does us," Desmond said. "Now come here and help me with these boots."

Minerva wanted to scream. How long did the two mean to stay, anyway? She tilted her head to look at Giles, who was calmly watching the edge of the screen. Wasn't he the slightest bit worried that they might be caught? That Ned might *use* the blade he was handy with? Giles acted as if he got into such dangerous situations every day.

Her blood ran cold. Perhaps he did. What if there was a reason he knew all these strange things? What if he were involved in some secret plot? He might even be a spy for the French, like Rockton!

Right. Giles as a spy. Her imagination was getting the better of her. Giles would never be a traitor. And England would never hire a rascal like him to do that sort of work. Besides, the war with France had ended ten years ago, so who would he spy on? Denizens of a gaming hell? The publican at his favorite tavern?

Ridiculous thought.

He caught her staring at him and his gaze darkened, then swept slowly down her in a heated glance that seared her wherever it touched. Suddenly she became very aware that she was sitting on his lap. It felt very . . . personal. Especially when his hand began to slide over her belly, back and forth, with a familiarity that made her blood race.

His very eyes invited her to sin as they fixed on her mouth and deepened to a cobalt blue. She jerked her gaze from his, but it was too late. Now she was all too conscious of him. The scent of his Guard's Bouquet enveloped her, mingling with the smell of sweat and dirt and pure *man*. His strong thighs flexed under her bottom, and she could feel his breath fanning the ribbons of her bonnet. Worst of all, his hand continued to move in slow, seductive circles on her corseted belly, rousing an acute ache for more.

What was he doing? He must be out of his mind. They were inches away from being discovered, and he was . . .

Oh, Lord. He was stealthily removing her bonnet. He handed it to her, then had the audacity to kiss her hair. This was madness!

This was intoxicating. To be held by a man like this. To be this close, this intimate. To feel the heat of his body against her own. She ought to be chiding him with a look, at the very least. She knew very well how to quell a man's advances that way.

Yet she sat here doing nothing, reveling in the excitement that coursed through her, the thrill of doing something dangerous.

The thrill of doing it with Giles. The fact that they were a hairsbreadth away from being discovered enhanced the thrill even more.

She could hear Desmond cursing at Ned to hurry, could feel when the first boot hit the floor, but all her concentration was on Giles, who was now kissing her temple, her cheek, her ear. His faintly whiskered chin scraped the delicate skin of her jaw, and she wanted so badly to turn her mouth to meet his.

Why did he have to be so good at this? And why must she melt into a quivering pudding whenever he began to caress her?

"Come on, let's go," Desmond said.

She jumped, afraid for half a second that he'd found them out. Giles stopped his caresses, cocking his head and setting his gaze once more on the end of the screen.

"We're losing daylight," Desmond went on. "I shouldn't have lingered to watch my cousin race."

Footsteps sounded, heading for the door. "Would've been worth it if you'd won some blunt off the bloody arse," Ned retorted.

"Don't remind me. I should have known better than to bet against Gabriel. Damned bastard probably fixed the race somehow."

Minerva tensed. Drat her cousins and their resentment of her family. Why must they always say such nasty things?

The door opened. The sounds of footsteps passing into the hall made her catch her breath. She only released it when the door closed, though the snick of the key turning in the lock had her groaning.

Leaping from Giles's lap, she said, "We have to follow them."

Giles rose with oddly stiff movements. "There's no way we'll even get back to my curricle before they've disappeared on the road. But if they're going to the estate, we can look for them there."

"I suppose that's true."

She tied her bonnet on as he headed for the door, his picklock in hand. "Either way, we need to get out of here before they decide they've forgotten something else."

Nodding her agreement, she watched as he picked the lock again. They left and headed for the stairs, only to halt when they heard Desmond's voice waft up from below. "What do you mean, you want me to leave? I paid good money for my room."

"I can't have your sort hanging about with important people staying here," the innkeeper said.

"*My* sort! I'll have you know—"

"I always thought you were a suspicious one, talking

about hunting grouse when there's none hereabouts. And his lordship's anxiety confirmed my suspicions."

"His lordship?" Desmond cursed loudly. "I suppose one of my cousins saw me and is causing trouble. If those Sharpes—"

"Sharpe isn't the man's name. You just be on your way, do you hear? Pack up and leave before he gets wind of your being here."

"Who *is* this man?"

"Lord Manderley, and a fine gentleman he is, too."

"Manderley is *here*?" Desmond squeaked.

Minerva's gaze shot to Giles. "I thought you made him up," she whispered.

His eyes gleamed with mischief. "Why invent things when the truth will serve? It just so happens that your cousin owes Manderley a lot of money."

"How do you know?"

He flashed her an enigmatic smile. "Your brother wanted me to look into Plumtree's finances. So I did."

She'd thought that Jarret had asked him to look into the situation involving Desmond and Gran's will, but she wasn't going to argue the point just now.

Desmond's panicked voice rose from below. "If Manderley is here, I'm leaving."

Oh, dear. She glanced to Giles, but he was already tugging her in the direction of their room. They'd barely gotten inside and shut the door when they heard Desmond stomping up the stairs with Ned.

Though she knew he couldn't see them, she caught her breath and held it until she heard boot steps passing down the other hall.

"We can't leave until they're gone," Giles said. "Can't risk running into them."

She eyed him with deep amazement. How did he manage to maintain such an unsettling calm? "While *I* stand here shaking, with my heart pounding and my entire body tense, you act as if this were all in a day's work for you."

A shutter came down over his features. "I don't know what you're talking about."

There he went again, behaving as if his actions were perfectly logical when they both knew they weren't. One way or the other, she was going to make him admit what he had been up to that day at Newmarsh's. It had finally occurred to her that she had the perfect way to do it: accuse him of the one thing she was certain he was not. The one thing he wouldn't like being accused of.

"Admit it, there's a reason you were in Lord Newmarsh's study that night, a reason you know how to break into inn rooms and stay calm in the face of danger."

"And what reason might that be?" he bit out.

"It's quite clear to me. You're a professional thief."

Chapter Seven

$\mathcal{G}$iles laughed, which made her frown. But he couldn't help himself, considering what he'd been afraid she was going to say. "A thief. You think I'm a thief. Based on nothing more than my ability to break into your cousin's room."

"And the fact that I saw you stealing something years ago. That you're comfortable sneaking into people's houses. And adamant about not being interested in my fortune. Clearly you have another source of income."

That banished his amusement. He strode toward her, anger fueling his movements. "Is it really so hard to believe I might make a decent living at what I do? That I might be clever enough to succeed as a barrister and command high fees?"

She stared him down. "Well, you must admit—"

"No need to admit it, when you've decided to admit it *for* me, with your vivid imagination and your talent for fiction." He backed her against the door. "So this is what you've been doing with that keen mind of yours: turning me into a criminal mastermind."

"I wasn't—"

"Yes, you were." He braced his hands on either side of her, his temper getting the better of him.

She met his gaze steadily, apparently not the least intimidated.

"What am I supposed to think when you break into rooms and lie so easily?"

"I'm not the only one who lies easily," he shot back. "You lie daily with your pen and think nothing of it."

"That's not the same—I'm telling stories. People know that."

"Do they? Everyone speculates that Rockton is your brother." He leaned closer. "And just a short while ago you played the part of Lady Manderley without a qualm, yet I'm not accusing *you* of being a criminal. I'm not questioning *your* character."

She sniffed. "I was only trying to help you find out about Desmond."

"Which I was doing for *your* family's benefit. And this is the thanks I get—accusations and insinuations." He glowered down at her. "You know what this is really about? You hate the fact that you're attracted to me. So you're inventing new levels of villainy in hopes that it will keep you from desiring me."

She drew herself up. "That is the most ridiculous thing I've ever heard. You're merely trying to distract me from asking perfectly sensible questions—"

He kissed her. What else could he do? He *was* trying to distract her from asking questions, and she was far too clever to fall for it. But there was some truth to his words, whether she admitted it or not.

He'd seen the flare of need in her eyes when he'd caressed her earlier, felt the sharp increase in her breath. She wanted him. And he damned well wanted her. He'd already spent half the day aching for her, tempted beyond endurance by her lush mouth and delicate wrists and the dainty ankle he'd glimpsed when she'd leapt into his curricle. Having her squirm on his lap had been the last straw.

God, she was sweet to kiss. For a woman with a reputation

for tearing men to ribbons with her tongue, she had the softest mouth he'd ever known. He could lose himself in it so easily.

He could lose himself in *her* so easily. And that would be a mistake. The last time he'd let his cock lead him, he'd nearly ruined two people's lives forever. So he should keep a firm clamp on his urges, not let them loose.

But how was he supposed to do that with Minerva? She shredded his control with every arch of her perfect body. Her hands were about his neck now, dislodging his hat, which went tumbling to the floor. He could feel her fingers in his hair, and it made him want her fingers in other places, doing other things . . . God save him . . .

"Intriguing as this is," she murmured against his lips, "it won't make me stop asking questions."

"Are you sure about that?" He dragged his mouth down and beneath the lacy ruff at her collar to suck her neck.

"Quite sure," she said, though she quivered beneath his lips. "I'm not . . . a flighty schoolgirl anymore."

He drew back to stare into her beautiful green eyes. "Not for one moment of your life have you ever been flighty."

"Then call it foolish." She tipped up her chin. "I was too foolish to realize I was merely a moment's amusement to you that night at the masquerade."

The pain in her eyes made him wince. He'd hurt her more than he'd ever realized. "Not that, either." He kissed her temple. "Just too young. And in the wrong place at the wrong time in my life."

"A likely excuse. I haven't been 'too young' for some time, and it's taken you nine years to even kiss me again. At this rate, you'll only advance to ravishing me when I'm forty."

He dearly hoped he'd be ravishing her at forty. And thirty-five and twenty-nine and the day after tomorrow.

Or today. That would certainly move this process along.

"If it's ravishment you want . . ." He lifted her in his arms and carried her to the bed, where he tossed her down onto it.

"What the devil!" she exclaimed. "You'll crush my favorite bonnet!"

She started to rise, but he climbed on the bed to lie half on her, his arm manacling her waist and his leg trapping one of hers. "Oh, I plan to do more than crush your bonnet, minx."

Her eyes sparked a warning. "Be careful, Giles. I might decide to scream."

He lifted one eyebrow. "Then you'd have a fine time explaining why you're screaming about your 'husband's' advances." He began to work loose the frogs holding her pelisse-robe together.

When he opened it to bare the upper swells of her breasts to his gaze, she dragged in a heavy breath. "Perhaps I'll tell the truth, then," she said shakily, though she didn't try to close her gown.

His pulse jumped into a frenzy. "That you're not really my wife? That you lied about that? Let me take a room for us? Let me get you alone? I should like to hear *that* conversation."

Warily she watched as he bent the cup of her corset down to reveal one linen-shrouded breast. His breath caught in his throat. It was every bit as pretty as he'd expected—full and pouty, with a rosy nipple that pebbled beneath his stare. He cupped the ample flesh in his hand, relishing the instant fire that flashed in her gaze.

"How clever of you . . . to make it be . . . my fault," she breathed as he lowered his head to suck at her succulent breast through her shift and tongue her hard nipple.

She gasped but didn't stop him.

"Shall I take the blame, then?" he rasped against the damp

linen, his throat raw with need of her. "For wanting you? For craving the taste of you? For trying to drive you as insane as you've been driving me?"

With a moan, she buried her fingers in his hair and urged him back to her breast. "Have I been driving you insane?" she whispered.

"You know you have." Why was she letting him do this? Why wasn't she protesting?

It didn't matter. Ever since that damned Valentine's Day ball, he'd had too many dreams where she lay beneath him, willing and eager. And now that he was living that dream, he wasn't going to stop.

He shifted his body so he could lift her skirts. "All I've been able to think of ever since we danced," he murmured, "is how I want to touch you." He slid his hand up under her petticoats to smooth it along her stocking-clad calves. "How I want to fondle you until you cry out your pleasure." He reached her garters and moved higher. "To plunder your soft body in ways you can't imagine."

Her chest rose and fell with her rapid breaths; her eyes were wide but not the least afraid.

She ought to be afraid. He was reaching the end of his tether. She felt so good beneath her skirts, her skin as silky and warm as rose petals kissed by the sun.

Finding the tender place between her legs, he slipped his fingers inside the slit in her drawers to touch her curls. She was hot and damp for him, and he might explode just knowing that.

When he bent his head to suck her breast again, she dragged in a harsh breath but still managed to murmur, "So tell me . . . the truth. Are you a thief? Or perhaps . . . something worse?"

At first her question didn't register. He was too caught up in filling his hands and his mouth with her lovely flesh. When at last her words sank in, disappointment crashed through him. So *that's* why she was letting him touch her. She thought to use her body to distract him, to get him to answer her questions.

He wasn't sure whether to laugh or groan. Clearly she didn't know whom she was dealing with; two could play this game.

Deliberately he cupped her between the legs, enjoying how her eyes went wide in shock. "Why do you care?" he rasped. "You don't intend to marry me anyway. So what does it matter if I'm a thief?"

Her breathing was unsteady. Good. He wanted her as unsettled as he was. "Perhaps it's . . . simple intellectual curiosity," she choked out.

"Like this little interlude? Is that what you're doing with me, sweet? Satisfying your intellectual curiosity?"

He dragged his finger up her delicate cleft until he found the luscious center of her passion, then thumbed it until she let out a cry of surprise.

"Oh . . . my word . . . Giles . . ."

"Or perhaps you're reconsidering the idea of marriage to me," he went on. "That's why it's so imperative that you know my true character."

Though she squirmed beneath him, her face growing flushed, she shook her head. "I want . . . to be left alone to . . . write my books."

"Then you shouldn't do things like this . . . let me touch you, taste you."

Nor should he. Since seduction hadn't been her purpose, he would be a true scoundrel to continue. But he was rapidly forgetting he wasn't a scoundrel anymore. She smelled too sweet, tasted too delicious. And he wanted her too badly.

Only half-conscious of what he did, he rubbed himself against her thigh, seeking relief for the rising ache in his cock.

She blinked and grabbed his hand. "What's that in your pocket? It's a pistol, isn't it? I *knew* you were up to something suspicious."

With a laugh, he forced her hand down to his "pistol" and rubbed it along his flesh, an action that was as much pain as pleasure for him, since he knew that was *all* he would get to do. "It's not a pistol, minx. It's what happens to a man when a woman arouses him beyond his control. Do you understand?"

The hot color rising up her neck told him that she had caught on. "I-I didn't realize . . . that is—"

A knock came at the door.

"Damn it all to hell," he gritted out under his breath. "What do you want?" he called out.

His tone must have been too sharp, for there was a long pause. "My lord, if I might have a moment of your time . . ."

With a sigh, he glanced down at Minerva. "Looks like you've been spared for now, sweetiekins."

Pushing off the bed, he walked slowly to the door to give his cock time to calm and her to fasten up the frogs on her pelisse-robe. He found his hat lying near the bed and put it on, then waited until she had left the bed before he opened the door. "Yes?"

"I just wanted to inform you that Mr. Plumtree is gone, my lord. So you needn't worry about encountering him in the halls."

"Actually, sir, we've decided to leave the inn ourselves," Giles said bluntly.

"What?" he squeaked. "Why?"

"My wife doesn't like the room."

As if on cue, Minerva came forward. Though he could

see she was shaken, she managed a theatrical sniff. "It has an unpleasant odor, sir. And I would swear I saw a rat run under the bed."

"I beg your pardon, my lady, but we do not have rats," the innkeeper protested. "And if there's an odor, perhaps another room—"

"Sorry, my good fellow, but we're leaving." Giles handed the man a number of sovereigns. "I hope this will make up for any inconvenience we've caused you."

The innkeeper stared at the coins, and his eyes brightened. "Yes, my lord. Thank you, my lord."

"Come, my dear," Giles said, holding out his arm.

As she took it, he dared another glance at her. The flowers on her bonnet were a bit crushed and her clothing a little disordered, but nothing that anyone would probably remark upon. She'd been lucky. She just didn't know how lucky.

As they headed down the stairs, he murmured, "Don't ever do that again."

Her gaze flew to his. "What?"

"Taunt me into losing control with you."

"Is that what I did? I thought I merely pointed out that you've been rather inattentive for a man who claims to want to marry me for something other than my fortune."

"Did you want me to be more attentive?" he asked seriously.

She wouldn't look at him as they headed back to the curricle. "Of course not."

"And now?"

"Do as you please. It matters nothing to me."

Yet something had changed between them. The air that had been charged with sensual energy before fairly crackled with it now. Until today, she'd been denying that she wanted him. She no longer could.

Her tone hardened. "You gave the innkeeper an awful lot of money. And there's that signet ring you're wearing. Tell me, how exactly did you come by all of that?"

"Are we back to your absurd suspicions?" he growled. "Hasn't it occurred to you that it would be difficult for me to find a fence for my goods when I'm working as an officer of the law? I'd risk exposure by any criminal who recognized me at the courthouse."

"Then what exactly are you—"

"I don't know whether to be flattered that you think me such a clever criminal mastermind, or insulted that you think me so devoid of good character." He steered her through the people still milling about near the course. "Except for when I took those papers, I'm not a thief, Minerva. I swear it on my honor." He shot her a long glance. "Unless you think me too much a scoundrel to have any honor?"

She looked embarrassed. "Well, no. But you still haven't explained why—"

"This conversation will have to wait for later," he murmured as he caught sight of his rig. "We have a more important problem to worry about."

"Oh?" she said testily.

"It appears that your brothers have found us."

She followed his gaze, then groaned.

Stoneville was sitting right in Giles's curricle, ignoring the tiger who was holding the horses and looking panicked. Jarret and Gabe lounged on either side of the rig, and the expressions on their faces as he approached with Minerva told Giles that his reprieve from a thrashing was about to end.

"Fancy seeing you here," Giles quipped.

Jarret's eyes narrowed. "We spotted your rig and figured you had to be about." He pushed away from the curricle, his expression murderous.

Minerva leaned into Giles, as if seeking his protection. It was most gratifying.

"And since you already told us you were calling on Minerva this morning . . ." Gabe continued with a threatening glare.

Stoneville leaped down from the curricle. "Her bonnet is askew. Doesn't her bonnet look rather the worse for wear to you, Jarret?"

"Definitely. And her gown, too."

"Not that it's any of *your* concern," Minerva snapped, "but my gown and my bonnet are mussed because we were hiding from Desmond."

That brought them up short.

"Desmond was here?" Oliver asked.

"Yes. And when Mr. Masters and I saw him, we followed him to find out why. That's how we ended up hiding in his room in the inn and nearly getting caught."

Jarret's gaze moved from Giles to Minerva. "Perhaps you should start from the beginning, Minerva."

"Very well." Quickly she launched into a brief version of their activities in the inn, though he noticed she hid the fact that Giles had broken into Desmond's room. Instead, she told them that the door was unlocked.

How very curious. She was lying to protect him. She might have some ridiculous notion that he was a thief, but she clearly didn't want him getting caught.

When she got to the part about their hiding behind the screen in Desmond's room, Jarret scowled at Giles. "What were you thinking, to let her go along while you followed him?"

"*Let* her?" Giles retorted. "Clearly, you don't know your sister very well if you think I could stop her once she decided to do something."

"You shouldn't have brought her here in the first place,"

Gabe pointed out with a hard stare. "For God's sake, man, have you no—"

"I *made* him bring me here," Minerva snapped. "Once I found out you were racing Mr. Chetwin—"

"How exactly *did* you find that out?" Gabe shot Giles an angry glance.

"Don't look at *me*," Giles said. "I didn't even know about the race."

"Freddy told me," Minerva said. Oliver cursed under his breath. "And once I heard you were planning to run that horrible course again, the whole English army couldn't keep me from trying to stop you. I only wish we hadn't arrived too late."

"I won, you know," Gabe said with a superior smirk.

Giles rolled his eyes. That was *not* the tack to take with Minerva.

She marched up to Gabe and stabbed her finger at his chest, startling him. "You're lucky you didn't end up dead, you fool. What were you thinking? After that last crash, I assumed you had the sense not to risk it, but no, we drive up to find you recklessly hurtling toward the boulders . . ."

Her voice caught as if on a sob, and Gabe's smirk turned to alarm. "Come on, Minerva, I was fine!"

"Yes, but you could have been killed!" When she drew out her handkerchief to dab at one eye, Giles wondered cynically if her tears were real. He'd seen his sisters manufacture tears often enough.

If she had manufactured them, it was a clever way to defuse her brothers' anger and draw attention away from what she and Giles had been doing. Gabe wore an expression of pure chagrin, and the other two exchanged nervous glances.

"And you, Jarret, of all people," she continued, rounding on that brother. Her tirade was drawing a crowd, but she didn't seem to care. "You *let* him do it, even after seeing him practically kill himself last time! You ought to be ashamed of yourself!"

"Now see here, sis," Jarret protested. "I tried to talk him out of it."

"Not hard enough. Perhaps you were more interested in wagering on the race than on keeping your brother from dying."

"Certainly not!" Jarret said, now on the defensive. "I didn't . . . I would never . . ."

"Then there's you, Oliver," she said, turning her heart-wrenching gaze on her eldest brother. "You know how badly he was hurt before. He could easily have broken his neck. Did you *want* to see him die?"

"Of course not!"

"Then why not demand that he stay home? Why come here and help him?"

"Someone had to make sure that Chetwin didn't cheat, and keep watch in case—" Oliver broke off with a grimace.

"He had an accident, like last time?" she said. "Is that what you were here for, to pick up the pieces afterward?"

"No . . . I mean . . ." To Giles's vast amusement, Stoneville sent him a helpless glance. "Would you please explain to my sister that a man has to stand by his brother, whatever choice he makes? What was I supposed to do, tie him up and never let him out of the house? He's a grown man, for God's sake."

When some of the onlookers watching their very public family spat murmured their agreement, Minerva rounded on Giles, her eyes flashing fire. "Don't you dare tell me you agree with them!"

He held up his hands. "I'm staying out of this fight. I brought you here, remember? I did my part."

"And anyway, it turned out fine," Gabe said irritably. "I don't know why you're making such a fuss. I didn't die, and I won the race besides. That's all that matters."

A new voice entered the fray. "Yes, that's always the only thing that matters to you, isn't it, Lord Gabriel? That you win."

They all turned to see a young woman standing there, accompanied by a gentleman who looked as if he wanted to be anywhere else but there. Giles tried to place the woman, who looked familiar somehow.

But apparently not to Gabe. "Who the devil are *you*?" he asked.

"Someone who hasn't forgotten the last victim of your recklessness," the woman said with great anguish in her voice. "But *you* have, haven't you? You've forgotten completely how you came to be called the Angel of Death."

Giles groaned as the truth registered, and the blood drained from Gabe's face.

"You're Miss Waverly," Gabe said, his eyes suddenly haunted.

"Exactly. Miss Virginia Waverly. And you killed my brother."

Chapter Eight

Minerva was thunderstruck. Virginia Waverly. She'd met the girl only once, at Roger Waverly's funeral, when Miss Waverly had been thirteen and quite unremarkable.

She wasn't unremarkable now. At twenty, she was a beauty, with a willowy figure, eyes of cornflower blue, and hair a mass of black ringlets set off by a pretty little straw bonnet with pink ribbons. And she fairly glowed with righteous anger as she confronted the man she saw as her brother's murderer.

Poor Gabe looked as if someone had struck him in the head with an ax. At least someone was trying to knock some sense into him, although the woman had no right to claim that he'd killed her brother.

"Miss Waverly," Minerva said, forcing a smile as she stepped forward, "I believe you're laboring under some misapprehension about your brother's death. You see—"

"Stay out of this, Minerva," Gabe ordered in an emotionless tone. "Miss Waverly has come here to get something off her chest, and I for one would like to hear it."

"Actually," Miss Waverly said hotly, "I came to see you race, Lord Gabriel. I couldn't believe you'd be so reckless again. That you'd risk another man's life after what—"

"Chetwin chose the course, not Gabe," Jarret put in. "As my sister said, you're laboring under a misapprehension."

"Would the rest of you just shut the hell up?" Gabe snapped. "This has nothing to do with any of you."

He approached Miss Waverly with leaden steps and a stricken expression that broke Minerva's heart.

"What do you want as recompense for your brother's death, Miss Waverly? Ask anything, and I'll do it. I've offered the same to your grandfather in writing many a time, but he won't even acknowledge my letters."

"He wants to forget," she bit out. "But I cannot."

"I understand. Roger was your brother. If I could go back and do it over—"

"What a lot of nonsense," she retorted in a bitter voice. "You're here today repeating history. I might have forgiven you before, but not now. Not when I heard that you meant to do exactly the same thing again. I learned of the first race against Chetwin too late to attend, but this one, I wasn't about to miss."

Gabe stiffened, his voice turning chilly as doom. "So you came to tell me that I'm a conscienceless bastard."

"No, I came to see you lose. But you never do, do you? Since you're so bent on risking everyone's lives on that wretched course, then you might as well race *me,* too. At least I can honor my brother's memory by succeeding in the one thing he wanted: beating the almighty Lord Gabriel Sharpe."

Gabe seemed as startled as the rest of them. "I'm not going to race you, Miss Waverly."

She set her hands on her hips. "Why not? Because I'm a woman? I'm an excellent whip, as good as my brother ever was."

"She really is, you know," her companion offered, a dark-haired fellow with an arresting face. "My cousin excels at driving four-in-hand. She even won a race against Letty Lade."

"I've heard," Gabe said tersely.

Minerva certainly hadn't. Letty Lade was the quite disreputable wife of Sir John Lade. Not only was she a notorious whip, but she was also rumored to have been the mistress to a highwayman before marrying her husband, who was famous as the founder of the Four-in-Hand Club. To beat Letty Lade would take a driver of much skill.

"But no matter how good you are, madam," Gabe went on. "I won't race you, and certainly not on this course. You'll have to take your revenge upon me some other way."

"You may change your mind after word gets around that a woman challenged you to a race and you refused," she said, her countenance calm. "I doubt you'll like being branded a coward by all your friends."

And with that cutting remark, Miss Waverly turned and walked off.

Her tall cousin paused a moment. "You do realize she's just angry and trying to provoke you."

Gabe stared after her, his eyes bleak. "She's succeeding."

"I'll talk some sense into her," her cousin said, then hurried after her.

"Good luck," Gabe muttered. Then abruptly he turned and headed away from where they stood.

"Where the devil are *you* going?" Jarret called after him.

"To get drunk!" he cried and strode determinedly toward the Black Bull.

"But Gabe—" Minerva began.

"Leave him be," Giles said in a low voice. "This isn't the time when a man wants his sister."

Some unspoken communication passed between Oliver and

Jarret, then Jarret nodded. "I'll keep an eye on him. You can go on home with Minerva."

"Do you think Gabe will be all right?" Minerva asked Oliver anxiously as Jarret left.

"Hard to tell," Oliver answered. "You know how he is."

She did indeed. Gabe fell into a chilling silence whenever Roger Waverly's name was mentioned and afterward invariably took whatever risky challenge anyone offered him. Lord only knew how he would react to *this*.

Oliver stared after his brothers another moment, then turned to Giles. "I think Minerva should ride back to Halstead Hall with me."

"Not a chance," Giles said in a voice of steely calm. "I brought her here, and I'll bring her home."

"If you think I'll let you have one more minute alone with my sister—"

"Oh, for goodness sake," Minerva told Oliver irritably, "we're in an open curricle and we'll be following right behind you. What could he possibly do to me?"

The last thing she wanted right now was to ride alone with Oliver while he tried to determine the full extent of what she and Giles had been up to at the inn. She knew better than to think he had taken her tale of the afternoon at face value. Oliver was wily that way.

Finally Oliver nodded. "You'll both give me a full report once we reach the house about what you've discovered concerning Desmond." It wasn't a request.

"Of course," Giles said.

When Oliver strode off for his own carriage, Minerva let out a long breath. Thank heavens he'd given in. She needed time to prepare what she would tell him about her and Giles.

Lord preserve her if he ever guessed the truth. Yes, she

wanted him to be concerned about her association with Giles, at least enough to talk Gran out of making her marry. But she didn't want Giles hurt. And Oliver would most assuredly hurt him badly if he learned that she'd just spent part of the afternoon being fondled and driven to distraction by the man.

It was going to be hard to pretend that her entire world hadn't just shifted on its axis. At last she knew firsthand some of what men and women did together once they moved past kissing. And now that she did, she had to wonder how any woman ever stayed chaste.

What had started out as acquiescing to Giles's seductions so she could get some answers from him had rapidly become the most thrilling afternoon of her life. Such new feelings he'd roused in her! And when he'd slid his finger inside her drawers . . . No wonder women threw themselves into bed with scoundrels. Men like him were a danger to any woman's composure.

Giles was a masterful seducer. Because he could rouse a woman's body so easily that she lost her mind to his delicious kisses and caresses. Because he could make a woman forget all her plans for the future.

No, not that. Never that. Though he'd heated her blood, that wasn't enough to build a marriage upon, especially when he had a habit of heating *every* woman's blood. She wasn't about to end up in Mama's situation.

Besides, after today she would surely be one step away from freedom. Gran would be alarmed after Oliver told her his concerns. Then Gran would cut her off for good—her and only her—leaving her free to write her books in a cottage somewhere. She already made enough money to support herself that way.

And that's all Minerva wanted. Her own life.

Still, when Giles took her hand to help her into the curricle, she couldn't help thinking of where that hand had recently been, exactly what it had been doing to her, and how wonderful it had made her feel. Worse yet, the heated glance he gave her told her that she wasn't the only one thinking about it.

And when he climbed up to sit beside her, she was painfully conscious of the warmth of his thigh against hers, the masterful way he took up the reins and set the horses going at a steady pace behind Oliver's rig.

"Are you all right?" he asked in a low voice.

She stiffened. Had he read her mind? "Why wouldn't I be?"

"Because you just heard a woman practically accuse your brother of murder."

Oh, *that*. "I'm fine. I'm just worried about Gabe." She thought of the stricken look on his face. "I understand why Miss Waverly is angry, but she had no right to blame Gabe for Mr. Waverly's death." When Giles said nothing, Minerva's temper sparked. "You don't agree?"

He cast her a searching glance. "Would you have blamed Chetwin if Gabe had died today?"

The remark caught her off guard. She searched her conscience. "Since he was the one to challenge Gabe . . . I suppose I might have. But Gabe didn't challenge Mr. Waverly to that race."

"You know that for certain? Has Gabe ever said so?"

She thought back through everything that had been said when it happened and let out a long breath. "No. I just assumed . . ." She looked at him. "Do you know?"

"No one knows, except a couple of their friends who refuse to say. Which leads me to believe that Gabe might have laid down the challenge. If Waverly had done it, the friends would have no compunction in saying so, since the man is dead."

She scowled at him. "I hate it when you're logical."

A faint smile touched his lips. "Only because you're blind when it comes to seeing your family clearly."

"And Miss Waverly isn't?"

"I didn't say that." He flashed her a brief, thoughtful glance. "But I'd think that you, of all people, would understand what it's like to want justice for someone you love, yet feel utterly incapable of gaining it through any legitimate means."

Something in the way he said "justice" and "legitimate means" arrested her, reminding her that his father had committed suicide after losing a great deal of money, probably by gambling it away. "Are we still talking about me and my family?"

His face closed up. "Of course. You want to know the truth about what happened to your parents, and you're willing to go to great lengths—like sneaking into Desmond's room—to get it. You and Miss Waverly are alike in that respect."

Why did she get the sense that there were things he wasn't saying? "She doesn't want justice—she wants revenge."

"You would, too, if you knew for certain that Desmond killed your parents."

"Perhaps." She eyed him closely. "So did you want revenge for your father's death?"

He wore a bland expression. "He killed himself—how can one get revenge for that?"

"I don't know—I'm asking *you*. You say I'm blind to my family's faults. I just wondered if you were equally blind to your father's."

"Hardly. I knew my father's faults as well as I know my own." His remote tone warned her not to pry.

"Oh? And what precisely *are* your faults, Giles? Aside from your tendency to spend your evenings in the stews and your inability to take life seriously."

A muscle ticked in his jaw. "Sounds to me as if you already know my faults. No point in my helping you add to your list."

She tapped her finger against her chin. "I wonder if I should consider your ability to pick a lock as a fault or an asset. Your amazing facility for lying convincingly is certainly a fault."

"One you share," he said drily.

She gaped at him. "I beg your pardon!"

He shot her a piercing look from beneath incredibly thick brown lashes. "You told your brother that Desmond's door was unlocked, and he believed you. So that makes you as convincing a liar as I."

She jerked her gaze from his. Well, he had her there.

He continued with apparent relish. "Revealing to your brothers that I possess such questionable talents would only have helped your cause. It would have sent Oliver right to your grandmother to protest our courtship. I can't imagine what you were thinking to pass up that opportunity."

"Neither can I," she said tartly.

The truth was, something had held her back from revealing that little tidbit. It certainly hadn't been Giles's flimsy excuses about how he'd learned to pick a lock. It hadn't even been the wary way he'd watched her as she'd told her tale, almost as if he'd been waiting for her to betray him.

No, something else kept her silent about his . . . peculiarities. She felt a strange kinship with him, borne of their shared secrets. Somehow she knew that whatever suspicious activities he was engaged in must remain between the two of them, at least until she could find out exactly what they were.

Careful now, her sensible self told her. *You said you weren't going to let him steal your heart this time. Yet you lied for him.*

A pox on her sensible self. Where had it been when Giles was sliding his hand under her skirts? It had no business chiding her.

"So you won't admit the real reason you lied about my lock picking," he drawled.

"What *real* reason?"

He shrugged. "You want to protect me. Despite everything you think you believe about me, you trust me."

That was uncomfortably close to being true. "I don't trust any man," she countered, "most especially not you."

"Then why did you lie for me?"

"Why did you steal those papers nine years ago?" When he said nothing, she primly smoothed her skirts. "You're no more willing than I to explain yourself. And until you are, you can hardly expect me to trust you. "

They were nearing Halstead Hall now, and Oliver's coach was already slowing in preparation to make the turn.

"Then perhaps I should show you a different side of me." Giles's voice held steely determination. "One more apt to make you trust me."

"Oh? And what side is that?"

He flashed her a crooked smile. "How would you like to attend a trial tomorrow, one where I'm barrister for the defense?"

An instant surge of excitement filled her chest. She'd never even been in a courtroom. "What sort of trial?"

"The kind you're sure to like, given the dark bent of your mind. I'm defending a man accused of killing his wife. Since I've spent the last few weeks determining that he didn't, tomorrow's trial promises to be most enlightening."

A murder trial—that *would* be fascinating. "How long will it take?"

"No more than a day, I expect, since we're the first trial up." His voice hardened. "Some trials are done in a matter of minutes. Justice is occasionally more swift than fair. Though I hope that's changing, as more people hire barristers to look after their interests."

He eyed her closely. "So what do you say? If you want to attend, I can send my carriage for you at whatever time you think you can be ready."

"I can be ready at dawn if it means having a chance to witness a murder trial!"

He chuckled. "Court doesn't go into session until eight o'clock. I'll send a carriage for you at seven."

"Someone will have to accompany me to town, though." She grimaced. "Propriety and all that."

"Perhaps one of your brothers could do it."

A slow smile lit her face. "Actually, I have a much better choice in mind."

Chapter Nine

"No," Stoneville told Minerva as the three of them sat in his study a short while later. "Absolutely not."

Giles couldn't help laughing. "What the hell did you expect him to say, Minerva? She's his wife."

"I expected him not to be a prig." Minerva scowled at Stoneville. "You know perfectly well that Maria would be thrilled to attend a criminal trial. She devours every issue of *The Proceedings of the Old Bailey* and *The Newgate Calendar*, not to mention my books. And it's not as if it would be dangerous. Mr. Masters will be there."

"He'll be preoccupied doing his job," Stoneville pointed out. "He won't be able to protect you."

"Then go with us," she said.

"I can't. My meeting with the tenants is scheduled for three days from now, and I have to prepare. I haven't met with them since my return from America, so I don't want to delay it."

"We'll take Freddy with us, then," she said breezily.

"That's hardly reassuring," Stoneville muttered.

Minerva's exasperation was evident in the stubborn set of her mouth. "I swear, Oliver, when did you become such a stick-in-the-mud?"

"I've always been a stick-in-the-mud." Her brother cast her a thin smile. "I just hid it beneath all the debauchery."

She sniffed. "I wish you'd hide it again. It's quite annoying."

Giles decided it was time he stepped in. "I promise, Stoneville, that your wife and sister will be perfectly safe."

"You may not know this, Masters, but Maria is bearing my child. I won't risk having her—or the baby—come to any harm."

"I'll have one of my clerks sit with Lady Stoneville and Minerva during the trial, and I'll accompany them wherever they go afterward. I swear upon my honor that I will protect them as well as you would yourself."

"*One* of your clerks?" Minerva interrupted. "You have more than one?"

"Most barristers of any consequence do."

"Oh."

That one word, spoken with such surprise, reinforced for him that this was a good idea. She needed to see him as something other than a rogue who couldn't be trusted. She needed to see him in his element, especially after the impression she'd gained this afternoon when he'd used his lock-picking skills.

"So you see," he went on, "you have nothing to worry about, Stoneville. I'll take excellent care of your womenfolk."

"The way you did today?" Stoneville snapped.

"Don't blame *him* for that," Minerva surprised him by saying. "Blame me. Besides, aren't you glad we followed Desmond and Ned? We learned more in one afternoon than we've learned in all the time since Mama and Papa died."

Stoneville crossed his arms over his chest. "Yes, perhaps it's time you tell me about that."

Giles had scarcely begun the tale when Jarret entered the study.

"I thought you were going to keep an eye on Gabe," Stoneville said.

"He gave me the slip. One minute we were drinking in the taproom and the next he was gone. I looked for him, but his rig had disappeared. Apparently he didn't like the idea of his older brother hanging about after him."

"Oh dear," Minerva said, worry plain upon her face.

Stoneville sighed. "He'll be fine, I'm sure. The lad just needs some time alone."

What Gabriel Sharpe needed was a swift kick in the arse, but Giles wasn't fool enough to say that aloud. For one thing, they would find it highly suspicious coming from him, and for another, Minerva seemed disinclined to agree. Besides, Giles rather suspected that Gabe had received precisely what he needed this afternoon in the form of Miss Waverly and her challenge.

"When I came in, you were talking about Desmond," Jarret prodded.

"Right." Giles told them everything he and Minerva had learned. When he got to the map, Stoneville sat up straight.

"Are you sure it was of the estate?"

"No," Minerva said. "That's the point."

"Give me some paper, and I'll draw it for you," Giles said.

As Giles sketched, he felt Minerva's eyes on him, and when he handed the map to her she gaped at him. "Why, this is it exactly, as far as I recollect. How did you—"

"Masters has always had an amazing memory for images and the written word," Jarret put in. "It's as if it's imprinted on his mind. That's how he managed to do all right in school even when he spent most of his time in dissolute pursuits—he could remember every line he ever read."

Minerva's eyes narrowed. "It seems that Mr. Masters has a number of interesting talents."

Giles smiled at her. "I keep telling you that. You just don't believe me."

Stoneville was examining the sketch. "If this *is* my estate, it's a map of how it looked decades ago, before Desmond was even born. The hunting lodge that Father built isn't on it, nor are the gardens on the east side that were put in by the fourth marquess. A map like this wouldn't be of much practical use to anyone now."

"And surely if he were sneaking about on the estate, we'd have noticed," Minerva said.

"Not necessarily," Stoneville pointed out. "We haven't been here much until recently. And the place is massive. That has always been the problem. It's just too damned big."

"But then where *is* he going?" Jarret asked. "And why has he started coming to Turnham in the last few months after all these years?"

"I don't know." Stoneville set down the paper. "Perhaps Pinter can find out."

"Oh yes, set Mr. Pinter on it," Minerva said enthusiastically. "He's a clever fellow and very good at his job."

Giles frowned. Pinter was also a *handsome* fellow and closer to Minerva's age. And the Bow Street runner was more the sort of man Minerva claimed she wanted, honorable and forthright.

Damn the man. "I'll see what I can find out at the courthouse," Giles said. "Perhaps some old records of the estate will show for certain if this is it."

"Pinter can take care of that," Stoneville said.

"I don't mind."

Stoneville's expression hardened. "All the same, I'd rather Pinter did it."

Awareness dawned. "You don't trust me."

"Don't get me wrong—I didn't mind when Jarret involved you in the legal aspects, but the issue of what really happened to our parents is more . . . personal. Family business. And none of your concern."

"But it's fine to involve Pinter in this personal family business?" he bit out, struggling to contain his anger.

"He's discreet."

"Ah. And you think I'm not." He rose. If he didn't leave soon, he would say things he'd regret. "Thank you for the vote of confidence."

Minerva stood up, too. "I'll walk you out."

"No," Jarret said firmly. "*I'll* walk him out. We have a few matters to discuss."

Great. Stoneville spoke to him as if he were some loose-tongued nitwit, and now Jarret was going to do the same. The Sharpe brothers were sorely trying his patience.

As they headed for the door, he stopped by Minerva to press her hand. "I'll see you tomorrow morning," he said.

She gave him a smile. "I'm looking forward to it."

"I wouldn't count on that, if I were you," Stoneville said.

"Oh, shut up, Oliver," she snapped. "Haven't you said enough? And I'll go where I please, thank you very much."

She probably would, too. That was one thing in his favor—Minerva was good at plaguing her idiot brother until he came around. She would never let him cheat her out of a chance to witness a real murder trial. That's why Giles had chosen tomorrow for her day in court.

As soon as they were out of earshot of the others, Jarret said, "I have a question for you that I expect you to answer honestly. What did you mean last night when you said there was more between you and Minerva than we realized?"

"I told you. You'll have to ask her."

"We did. She said something about your having danced together that one time. But that's not what you meant, is it?"

Giles just kept walking.

"Look here, old chap, you can tell me. I thought we were friends, after all."

His anger boiled over as he halted to stare Jarret down. "So did I."

Although Jarret was five years his junior and Stoneville only two, Giles was closer to the younger man. Stoneville had always had a bleaker view of the world than Giles—Jarret's view had been pragmatic, like his own. He'd assumed that Jarret understood him.

Until now. "I thought you knew me well enough to trust me around your sister. I thought your brother knew me well enough to know I'm discreet. Apparently I was wrong on both counts."

Jarret had the good grace to look guilty. "Oliver has always been damned secretive—you know that. And I've seen how you are around women too many times—"

"I've seen the same of you," Giles said curtly. "Does that mean you're not being faithful to your wife? That you can't be trusted to treat her well?"

"Of course not," Jarret said with a scowl. "But it's different for me than for you."

"How so?"

He threaded his fingers through his hair, then glanced away before lowering his voice. "I didn't gain a fortune by marrying Annabel."

"No, but I gather that your wife's family business played a part in why Plumtree Brewery is thriving once more. Plus, you gained your grandmother's goodwill. Those are tangible advantages. Is that why you married her?"

"Certainly not!"

Giles let his point sink in. "I'm not marrying Minerva for her money, and that's the last time I'll say it. Choose to believe me or not, but you have no say in her affairs. She's of age. We'll marry if we wish." Simmering with temper, he walked off.

"We could help you," Jarret called after him.

Giles paused.

"My brothers and I." Jarret came up beside him. "We could stop opposing you, give you some room to breathe, make it easier for you to court her."

He snorted. "They won't agree to that. You know damned well that Oliver won't."

"I'll make them agree to it, I swear." Jarret stared him down. "But first I have to know what lies between you and Minerva."

Giles debated what to say. He dared not tell Jarret about the issue with her books—that would send the man looking into matters he shouldn't. But there was one thing he could say. Unfortunately, it might make Jarret more opposed than less.

Still, it was worth the risk. It was hard to court Minerva when she kept taunting her brothers and they kept rising to the bait.

"Nine years ago, I kissed Minerva."

Jarret stared dumbly at him. "What?"

"I kissed your sister."

"You *kissed* her?"

"That's what I said."

"*Minerva.* Our Minerva."

"The very one," he said irritably.

To his shock, Jarret burst into laughter. "Oh, that's rich. I can well imagine how *that* went. You kissed Minerva, and she gave you a setdown to blister your ears."

"Not exactly."

Jarret's amusement vanished. "What do you mean?"

"She asked me to kiss her, so I did. Then she looked up at me all starry-eyed, and I panicked. I said something rather cutting, and she . . . didn't take it well."

"She wouldn't." Jarret stared off down the hall. "Well, that explains the way she talks about you, at any rate."

Giles scowled. "How does she talk about me?"

"With a great deal of vehemence. Or she did until you started courting her." Jarret's gaze swung back to him, full of curiosity. "Why is she letting you court her if your last encounter ended badly?"

"To provoke your grandmother into rescinding her ultimatum, of course."

"That does sound like Minerva. So why did you agree to help her in that?"

"I didn't. I agreed to court her. My desire to marry her is real, whether she accepts it or not."

"Ah. Is that why you're so eager to help us investigate Desmond? Are you hoping it will soften her toward you?"

"Something like that."

Jarret cast him a pitying look. "Good luck. Minerva has a tendency to hold a grudge. She's not going to change her mind about you easily."

"How well I know," Giles said ruefully. "Any advice you'd be willing to give me?"

"On how to capture my sister's heart?" Jarret let out a sharp laugh. "Minerva keeps it behind a thicket of thorns a mile high. I'm not sure there's any way through."

"No easy way, perhaps," Giles said quietly. "But thorns can be cut down. Or tunneled under."

"And you're willing to do that to gain her?"

"If that's what it takes."

He told himself it was because he needed to end this nonsense of her writing about him. He needed to have a wife, and she was a logical choice. But he feared it ran deeper than that.

He balked at the thought. That was nonsense—what he needed was her in his bed. This was simple lust, nothing more. If he could only satisfy that desire, he would feel more himself, less vulnerable, less . . . susceptible. He didn't like knowing that at any moment, Minerva might upset his apple cart.

Only by marrying her could he have some order in his life. Only then could he tie up the loose ends of his secret second life before going on to become a King's Counsel. It was nothing more than that.

And by the time he left Halstead Hall, he almost believed it.

Chapter Ten

$\mathcal{M}$ inerva could scarcely contain her excitement at being in the Old Bailey. She was going to see a real murder trial! It appeared there were *some* advantages to being the pretend fiancée of a barrister.

"It's much smaller than I thought it would be," Maria said beside her.

Maria had been the one to talk Oliver into letting them go. He was putty in his wife's hands, as he had been practically since the day he'd met her. Minerva loved that her sister-in-law could always get around Oliver—it was about time some woman took him in hand, since none of the rest of them had any luck with that.

Oliver had even acquiesced to letting Freddy be their protector. Freddy had been unable to talk his own wife into coming, since Jane was afraid there'd be discussions of blood and gore. Jane was a bit squeamish.

"It's surprisingly well lit," Minerva pointed out. "Four chandeliers, of all things." She turned to the clerk sitting to her right on the bench, who'd met them in front and announced he would sit with them during the trial. "Why is there a mirror above the defendant's box?"

The chubby-cheeked Mr. Jenks, who mopped his damp

brow frequently with a handkerchief, leaned close. "It's to reflect light from those windows onto the accused, my lady, so the jury can see how he reacts to testimony."

Fascinating! She drew out the notebook she'd brought along and jotted down his explanation. This was *definitely* going into a book.

Members of the jury filled the seats in the box below them, and Mr. Jenks explained that the same jury decided several cases. He expected this particular trial to be over by midafternoon, but sometimes as many as fifteen trials were held in one day.

That was probably why more than one judge now filed into the room, followed by several barristers, all dressed in black gowns and powdered wigs and looking terribly important.

"There's Mr. Masters!" Maria whispered. "Isn't he handsome in his gown and wig?"

Freddy, who sat on the other side of Maria, snorted. "Can't believe he's not ashamed to be seen in it. Someone should tell him and those other fellows that wigs are out of fashion these days. Wouldn't be caught dead in one myself." Freddy tended to be obsessive about looking sharp.

"Actually, the English have worn powdered wigs in the courtroom for centuries," Minerva explained. "Think of it as tradition more than fashion."

And Giles *did* look good in his, though it was hard to reconcile his solemn expression with the teasing Giles she knew. He didn't even glance their way as he took his seat at the barristers' table with the other attorneys.

A man in his late thirties was brought into the room from a passage connected to Newgate prison, where he'd been awaiting trial for the past five months.

"That's Mr. Wallace Lancaster," Mr. Jenkins said as the man

went to stand in the defendant's box. "He's a wealthy cotton merchant accused of murdering his wife. She was found floating in the River Lea last winter on a day when he was away from his home in Ware. The coroner asserts that she was killed the day before and thrown into the river by the defendant, with whom she'd quarreled."

"Do you think the coroner is right?" Minerva asked.

"We hope to prove that he's not. If anyone can do so, it's Mr. Masters."

The clear awe in his voice gave her pause. "I take it that you like your employer."

"Oh, yes, my lady. I've learned a great deal from him over the years." He puffed out his chest. "He says he'll take me with him when he becomes a King's Counsel."

Minerva gaped at him.

"King's Counsel?" Maria leaned forward to ask. "What's that?"

"It's the barristers who prosecute important cases for the Crown," Minerva said. She couldn't believe that Giles, of all people . . . "What makes you think that Mr. Masters will become a K.C.?" she asked Mr. Jenkins.

"Because he's already being considered. He wins far more cases than he loses, and that hasn't gone unnoticed."

She sat back against the bench to stare down at where Giles was reviewing a notebook. Good Lord, a K.C. It was the most prestigious position a barrister could attain without becoming a judge or someone high in His Majesty's government, like attorney general or solicitor general.

She'd had no idea Giles had risen so far in his profession. No wonder he got angry when she called him a scapegrace.

No wonder he didn't want her writing about him in her books.

A shiver wracked her. He had much to lose if people learned about his stealing. She should have realized it before, and this made it even clearer.

The court was called to order, jolting her from her uncomfortable thoughts, and she forced herself to pay attention. As the trial commenced, she began taking notes fast and furiously.

First on the witness stand was the coroner. He explained why he believed Mrs. Lancaster had been murdered and thrown into the water. There'd been no water in her lungs, and there was bruising about her neck. As the prosecuting attorney, Mr. Pitney, sat down, Giles rose to cross-examine the coroner.

"Tell me, sir, what education do you have that qualifies you as a coroner?" His voice held an edge she'd rarely heard.

"I'm a surgeon by trade."

"And how many cases of drowning have you examined in your years as coroner?"

The man colored. "Three, sir."

"Three," Giles repeated, his voice condescending. "I suppose you read the important works about your profession?"

The coroner began to fidget. "I try to, sir."

"Are you familiar with *Elements of Jurisprudence* by Mr. Theodric Beck?"

"No, sir."

"Can't blame him for that," Freddy whispered to Maria. "It sounds as tedious as that play your husband took us to, the one where the chap droned on forever about whether to be or not. 'Be what?' I ask you. Made no sense to me."

"Hush, Freddy," Maria whispered. "We can discuss *Hamlet* later."

Minerva bit back a smile. Thank heavens the courtroom was

rather noisy. Nobody down on the floor could probably hear Freddy's ramblings.

Giles strode up to the witness box and fixed his gaze on the coroner. "Mr. Beck asserts in his book, based on his knowledge of experiments performed by several men of science, that a person may drown and still not have water in the lungs."

The coroner wrung his hat in his hands. "I had not heard of it, sir. But the bruises around her neck were pronounced."

"And was Mrs. Lancaster wearing anything when she was found?"

"Yes, sir. She was fully clothed and wore a cloak."

"So isn't it possible that the ties of her cloak could have tightened around her neck as the current tossed her body about?"

"I suppose, but I don't think—"

"Thank you, that will be all."

As the coroner left the witness stand, Maria leaned across Minerva to ask the clerk, "That book he's talking about—does it really say all that about drowning?"

"There's an entire chapter on how often drowning is misinterpreted by coroners. Experiments have been performed on animals, and cases examined where people were seen to drown, yet had no water in their lungs afterward. A lack of water in the lungs is no absolute indicator. And bruising is common in cases of drowning, especially in a river where people are fighting a current or their bodies can knock against rocks."

A pretty young woman named Miss Tuttle was called to the stand next. According to Mr. Jenks, she was a close friend of Mrs. Lancaster's. After she was sworn in, Mr. Pitney asked her for her testimony. She said that she had last seen Mrs. Lancaster the night before her death, and the woman had mentioned quarreling with her husband. When Miss Tuttle had heard the next day that Mrs. Lancaster was dead, possibly by her husband's hand, she'd remembered their conversation and told the authorities of it.

Minerva watched Giles the entire time the woman was speaking. He wore a steely look that gave her shivers. Miss Tuttle squirmed beneath it.

When it came time to cross-examine, Giles rose in a leisurely manner that belied his cold expression. He walked in front of the witness box, paused, walked back to refer to his notes again, then faced her with a tight smile.

"You say that you were a close friend of the deceased."

"Yes, sir."

"And how long had you known her?"

"About seven years, sir."

"Did she often walk over that footbridge near Ware?"

"Yes. Her mother lived on the other side."

"Could she swim?"

"No, sir."

Freddy snorted. "Damned foolish of her, then, to be walking over a footbridge."

"Shh!" Minerva didn't want to miss a word of Giles's cross-examination.

Giles paced before the witness box. "How was the weather that day in Ware?"

Miss Tuttle cast him a nervous glance. "It was cold."

"Did the footbridge have ice on it?"

"It might have. I-I'm not sure."

"So Mrs. Lancaster could easily have slipped off the bridge into the river."

Miss Tuttle glanced to the prosecutor, who lifted an eyebrow at her. "I suppose."

Giles paused. "Where were you when you heard of the drowning?"

Miss Tuttle blinked. Clearly she wasn't expecting *that* question. "I was at the market in Ware."

"Is it true that upon hearing of it, you said to the woman selling you fish that you couldn't believe it, because you had just spoken to Mrs. Lancaster that morning?"

When the young woman paled, Minerva pursed her lips. Very interesting.

"I . . . I don't recall saying that, but—"

"If you like, I can call the fishmonger to the stand. You may have noticed her waiting in the witness room."

Miss Tuttle chewed on her lower lip. "No need to call her. I remember now. But I must have confused the previous day with that one."

"Do you make a habit of mixing up your days?" Giles persisted.

"I was very upset to hear of my friend's death."

"Upset enough to lie about what she said to you the night before, which was supposedly the last time you saw her?"

"Certainly not!"

He stared hard at her, then returned to his notes. "Please tell the court about your relationship with the defendant's brother, Mr. Andrew Lancaster."

"Oho," Freddy said, "now he's got her. There's some treachery afoot here."

"Freddy!" Minerva and Maria hissed in unison.

With a roll of his eyes, Freddy crossed his arms over his chest.

Miss Tuttle didn't speak for several moments. A frightened look crossed her face. "I-I don't know what you mean."

Giles arched an eyebrow. "So you haven't been meeting him late at night in his cobbler's shop?"

"He's betrothed to another lady!"

"I am well aware of that. Answer the question, if you please."

She drew herself up with great indignation. "I'm a good girl, I'll have you know! I take care of my parents, and I—"

"That isn't what I asked, Miss Tuttle. I *asked* if you've been meeting him at his cobbler's shop late at night. And remember that you're under oath."

Her lower lip trembled, but she didn't speak.

"If you like, I can put the younger Mr. Lancaster on the stand to confirm whether the two of you have been meeting."

Mr. Pitney groaned and barked a terse command to his clerk, who began frantically leafing through papers.

"Mr. Andrew Lancaster is a friend of mine, yes," Miss Tuttle said stiffly.

"Is your friendship of a romantic nature?" Giles asked.

When Miss Tuttle looked panicked, Mr. Pitney rose to address the judge. "My lord, I fail to see what significance this has to the case at hand."

"I am coming to that, my lord," Giles said.

"Then get on with it, Mr. Masters," the judge said.

"Please answer the question, Miss Tuttle. Are you and Mr. Andrew Lancaster romantically involved? I have two witnesses who are willing to testify that they saw him kissing you outside the cobbler's shop one night."

She slumped in the witness box. "Yes. Mr. Lancaster and I are romantically involved."

The courtroom was very quiet now. Everyone hung on Miss Tuttle's words.

Minerva felt a little sorry for her. Giles was being rather ruthless for no reason that she could see. Then again, it was his job to get at the truth.

"And is Mr. Lancaster's fiancée wealthy?" Giles asked.

"I wouldn't know, sir."

"But it wouldn't surprise you to learn that she has a dowry of several thousand pounds, would it?"

"No," Miss Tuttle said wearily.

A low murmur began in the courtroom all around them.

"And if the defendant is found guilty of murder, do you know who will come into his fortune?" Giles asked.

Miss Tuttle hesitated.

"Come now, madam, it should be fairly obvious who that would be, since the defendant has no children."

Mr. Pitney leaped to his feet. "My lord, as Mr. Masters knows perfectly well, the law states—"

"Sit down, sir," the judge ordered. "I wish to hear Miss Tuttle's answer."

"I repeat my question, Miss Tuttle," Giles said. "If the defendant dies, who will inherit his fortune?"

"Answer the question, Miss Tuttle," the judge said.

She glanced from the judge to Mr. Pitney, then said in a small voice, "Mr. Andrew Lancaster, sir."

"So you might see it as convenient if the defendant is hanged as a result of your false testimony. Then his brother would inherit his wealth and wouldn't have to marry for money. Andrew Lancaster could marry *you* instead of his rich fiancée."

"My lord!" Mr. Pitney interjected again. "Mr. Masters is deliberately misleading the witness!"

"And doing it rather effectively," the judge drawled.

"If my lord will permit me," Giles put in, "I would now be happy to explain the situation to Miss Tuttle."

"Oh, please do," the judge said drily. "I wait with bated breath to hear it."

The prosecutor released a pained sigh.

"Miss Tuttle, the fact is that convicted felons forfeit their property to the Crown," Giles said in a hard voice. "So if the defendant is found guilty of murdering his wife and is hanged, his brother gets nothing. And he will lose any chance of ever inheriting money from the defendant."

The blood drained from Miss Tuttle's face. How clever of Giles to figure out that she didn't know the law, for otherwise she would have had no motive for lying about Mr. Lancaster's behavior.

"So you may wish to reconsider your testimony," Giles told her, "remembering that lying to the court is called perjury and is a crime for which you can be prosecuted."

"Lord bless me," she muttered, her eyes huge.

"So I must ask you, Miss Tuttle," Giles went on, "and I advise you to answer honestly this time. When did you last see Mrs. Lancaster alive?"

The whole courtroom held its breath.

Miss Tuttle glanced to Mr. Pitney, but he now watched her with the same cold look as Giles.

She gripped the front of the witness box. "I saw her the morning of the day she drowned. I paid her a call to bring her a gown I'd borrowed."

The spectators' section erupted into cries of outrage, which had to be squelched by a command from the judge.

Giles stood there perfectly calm, waiting until the noise died, then said in his controlled tone, "So it would be impossible for the defendant to have killed his wife, since he was out of town, would it not?"

"Yes, sir."

"Did you have any part in her drowning?" Giles asked.

"No!" Glancing around at the unforgiving faces in the courtroom, she admitted, "I just . . . well, when the coroner said it wasn't a drowning and Mr. Lancaster had to have murdered her, I thought . . . They *did* argue sometimes."

"I daresay many couples argue," Giles retorted. "But that doesn't make it acceptable for you to imply that an innocent man committed murder, just so that you might gain a husband."

A look of pure chagrin crossed her face. "No, sir."

He flashed her a thin smile. "Thank you for telling the truth at last, Miss Tuttle. That will be all."

The rest of the trial was mercifully quick. Andrew Lancaster was brought to the stand to confirm that he'd been romantically entangled with Miss Tuttle, though he swore he'd had no idea of her plan to effect a marriage with him by getting his brother hanged. The defendant was then allowed to protest his innocence, which had more weight now that Giles had shown it to be the truth.

In Mr. Pitney's closing summary, he tried to hang his case on the word of the coroner alone and to assert that Miss Tuttle had been bullied by Mr. Masters into contradicting her earlier testimony, but it was no use. Giles had proved his case. And the jury confirmed it by coming back in a scant few minutes with an acquittal.

The crowd cheered, as did they. Seeing innocence prevail gave Minerva a decided thrill, especially because it was Giles who'd brought it about. How strange that she should even care if it was him. Hadn't she fortified her heart against him better than that?

Giles and Mr. Lancaster walked out the door together, while Mr. Jenks brought Maria, Freddy, and Minerva out the side door to meet them in the hall. Mr. Lancaster was understandably ecstatic. He thanked Giles over and over for gaining him his freedom, then left with his brother to return to his home in Ware.

Before they could speak to Giles, Mr. Pitney came out,

walked up to him, and held out his hand. When Giles shook it, he said, "I'm looking forward to the day when you are on our side of the table as a K.C."

Giles smiled. "Are you sure that day will come?"

"Everything I've heard says that it will, and soon."

"Well, *I'm* looking forward to the day when coroners know enough about their business to give reliable testimony," Giles said drily.

Mr. Pitney sighed. "I shall have to find that book you spoke of. Seems it's no longer enough just to know the law, eh, sir?"

"Very true."

With a bow, Mr. Pitney headed outside, leaving Giles to them. They crowded round him.

"Remind me never to try lying to you," Minerva teased. "You have a scary ability to sniff out the truth."

"You were brilliant!" Maria gushed. "Absolutely brilliant!"

"Was I?" he drawled, casting Minerva a questioning glance.

"You know perfectly well that you were," she told him. "Don't pretend to be modest about it."

His eyes twinkled at her. "Does that mean I've managed to impress you?"

"Perhaps a little," she said with a smile.

"That deserves a celebration." He glanced around at them. "This was my only trial today, so I'm free for the afternoon. I need to return to my office so I can change my clothes, but after that I thought that the four of us might wish to have a late lunch. I know the perfect place for it."

"Thank God," Freddy said. "I'm famished."

"You're always famished," Maria said.

"Mr. Jenks should join us, too," Minerva put in, noticing the clerk's downcast look, "since he's been so helpful today. It hardly seems fair to leave him out."

"Very well," Giles said. "Jenks, you're going with us."

"Thank you, sir!"

As she took the arm Giles offered and they headed out the door, he bent to whisper, "You just made a friend for life. Law clerks don't earn much, and they do love a good meal at someone else's expense."

"Well, you've made a friend for life in Freddy. He loves a good meal no matter how much money he earns."

Their coachman brought the carriage round, and they all squeezed in. After they set off for Giles's office, Maria said, "Mr. Masters, thank you so much for inviting us to see the trial."

"Was it exciting enough for you, Lady Stoneville? I hear that you like a great deal of blood and gore in your trials."

Maria blushed. "I suppose it *was* a bit lacking in that area, but it was still terribly interesting. And how clever of you to guess that Miss Tuttle was lying."

"It wasn't a guess." He took off his wig to reveal hair that was endearingly mussed. "Jenks and I spent a few hours in Ware and learned that matters weren't quite as they seemed."

"But how did you even know to examine the situation more closely?" Minerva asked. "Most people would have taken the facts at face value—accepted what the coroner said and assumed that the witness was telling the truth."

"Not Mr. Masters," Mr. Jenks put in, a hint of pride in his voice. "He never takes anything at face value."

"My client protested his innocence from the beginning," Giles explained, "and I already knew that drowning is harder to prove than many assume. I figured that in a town like Ware, where everyone knows everyone, you're bound to get at the truth if you ask the right questions. It only took me a few hours. It wasn't any great effort."

"But I daresay many attorneys wouldn't bother to do *that* much," Maria said.

"Certainly Mr. Pitney didn't," Minerva said. "And he's the one who should have fought hard to get at the truth."

"I agree, Lady Minerva," Mr. Jenks said stoutly. "It was sloppy work on Mr. Pitney's part. At the very least, he should have questioned Miss Tuttle more thoroughly."

"We'll see if you still say that when we make it to the Crown offices," Giles said with thinly veiled amusement. "From what I hear, they work the King's Counsels like dogs. They probably don't have the time to investigate the way we do."

"Then why do you want to become a King's Counsel?" Minerva asked. "I imagine it's more political than lucrative."

His gaze burned into her. "I want to do something beyond just collecting fees. I want to see justice done. More importantly, I want to see it done fairly, which doesn't happen nearly often enough. There are too many crimes going unpunished in this city, and too many people being punished for the wrong crimes."

"Hear, hear, Mr. Masters!" Maria said. "They'll be lucky to have you."

Minerva thought so, too. Giles had this astonishing ability to take a hard look at a crime and uncover things that no one else might have.

Her gaze narrowed. Yes, he did, didn't he? Hmm.

"What I don't understand is why the younger Mr. Lancaster didn't realize what his sweetheart was up to," Maria said. "Did he *want* his brother to hang?"

"No, but it didn't occur to him that she was misguided," Giles said. "Everyone looking at the case knew what the penalty for murder was—they just assumed that she did, too. Lawyers often forget that the average person doesn't know the law."

"Mr. Masters is always saying, 'Don't forget that people are often more stupid than you expect,'" Mr. Jenks put in.

"Isn't that rather cynical?" Minerva teased Giles.

He shrugged. "Perhaps. But you haven't seen the slice of humanity I see every day—seasoned gamblers taken in by sharpers, shopkeepers fooled by swindlers, young women ruined by smooth-talking scoundrels. We had a bigamist in court last week—he'd managed to live two entirely separate lives and support two different families for eight years without either family catching on. His business partner uncovered the crime. These people stupidly trust those whom they shouldn't."

"Oh, but you're mixing up stupidity with love," Maria said. "Miss Tuttle was blinded by love. The women ruined by smooth-talking scoundrels and the bigamist's wives—they trust because they love. It's awful that their love was betrayed."

"*Blinded* is the key word," Giles said. "That's why love is so often betrayed. No one with any sense should ever let love blind them."

Mr. Jenks steadied himself as they made a sharp turn. "That's another thing Mr. Masters is always saying: 'Love is for fools and dreamers. The only people who benefit from it are flower sellers and Valentine artists.'"

"How romantic of you, Mr. Masters," Minerva said with feigned sweetness.

Giles winced. "Mr. Jenks, did I fail to mention that Lady Minerva is my fiancée?"

Mr. Jenks turned an interesting shade of purple. "Oh, sir, I'm sorry, I—"

"It's all right," Minerva interrupted. "Mr. Masters and I have a more practical sort of engagement."

"Do we?" Giles brushed her foot with his as if to remind her of the less . . . practical side of their association. "And here I thought you were mad for me."

"I always say that love is like the meat in a pie," Freddy put in. "The crust is what people see—the practical things that hold a couple together. But love is the important part—without it you've got a meatless pie, and what's the point of that?"

"Why, Freddy," Minerva said, "that was almost profound."

"Freddy is always profound when it comes to pie," Maria remarked. Then she turned pensive as they drew up in front of an imposing building of gray stone. "But I think love is like the ocean. The surface may be stormy or ruffled by wind, rain may fall on it or lightning strike it, but if you sink down where the water is deep and steady, no matter what happens on the surface, you can always have a marvelous swim."

At those words, a long silence fell upon the carriage.

Then Giles cast Maria a cynical smile. "Rather like a porpoise."

Everyone laughed.

Except Minerva. She didn't know how she felt about love, but she couldn't mock it as easily as Giles. Because some part of her still believed that it existed, that it was as beautiful and special as Maria made it sound.

Some part of her wished she could have that with *him.*

It was impossible, of course. Giles was a practical man, and this courtship was a practical matter. She'd realized it even more after watching him in the courtroom. He was destined for greater things than she'd ever imagined. That's why he was pretending to court her—to get her to stop writing about him so his future could be secure.

And if by some chance he decided he really did want to marry her, it would be for practical reasons, because he thought he could mold her into the kind of wife he wanted. But a King's Counsel required a wife of pristine reputation, and she could never be that. A King's Counsel needed a woman who had no interests beyond furthering her husband's career, and she couldn't be that, either. No matter what Giles claimed, he would grow to resent her need to write. It didn't fit his world.

As she watched him deftly answering Maria's questions and subtly deflecting Mr. Jenks's obvious hero worship, sadness stole over her. It had been so much easier to dismiss him when she'd thought him merely a rogue. But now that she realized he was so much more . . .

No, she mustn't think that way. She had a plan for her own future that didn't involve marriage. Giles was instrumental to getting Gran to leave her alone, that's all. So no matter how brilliant or responsible he was, she mustn't let him get in the way of that.

Chapter Eleven

$\mathcal{A}$s they left Stephen's Hotel, where they'd eaten lunch and parted from Mr. Jenks, Giles was fairly certain his plan to impress Minerva had worked. Still, it hadn't seemed to soften her toward him overly much. She certainly hadn't been her usual talkative self.

He wasn't the only one who'd noticed. Maria took Minerva's arm and said, "You've been very quiet. Are you thinking about how you can use those notes you took during the trial? Do you think you'll put any of it in your books?"

"Nothing specific, just general information about how a court is run." Minerva cast him a quick glance. "I keep telling you and Oliver—I only used variations on people's real names for fun. Other than that, I don't put anything from my real life into my books."

"That's not entirely true," Maria countered. "I read that scene from *The Ladies Magazine* to Oliver, and he was quite put out. He was sure it was about some scandalous masquerade party attended by him and Jarret and Gabe"—she paused to look at Giles—"and probably you, Mr. Masters, since you four used to go everywhere together."

"No, Giles wasn't at the party," Minerva said hastily.

God help him. Minerva might be able to play a part well, but she wasn't a good liar in general.

"So you *did* use that party in your book!" Maria cried in triumph. "But how would you know if Mr. Masters was there? For that matter, how would you have known enough about it to describe it? From what Oliver told me, it wasn't the sort of party a respectable lady attends."

Minerva colored. "Of course I didn't attend it, but I heard all about it from . . . various people. As for Giles, my birthday party was that same day, and he couldn't come to it because he was in the country with his mother, so I know he couldn't have been at that other party, because he wouldn't have—"

"Ah, there's Gunter's," he interrupted. "Should we have some ices?" He had to stop her babbling before she spilled everything. Though she was saying all this to help *him,* it would have been better for her to play dumb.

Then again, unlike him, she wasn't used to playing dumb.

Fortunately the conversation turned to ices and how Maria hadn't ever had one until she'd come to England, and he was easily able to steer it further afield from there.

But later, as they strolled down Oxford Street so Maria and Minerva could shop, Giles worried when he caught her whispering with Maria more than once.

They seemed thick as thieves. He could only hope they weren't continuing the discussion about the masquerade party.

Then, just as the four of them were entering a shop for caricatures, Minerva held him back, as if she wanted to show him something in the window.

"I'm sorry about handling that business about the party so badly," she murmured under her breath as they stood looking into the shop window. "It threw me off guard when she said Oliver had recognized it. I never dreamed he would."

"Well, you did mention a Marie Antoinette costume in that passage, and Oliver has never forgotten that some chit dressed that way claimed he'd given her the pox."

Minerva turned an interesting shade of red. "Oh, Lord, you *knew* about that?"

When he saw Maria glance from inside the shop at them, he pretended to be examining a caricature. "He's mentioned it more than once, yes." It always made Giles laugh, though he could never admit to Oliver the real reason for his amusement.

"I should have known better than to put all that in the books."

"Yes, you should have. But it's out there now. Nothing you can do about it." With any luck Newmarsh would never see it, and even if he did, would never assume that Giles had been involved with it. So far, Minerva's hints about him had been subtle enough that he didn't think too many people would recognize him. Although Ravenswood had.

Maria came out of the shop with Freddy in tow, and they continued down Oxford Street. As they approached Hyde Park, Freddy said, "How much longer are we going to tramp about town, Lady Minerva? I'm about to faint from exhaustion."

"It's fine if you want to return to the carriage," Minerva said. "I'd like to walk with Mr. Masters through the park, but there's no need for you to exert yourself. You can drive round and pick us up by the barracks on the other end."

When Minerva exchanged a meaningful glance with Maria, Giles's eyes narrowed. Something was afoot.

"I believe I'll go back with Freddy," Maria said smoothly. "I'm tired, too." She cast Minerva a cautioning glance. "But remember that night will be falling soon, so don't be too long."

"We won't be," Minerva assured her.

Giles exulted as Maria and Freddy headed off, leaving

them to themselves. There was something to be said for this betrothal business. It allowed him to walk through the park alone with Minerva without reproach.

As they headed into it, Giles said, "That was neatly handled."

Minerva colored. "What do you mean?"

They were near a wooded area surprisingly devoid of walkers. He laughed. "I do love it when you play coy." Glancing about to make sure no one was around to see, Giles pulled her into the woods and kissed her.

She drew back, startled, but he pulled her close again for a deeper kiss. To his delight, she let him plunder her mouth for several long moments. When at last she broke the kiss, her eyes were glazed and her lips charmingly reddened.

He brushed his mouth over her ear. "I've been wanting to do that from the moment you showed up in the courtroom this morning." He kissed his way down to her throat, the only part of her neck showing in the V of the frilly lace collar she wore.

Tilting her head back, she gave a shaky laugh. "That would have provided an interesting counterpoint to the trial, don't you think?"

"It probably would have had me disbarred," he murmured against her porcelain skin. "But it would have been worth it."

"Flatterer," she whispered.

He pressed her up against a tree and proceeded to kiss her again, this time more thoroughly. She smelled and tasted of the lemon ices they'd had at Gunter's, tart and sweet and fruity. It made him light-headed. Or perhaps just having her in his arms again did that.

She was soft beneath him, her mouth deliciously eager to return his kisses. Though she wore the usual female layers—a violet carriage dress with petticoats and a corset and God knows what else underneath—they were all of thin fabrics because of summer. So when he slid the palm of his hand lightly over her breast, she definitely felt it, for she moaned low in her throat. But when he thumbed the nipple to a hard tip, she pushed him away, her cheeks going rosy.

"This wasn't what I had in mind when I brought you to the park, Giles. I have to talk to you about something."

"Talk?" he muttered, the fever to touch her burning high in him as he reached for her again. "Must we?"

"Yes, we must." She slid from between him and the tree. "It's important."

Bloody hell. He didn't know how much longer he could stand this cat-and-mouse game. Last night he'd thought of nothing but having her in his bed, her hair twining around her curvy body, her hand on his cock as it had been in the inn yesterday, and her breasts served up for his mouth like a pair of plum puddings with currants on top.

Fiercely he willed his erection to subside and offered her his arm. "If it's talk you want, then let's talk." *So I can get it out of the way and return to more important things. Like making you mine.*

"Thank you." Taking his arm, she led him back toward the path. "It's about Mama and Papa."

That banished the remains of his arousal. "Surely you haven't had time to hear anything more about Desmond."

"No." She clutched his arm. "But it occurred to me today as I watched you work that you might . . . well, notice things about what happened to my parents that no one else would."

"*Notice* things?"

"At the hunting lodge." When he looked blank, she added, "You know. Where they were murdered."

"We still don't know for certain that they *were* murdered, at least not by someone else."

"That's precisely my point. We know very little." She gazed up at him with those beautiful green eyes, fringed with gold-brown lashes and dark with a sudden sorrow that clutched at him deep inside. "We ought to know more. But Gran was so eager to cover up the scandal that she never fully examined the scene."

"Surely the authorities did so," he said as they headed across a swath of green toward the path that skirted the Serpentine.

"The local constable and the coroner, yes, but you proved today that such people don't always uncover the truth. Gran told them her version of events, and they saw enough to confirm that. According to Oliver, they took the scene at face value, helped along by her bribes." She stared at him as if he held the key to everything. "But you wouldn't do that. You would look at it through fresh eyes. You might notice something no one noticed before. You might see—"

"After all these years, my dear, I doubt I could see much of any use," he said noncommittally, remembering how Stoneville had reacted to the possibility of his involvement.

"Oh, but I know you could! Except for the blood being cleaned up and the place set to rights, the lodge is virtually the same as it was then, so surely you—"

"Wait a minute. Are you telling me no one has been back to that hunting lodge in all these years?"

She nodded solemnly. "Oliver closed the estate down immediately after the 'accident,' as we were taught to call it. The family wasn't even at Halstead Hall until Oliver opened it back up a few months ago, and none of us have wanted . . . that is, it's just so . . ."

"I understand." Oh yes, he understood. He still couldn't bring himself to go into the library where his father shot himself nine years ago. "So you want me to examine the scene alone."

"No! I wouldn't ask you to do that. I would go with you, of course." She gave him a sad little smile. "People in town say it's haunted, you know. They've heard noises near the lodge, seen mysterious lights and such."

"Are you sure you're up to it?"

"Of course I'm up to it. Why shouldn't I be? I don't believe in ghosts."

There was that bravery that had always impressed him. He could still remember the stubborn tilt of her chin at nine, when she'd steadied herself to view her parents' caskets.

"Stoneville wouldn't approve."

She tipped up her chin. "I don't care. He's behaving like an utter ass to you."

He bit back a smile. "True."

"If anyone knows how discreet you can be about things, it's me. You're as secretive as he is, if not worse. I know you won't speak of it to anyone."

"Very well. Give me a day to see what I can find out about the official report."

"That might be difficult," Minerva said. "I asked Oliver about it last night, and he said Mr. Pinter inquired about it but was told it would take weeks to locate."

Giles arched one eyebrow. "What else would they tell him? He's operating behind your grandmother's back. The constable isn't going to act without asking her about it first. And if Pinter made it clear that he didn't want her brought into it . . ."

Her mouth formed a perfect O. "You see? You're already proving helpful!"

"I hope Stoneville feels the same way when he finds out that I went against his express wishes."

"You let me handle my brother. If we come up with something useful, he won't be too angry."

They walked along the path in silence a moment, watching the ducks glide along the Serpentine.

Giles shot her a long look. "And you're not worried about meeting me in secret, alone, in a remote part of your brother's estate?"

Though she colored, she smiled up at him. "Should I be?"

"Absolutely," he said, perfectly serious. "There's only so much temptation a man can endure before he starts taking advantage of a situation."

"You know better than to ruin me, because you know what it would lead to," she said lightly. "You've no more desire to be leg-shackled than I, and you won't get me to stop writing about you in my books if you take advantage of me."

He suppressed the urge to declare himself right then and there. That would only drive her farther away. She still had some notion that this wasn't a real courtship, and he could accomplish far more by courting her without her knowing it.

Still, he felt compelled to warn her that he wasn't going to play nice just because she had declared that he should.

"I assure you, Minerva, a man can cover a great deal of ground between taking advantage and ruination." He covered her hand with his. "A very great deal."

"Oh?" she said, her eyes shining with mischief. "How so?"

He glanced around at the people they were passing—a young couple sitting arm in arm on a bench, a man feeding the ducks, an older woman walking briskly along the river—and lowered his voice. "If we were alone, I would remove your bonnet and lace collar so I could see your neck. I love your neck. It has the most interesting dips and curves, and it's quite elegant when it's bare."

Her fingers tightened on his arm and she stared straight ahead, two spots of color pinkening her pretty cheeks.

He kept his voice low, husky. "Then I'd unbutton your gown very slowly, so I could kiss your back through your shift after every button was undone. I wonder if your back is as lovely naked as it seems to be when clothed."

"I'm afraid you'll just have to keep wondering," she said a bit unsteadily.

"Will I? There's no reason I can't look at your naked back. It certainly wouldn't ruin you. Indeed, there are a great many parts of you I can touch and caress and kiss without doing the dirty deed. Like that delicate stretch of skin on your inner thigh just above your knee. I could put my mouth there, kiss up the inside of your leg until I reach the forbidden—"

"Stop," she whispered. "You're embarrassing me."

"I'm arousing you. Not the same thing at all."

She swallowed. "You're trying to seduce me with words."

"Is it working?"

A couple passed near them, and she remained quiet until they were out of hearing. "I won't let you seduce me, Giles. Put that right out of your mind."

"What a pity," he said softly. "You badly need seducing, Minerva Sharpe."

Her gaze shot to him, hot and irate. "Why on earth would you say that?"

"Because you see marriage as a loss of independence, without taking into consideration its benefits. I daresay if you had a really good taste of them, you would be less inclined to throw out the baby with the bathwater."

"I thought you already gave me a taste, in that inn."

"That was more a sniff than a taste. What I intend would go beyond a few brief touches. You would end with as thorough a knowledge of that particular benefit of marriage as I could offer without ruining you. That is, if you'd allow me to give it to you. Is that possible?"

She blinked, then jerked her gaze away. When she remained silent, his pulse quickened.

"Suppose I were to . . . let you give me a taste," she said at last. "Only a taste, mind you. Not anything that would cause me trouble later. Would you be willing to do so without . . . 'doing the dirty deed,' as you call it?"

His body responded instantly to that remark, and he groaned. "Must you say things like that in public, for God's sake?"

"What do you mean?"

He lowered his voice to a hiss. "Remember yesterday at the inn? My 'pistol' is making an appearance, thanks to you."

She glanced down at his trousers, which only made them bulge more obviously. Then she lifted a mischievous gaze to his face. "Whatever will you do, now that you're in this . . . state?"

"Conjugate Latin," he said tersely. "Think of England. Think of anything but you and me doing— Bloody hell, there it goes again, and we're nearly to Rotten Row." He stopped short and stepped behind a bench with a high back that sat near the river.

She stood next to him, pretty as the proverbial picture, her eyes dropping to his trousers with virginal curiosity.

"Would you stop looking at me *there*?" he growled. "You're not helping."

She laughed. "You're the one who started it by trying to seduce me with words. Serves you right if you have to suffer for it."

"You, my darling, are a tease."

Her smile faltered. "Am I?"

"You know damned well you are. You only mentioned my giving you a taste in order to plague me."

"Actually, I was serious. And you didn't answer my question." She swallowed. "If I let you . . . give me a taste, could you control yourself and not go beyond that?"

"I'm not the one you should worry about."

She cast a condescending look at his groin, which did more to dampen his arousal than conjugating Latin ever had. "I think you've proved that you're *not* in perfect control of your . . . faculties, shall we say?"

"Trust me, a man is always in control of his 'faculties' when it comes to the point of no return. The question is whether *you* can control *your* faculties. Because I promise I would never seduce you against your will, my darling."

Her breathing grew erratic. "And I would never give myself willingly to you. It would destroy all my plans."

"Then you have nothing to worry about," he said smoothly. "If what you want is just a taste, you can have it." He lowered his voice. "As long as I get mine, too."

"You are such a rogue," she said.

"Only a rogue would agree to what you're proposing." With his arousal firmly in check, he took her arm and headed back to the path.

She said nothing as they strolled along Rotten Row. She merely smiled and waved at the few people still promenading in their carriages near dusk.

When they were headed toward the barracks, she looked up at him with a serious expression. "I don't understand you. How can you be a clever and responsible barrister who's a prospective K.C. one moment, and a rogue the next?"

"Practice." She had no idea how true that was.

"That's not what I mean, and you know it. Which one is the real you?"

"Why can't I be both? They're not mutually exclusive."

"Aren't they?"

He shrugged. "Obviously *you* don't think they are. You have Rockton playing the rogue and a spy at the same time."

"Only to heighten the drama in my story. But it's not a good idea to heighten the drama in real life. It makes things far too complicated."

That was certainly true. "Look at it this way. I spend my days in a serious business, making sure that justice is meted out to those who deserve it. So at night I need to be less serious, even a little wild. Otherwise I would run mad through the streets."

"So which half of your life am I a part of? The serious half or the wild half?"

"Today? Both."

They were walking through a copse of woods, so he pulled her behind a tree and kissed her hard on the lips. "Tell me the truth. Are you sure you want me to give you a taste?"

She swallowed hard. "Yes."

As his pulse jumped, he ran his thumb over her lower lip. "Then tomorrow morning, I'll see if I can find out more about the official report. In the afternoon, I'll meet you at the—"

"No, not tomorrow. The day after, when Oliver is meeting with the tenants at a tavern in Ealing. That way we have less chance of running into him."

He nodded. "I'll have to rearrange some appointments, but I can manage it. I'll meet you at the hunting lodge at ten, day after tomorrow."

"Do you know where it is?"

"Yes. We lads used to play cards there before—" He caught himself. "I'll look at the scene and deduce what I can. Then you and I will have a lovely picnic somewhere we're unlikely to be discovered, and I'll give you the taste you crave." He cupped her face in his hands. "But I warn you—if you should find yourself 'willing' to be seduced after all, I'm not sure I'll be able to say no."

"Don't worry. That won't happen."

He was tempted to kiss her and remind her how easily it *could* happen, but that would ruin his plans. Besides, she'd find it out for herself soon enough.

"Day after tomorrow, then," he said, brushing his lips over hers.

"Day after tomorrow," she agreed.

Tomorrow was going to be the longest damned day of his life.

Chapter Twelve

$\mathcal{M}$inerva headed downstairs for breakfast early on the appointed day in hopes that few of her family would be up.

No such luck. Celia and Jarret were debating the merits of the new Manton breechloader Celia had just purchased, and Oliver and Maria were explaining to Gran why they believed that Mama's old bedchamber would make a better choice for a nursery than the one the Sharpe children had been raised in.

"We want the baby close by," Maria said. "And I don't use the bedchamber anyway."

Jarret stopped to quip, "No doubt my brother keeps you far too busy in *his* bed to allow you time to sleep in any other."

"Sleep? What's that?" Oliver drawled, and the two idiots laughed together.

Maria rolled her eyes. "The point is, your mother's bedchamber could easily be refitted as a nursery. It's huge, and it's not far from Jarret and Annabel's room, so it would be suitable for the child they're expecting, too, as long as they're living here."

With a sigh, Minerva served herself some ham, cheese, and toast from the sideboard. The endless discussions of the two impending babes were beginning to get on her nerves.

Not that she didn't like children. She did. But the thought of being responsible for a tiny life—the thought of failing a child the way Mama had in the end—gave her shivers.

Then there was everything she would have to give up to be a good mother. She remembered only too well how wistfully Mama had talked of writing and how opposed Papa had been to it.

Giles wouldn't be opposed.

She frowned. He said that, but she wasn't sure she could believe him.

So why was she planning such a daring escapade with him? Had she lost her mind?

Perhaps. Or perhaps she just wanted to experience the madness of having a man touch her, caress her, see her as someone desirable in her own right, and not merely as a means to an inheritance. She didn't know why, but she wanted to believe that her money really didn't matter to Giles.

She was an utter fool. She was playing with fire. And she didn't care.

Last night she'd barely slept for excitement about seeing him today. The very idea of being alone with him in the woods had ramped up her imagination to feverish heights. The way he'd spoken to her, the things he'd said . . . Would he really put his mouth on the inside of her thigh, so close to . . . to *there*? He'd put his hand there at the inn, and it had been quite delicious.

"Will we be seeing Mr. Masters today?" Celia asked.

Minerva nearly jumped out of her skin. Her sister had the most uncanny ability to sense the direction of her thoughts. Hopefully not the *entire* direction.

She pasted a smile to her lips as she took a seat at the table. "I doubt it. He's in court." It was the only plausible excuse she could think of for his not paying a call on her.

"Is he?" Jarret said. "He didn't mention it when Gabe and I saw him yesterday morning on our way into town."

"You saw him?" she asked, then cursed herself for sounding like some lovestruck schoolgirl wanting news of her latest beau. She forced herself to butter her toast nonchalantly. "Where were you?"

"Ealing, actually," Jarret said. "It's so close by I thought he might be headed this way, but he said no, he had business there that would take him most of the day."

He'd been trying to get the report from the constable, no doubt.

Jarret eyed her thoughtfully as she ate a piece of ham. "He did say that we should give you his love."

It's a figure of speech, she reminded herself when her pulse gave a little flutter. Love *isn't a word in Giles's vocabulary—it's for "fools and dreamers," remember?*

"Did he?" She squirmed under her brother's continued scrutiny. Jarret had been watching her the past two days with a peculiar concentration that made her extremely nervous. "How sweet of him."

"What business could Giles Masters possibly have in Ealing?" Oliver growled.

"I believe he has a client there," she lied, then kicked herself for it. There she went again, lying for him. What if Oliver asked him about his client? Worse yet, what if Oliver asked in Ealing if anyone knew what Giles had been doing?

She had no business trying to cover his tracks. He was a grown man—he could take care of himself.

Folding her buttered toast around slices of ham and cheese, she ate it like a sandwich. "I thought you had a tenants' meeting today, Oliver," she said brightly, determined to turn the conversation away from Giles.

"It's tomorrow. We had to put it off because of an issue with the new calves."

Her gaze shot to him. Oh Lord. She'd counted on Oliver not being on the estate.

"What are you doing today?" Oliver asked conversationally.

"Writing." Not wanting him to probe into the when and where of it too deeply, she said, "So you're thinking about turning Mama's bedchamber into a nursery, are you?"

"We have to do something. The child will be here before we know it, and our old nursery is too cold and far away from the rest of the rooms for our liking."

He and Maria exchanged a warm glance, and a sudden stab of envy pierced Minerva's heart.

Envy? That was ridiculous. She had exactly the life that she wanted.

"Perhaps you could help with it," Maria said. "I could use another woman's opinion."

Minerva tamped down her panic. "Sorry, Maria, but I'm taking a long walk after breakfast."

"I could go with you, discuss ideas for the nursery—"

Everyone burst into laughter.

"What?" Maria asked.

"When Minerva announces she's taking a long walk," Oliver explained, "that means she definitely doesn't want company."

"If she wants company," Celia put in, "she says, 'Is anyone up for a walk?'"

When Maria looked bewildered, Jarret said, "Minerva walks when she's having trouble with the book she's presently writing." He grinned. "She walks *a lot.*"

"It helps me think," Minerva said defensively. And for once, her predictable habits would keep her family out of her hair.

"Perhaps I could help you this evening," she went on. *After my adventure in Giles's arms.*

No, she mustn't think of that. It would surely show on her face.

She glanced at the clock—it was nearly nine-thirty, and she still had to get to the lodge. She gulped some tea, then rose. "Well, I'm off. I'll see everyone later." And before anyone could stop her, she tied her bonnet on over her morning cap and headed out the door.

The woods teemed with birdsong as she walked briskly down the path. Taking a horse would have been quicker, but that might have been noticed. Walking aimlessly about the estate was less suspicious, though if anyone saw her this far afield, they might find it odd. She generally kept to the gardens.

As she approached the lodge, her heart faltered. The horse tethered by the door told her that Giles had already arrived. Since he wasn't out here, he must have found a way inside. Given his propensity for picking locks, that wasn't surprising.

But that wasn't what made her hesitate. She was here again. Here where her parents had been killed.

She stood there a long moment, gathering her courage. She'd lied to him yesterday when she'd said that no one had come here in nineteen years. *She* had come here a few months ago, after Oliver reopened the estate. Some compulsion had led her to see if she might spot the "ghost" the local populace talked about. To see if she could sense the presence of her parents.

But she hadn't been able to bring herself to go inside. The idea of being alone in there, of possibly seeing some . . . specter of them in the throes of death had kept her frozen in front. After staring at the entrance for twenty minutes, she'd fled.

She couldn't do that today. Not if she wanted answers.

There's nothing to worry about, she told herself. *Giles is inside, ready to dispatch any spooks with his logic. Really, it's just an ordinary little lodge, made to accommodate sportsmen. There's nothing threatening about the place itself.*

Giles's horse snorted, making her jump. Good Lord, she was being ridiculous. There was no such thing as ghosts. This was what came of writing about them all the time. One began to believe one's own fiction—a dangerous tendency for someone with stories as dark as hers.

She forced herself to enter and walk toward the drawing room, where she'd been told her parents had died. Halting on the threshold, she glanced inside, looking for Giles. He wasn't there. And something about the cloth-shrouded furniture and stifling air made panic well up inside her.

"Giles?" She headed back toward the foyer, feeling her heart pound harder with each step. "Giles, where are you?"

"Up here!" he called down the stairs. "In the master bedchamber!"

Oh, thank heavens. Holding her hand to her chest to steady her heart, she climbed the stairs. She found him standing in the middle of the marquet floor of what had been her parents' room whenever they stayed here.

He was standing by the window he'd apparently opened, for a balmy breeze ruffled his hair. His air of normalcy helped soothe her agitation. He was tapping his hat idly against his thigh, his brow furrowed in thought. Dressed in buckskin riding breeches and a jaunty green riding coat, he looked carefree and just a tiny bit wild.

When he turned to her, his eyes held the same native intelligence that had always attracted her. "We know one thing for certain already."

"Oh?"

"The constable's report, which mostly contains your grandmother's tale of what happened, can't possibly be true."

She blinked. "You *saw* the report? However did you manage it when Pinter couldn't?"

He cast her a self-satisfied smile. "I gave the current constable a letter from your grandmother authorizing me, as her attorney, to look at it. I told him I needed the report to figure out certain matters concerning the inheritance."

She gaped at him. "But Giles, how did you get Gran—"

"I didn't. I've been poring over her will for weeks—it was a simple matter of copying her signature." He grinned at her. "Unlike Pinter, I'm perfectly willing to break the rules to get what I want. He has no leverage, since he's investigating behind your grandmother's back. I, on the other hand, made sure that I appeared to be on her side, and since she's well respected in this area, the constable was more than willing to hunt up the report."

"You wicked devil!" she said, impressed and shocked at the same time. "One of these days someone is going to catch you doing these havey-cavey things, you know."

"I doubt it. The only person who has ever caught me is you, and I don't mind when *you* catch me, darling. Especially if I get a kiss out of it."

There he went again, calling her "darling." She wished he wouldn't do that. She liked it entirely too much. And the way he was looking at her . . .

Faintly embarrassed, she turned to glance about the room that she hadn't entered in years. The furniture here was covered with cloths, too, giving it an unreal appearance.

As a child, she'd come here often. Mama had liked to escape the oppressive grandeur of Halstead Hall from time to time, and Minerva often begged to come along. Mama had let her, because she'd known Minerva would sit quietly and read, unlike her brothers, who always ran roughshod over the place. She and Mama would cuddle in the bed and read together for hours.

Tears stung her eyes. She'd forgotten entirely about that.

Fighting back the memories, she forced her voice to sound light. "So what did the report say?"

"Not much. Most of it goes right along with what I understand is the public account of what happened—your mother was awakened by the sound of an intruder, went downstairs, and shot him, then shot herself while grieving over what she'd done."

"Most of it?"

"I learned a few new things. According to the report, she used a loaded pistol that her husband kept in a bedside drawer in this very room for protection."

"Where's the pistol now?

"The constable has it. And it's not a multibarreled pistol, so she would have had to reload it before shooting herself. Unless your mother was a markswoman—"

"As far as we know, she wasn't. And Celia has already pointed out how unlikely it was that Mother knew how to load a pistol."

"There are more inconsistencies than that in the account, I assure you." Giles walked toward her. "I've been up here listening for you for the past few minutes. I didn't hear the door open or close, and I didn't hear you enter or walk around. I heard nothing until you called out my name, and that was faint at best."

He strode over to the wall and knocked on it. "These are very solid, and this room is at the end of the hall. No one, especially someone sleeping, would hear a person sneaking in downstairs."

"Perhaps Mama was sleeping in another room."

"And she came in this one to get the pistol? Why would she take the time? For that matter, why would she confront an intruder with a pistol at all, when she could have just gone down the servants' stairs and out the back door for help?" He returned to the window to look out. "And there are other inconsistencies."

She followed him over and looked out herself.

"The stables are close enough to this window that anyone would easily hear a horse being stabled," Giles went on. "And what intruder stables his horse? The minute she heard someone doing that, your mother would have assumed it was your father or some other member of the family."

"Unless he'd walked here. I walked today."

"The report said that both their horses were in the stables."

"Oh."

"You see? Too many inconsistencies." Clapping his hat on his head, he walked toward the door. "And another thing."

She followed him out into the hall.

"Even assuming that the story is correct, your mother would have had to creep down this hall to get to the stairs." He took a step, and a board creaked loudly. "Your father should have heard this—it lies directly over the drawing room, and you can't go from *any* of the bedchambers without passing this way."

"Perhaps she stepped around it?"

"Roused out of a dead sleep, she thought to grab a pistol and step around a creaky board? Does that sound logical to you?"

"No, none of it does." Minerva sighed. "And that means Oliver might be right that she killed Papa on purpose. That she laid in wait for him here."

Giles's gaze narrowed. "Why would he think that?"

"I-I can't tell you—he would never forgive me. All I can say is that Oliver argued with Mama and gave her good reason to be furious at Papa."

"Ah. Jarret seems to think that Desmond might have shot them both."

"I know."

Giles pinched the bridge of his nose. "The trouble with that theory is that Desmond had no motive for killing them. He wouldn't have inherited anything."

"Perhaps he didn't do it for money." She much preferred believing that Desmond had killed them to thinking that Mama had lain in wait to murder her husband. "Perhaps he had some personal reason for killing them."

"I considered that." He headed for the stairs, and she followed him. "I just can't imagine what it would be."

When they got downstairs, he walked toward the drawing room. Reluctantly she followed.

"I only wish I knew more about how they were situated when they were found," Giles said. "I mean, I know roughly how they were, but—"

"You do? How?"

He entered the drawing room. She hesitated before going in after him. *You wanted this, remember? You asked him to come here and do this.*

But she hadn't thought it would be so difficult. She'd never seen the scene, yet she could well imagine it—Mama facing Papa, Papa's shock as the pistol was leveled on him.

"One of them fell here," Giles was saying as he walked to a bare stretch of floor.

She hadn't noticed before, but a rug had been pulled aside.

Giles knelt down to tap the wood. "When I first arrived, I went through this room. The blood has been cleaned away, but one can never get it completely clean. Blood that sits a while stains the wood, so I looked for any spot that might have been covered, and I found this. It tells me that one of them fell here."

He rose to go to another part of the room, but she was no longer listening. She could only stand there, staring at the wide patch of wood that was a ruddier brown than the rest of it. Seeing the stain made it all more real somehow.

Images rose in her mind that she'd struggled all her life to banish from her imagination: Mama firing the gun at Papa, shattering his face . . . him falling to the floor as Mama fumbled to reload the pistol . . . Mama putting the pistol to her chest . . .

"Giles . . ." she whispered as her vision started to narrow, and sweat broke out on her brow.

He was talking, not paying attention. "It was probably over by . . ."

"Giles . . . I think . . . I think I'm going to . . ." She felt her knees buckle, then the room faded to black.

Chapter Thirteen

Giles turned just in time to see Minerva crumple. Alarm gripped him as he hurried to scoop her up. Cursing himself for being oblivious, he carried her outside. While he'd been spouting off about Lewis and Prudence Sharpe's deaths like some pompous fool, he'd forgotten the most essential thing. They were *her* parents. It had been *her* tragedy as much as anyone's.

Much too late, he remembered the nine-year-old Minerva balking at entering the chapel for fear of what she would see there. And he'd just made her think about all of that again. What an idiot he was.

The sight of her insensible in his arms did something terrifying to his insides. She looked so fragile in her thin white muslin, like an angel shot down by some errant hunter.

God save him, he was spouting poetry again. He was getting in much too deep with her. And he couldn't seem to stop.

She stirred, her eyes fluttering open to stare up at him in confusion. "Wh-what happened?"

"You fainted," he murmured, his heart still in his throat. "I'm afraid I got carried away talking about your parents' . . . um . . ."

"Deaths. You can say it." Her voice was a little steadier. "Put me down. I'm all right now."

Reluctantly, he did as she asked but kept his hands on her waist. "I'm sorry, I—"

"No, no, it's fine. It's ridiculous, really. I've never fainted. I don't know why I did." Her words tumbled out of her too quickly to be normal. "It's been nearly twenty years, and it's not as if I'd been there to see it happen or anything, and I'm not—"

"Shh, darling." He urged her down onto the entrance steps and sat beside her. After fumbling in his coat pocket, he pulled out his handkerchief to mop her clammy brow, no easy task with that enormous bonnet she was wearing. "Steady now. Breathe deeply. Do you have smelling salts?"

She shook her head. "As I said, I'm not the fainting sort. It's just that being there, in the place where they died, knowing *how* they died and seeing the blood . . ."

"It's not your fault," he said, folding her hand in his. "I shouldn't have been so blunt. I got caught up in solving the puzzle and forgot how much more it means to you."

"But I *wanted* to be there and hear what you noticed. I can't believe I behaved like such an idiot."

"There's no shame in fainting, Minerva." And she was the only woman he knew who'd be embarrassed by it. "There's certainly no shame in balking at seeing the place where they died. Your reaction is perfectly rational."

"But you don't understand." She gripped his hand as she stared down at her lap. "I-I write about these things all the time. I shouldn't—"

"It's not the same. You write about them from the safety of your secure home. They're not real."

"That's not true. They're real to me." Her voice grew choked. "Sometimes I wonder if . . . well . . . there's something wrong with me. Why do I revel in the blood?" She frowned. "No, I don't revel in it. It's just that I feel compelled to create it, to write about it, to . . . to lay it out in all its horror."

"And then to destroy it. Don't you see? You control the violence. You dictate what happens to whom." As awareness dawned, he squeezed her hand. "Perhaps that's *why* you do it. Because in writing, you have power over monstrosities. You can banish them with the stroke of a pen. You can gain justice for its victims in your books."

She stared up at him, wide-eyed. "I'd never thought of it like that. Still, you'd think that with my parents dying so horribly, I would balk at describing such things."

"Actually, I think it's just the opposite. Children are impressionable, especially at the age you were when your parents died." He rubbed her knuckles with his thumb. "You heard about their horrific ends, and you couldn't get it out of your mind. So you found a way to deal with it, to regain the power that was ripped from you in life. That just shows how strong you are."

"Do you really think so?"

"I wouldn't be here if I didn't."

With a grateful smile, she released his hand. "I-I think I can manage now. We can go back in, and you can finish what you were showing me."

"No need." He would cut off his right arm before he forced her to relive the horrors again. "It's not cowardice to avoid those things that will damage your ability to cope." He debated whether to say more, but her haunted expression decided him. "I haven't set foot in the library since my father shot himself there. I was a grown man at the time, yet I still can't bring myself to go in."

Compassion flooded her features. "You weren't the one to find . . ."

"No. I almost wish I was." His voice hardened. "Mother got there first after we heard the shot. She was still screaming when I ran in."

He glanced away, remembering the scene. "I happened to be visiting at the estate when Father received the news that—" *He'd lost everything to the schemer Sir John Sully*. No, he shouldn't tell her that. It would lead to other questions. "Father received some bad news. My brother had been called away to town, so it was just Mother and I." He fought for control over his voice. "I was the one to contact the constable, to deal with the coroner, to make sure that the library was cleaned up properly afterward."

"Oh, Giles," she whispered as she took his hand in hers once more. "That's why you know about bloodstains."

"Yes. There was one in our library. Mother had the floor redone, but I've never seen it. I don't . . . go in there. I let David or a servant do it." A breath shuddered out of him. "I tell myself that I'm being foolish, that there's no reason to avoid it, that it's not as if his ghost haunts it, and yet—"

"You see it all again in your mind's eye, and you don't want the image to plague you any more than it already does."

"Exactly." He softened his voice. "It was wrong of me to expect you to do what I couldn't manage myself."

"You didn't expect it. I asked you to do it. And I still want you to—"

"There's no point. I've seen all I can for now, anyway. I need to know more before I can explore further."

She nodded. "I remember. You said something about . . . needing to know what position the bodies were in when they were found?"

"That would tell me a great deal. Unfortunately, given your grandmother's involvement, I can't trust that the constable was allowed to see the scene exactly as it was. The only person who knows the truth about how they were is your grandmother, and your brothers are reluctant to involve her as long as they suspect Desmond. I gather she's had some illness, and they don't want to upset her with baseless theories."

"Actually . . ." She bit her lip, as if trying to decide whether to tell him something. Then she let out a long breath. "Actually, Oliver knows how Mama and Papa were positioned. He was the one to find them."

Giles narrowed his gaze on her. "He was?"

Though she avoided his gaze, she nodded. "He didn't kill them. He would never do that. He found them, that's all."

"I know your brother didn't kill them," Giles clipped out. How could she think he would believe such a thing? "I knew him long before they died. He was the last person on earth I would have thought capable of murder. He despised your father for his adulteries, true, but he admired him for his handling of the estate. And your mother . . ." Giles shook his head. "Nothing on earth would have persuaded Oliver to shoot *her.*"

Her eyes searched his face. "The gossips said he shot her by accident when she came between him and Father."

"The gossips are idiots. They also say that he shot your father to gain his inheritance. If he did, he certainly behaved oddly afterward—closing up the estate, setting out to destroy himself with drink and women. That's not the behavior of a man who got the inheritance he wanted."

She cast him a watery smile. "You're an absolute dear to say that."

"And that's the nicest thing you've ever called me." He smiled in return.

"I've been really awful to you, haven't I?"

"Not too awful." And now that he knew how badly he'd hurt her that night at the masquerade, he understood why. He went back to what they'd been discussing. "Do you think Oliver would tell me what he saw that night?"

She shook her head. "It took him years to speak to *us* about it, and every word was hard won. I can't imagine his agreeing to detail the how and where."

"Never mind, then," he said as her tone grew mournful again. "We'll consider how to handle it another time." He stood and held out his hand to her. "Let's leave this place, shall we? We've had enough of death and blood and bad memories for one day."

"We certainly have." When she let him pull her up into his arms, he nearly kissed her right there.

Then he glanced behind her at the lodge and thought better of it. This wasn't the place for that. Instead he turned to untether his mare. Offering her his arm, he led her and the horse across the field.

When he stopped on the edge of the woods to tie up his horse and remove the saddlebags that contained their picnic lunch, she asked, "Where are we going?"

He slung the saddlebags over his shoulder and led her into the woods along a well-trod path. "To the pond where we lads used to swim."

"There's a pond on the estate?"

"It's more like a puddle aspiring to be a pond. But it's pretty and private enough for our picnic."

When he cast her a meaningful glance, she looked away.

His pulse faltered. "Unless you've changed your mind," he added.

She flashed him a look of wide-eyed innocence. "About what?"

He frowned. "You know damned well about what. You said you wanted a taste."

"Well, of course," she said, her eyes bright with mischief. "That's what picnics are for, aren't they? Tasting things?"

"You're tormenting me on purpose, aren't you?"

A wicked smile crossed her lips as she released his arm to dance merrily along the path ahead of him. "Me? Torment you? I can't imagine what you mean."

"Then perhaps I should remind you of exactly what you *said* you wanted," he growled, and lunged for her.

Laughter bubbled out of her. "You'll have to catch me first." Then she turned and ran.

He lengthened his stride but didn't bother to chase her. The path came to a dead halt at the pond, so unless she meant to thrash her way through the underbrush around to the other side, which he highly doubted, he would get her in the end.

Just as he'd expected, as he broke free of the woods, he found her pacing before the pond, looking for an escape and not finding one. "The woods are thin on the other side, minx—that's the only way out." He opened a saddlebag and removed a small blanket to spread on the ground. "Unless you know how to swim?"

She faced him with a sparkle in her eyes that made his blood roar through his veins. "I'm afraid that isn't one of my skills, sir."

"Would you like to learn?"

A look of pure longing crossed her face. "That would be marvelous." She then seemed to catch herself. "No, we can't. If I go home with my clothes wet, everyone will *know* I've been up to something naughty."

"Very well." He tossed down his hat. "So take them off."

HETTY WAS SITTING in the library, thoroughly enjoying her discussion with Maria and Oliver about plans for the nursery, when the butler announced a visitor.

"Mr. Pinter!" Hetty said with genuine pleasure as she rose to greet him.

"Mrs. Plumtree," he murmured with a courtly bow.

The young man was always unfailingly polite, a mark in his favor. He'd served the family well so far, and for that she was grateful.

"Tell me, what brings you out to see us?"

With a furtive glance at Oliver, he said, "I'm here to report on the matter you discussed with me a few days ago."

"What matter?" She searched her mind for what had been going on a few days ago. "Oh, right. Giles Masters."

Oliver's head shot up. "What about Masters?"

When Mr. Pinter stiffened, she said, "It's all right. I don't mind if Oliver knows."

Mr. Pinter acquiesced with a nod. "Your grandmother paid me to look into Masters's personal and financial affairs, since he's courting Lady Minerva."

Oliver leaned back in his chair. "And?"

Mr. Pinter removed a notebook from his coat pocket. "Masters is very successful in his profession."

"Not that it matters, since he gambles it all away."

"Actually, that's not true," Mr. Pinter said. "Everywhere I went in the clubs, people spoke of his wild gambling, but no one could remember the last time he'd lost a truly large sum of money. He seems to gamble a bit here and there, but not enough to create any serious financial problems for himself. He's having a house built in Berkeley Square that's nearly completed, and you know that takes some money."

"That's good to hear," Hetty said, though she wasn't surprised. She was beginning to think there was more to Giles Masters than met the eye.

"Rumor also has it that he's the most likely candidate to be appointed the next King's Counsel," Mr. Pinter went on. "He's very highly regarded in the Inns of Court."

Oliver cocked his head. "I knew he'd handled some important cases, but King's Counsel . . . are you sure? You'd think he would have bragged about it."

"I forgot to tell you," Maria put in. "His clerk told me and Minerva the same thing. And he really was quite amazing in court."

"Was he?" Oliver said with a frown.

"Oh, don't look at me like that," Maria teased. "I'm only speaking of his legal prowess, and you know it."

"What about his personal life?" Oliver asked Mr. Pinter. "Does he have a mistress?"

"Not that I could find."

Hetty smiled. This got better and better.

Oliver mused a moment. "Any idea why he might have been in Ealing yesterday?"

"None, I'm afraid. After your brother mentioned to me yesterday that he'd seen Masters there, I thought I should follow him today to see what he was up to, but when he reached Ealing he didn't stop. He just came on here, so I suppose it's possible he really did just have business—"

"What do you mean, he came on here?" Oliver interrupted.

Hetty's eyes narrowed. Minerva had been in an awful hurry to go for her walk.

Mr. Pinter looked perplexed. "He's paying a call on Lady Minerva, isn't he? When I realized he was headed here, I pulled back, not wanting him to see me. I returned to Ealing and asked a few questions there, then came on here to give my report."

Oliver rose with a black scowl. "You're sure he was on his way to the estate."

"I saw him take the road to Halstead Hall. I suppose he could have passed it by, but I can't imagine why he would have."

When Oliver met her gaze, Hetty knew he'd come to the same conclusion as she. "That little weasel," he growled. "Minerva was acting peculiar at breakfast, too. He's seeing her in secret. And you know damned well there can only be one reason for that."

"Now, Oliver," Hetty began, "you cannot blame the man if he wants to spend time alone with her. You are such a bear when he is around."

"Because I know what he's up to!" Oliver shouted. "It's what *I'd* be up to if I were in *his* place." He marched toward the door. "I knew I should have beaten some sense into that rogue while I had the chance."

"What are you planning to do?" Hetty called out.

"Find them, even if I have to send the dogs out after them. He is *not* going to ruin my sister, damn him!"

"I am coming with you." Hetty looked around for her cane.

Celia chose that moment to enter the library. "Who is Oliver sending the dogs out after?"

"Mr. Masters and Minerva," Hetty replied as she found her cane. "Mr. Pinter saw Mr. Masters headed this way, but since he never showed up, we think they may be meeting privately on the estate."

Celia's gaze swung to Mr. Pinter, then darkened. "So Gran's got you spying on us now?"

"Not all of you," he said. "Just the ones who cause trouble."

The flippant remark gave Hetty pause. Mr. Pinter was never flippant. Pretending to be looking for her shawl, she kept an eye on the pair.

A light flush stained Celia's cheeks. "I suppose you include me in that number."

Mr. Pinter smiled, but his eyes did not. "If the shoe fits, my lady . . ." he drawled.

"I'd be careful, Mr. Pinter," Celia said coldly. "If you take to spying on *me*, you're liable to find yourself at the wrong end of a rifle."

"Trust me," he said in a voice of silk over steel, "if I take to spying on *you*, you'll never know it."

Hetty had heard enough. "Come, Celia. I think you'd better go with me and Oliver to look for Minerva."

With a sniff, Celia headed for the door. Hetty observed Mr. Pinter watching Celia walk away. When his gaze dipped down to her bottom in a look of frankly male appreciation, Hetty groaned.

It appeared that she might have a problem. She liked Mr. Pinter, truly, she did. But when Oliver had suggested hiring him, she had made some inquiries, and she had learned a few things that she suspected even Oliver did not know. Like the fact that he was a bastard, with a whore for a mother and an unknown father.

Hetty had been fine with Oliver's marrying a Catholic American of no rank, and Jarret's marrying a brewster with a bastard son. Maria was an heiress, after all, and Annabel was of a good family. Even the rogue Mr. Masters was the son of a viscount.

But Hetty wasn't so sure she wanted the bastard son of a whore in the family. Then again, Celia didn't seem to like Mr. Pinter, so perhaps she was worrying for naught.

"Are you coming or not?" Oliver roared from down the hall.

"We're coming!" Hetty called out.

She would have to decide what to do about Mr. Pinter later.

Chapter Fourteen

*M*inerva gaped at Giles. Surely she'd misheard him. "What?"

"Your clothes. Take them off." His eyes shone with promise as he shed his coat and waistcoat, then tossed them down on the blanket. "You can swim in your shift and drawers. They would dry in no time."

"But my hair—"

"Stuff it up beneath that cap of yours afterward, and no one will be the wiser."

Heat rose in her cheeks as he removed his boots, then his trousers and stockings. This was a bit more than she'd bargained for.

Then again, the idea of stripping down to her shift, of being in a pond in the outdoors, half-naked, gave her delightful shivers. How did he always manage to find the one thing that would make her *want* to be wicked?

Especially when he yanked his shirt off over his head and tossed it onto the blanket. My oh my oh my. She'd seen her brother's bare chests by accident a time or two, so she knew how a man's chest was supposed to look, but a shirtless Giles was a wonder to behold. He had the most glorious muscles, covered with a sprinkling of brown curls that narrowed to a line down his belly, disappearing beneath his drawers.

His prominently bulging drawers.

She jerked her gaze up to find him looking her over, too, as if imagining her undressed. "I'd do almost anything to see you in your shift, darling. Hell, I'd do almost anything just to see your hair unbound."

He made her feel like a wanton. It was a feeling she rather enjoyed. "You mean, like this?" she said and removed her bonnet and cap, then took her pins out one by one and dropped them into her bonnet.

His eyes darkened to slate as her hair tumbled down about her shoulders. "God, it's even more beautiful than I imagined."

He strode up to fill his hands with her hair, and his voice dropped to a husky murmur. "I've been waiting to see your hair like this for six years, ever since that house party at our estate in Berkshire. Do you remember? The one you attended with your brothers?"

Her pulse leapt. "I'm surprised that *you* remember."

Looping her hair over one shoulder, he turned her around so he could work loose the fastenings of her gown. "I can't forget," he admitted. "The first night we were there, you wore an elegant dinner dress that was cut low enough to bring any man to his knees."

He pulled her gown down until it fell into a puddle of muslin at her feet, then dispensed with her single petticoat. "Your hair was put up, but you had one long sausage curl draped just here." He trailed his fingers down the front of her from shoulder to corset, making her blood heat. "I had this fanciful notion that if I just pulled it, your entire coiffure would unravel like a skein of yarn, and I'd finally see you with your hair down."

For a moment, the thrum of need in his voice seduced her. Then memory returned. She pivoted to face him. "Your fascination with my hair didn't last long. That very evening you disappeared with a widow, and we didn't see you for the rest of the visit."

He blinked. "That's only because—"A look of chagrin crossed his face.

"Because what?" she asked coldly.

His lazy smile was decidedly false. "Because *you* weren't available."

That wasn't what he'd been about to say. She was almost sure of it. With a skeptical expression, she turned away, but he caught her about the waist and pulled her close so he could work loose the ties of her corset. "Don't you remember? That's when that fool Winthrop was courting you. Never left your side the whole weekend."

She'd completely forgot about Lord Winthrop, the man with five children who was determined to find a mother for them. "I thought I'd never get rid of him. He followed me everywhere like a lap dog."

When Giles had finished removing her corset, she faced him once more. "But you know perfectly well that even if he *hadn't* been around, you wouldn't have made any attempt to be near me."

"True," he said. "You had a tendency to snap my head off in those days."

She opened her mouth, then closed it. He was right.

"And you're going to snap my head off in a minute, too," he went on.

"Why?" she asked.

He grinned at her. "Because of this." Without warning, he picked her up and headed for the pond.

"Giles Masters, don't you dare!" she cried, trying to wriggle out of his arms. "I told you, I don't know how to—"

He tossed her into the pond. She felt a moment's panic as she went underwater, but it vanished when her leg hit the bottom and she realized the water was only about four feet deep.

She rose out of the water to glare at him. He was standing calf-deep in the water and laughing heartily, the wretch.

"You think that's funny, do you?" Walking toward him, she glanced at a spot behind him. "You're not going to find it so amusing when that snake gets you."

He turned his head, and she lunged forward to grab his calf and pull hard. He struggled to regain his balance, but it was no use—he couldn't gain purchase on the slippery pond bottom. He slid right into the water at her feet.

He came up sputtering and laughing at the same time. "You're going to pay for that, sweetiekins."

With a grin, she backed into the pond. "What will you do? Drown me in four feet of water?"

His smile faded. "Actually, there's a drop—"

She heard him dimly as she plunged under the water. But before she could even think to panic, he had her and was lifting her so her head was above water.

He pushed the hair from her face. "Thought you'd start the swimming lessons without me, did you?"

Though she could just touch the bottom with the tips of her toes, she clung to him. "I learn from doing."

"Yes, well, you'd learn from drowning, too, but I don't think sink or swim is the most effective way to learn."

"So you *are* going to teach me?" she asked, though her heart was racing, both from her near mishap and the feel of his hands on her waist, holding her above the water.

"Whatever my lady wants," he murmured, eyes gleaming.

For the next half hour, he showed her how to float, how not to panic in the water, how to propel herself through it. It was exhilarating—she'd never been afraid of the water, but neither had she ever been entirely comfortable in it. He made it seem as if navigating it was nothing.

They were standing shoulder-deep in the pond when something slithered over her foot. She shrieked and grabbed onto his shoulders. "Something touched me!"

"It's probably just a fish." Then his gaze dropped to her mouth, and the next thing she knew he was kissing her deeply, thoroughly, boldly. The "fish" was forgotten as she dug her fingers into his shoulders . . . his masterful shoulders, thick with muscle. She could hardly breathe—he was making her blood run too hot.

One of his arms encircled her waist, anchoring her to him. "Look what I've got," he murmured against her lips. "A water nymph, out for a gambol." His free hand fondled her breast, so sweetly, so softly.

"If I'm a water nymph," she breathed, "then what are you?"

"The man who's going to give the nymph whatever she wants." He bent his head to tongue her nipple through her shift. "What do you want, sweet nymph? This?" He sucked her breast, making her gasp. "Or this?" His hand slid down to cup her bottom and pull her hard against him.

"I want you to . . . touch me the way you touched me in the inn," she choked out.

His breath quickened. "Where?"

She hid her flaming face against his shoulder. "You know. Down there. I-in my drawers."

With a chuckle, he slipped his hand around to the front of her and under her shift. She parted her legs to allow him access. As his hand found the tender place between her thighs, he bent her back over his arm so he could tease her breasts with his mouth.

"Yes," she whispered. She grabbed at his shoulders to keep from falling back into the water as her eyes slid closed. "Like that. Oh, Giles, you are very wicked."

"So are you, my lady," he murmured against her breasts. He fingered her devilishly, making her squirm. "A naughty nymph that a man could drown in."

He slid a finger inside her, and her eyes shot open. "Are you sure you should be doing that?"

"Absolutely certain," he growled, then slipped another finger inside her.

A shuddering breath escaped her. It felt too good to be believed, even better than when he'd cupped her there in the inn.

"Hook your legs around my waist," he said in a guttural voice, "and hold on to my neck."

It took her a moment to get the position right, but when she was situated as he'd ordered, she realized she was fully open to his hand, his clever hand that was exploring between her legs in a most exciting fashion.

Giving her deep, soul-searing kisses, he worked her with his fingers and thumb. The water eddied over and around his plunging fingers, as if conspiring with him to caress her. It lapped over her breasts, making her nipples tighten and her body feel fluid, part of the pond, part of *him*.

And then she felt a tide inside her body, rising along her nerves, swamping her senses, making her want and ache and feel the most exquisite sensations. She tore her mouth from his, seeking breath, afraid of drowning. His hot gaze scorched her as she undulated against his fingers.

"That's it, minx," he rasped. "Ride my hand. Find your pleasure. Oh God, you're so beautiful when you're aroused."

"Giles . . . please . . ."

"Whatever you want," he whispered. "Take what you want. I give it to you gladly."

The tide within her rose higher until she couldn't distinguish the water she was in from the water that was building to a flood inside her, threatening to overwhelm her. Then it crashed over her in a giant wave that had her gasping and crying out and tightening her legs convulsively about his waist.

She hung there on him, shaking, weak-kneed, feeling as boneless as the water itself. "Good Lord, Giles . . . my word . . . what was that?"

"You found your pleasure," he murmured. "Women find pleasure in lovemaking just as men do."

Well, *that* certainly explained a few things. Like why women would want to be naughty. And why every time he touched her, she disintegrated into a mass of roiling need.

Then something occurred to her. "Did you . . . find your pleasure?"

"Not yet."

That's when she realized that her privates were resting upon the very obvious bulge in his drawers. "Could I . . . do anything to help that?"

He gave a choked laugh. "You could touch my privates the way I touched yours. God, what I'd give to have you caress me with your hand."

Would you give your heart? The errant thought brought her up short. What was she thinking? Giles didn't believe in hearts. He didn't believe in love. He could only give her pleasure.

Still, he *had* done that, so the least she could do was give him the same.

"You mean, like this?" she asked, stroking along the hard

length of him. Lord, but there was a lot of him there. Quite a lot more than she would have imagined.

"Yes, but harder," he muttered. When she did as he bade, he gave a heartfelt groan. "Yes, like that. But put your hand inside my drawers. Grab hold of me."

It was a little awkward to do that with her legs still locked about his waist, so she let go and stood on the pond bottom.

When she dipped her hand inside his drawers to close her fingers around him, he released a shuddering gasp. "Yes, darling, that's perfect. God save me. Pull on it, up and down . . . a little harder . . . yes . . . like that . . . more . . . more . . ."

Suddenly his flesh spasmed in her hand, and he threw back his head and crowed, "Oh, God, yes! Minerva . . . my nymph . . . my sweet, beautiful nymph . . ."

He took her mouth then, kissing her with a tenderness he'd rarely shown before. It touched something deep inside her and made her want to weep. This was the Giles she'd fallen in love with years ago—not the self-controlled, cynical man she now knew who kept secrets. Why could he only be the old Giles when they were doing this?

And which one was the real one?

"That was wonderful, minx."

It had been wonderful for her, too. That was the trouble. "What now?" she asked. *What does this attraction between us mean? And does it end with this?*

An odd, unreadable expression crossed his face as his eyes bore into hers. For a moment she was sure he knew exactly what she was asking.

Then he gave her a noncommittal smile. "Now I'm going to feed you."

She let out a long breath. It was probably just as well that he didn't answer her questions. She didn't even know what she *wanted* to have happen. A secret affair? More of these dangerous adventures, knowing that in the end they ought to part?

Really, she shouldn't marry him. Even if she was certain that he wanted to, it wouldn't work. He would never let her close enough to really know him. Nor did she want a life where she was nothing more than the ornament in his professional crown.

Still, when he unpacked the picnic basket, revealing several of her favorite foods, it was hard to believe it couldn't work. He could be so sweet and considerate.

Except when he's hiding things.

She sighed. Yes, that was the trouble.

They ate quickly, famished after their bout of swimming and . . . other things. When he lay back and pulled her down next to him to hold her in his arms, she couldn't resist resting her head on his chest and listening to the steady beat of his heart.

"This is a very pretty spot for a picnic," she murmured. "I can't believe I never knew it was here."

"We lads were careful to keep it a secret. Didn't want a bunch of children spoiling our fun."

"Well, we wouldn't have wanted to play with fellows as old and decrepit as you lot anyway."

"I'm not *that* much older than you," he said with an edge in his voice.

She glanced up at him in surprise. He was self-conscious about his *age,* of all things. How delicious! "No, not that much older. I daresay you have a couple of years before you have to resort to false teeth."

"A couple of years!" When she grinned at him, he frowned. "That is *not* amusing."

"Wait, is that a gray hair I see?" she teased, reaching up to touch his decidedly brown locks.

"Watch it, minx," he growled, "or I'll treat you like the child you are and take you over my knee."

"A spanking?" she said. "Oh, that *does* sound interesting."

Shock lit his face. Then he laughed. "I swear, you aren't like any woman I know."

"Is that a good thing?"

"It's a very good thing." He brushed a kiss to the top of her head.

They fell silent. After a while, the hot noon sun and the chirping of the birds lulled them both into a state of pure drowsy contentment. Then they dozed off.

Chapter Fifteen

The unmistakable sound of a rifle being cocked brought Giles instantly awake. He looked up into the implacable face of the Marquess of Stoneville and then lower to the barrel of a Manton breechloader aimed right at his head.

This was bad. Very, very bad.

He felt Minerva stir beside him, then cry, "Oliver, what the devil do you think you're doing? Put that away! You might hurt him!"

Stoneville's gaze bore into Giles's, cold as death. "What a pity *that* would be."

"This isn't how it looks," Minerva said.

Giles tamped down a manic urge to laugh. "I doubt he believes that, minx."

"Minerva," Stoneville said, "you have about one minute to put some clothes on before everybody else gets here."

"Everybody else?" she squeaked.

"Oliver, what do you think you're doing?" cried an aged voice from the path.

"Too late," Stoneville muttered.

Everything happened at once. With a shriek, Minerva dived for her clothes. Several dogs burst into the little space, dragging along Halstead Hall's gamekeeper and an assortment of servants. Lady Celia came after them.

And Mrs. Plumtree appeared at Stoneville's side. "You cannot shoot Mr. Masters!"

"Oh, I'm fairly certain I can," Stoneville drawled. "I've got a pretty good bead on him."

Giles groaned. His life definitely hung in the balance. If he'd found some scoundrel lying half-naked on the ground with *his* sister, he would have reacted exactly like Stoneville. Only he would have aimed lower. And he would have fired by now.

"But if you shoot him, how can he be any good to Minerva?" Mrs. Plumtree said.

"I'm not sure he can be anyway," Stoneville snapped.

"I can if I marry her," Giles said. "And I *will* marry her."

"I don't know if I *want* you to marry my sister," Stoneville growled.

"And I don't know if I want to marry *him*," Minerva said hotly.

Giles's heart sank as she came up to stand beside Stoneville, her eyes flashing fire. She'd managed to struggle into her petticoat and gown but had abandoned her corset and apparently couldn't fasten her gown, which hung loosely on her.

Bloody, bloody hell. This wasn't how he'd meant this to happen. Minerva hated being forced almost as much as he did. She was bound to be stubborn about this.

"If you are willing to roll about on the ground half-naked with the man, then you had better be willing to marry him," her grandmother said in a hard voice.

"I'd rather shoot him," Stoneville said. "Either now, or at dawn tomorrow."

"You're not going to shoot Giles," Minerva snapped, "so just get that idea out of your head." Walking over to her brother, she shoved the rifle to the side.

It went off, spitting a bullet into the ground a few inches from Giles's head.

Giles sprang to his feet. "What the hell—"

"Don't ever do that again!" Stoneville shouted at his sister as the blood drained from his face. "That rifle has a damned hair-trigger, for God's sake!"

"Are you *trying* to get me killed, Minerva?" Giles growled.

"I-I thought it wasn't really loaded," she said, her face ashen.

Giles strode up to her. "Next time someone has a gun trained on me, would you please let *me* handle it?"

"But you *weren't* handling it!" Minerva protested. "You were just lying there, looking as if you thought you were about to die."

"Because I *was,* damn it! Thanks to you, I nearly did!"

"Quiet, both of you!" Mrs. Plumtree cried. "Good Lord, you sound like a married couple already." Her gaze shifted to Giles, who was struggling into his riding breeches. "Are you going to marry her?"

"Of course," Giles said just as Minerva said, "There's no need for that."

Minerva stared at her grandmother. "This is all a terrible misunderstanding. We merely went for a swim and had a picnic lunch. Then we fell asleep. I'm still chaste."

"Save your breath." Giles tugged his shirt on. "They're not going to believe you."

"And how did you find us anyway?" Minerva went on, ignoring Giles.

"That blasted Mr. Pinter has been spying on Mr. Masters for Gran," Celia said. "He followed Mr. Masters to the estate this morning."

Giles groaned. When Mrs. Plumtree had said she'd have Pinter look into his finances, it never occurred to him that the man might go beyond that. And how had he not noticed the fellow following him?

But he knew how. He'd been thinking of only one thing— meeting Minerva and giving her the taste of passion that she wanted. That they both wanted.

Damn it, this was what came of following his cock.

Minerva was gazing at her grandmother, perplexed. "Why would you have Mr. Pinter spy on Giles?"

"To make sure he was good enough for you," Mrs. Plumtree said, a trifle nervously.

"I see." Minerva planted her hands on her hips, which only made the gown droop more. "And what did he discover?"

"Mr. Masters is financially sound and is doing very well in his profession. He is even building a house in Berkeley Square. So you see, girl, he is not marrying you for your fortune. There is no reason not to accept him."

"Ah, but there's a very good reason," Minerva said in a heart-wrenching voice. "He's being forced into it. And I don't want a man who has to be forced to marry me."

"But he's *not*," Mrs. Plumtree cried. "He truly wants to marry you. He assured me of it himself that day when you first announced the engagement."

"Of course he did. I told him to." Minerva sighed. "Don't hate me, Gran, but this whole thing has just been a ruse to—"

"Alarm me into rescinding my ultimatum," Mrs. Plumtree said. "I know. He told me. He also told me that it wasn't a ruse for him. That he truly wanted to marry you."

Giles cursed under his breath. Could this possibly get any worse?

"You told her *what*?" Minerva said with a look of pure betrayal.

He stepped forward to grab her arm. "If you lot will excuse us, I think it's time I had a private word with my fiancée."

MINERVA'S MIND WHIRLED as they headed into the woods, her gown still deplorably half-fastened. Why had Giles told Gran about her subterfuge? And did that mean he'd really been serious about marrying her from the beginning? That he *hadn't* simply been going along with her plans to shock Gran so he could get her to stop writing about Rockton?

What it meant was that he was every bit as devious and sly as she'd feared. And he had a plan of his own. She just had to figure out how she fit into it.

She stopped and faced him, noting the look of guilt on his face.

No, she had to figure out how to *use* it to her benefit. Because after this afternoon, there was no point in denying that she wanted him—as a man, as a companion, and yes, as a husband. But on her terms, not his. It was time that Giles Masters—and Gran—learned that she wouldn't tolerate their planning out her life for her.

She stared him down with the cold expression she'd perfected for unsavory suitors. "Is it true? Did you tell Gran that I intended our engagement to be only pretend?"

His guilty look deepened. "It's not as bad as it sounds."

"Really? Because it sounds as if you've been conspiring with my grandmother to gain my hand in marriage. Even though I distinctly remember telling you that I did *not* want to marry you."

He winced.

A horrible thought occurred to her. "You didn't engineer this little scene of discovery by my family just so you could force me to marry you, did you?"

"No! I had no idea Pinter was following me."

She eyed him askance.

He looked a little ill. "I swear to God I didn't plan this."

"And how am I supposed to believe you, when you've been lying to me all along?"

"I haven't lied to you," he said. "I've merely left out parts of the truth."

She scowled. "I specifically recall asking you if you'd told Gran about my subterfuge."

"Then you should specifically recall how I answered."

She thought back to that day. What had he said? Oh yes. *You promised to kill off Rockton. Why would I jeopardize that by scheming with your grandmother?*

He really *was* a sly one, answering her question with a question to avoid lying to her.

What's more, she remembered what he'd said when she'd asked what he'd told Gran: *I told her I wanted to marry you. That I admired and respected you. That I could support you.*

From what Gran had implied, that probably wasn't a lie, either.

"If you didn't quite lie, you certainly bent the truth. You knew what I thought."

He stepped close to her. "I also knew you had a lot of baseless opinions about me that would keep you from agreeing to marry me. I wanted time to prove that you were wrong about me. To prove I could be a good husband to you." Taking her hands in his, he pressed them to his lips. "Haven't I proved that yet?"

Oh, he could coax the birds from the skies with all his sweet words. "All you've proved is that I can't trust you. That you will always be scheming to run my life."

"I have enough trouble running my own life, minx," he said drily. "I've no great desire to run yours, too."

"So this wasn't about trying to get me to stop writing about Rockton? It has nothing to do with that?"

He started, then glanced away with a curse.

"That's what I thought." She jerked her hands from his, but he caught her about the waist, refusing to let her go, even when her gown slid half off her shoulder.

"Listen to me, darling," he said in that low thrum that always made her insides flip over. "I came to Halstead Hall that day because I wanted to marry you. And yes, partly for the reason you say. But that wasn't the only reason." His voice grew husky. "I've wanted you from the day we first kissed. I just couldn't find a way to fit you into my life until now."

She stared him down. "How exactly *am* I supposed to fit into your life? I'm drenched in scandal. My parents' deaths, my family's present situation . . . my books—none of it fits into the life of a prominent barrister well on his way to becoming a K.C."

"It *can*," he said. "All you have to do is—"

"Stop writing."

"No! I told you—that doesn't matter to me."

"It will eventually."

He scowled at her. "What about your favorite author, Mrs. Radcliffe? She was married for her entire career, and her husband was a newspaper publisher. It didn't appear to harm *his* reputation or profession."

"But she wasn't the wife of a K.C. You and I both know that K.C.'s often go on to become judges or statesmen." Her voice faltered. "You are destined for great things."

"I don't care. And you *shouldn't* care."

"Then there's the matter of children. Mrs. Radcliffe had no children, did she?"

At the word *children,* he caught his breath.

"You *want* children, don't you?" she asked, her heart beating triple-time.

"Of course." His voice thickened. "You do, too, admit it. No one could write about children so fondly in her books and not want some of her own."

"The point is—"

"Enough excuses," he said. "The Minerva I know can make whatever sort of life she chooses. She's strong and fearless and capable of bringing public opinion around to her side. That's the Minerva I want, the Minerva who isn't afraid to take a bull by the horns."

Oh, he knew just the right things to say, the devil. It really was most annoying of him.

He reached up to cup her cheek. "We can make a good life together—we can make it work. I'm convinced of it. For once, trust me to know what I'm talking about."

"Trust you? When you evade the truth at every turn? When you still won't even tell me why you stole those papers years ago? Something that small, and you refuse to reveal—"

"It's not small, all right?" he gritted out. Releasing her, he turned to stare into the woods. "It's personal, having to do with my family."

"They will soon be my family, too, if I marry you. Which is doubtful, when you continue to keep secrets from me at every turn."

He pinched the bridge of his nose, then pivoted to face her. "I can't talk about it to you. All I can tell you is that it involved my father and the loss of a great sum of money."

"Oh, Lord!" She put things together in her mind. "That happened around the time of the suicide, didn't it?"

"Yes," he said warily. "Why?"

"Well, the newspapers never said why he killed himself,

but I assumed . . . that is, men who lose at the gaming tables often . . ." She took a steadying breath. "You were stealing gambling vowels, weren't you?"

Shock filled his face. "Gambling vowels?"

"Of your father's. You weren't stealing money, so it had to be IOUs." When he scowled, she added, "I know matters were difficult for your family then. That's why your brother had to marry an heiress, right? I heard my brothers talking about it."

"Your brothers are far too chatty."

"No, I'm just an eavesdropper." She tipped up her chin. "In any case, it's nothing to be ashamed of."

"Stealing is nothing to be ashamed of?" he said, one eyebrow raised.

"Well, stealing isn't good, of course, but I've always thought it horrible that a man's debts of honor should pass on to his children after his death. They didn't contract them, after all. Why should they have to suffer for *his* sins?"

He crossed his arms over his chest. "Why indeed?"

"Well, is that it? Is that what you were stealing?"

"It sounds as if you've figured it out perfectly well on your own," he bit out. "I don't know what else I can say." When she was about to press him for a more definitive answer, he added, "Except that despite what you seem to think is acceptable behavior, the bar would be alarmed to hear of it. My career would be ended."

Well, of course it would. That's why he'd been so angry over her writing about him. She'd figured that out already. "I'm not going to tell anyone. That would be rather foolish of me, don't you think?"

He eyed her cautiously. "How so?"

"I'm not going to ruin my own husband's career."

It took him a moment to grasp what she was saying, but

when he did, the look of hope in his eyes went a long way to reconfirming that she was making the right decision.

"You're going to marry me? You mean it?"

He started to reach for her, but she held him off. "Not yet. I have some conditions."

A laugh escaped him. "Of course you do. I'd expect nothing less."

"First, you have to swear that you'll never forbid me to write my books."

"Forbidding you to do things is a choice?" he asked sarcastically. "Truly?"

"Giles, be serious!"

He laid his hand on his heart and gave her his most lawyerly look. "I solemnly swear never to forbid you to write your books, so help me, God. What else?"

"You have to swear to be faithful."

His eyes turned solemn. "I told you once, I'm not your father. I believe in marriage, Minerva. That means I believe in fidelity and till death do us part. You'll never have to worry that there's any other woman in my life but you."

The words were so sweet that she was a little wary of trusting them. "I suppose if you were inclined to misbehave, you wouldn't exactly tell me the truth anyway."

"Darling, you have a brother fond of holding a gun on me, a sister who can shoot anything that moves, two other brothers who've repeatedly threatened to thrash me, and a grandmother who buys off constables. Do you really think I'm fool enough to antagonize them by committing adultery?"

It was hard not to smile at that. "An excellent point."

"I think so."

She stared at him a long moment, debating. "I have one more condition. You're not going to like it."

"I have to swim naked with you at least once a week in the pond?" he said hopefully.

"You have to be truthful with me."

He sucked in a breath. "About what?"

"Everything. Papa engaged in all sorts of wicked behavior behind Mama's back, and it made her life a misery. I will not suffer that sort of deceit to go on in our marriage."

His gaze bore into her. "There are things in my past that I can't talk about with you. Things I've done. Things I've been. And I'll be damned if I lay them all out for you just so you won't worry that I'm like your father. I'm not even sure you'd want me to."

She swallowed. It really *was* a lot to ask. If they were in love, perhaps she could demand it, and he might feel comfortable enough to talk. But they weren't.

Were they?

She stared at him. She didn't want to be in love with him, but every time she was near him, it became easier to trust him, easier to believe in him. Easier to consider loving him. That was the trouble with Giles. He had this way of making a woman want him . . .

But he certainly didn't love *her*. Even now, when he appeared to want to marry her, he said nothing about loving her.

Very well, she could do without that. They could still have a very good, contented marriage. Plenty of people did, with merely a deep affection to bind them. And he was the only man she'd ever even *considered* wanting to marry. She mustn't be greedy and expect love. Not under these circumstances.

"Fine," she said softly. "Then will you promise to be truthful with me about everything from now on?"

Relief flooded his features. "That I can promise." He took

her hand and entwined it with his. "So are we done? We're agreed?"

"One more thing."

"Oh, for God's sake, Minerva—"

"Would you please fasten up this gown for me?"

He blinked, then burst into laughter. "Absolutely."

Chapter Sixteen

As Minerva stood beside Giles in the Halstead Hall gardens, greeting the guests at their wedding breakfast, the gold ring on her finger felt heavy and cold, and making polite conversation with the steady flow of gentlemen instrumental to Giles's success began to wear on her. Scarcely more than two weeks had passed since she'd proclaimed this scenario impossible, and only a week had passed since she'd agreed to it. How Giles and Gran had managed to get so many important people here at such short notice was beyond her. Why, even the undersecretary of the Home Office himself, the Viscount Ravenswood, was here.

She'd had no idea that her husband had such connections. She cast Giles a furtive glance as he spoke to some judge, her heart skipping a beat at the sight of him so finely dressed. Lord, but he was handsome in his profusion of blues—the dark blue coat of superfine, breeches of light blue silk, and his beaver hat dyed blue. Though the whites of his silk waistcoat, cravat, shirt, and stockings stood as a stark counterpoint to all those blues, it was still the blue that one noticed first—bringing out the eyes that burned bright whenever he looked at her.

It was fitting, in a way—most of the people were here to see *him*. Was this to be her life now, always playing the cordial wife, watching every word she said for fear it would hurt Giles's chances at becoming a K.C.? If it hadn't been for his presence beside her, she might have turned tail and run. But the touch of his hand on her lower back steadied her nerves.

She'd missed him this week—there'd been far too much to do for them to spend time together. He'd been willing to wait for a proper wedding, but Gran had insisted on a quick wedding, probably out of fear that her granddaughter would change her mind. Or worse yet, worry about what Oliver was convinced had happened at the pond.

So Gran and Giles had compromised. They'd gained a special license, invited fewer people, and had the wedding and the breakfast at Halstead Hall. It had thrown Maria into quite a tizzy—it was the first time she and Oliver had entertained at the crumbling old mansion.

Giles had set Maria at ease by insisting that she and Oliver not make much fuss. As he put it, Halstead Hall was famous for being a moldering old pile—no one would think twice about a few frayed linens, and everyone would count themselves lucky to be invited. As it turned out, he'd been right. Even with the short notice, nearly everyone they'd invited had come.

At last the guests had all passed through the receiving line and were happily filling their plates with the ample dishes provided by Gran's French cook from town. Giles's mother, the elder Lady Kirkwood, who stood on Minerva's other side, faced her with a warm smile. "Giles tells me that you're taking your wedding trip to Bath."

"Yes," Minerva said, "though tonight we're staying in the Berkeley Square house." Which she still hadn't seen. Giles's builder had been working like a demon to get enough of it ready so they could inhabit it. She wondered if her mother-in-law had been there yet.

Her *mother-in-law*. Good Lord, she couldn't believe she had one. She probably ought to stop writing wicked mother-in-laws like the one in *The Stranger of the Lake*. No point in antagonizing her husband's mother when she barely knew the woman.

"Our wedding trip will be short, I'm afraid," Giles said. "I have some trials going on right now, so I couldn't leave town for long." He gazed down at Minerva with a softness in his eyes that made her blood sing. "But I've promised my wife that we'll take a more extended trip to Italy once I can get away."

My wife. That sounded perfectly wonderful.

"And what do you intend to do about your novels, my dear?" Lady Kirkwood asked.

Minerva stiffened. "I intend to keep writing them, of course."

"But surely, now that you're married—"

"Now that she's married," Giles interrupted, "she'll have a more extensive experience of life from which to draw her fiction."

Minerva wanted to kiss him.

Lady Kirkwood's smile was brittle. "Of course. And will you be . . . writing them under your married name?"

"No. I'll keep the same name as before." She'd discussed it at length with her publisher. She didn't want to risk losing readers.

"So do you . . . er . . . intend to go by Lady Minerva Masters everywhere else?"

"Mother, please," Giles interrupted. "Must we do this today, of all days?"

"I need to know how to address invitations to affairs in the future," Lady Kirkwood said with a sniff. "With such a hasty wedding, there was no chance for us to discuss these things. I was fortunate we could even arrive from Cornwall in time for it."

One of Giles's sisters lived in Cornwall, and that's where his mother had been until late last night.

"I plan to use the name Mrs. Giles Masters," Minerva said quickly. Though she had the right to retain her courtesy title since she was marrying a man below her in rank, she thought perhaps it was time she separated her writing life from her private life.

"Well then, that's all right, isn't it?" his mother said, beaming at Minerva.

Clearly Minerva wasn't the only one who thought it was time she make that separation. Suddenly she felt sorry for Lady Kirkwood. The woman had endured plenty of scandal in her own life—her husband's suicide and the murder of her eldest son's first wife. Watching her youngest son marry a character as scandalous as Minerva might not be easy for her to swallow.

Perhaps it was time for a little daughterly chat. "Lady Kirkwood," Minerva said, "would you like to see our maze? I understand that your other son is putting one in at your estate in Berkshire."

Lady Kirkwood brightened. "He is, indeed. And I would love to see yours."

Minerva pressed a kiss to Giles's cheek. "We'll be back shortly, my dear."

As they made their way down the path to the maze, Minerva said, "I want you to know, madam, that I intend to be a good wife to Giles. You needn't worry that I'll embarrass your family."

"Thank you." Lady Kirkwood sighed. "I don't mean to be rude. It's just that Giles finally seems to be settling down, and then this wedding comes out of the blue—"

"I know. It took both of us by surprise as well." That was certainly an understatement. "But I would never do anything to harm his career or his reputation."

"You can't do anything worse than he's done himself, I suppose. All that gambling and nonsense. He should have grown out of that years ago."

"I quite agree."

His mother patted her arm. "I do hope you will be a steadying influence on him." She spoke it more as a command than a wish.

Minerva smothered a smile. "I shall certainly try." That was one thing she should have thought to demand of him— that he not gamble—but that seemed a bit unfair, given that practically every man of her acquaintance did.

Besides, according to Gran, Mr. Pinter didn't seem to think it as much of a problem as she'd first feared. "Many men gamble, you know. He's merely following in the footsteps of his father and all the gentlemen he—"

"Not his father," Lady Kirkwood broke in. "My husband didn't gamble a day in his life."

Minerva eyed her skeptically. "No?"

"Certainly not." Her voice turned cold. "Unless you include his reckless investments in businesses he knew nothing about. That was his undoing."

Forcing a smile, Minerva led her into the maze. "I see."

She showed her mother-in-law around it, keeping up a constant chatter about their plans for the new house, but meanwhile her mind was reeling. Lady Kirkwood might simply be one of those women who had no idea of what her husband was up to. Or she might just be embarrassed to admit that her husband had gambled.

But she didn't seem the type to be unaware, and she certainly didn't seem the type to be embarrassed. She'd just finished complaining about Giles's gambling—why would she hide her husband's?

And if her husband hadn't been a gambler, then why had Giles told her . . .

She thought back to that day a week ago and groaned. He hadn't told her anything. Once again, he'd let her draw her own conclusions without admitting or denying anything. That was becoming a bad habit of his—she would have to nip it in the bud if they were to have any sort of marriage.

First chance she got, she would confront him with the truth—

What truth? That his father never gambled? She wasn't even sure that was the case. Besides, he'd already said he wouldn't talk about the past with her.

She ought to let it go. He'd promised to be truthful with her now, and that was all that mattered.

But it *wasn't* all that mattered. His past shaped who he was as surely as hers did. He was only letting her partway into his life. Why? What was he hiding?

Well, one thing was certain. She wasn't going to learn the truth by asking *him*. He'd either refuse to tell her anything or lie to her, which would break her heart. She would have to find another way to discover the truth.

As they left the maze she spotted Mr. Pinter talking to Oliver, and her eyes narrowed. Another way, indeed. Perhaps it was time she got some help.

She sighed. But she'd have to tell Mr. Pinter everything, even about the stealing—it was the only way to get at the truth. Did she dare? Was it too reckless of her? What if somehow it came back to harm Giles?

No, how could it? Mr. Pinter knew exactly how to handle

these things. He hadn't revealed any of her family's secrets heretofore, and their secrets were certainly darker. He was discreet and thorough, and he knew more about Giles already than anyone. And now that she was married to the man, Giles's secrets became her family's, too, whether Giles accepted that or not.

Very well. She would see what Mr. Pinter could learn. It was time she found out exactly what her husband was hiding from her.

GILES WATCHED AS his new bride left his mother's side. When she didn't come straight back to him, he scowled. He was being ridiculous, of course. They weren't shackled at the leg, no matter what the saying said. Still, he missed her. He'd hardly seen her at all this week, and the mere thought of what they'd be doing tonight stole the breath from his body.

It was hard not to think of it with her looking like an angel in that gown of frothy white silk. Dainty red and green rosettes on the hem danced about her ankles, and her throat held only a single gem—an emerald that was no match for her sparkling eyes. He couldn't wait to see those eyes shining up at him as he took her, to see her smile only for him, and not for all these fools who'd come to see the "scandalously hasty" wedding.

Then he saw where she was heading, and he tensed. What did she want with Pinter? The far too handsome, amiable, and upstanding Pinter?

He was just about to see for himself when a familiar voice arrested him.

"Glad to catch you alone at last."

Giles turned to face the Viscount Ravenswood. "Thank

you for coming. I was rather surprised to see you accept my invitation. I wasn't sure if you could make the time for it."

Ravenswood's smile was strained. "Actually, I hadn't planned to come, but my superiors wanted me to speak to you."

"About what?"

"Continuing with your work as an operative. They're willing to offer you some strong inducements to stay—a title, more pay . . . a few political favors, if that's what you wish."

He sighed. "Ravenswood, I don't want—"

"I know. I told them you'd refuse. But they wanted me to ask." He stared off across the lawn. "Unfortunately, we do have one more piece of business we need to discuss."

Giles went on the alert. "Oh?"

"I received a letter from Lord Newmarsh."

A weight settled on Giles's chest. That was one name he'd thought he was done with for good. "Is he still living abroad, as agreed?"

In exchange for his help in unveiling Sir John Sully's fraud, Lord Newmarsh's name had been kept out of the affair and he'd been given a pardon . . . on the condition that he leave England permanently.

"He is. He's in France. His letter said that he wishes to meet with you."

Giles stared at him, his gut twisting into a knot. "Me? Why would he ask you to set up a meeting with me? Does that mean—"

"That he knows you stole the papers from his house that were instrumental in convicting Sir John Sully?" A pained expression crossed Ravenswood's face. "Yes. He says that if you don't come, he'll tell the press about what you did."

The blood roared in his ears. Damn, this couldn't be happening. "How did he find out?"

"I don't know. He didn't say in his letter."

Giles raked his fingers through his hair. The one man who had the most reason to see him ruined now knew what he'd done. There was only one way he could have learned of it. From Minerva's books.

But that made no sense. Surely there weren't enough clues for him to have put all that together. And why would he be reading gothic novels, anyway?

Ravenswood took a sip from the champagne glass in his hand. "He wants you to meet him in Calais. He said he'd give you until next week. There's a steam packet service that can have you in Calais in eleven hours."

Frustration roiled in his belly. "I just got married, for God's sake."

"You don't have to go. I suspect he's bluffing. Why would he stir up all that old business again by going to the papers? He got out of it without his name and reputation being blackened, and he'd risk that happening now? Never. From all reports, he's made a comfortable life for himself in Paris. He doesn't need this."

"I can't take the chance."

"It could be a trap. He might want revenge."

"Newmarsh? I doubt that. He was never a violent man. More likely, he wants something from me. This is blackmail, pure and simple. I have to see what he wants."

They stood a moment in silence. Giles watched his wife having an intense conversation with Pinter, and despair rolled through him. He'd sworn to be done with secrets, and he'd meant it.

But he couldn't tell her this. If by some small chance it *had* happened because of her books, she would blame herself.

"You could always take your wife with you to Calais."

He could. It would be easier to pass off a change in their

wedding trip plans than to explain why he was abandoning her for a couple of days right after their wedding. "I may just do that. If I can figure out a good excuse for it."

"Masters, I realize I told you that you can't speak of your connection with us to anyone, and I certainly wouldn't want you spilling any state secrets, but I know I can trust you to be discreet in what you say. She *is* your wife, after all. Besides, the matter with Newmarsh happened before you started working for us. You have every right to speak of *that* to her. If you feel you can trust her—"

"It's not that."

But it was. Minerva wasn't used to keeping secrets—look at how she'd spilled her own family secrets to *him*. All she would have to do is let something slip to one person, and his past could very well unravel. Plus, Minerva had a tendency to use things in her damned books.

She wouldn't if you asked her not to.

Wouldn't she? How could he be sure? "I'd just . . . rather not tell her. It'll be over after this. It will all be behind me."

That way he didn't have to risk that she'd let his secrets slip. He wanted a fresh start with her. He could have it, too. All he had to do was hide his activities this one time. It was really only a small deception.

So why did it seem like an enormous one?

He gritted his teeth. For God's sake, why was he even worrying about this? Any other man would tell his wife to mind her own business and be done with it.

But he wasn't any other man. And Minerva definitely wasn't any other woman.

"One more thing," Ravenswood said.

Giles eyed him askance. "That wasn't enough to ruin my wedding day?"

"It's nothing like that. I just thought you'd like to know about that map you asked me to look into."

"The one Desmond Plumtree had." Having found nothing in property records, Giles had drawn up a copy for Ravenswood and asked for his help.

"One of my men says he recognizes it. He just can't remember from where. He's going to look into it and let me know. By the time you come back, we should have some answers for you."

"Good." It was very good. Perhaps it would be enough to make his wife forgive him if she happened to find out that he'd kept one small secret from her.

No, nothing would make her forgive him after the way she'd made him promise to be truthful.

So he'd just have to make sure she didn't suspect anything. He'd put this matter of Newmarsh behind him without involving her; then he could have his life back at last.

Chapter Seventeen

$\mathcal{I}$t was nearly evening by the time they left the wedding breakfast. As soon as their carriage was headed to London, Minerva glanced over at her new husband. Her *husband*. That would take some getting used to.

Especially since he seemed distracted. "Are you all right?" she asked.

He blinked, as if jerked from some deep reverie, then smiled at her. "Perfectly all right." Taking her hand, he slowly peeled off her glove. "I'll be even better once we reach the house." He kissed each finger. "When I can show you exactly how all right I am."

"You could show me now," she said, emboldened by the fire in his gaze.

"Sorry, darling, but I'm not going to bed you for the first time in a carriage." His gaze trailed down her with leisurely appreciation. "Much as it tempts me, I want you to be comfortable."

"I doubt that waiting will help me be comfortable," she said tartly. "From what I hear, the first time is always difficult for a woman."

"Are you frightened?"

"Of that?" She snorted. "Hardly. If it were so very awful, my sisters-in-law wouldn't be leaping into my brother's beds with astonishing regularity." When he laughed, she added, "Besides, I trust you. I know you'll do your best to make it easier."

He squeezed her hand, then released it. "Can we talk about something else? All this discussion of what we aren't going to do until we reach the house is only making me think about it more."

She looked down to see his breeches looking rather fuller than before. "Perhaps I could help with that," she teased, reaching to touch him.

Grabbing her hand, he pressed it back into her lap. "Not now," he said firmly.

With a sniff, she settled back against the seat. "I do hope you're not going to turn into a stick-in-the-mud like Oliver."

"Turn into one?" he echoed, a peculiar note of irony in his voice. "I don't think you need worry about that."

"I don't know—you have a lot of very high-in-the-instep friends."

"Like who?"

"The undersecretary of the Home Office. I had no idea you knew such lofty people."

He seemed to withdraw into himself. "Ravenswood and I went to school together. We've known each other for years."

"So it's not a . . . business thing then?"

A strange look passed over his face. "I've never had to represent him as a barrister, if that's what you mean."

"Your conversation at the wedding didn't look entirely pleasant, and you spoke to him quite a while."

"I could say the same about you and Pinter." He scowled at her. "What were you two discussing, anyway? You seemed awfully chummy."

She eyed him askance. "Don't tell me you're jealous of Mr. Pinter."

"Certainly not," he said stiffly. "You'd never be attracted to such a 'stick-in-the-mud.'" He shot her a sidelong glance. "Would you?"

Oh, that was too good to pass up. She pretended to contemplate the idea. "I don't know. He's quite good-looking. And there's something very enticing about officers of the law . . . all that masculine energy devoted to seeking justice."

"*I* seek justice," he said.

"But you're an attorney—it's not the same."

"You mean, it would be more *enticing* if I pranced around town waving a pistol and hauling people out of taverns whether or not they'd done anything wrong."

"I give you fair warning—if you ever start prancing about town, I shall leave you." She burst into laughter. "I'm teasing you, you clodpate. Surely you can tell by now that I won't ignore any chance to tweak your nose."

He stared hard at her. "You haven't answered my question."

No, she hadn't. She was hoping he'd forgotten. The last thing she wanted to do was lie to him. "Mr. Pinter and I were discussing the work he does for Gran—you know, the investigative work."

"Ah. Has he found out more about Desmond?"

"No." She figured that was true, since they hadn't discussed it. "But I understand that *you* did." Desmond and his family had been at the wedding, of course, and given what they all suspected of him she'd found it hard to be civil. But Giles had turned it into an opportunity. "Jarret told me you asked Desmond a number of questions in the guise of a newcomer to the family. Did you learn much?"

"Just that he claims not to have been on the estate in twenty years."

"And you think he's lying."

"Don't you?"

She sighed. "Probably. But Oliver hasn't found anything in the estate papers that resembles that map."

"Well, we'll know soon enough if he's been going to the estate."

"What do you mean?"

Giles smiled. "I set a trap for him."

That got her attention. "How?"

"I told him I'd discovered that Lord Manderley was planning to buy a house near Turnham and would be moving into it in a month or so. Plumtree is *not* going to want to run into a fellow he owes money to. So he'll step up his efforts to finish his project, whatever it is."

"What do you plan to do, lie in wait for him every day at the Black Bull?"

"No need. I paid the inn a visit earlier in the week and engaged the services of one of the grooms. He'll let me know when Plumtree shows up. Then I'll follow him and find out what he's up to."

"Oh, Giles, what a brilliant plan! You're always so clever." She smiled up at him. "If you want, I'll get Celia to send me a current map of the estate so you can compare it to what you remember of the other one."

"That would be useful."

They both fell silent. She wished he would sweep her into his arms and kiss her. Or, for that matter, tease her. He seemed too solemn. It worried her.

So she tried to pass it off by making small talk. "What time do you plan for us to leave for Bath tomorrow?"

He shifted on the seat. "Actually, I was thinking we might change that plan."

"Oh?"

"Bath is hot in the summer. Certainly too hot for us to spend standing shoulder-deep in a pit of steaming water. So I thought you might prefer something more interesting."

That certainly raised her curiosity. "Like what?"

"France."

She broke into a broad smile. "Paris, you mean? Oh, that would be wonderful! I've always wanted to see the Champs-Élysées. And the Louvre . . . But wait, I thought you said you couldn't leave London for that long."

A look of chagrin crossed his face. "I'm afraid that's true. Paris is too far, but I was thinking . . . perhaps Calais?"

It was hard to hide her confusion. "But is there anything to see of note in Calais?"

"There's the ramparts and Calais's Notre Dame church. It's not as impressive as the Notre Dame in Paris, of course, but still pretty. Best of all, they have French food and French shops and some very nice hotels."

"I suppose." At least in Bath there would be dancing and plenty of sights.

His smile turning heated, he took her hand again. "I'm not sure we're going to *want* to do much looking about, anyway." Lifting her hand to his lips, he kissed her wrist, making her pulse dance madly.

Ah, so that's what he was about. In Bath there would be a great many important people who would expect to visit with them. Perhaps he wanted to be somewhere it could be just the two of them, enjoying themselves. The more she thought about it, the more intriguing it sounded.

He went on in a low, coaxing voice. "You do, after all, have Rockton acting as a French spy. You should get a flavor for the country before you write any scenes where he visits France."

Her eyes narrowed. "I thought I wasn't supposed to write about Rockton anymore."

He shrugged. "You don't *have* to stop writing about him. Just make him less . . ."

"Like you?" she said, smothering her smile.

"Exactly."

"Are you sure you don't want me to kill him off? I could give him a spectacular death, with blood and guts spilling all over the place, and a dying speech to rival one of Shakespeare's."

He frowned. "You said that with entirely too much relish."

"Oh, dear. I must strive to better hide my murderous intent. It wouldn't do to have you guess the many ways I could—"

He kissed her—a quick, brusque kiss. Then as she stared up at him, a teasing smile on her lips, he cupped her head in his hands and kissed her with the leisurely enjoyment of a man who knows what he wants and how much time he has to gain it.

When he drew back, she murmured, "I thought you said we couldn't do this until we reached the house."

"I changed my mind." He proceeded to nibble on her ear, his breath tickling her cheek. "Think of this as the first course to an all-night feast."

"Oh, no," she said in false solemnity. "I think we should wait until we reach—"

This time his kiss was all-consuming, the kind that made her want and ache and need more. She slid her hands up about his neck, and he pulled her onto his lap.

"You were saying?" he murmured.

She kissed him, and that was all it took to have him devouring her mouth and fondling her breast through her gown and generally driving her to utter distraction. This part of marriage might make the rest of it worth it.

Still, she noticed he practiced restraint in the carriage. He kissed and caressed her, oh yes, until they were both breathing heavily and his arousal was stiff enough beneath her bottom to bludgeon someone with. But he touched nothing beneath her clothes.

It was driving her insane. "For a rogue, you're very circumspect," she whispered against his mouth.

"And you aren't circumspect enough, *mon petit mignon*," he murmured. "I will have to walk into our house, you know. No one can tell what state *you're* in beneath your clothes, but everyone will be able to see what state *I'm* in."

She cast him a solemn glance. "Good. I like you better when you have no secrets."

He drew back to stare at her with a shadowed gaze. "You like me better under your thumb, you mean. But if you think you're going to drag me about by my . . . er . . . arousal, Minerva, think again."

"Trust me," she said earnestly, "if I wanted to do that, I could do it as easily as this." She snapped her fingers.

"You think so, do you?"

"I know so." Not for nothing had she watched her sisters-in-law handle her brothers. Giles liked her for her body. And she would make good use of that if she had to.

"I haven't been *that* susceptible to a woman's charms in years, minx," he drawled. "I want you very badly, but I'm not the sort of man to lose his brains to desire. I made that mistake once. I'll never make it again."

She eyed him closely. "When did you make that mistake? Or is that another thing you refuse to tell me about your past?"

The carriage rumbled into London. Though the noise of workers going home and calling to one another filled the air, inside the carriage all was silent as a snowfall. Giles shifted her off of his lap, then angled himself so he could stare into her face. "Do you really want to know about something I did with another woman?"

She hesitated. But if it helped to explain him to her . . . "Yes."

"All right. You'll probably hear about it eventually, anyway." He crossed his arms over his chest. "How well do you know my brother's wife, Charlotte? Who used to be Mrs. Harris?"

Her blood stilled. "I've met her a few times, and of course I saw her at the wedding today. I know she created the School for Young Ladies in Richmond, the one everyone calls the School for Heiresses." Until now Minerva had admired the woman, not only for her keen mind and kind spirit, but also for her perseverance in building up her school from nothing.

"What most people don't know is that she and my brother were on the verge of marrying nearly twenty years ago. It was the summer of the year your parents died, when I was eighteen and she and her family came to visit. She and David were getting along very well. Until I did something stupid that broke them apart."

A pressure built in her chest. "You and she didn't—"

"No," he said hastily. "I doubt my brother would have forgiven that. But as you know, he and I resemble each other a bit. David had given me his dressing gown while Charlotte was visiting, but she didn't know that. It was fairly distinctive, and she'd only seen David wearing it."

He glanced out the window. "We had a maidservant who was very . . . loose with her affections. Molly had worked her way through most of the footmen and had decided I was going to be her next conquest. She asked me to meet her outside on the terrace late one night. I did, and we . . . coupled." A muscle worked in his jaw. "That probably shocks you."

"No," she lied, but it did. Her brothers were rogues—or had

been—and her father had been the worst rakehell ever, but to her knowledge none of them had ever trifled with the servants, not even Oliver when he was in his wild phase and had lived in a bachelor house of his own. Only the worst of the worst toyed with servants.

Then again . . . "You were young," she said softly. "Men do stupid things when they're young."

"Kind of you to excuse it, but we both know it was unconscionable. That wasn't the worst part, however." He dragged in a heavy breath. "Charlotte saw me and thought I was David."

"Oh dear."

"Exactly. For complicated reasons that I won't go into, Charlotte didn't speak to David about it. She just broke off their association in a rather dramatic way. She sent him a letter that somehow ended up in the papers—"

"Wait, I remember this! That was quite a scandal—that anonymous letter that everyone figured out was about your brother. *She* wrote that? Good Lord. But it didn't say anything about . . . well . . . seeing him doing . . ."

"No. That's why for years, I wasn't sure if I was responsible for their rift. I told myself I wasn't." He gave a harsh laugh. "But some little part of me always knew . . ." His gaze met hers. "It was the one and only time I ever let my physical urges lead me to do something so foolish, and it destroyed their lives for *years*. I never dreamed . . ."

"Of course not," she said, his clear guilt making her wish she could wipe it away with a word. "How could you anticipate that?"

"Once I learned of it, I made a solemn vow never to let myself be so carried away by desire that it impinged on my duty to my family. Never to let it make a fool of me again."

Her heart twisted in her chest. "Is that how you see our desire for each other? As making a fool of you?"

That seemed to stymie him. "No, that's not what I meant. I meant that . . ."

"You don't like to be manipulated with it."

He let out a breath. "Exactly."

"And you haven't been trying to manipulate *me* with desire at all," she said, baffled by his logic.

That arrested him. "What do you mean?"

"From the moment we began our faux courtship—or what *I* saw as our faux courtship—you kissed me senseless every chance you got. Assuming that you weren't letting desire run away with you—as you've said quite clearly—you must have been trying to use it to make *me* amenable to your suit."

"Perhaps a little." He shifted uncomfortably on the seat. "But it's not like that between us. I wasn't just trying to manipulate you. Our desire was a natural manifestation of our affection for each other. And we were always sensible about it. We didn't let it drive us to do stupid things. We should continue in that fashion."

She nearly pointed out that they hadn't been very sensible about it the day they'd gone to the pond. Or in the inn. Or even when they'd been walking in Hyde Park. But perhaps logic wasn't the way to handle this.

Because he didn't sound logical. He sounded more . . . panicked than anything. Men did get panicked with women. She'd recently begun to understand that. Certainly her brothers had panicked when they'd started caring about the women who'd become their wives. She would swear that Giles was starting to care about her. And clearly it panicked him, too, a bit.

"The point is," he went on, "do not think to use our hunger

for each other to twist me about your finger, Minerva. It won't work with me."

She doubted that very much, but he needed to believe it. He needed to think he was in control. Still, the very fact that he'd told her this little part of his past meant he was already opening up to her. It reassured her as nothing else had that they could have a good marriage.

"Well, there goes my dastardly plan," she said lightly. "You really are a spoilsport, Giles."

His low chuckle sounded relieved. No doubt he'd expected her to fight harder. And she would. Just not the way he thought.

"Anything else you want to warn me about?" she went on. "Any hidden vices like knuckle cracking or sleepwalking?"

"Nothing you can't handle, I expect."

He had no idea. She was ready to handle just about anything from him. She might have been forced into this marriage by her own recklessness in succumbing to her desires, but now that she was here, she meant to make the most of it.

GILES WAS STILL cursing himself as they drew up in front of the house. What had possessed him to tell her about that night with Molly? For God's sake, this was his wedding night. He was supposed to be sweeping her off her feet, not spilling his unsavory secrets.

He stepped down from the carriage. And why had he bristled so at her assertion that she could have him do her bidding if she wanted? She couldn't. He knew that.

Well, he knew it intellectually, anyway. Physically . . .

Just helping her out of the coach was having the same potent effect on him she'd been having for weeks, even months, ever since their Valentine's Day dance. Her hand in his, so dainty, so . . . naked without her glove on, had the perverse effect of making him want her even more. God, he was in trouble.

They got to the top of the steps, and the door opened as his new butler strove to impress the new master and mistress. Giles stopped her just before entering. "Oh, no, darling, we're going to do this right."

When he swept her up in his arms and carried her across the threshold, she laughed. It made her beautiful eyes sparkle, and her cheeks shine a rosy pink that had his blood roaring in his veins. He must have been mad to tell her she couldn't manipulate him with desire. She could do anything she pleased when she looked at him like that.

"Finch," he said, "you're dismissed for the evening. You and all the servants."

"Yes, sir," Finch answered, barely hiding his smirk.

Then Giles carried her toward the stairs.

"Put me down!" Minerva said, her eyes twinkling up at him. "You'll break your back hauling me about the house! I'm heavier than I look."

"Ah, but I'm stronger than *I* look."

"All the same . . ." She wriggled out of his arms to cast him a coy glance. "You need to save your strength." With another laugh, she darted up the stairs.

"So *that's* how it's going to be, is it?" he called out as he followed her leisurely.

It wasn't as if there were many places for her to go. The house was large enough to be comfortable but nothing like the mansion she was used to. She could hardly get lost in its rooms, and with scarcely any furniture yet there were few places she could hide.

So when he reached the first floor he wasn't surprised to find she wasn't even trying to hide. Instead she stood motionless in the doorway of a room that was *not* the bedchamber.

He smiled as he realized which room it was. Perhaps it would make up for how he'd bungled things in the carriage.

"What is this room?" she asked as he walked up beside her. "Is it your study?"

"No. My study is downstairs. *This,* my dear, is your wedding present. It's your own study. For writing."

"For writing my books?" she said, almost disbelievingly.

"Unless you've been writing something else I don't know about. Please tell me Rockton isn't going to appear in a play."

"Don't be silly." Her eyes filled with tears that she brushed away, as if embarrassed. "Oh, Giles, that is the sweetest thing you could ever have done for me!"

When she broke into a blazing smile, his heart flipped over in his chest. At that moment he would have given her whatever she wanted.

Careful, man. Don't be a fool.

But it was hard not to when she was so excited. Hurrying to the center of the room, she twirled like a little girl, then walked about, examining the bare bookshelves, the desk he'd fitted up with writing materials, and the comfortable couch he'd placed near the fireplace.

"It's still a bit sparsely furnished," he said, "but I figured you'd rather do that part yourself anyway."

"It's perfect, absolutely perfect." She spotted something and let out a cry. "Oh, and you've even had my books and papers brought up here!" Rushing over to the trunk, she began to remove things. "I can put the novels on that shelf, and the papers—"

He caught her about the waist. "This wasn't quite what I had in mind for tonight, darling."

Startled, she gazed up at him, then flashed him a teasing smile. "I can't imagine what you did have in mind that would be more important than unpacking my books."

He took her hand and drew her toward the door. "Can't you?"

"Well, you already said that you wouldn't let desire rule your life, and I don't see why it should rule mine, so if I want to set up my study—"

He kissed her square on the lips. "All right, you made your point. I'm an idiot."

She looped her arms about his neck. "Yes, you are. But I rather like that about you. Clearly, there's something seriously wrong with me."

He picked her up and headed for the bedchamber. "Absolutely. You resisted marrying me, didn't you?"

"True. I don't know what I was thinking."

"You were skittish, that's all. Some maidens are." He stared down into her face as he angled her through the door. "I've never bedded a virgin, you know."

"Well, that's good, because neither have I. So it should all work out."

He laughed. "You do realize that any other man wouldn't find that amusing."

"Ah, but you aren't any other man, are you?" she said, eyes bright.

Unfortunately, he really was concerned about bedding a virgin. From what he'd heard, some women had more difficulty the first time than others did. What if he hurt her? Or God forbid, made her afraid of him?

It would kill him to see Minerva look at him in fear.

Then there was his other concern, one that he'd been thinking about quite a bit the past few days. Minerva's only lover had been the imaginary Rockton, whom she'd described as a consummate lover more than once. He wasn't sure what that meant to a virgin. And he damned well didn't like the idea of failing to live up to his alter ego's fictional reputation.

So he wouldn't fail. He would keep his desire in check until he could bring her so much pleasure that she would find their joining well worth it, despite any pain she suffered. Because he was *not* going to disappoint her on her wedding night. He was going to outperform Rockton, even if it killed him.

Chapter Eighteen

From the moment Giles set her down near the bed, Minerva's heart jumped into a stammering that wouldn't be quelled. Not that she wanted to quell it. This was the night she'd been waiting for half her life. Giles was going to make her his wife, and she could scarcely contain her excitement.

But when she reached up to remove her veil, he said, "No. Let me do it."

Ooh, he was giving orders now. How perfectly delicious. Who could have dreamed that such a thing would thrill her?

He took it off, then let down her hair, pausing to kiss a coil of it and give her more delectable shivers. Then he turned her around and unbuttoned her gown slowly. Too slowly.

She wanted him to take her with abandon, to fall on her like a hungry animal, to show her that she inspired him to heights of reckless passion. This aching sensuality unnerved her.

"Giles, please . . ."

"Do you know how often I've imagined this, Minerva?" he said in a guttural voice. "Imagined undressing you piece by piece, unveiling your perfect skin, your lovely back . . ." He pressed a kiss into her back, then pushed the gown aside so he could do the same to her shoulder. "Your fine arms . . ."

"You can't have imagined it *too* often," she snapped, "or you wouldn't be doing it so slowly. Besides, you already unveiled my perfect skin at the pond. I should think you'd want to unveil something a little more . . . intimate."

"Patience, darling," he said, laughter in his voice. "There's something to be said for the pleasures of anticipation."

"Is that what you've learned from all your . . . I mean, they say you've been with hundreds . . ." Now, why had she brought that up?

Probably because his careful seduction was reminding her that he'd done this far more than she had. That she couldn't possibly measure up to his others. Not that she was jealous of those other women. She wasn't.

Oh, all right, she was.

"Not hundreds," he countered. "The number is a good deal smaller." He dragged her gown down her body to fall in a puddle of shimmering silk at her feet, then dispensed quickly with her petticoat. "And they were mere ciphers compared to you."

Him and his silver tongue . . . no wonder he was such a good barrister. "Gran told me that you didn't . . . *don't* have a mistress."

His hands stilled on her corset ties. "How did she know that?"

"Mr. Pinter found it out."

He hesitated a moment, then continued working her laces loose until he could shove her corset off, too. It landed atop her gown and petticoat. "Your grandmother was very thorough in her investigations."

Except that Gran hadn't found out about his stealing. Or if she had, she hadn't said anything to Minerva. "Gran is always thorough. She wanted to be sure I wasn't giving myself to an out-and-out scoundrel."

"I take it that she decided you weren't, or she wouldn't have let you marry me."

"Gran had no say in that," she said stoutly. "I chose to be here. I hope you realize that."

His answer was to reach around and cup her breasts.

Her knees went weak. "So . . . was Mr. Pinter . . . right? You don't have a mistress?"

Why was she harping on this? She knew he didn't. Yet she wanted to hear him say it. If she couldn't have words of love from him, she wanted reassurance that he really did want her and only her.

"I don't have a mistress," he said with an edge to his voice as he dropped his hands from her. "Truth is, I've only had a couple in my life, and only when I was young."

"Truly?"

"Once I became successful, I had no time. It was less complicated to have the occasional . . . Good God, must we discuss this on our *wedding night*?"

She turned to face him, contrite. "No. I just want to know that—"

"That I chose to be here, too. That I chose you over any others."

"Yes," she said, relieved that he understood.

His eyes burned into hers. "Do you see that bed behind me?" he said as he tugged her against him.

She hadn't noticed anything but him when they'd entered the room, but now she looked past him at the bed.

It was a truly fine example of a Chippendale four-poster, but the part she paid particular attention to were the hangings and coverlet of spring green figured silk. They seemed a bit . . . extravagant for a man.

"I had you in mind when I picked it out weeks ago, even

before we began courting," he said. "I kept thinking of you in it, on it, with your hair spread out about your luscious shoulders. The bedclothes are the exact color of your eyes, which I imagined shining up at me as I made love to you." He swept his hands down her body. "Does that answer your question?"

She couldn't speak. Her throat was too dry, and her heart pounded like a timpani.

He bent forward to whisper in her ear, "I've wanted you for a very long time, Minerva. You, and only you. And if you haven't figured that out by now, then you're not as clever as I thought."

There was a truth to his words that she simply couldn't deny. But wanting her body was one thing, wanting *her* was quite another.

Still, when he took her mouth, kissing her with deep, bold strokes of his tongue, she forgot anything else but him. At least he *did* want her body. Lord knew she wanted his. And his kisses were perfect, fiercely passionate, making her eager for their bed.

Except that he was not taking her *to* their bed. His hands lingered over her, touching and caressing until she thought she'd go out of her mind. He tore his mouth from hers only so he could tug her shift up and untie her drawers. When they slithered down her legs, she dragged at his coat lapels, and he shrugged off his coat. But before she could do more, he stripped her shift off over her head, then lifted her in his arms and took the few steps to the bed, where he laid her down.

At last. He was going to make her his in every way.

But he didn't. He just stood back to rake her from head to toe. She shivered, unsettled by the thought of being completely naked in front of him. She felt exposed, not just in body but in soul, as if he could see into all the secret parts of her. She wondered what he saw with that raw, piercing glance.

"Giles?" she asked, coming up on her elbows.

He blinked, as if she'd jerked him out of some reverie. Then his gaze warmed.

"Now that's a sight to make a man's blood rise," he rasped, his eyes continuing to devour her as he untied his cravat, tossed it aside, then unbuttoned his waistcoat. "My water nymph has turned into a seductress."

"Not a very good one, if all I inspire you to do is look," she said in a low, sultry voice.

"Trust me, minx, you inspire me to do far more than that."

"But you're taking too long. And I want to look at *you*, too."

He flashed her his crooked smile, the endearing one that always arrowed straight to her heart. "Whatever my seductress wants." He stripped down to his drawers in measured motions that made her want to gnash her teeth with frustration, but when he finally shucked them, too, she caught her breath.

His flesh was stiff and imposing. It stuck out from its bed of dark curls like a night watchmen's staff, a palpable threat that she somehow hadn't expected.

"Good Lord," she breathed, "it's huge." And for some perverse reason that made it grow even larger.

He laughed. "Not really. But probably bigger than you expected."

That was an understatement. It certainly hadn't felt that big in her hand. Then again, she'd been a little preoccupied when she'd had her hand in his drawers. "It's *definitely* bigger than I expected."

"Trust me, darling," he said drily, "you'll be glad of that in the end."

She wasn't at all sure about that. No wonder people said that the first time always hurt. Now she wondered whether the second, third, and fourth times hurt, too.

He climbed onto the bed, and she actually scooted away from him.

"Oh, no, you don't, minx," he said huskily as he threw one leg over hers. "You're not getting out of this that easily."

Then he kissed her again, and that soothed her a little. Especially when he began to knead her breast and fondle her below, as he had before. This part was quite enjoyable, and he did it quite well. Perhaps she shouldn't have been in such a hurry to move things along—she could easily keep doing this part forever.

Within a few moments, he had her squirming beneath his hand, and the same strange sensation that she'd felt at the pond rose from between her legs, like heat stealing through her veins, tingling over her skin, making her arch into him for more.

Then abruptly his hand was gone. She opened her eyes—she wasn't sure exactly when she'd closed them—to find him moving down her body. What on earth?

He kissed her belly, then moved lower still. She grew self-conscious. Did he have to look at her *there*? It wasn't a particularly pretty part of her, though she had to admit his admiring stare was making her hot and bothered.

Then he kissed her thatch of curls, and she nearly shot up off the bed. "What the devil are you *doing*?" she cried and tried to pull her legs together.

But his hands now gripped her thighs, holding her open to his rakish gaze. "Relax, darling. You'll like it."

"Oh, you think so, do you?" she said as he covered her there with his mouth. "I can't imagine why I would . . . why I might . . . oh . . . Oh my . . . Giles . . . Oh, my word . . . oh, Giles!"

He just chuckled and kept doing wicked things to her with

his mouth and teeth. She wanted to be angry at him for being so dratted in control while she was writhing and moaning, but it was hard to be angry when the most amazing feelings were rocketing through her. She was sure she was about to explode. She *wanted* to explode, but before she could, he left her hanging and moved back up over her.

"No, Giles, not yet!" she cried out.

"Don't worry, darling, I mean to give you everything you want. But I want to be with you when I do."

She blew out a frustrated breath. "I don't see how *that's* going to help anything." Her whole body felt strung tight, like a fiddler's bowstring ready to snap. "But I suppose you're going to do it anyway, aren't you?"

"Not unless you don't want me to," he said, his voice sounding decidedly strained. His eyes were a brilliant blue, sharp and hard like faceted sapphires, and his jaw was set, as if he struggled to contain himself.

That small sign of a break in his control reassured her a little. Perhaps he was having a difficult time of it, too—though she couldn't imagine how, given his vast experience in bedding women.

The thought made her scowl. And lie. "Of course I want you to. I'm your wife, aren't I?"

"Not entirely," he choked out. "But you will be."

Then he pressed himself inside her. It was quite unnerving, but before she could tell him so, he began mating his tongue with hers in that slow dance that she so enjoyed. At the same time he filled one hand with her breast, teasing the nipple until the sweet, hot honey of desire trickled through her again.

And all the while he inched farther inside her. Her body actually accommodated him. Not *well,* mind you. It wasn't as comfortable as she would like, but it was . . . interesting.

When she reached up to clutch his shoulders, he tore his mouth from hers to whisper, "It feels amazing to be inside you, darling. You're so soft."

"I wish I could say the same about you," she retorted.

Her curst husband actually had the nerve to laugh. "No, you don't. Trust me."

"I'm trying to trust you, but you're making it awfully difficult."

"Lift your knees," he said. "That will help."

She did as he said, and he slid into her another couple of inches. "Help who?" she muttered under her breath. But then she felt it—the way he now pressed against the part of her he fondled whenever he was trying to drive her insane with lust. "Ohhh," she murmured. "That's intriguing."

"Hold on," he murmured, then gave a decided push that planted him inside her to the hilt.

She felt a faint burning, but it was over quickly. "Was that it?" she asked.

"What?" He drew back to look at her. The faint sheen of sweat on his brow and the muscle ticking in his jaw told her he was fighting for control.

"My maidenhead. Is it gone?"

"I imagine so," he bit out. "Minerva, I want to move. I have to move."

"All right. It's fine."

He laughed. "That's my wife." He brushed a kiss over her forehead. "But now the good part begins."

He began moving. Inside her. How . . . intimate, the most intimate thing she'd ever known. Giles was joined to her so thoroughly that she didn't know who was moving, him or her or both at once.

He drove into her with slow, silky thrusts that left her

breathless. It felt odd at first, then became quite warming, and soon that strange whisper of a tingling began again down below, making her squirm. Whenever she squirmed, the tingling intensified until it grew into a dark and atavistic thrill.

Lord, but that was . . . actually quite good.

"Better?" he asked, his voice low, guttural.

"Oh yes."

His triumphant smile speared her. "I thought it might be."

Once he was satisfied that she was finding more enjoyment by the moment, he deliberately acted to heighten her pleasure. He kissed her deeply, heatedly. He fondled her breast, then slid his hand down to finger the place where they were joined until she was gasping and aching and dragging her fingernails along the bunched muscles of his shoulders.

Then inexplicably he slowed his thrusts.

"Giles . . . please . . ."

He pressed his mouth to her ear, his breathing coming in quick, hard gusts. "What do you . . . want, minx?" he rasped. "Do you want . . . me to stop?"

"No!" She could feel the tension rousing again, his every thrust like a fiddler tightening a string, winding it until it shivered with the promise of music.

He tongued her ear. "Are you ready . . . for more?"

"Yes. Lord, yes!"

He nipped her earlobe, sending a frisson of excitement along her nerves. "Then hold on, sweet nymph, and we'll finish this."

So she did. He quickened his pace again, pounding into her, every stroke another tightening of the string. Soon she was arching up to meet his thrusts, her feet now locked behind his knees. She felt the humming of the tautening string, hovering on the edge of her consciousness, making her strain toward it. . . .

"Oh, God, Minerva . . . my darling . . . my wife . . ."

Suddenly, it was as if the string was plucked, and a note sang high and sweet, piercing her with pleasure, making her cry out and clasp him to her as her body vibrated with the intensity of her release.

Then with a strangled groan, he drove deep into her to reach his own release. Giving a shudder that rocked them both, he spilled his seed inside her.

And as her body thrilled to the ecstasy, as he collapsed atop her, his warm body enveloping hers, she realized she couldn't lie to herself any longer.

She loved him. She'd never stopped loving him. She'd just been angry with him for a while. Worse yet, now that he was hers, she knew she'd never be happy until she'd made him love her, too.

And she feared that might prove impossible.

GILES GLANCED OVER at his wife to see if she was asleep yet. She was, and she slept very fetchingly, too. She did everything fetchingly. That was the trouble. She'd wriggled under his skin when he wasn't looking, and now he didn't know what to do about it.

He'd seen the heartache his brother had gone through when love had first seized him by the balls. Giles wasn't going to allow that. A man should never let himself be driven to madness by a woman—that's when he made mistakes that cost him dearly.

And Minerva was just the sort of female to attempt riding roughshod over her husband. Clearly she'd run roughshod over her entire family for quite some time.

She gave a little sigh in her sleep, and something caught in his throat. He scowled. He was going to have to watch this. He wanted her far too much. He *liked* her far too much. Better be careful.

But he didn't want to be careful. He wanted to sink into marriage with her and drown there. If he didn't maintain control of this situation, everything would go to hell.

Which was why, much as he wanted to join Minerva in sleep, he couldn't. He had work to do yet.

Leaving the bed, he pulled on his clothes and went to his study. Ravenswood had promised to send over the letter Newmarsh had written. Sure enough, there it was on his desk, waiting for him in a sealed envelope. He broke the seal to read it before he set off for Calais.

They set off for Calais. With a groan, he set the letter down. He'd managed not to flat out lie to her so far, but once they reached Calais . . .

No, somehow he would manage it. He would meet with Newmarsh at the man's lodgings, and he would do it without Minerva knowing or fretting over it.

"What are you doing?"

Steeling himself to show no surprise, he glanced up to see Minerva standing there, dressed in nothing but her thin shift. Her hair hung in a tangle to her waist, and the swells of her breasts were plainly visible.

His blood surged again in his loins. This was exactly what he worried about—that just seeing her made him want to unburden every secret in his soul.

"I thought you were sleeping," he said, "and I have a few business matters to attend to before we leave tomorrow, so I came down here."

"I think I roused the minute you opened the door," she said with a soft smile that fired his blood. "I'm a light sleeper. It's been the curse of my life." She leaned against the doorframe.

"Celia can sleep through a hailstorm, but even a gentle rain wakes me."

Was that a warning to him? Or just a statement of fact?

Knowing her, it was probably both.

She didn't look the least bit changed by their lovemaking. She still bore that air of complete self-assurance that said nothing would keep her from being herself. No *man* would, anyway.

But then, he liked that about her.

"Go back to bed, darling," he said. "I'll be there shortly."

She cast him a sultry look that set his blood afire. "Don't be too long."

When she left, he laid his head back against the chair and cursed Ravenswood long and loud. He wanted to be done with this. He didn't want to have to hide things anymore, especially from her.

I am trying to trust you, but you are making it awfully difficult.

He wanted her to trust him. And if she ever found out he'd broken his promise to her—

She mustn't, that's all. He merely had to do this one thing. Then the whole sordid business would be behind him, and he wouldn't have to worry about her letting something slip or creep into her books that might unmask him.

Just look at how David had suffered after Charlotte had written those cruel things about him that had ended up in the papers. Granted, she hadn't meant that to happen, and she'd misunderstood the situation in the first place, but it had blackened David's name for a long while.

Women let their emotions guide them, and it got them into trouble. Giles had seen his family be dragged through scandal one too many times—he wasn't going to let it happen yet again because of him.

So he'd just have to pray he could keep his secrets for a couple of days more.

Chapter Nineteen

The next day Minerva and Giles arrived in Calais at ten in the evening. They then worked their way through the customs house and the police station to have their bags examined and their passports stamped. It was well after midnight when they reached the Hotel Bourbon, where they ate a quick dinner consisting of a roast chicken, a sweet omelet, and some very fine wine. By the time they got to bed, they were too tired to do anything but collapse into sleep.

The church bells calling parishioners to morning mass awakened Minerva early. She lay there a moment listening, then laughed to herself when she realized the bells were playing a waltz. Only in France.

The sound must be coming from that Notre Dame church Giles had mentioned. She'd seen enough of the town the night before to pique her interest, and she wouldn't mind visiting the church. But when she turned over to ask Giles about it, she found him still asleep.

A smile crossed her lips. He was such a sound sleeper. And a neat one, too. She always churned her bedsheets while she slept, taking her rest by fits and starts. But from what she'd seen of him after two nights of marriage, Giles fell into one spot, lying on his back, and stayed there until something or someone forceful roused him.

Should she attempt to wake him? Or perhaps . . . A slow smile curved up her lips. Why not take a peek at his "thing" while he slept? She'd been too nervous on their wedding night to notice anything but how large it was, and she was curious to see it in its natural state.

Carefully she raised his nightshirt. She would have to get his drawers open somehow. Did she dare? What would he do if he woke to find her being so free with him?

Well, he was her husband after all. She should be able to look at him whenever she wished, right?

She touched the first button, then froze, surprised to find him hardening beneath her hand. So much for seeing him in his natural state. She slanted a glance up at him, but his eyes were still closed. So she cautiously unbuttoned his drawers to unveil his member, which grew impressively harder by the moment.

Did men do these things in their sleep, for goodness sake? That seemed rather alarming. What must it be like to awaken with one's flesh sticking up, quite by accident?

Now that she had his drawers entirely opened, his member spilled out to spring to life before her gaze. She examined it with great curiosity. It was such a strange appendage. It wasn't at all attractive, with its thick veins and bulbous head, yet inexplicably it fascinated her. It was just so . . . reckless and impudent, like a standard men bore into battle with the female sex in another attempt to cow them.

"Enjoying yourself?" said a rumbling male voice, and she jumped.

Heat rose in her cheeks. "Giles! How long have you been awake?"

He flashed her a lazy smile. "Since you lifted my nightshirt."

She swallowed. "I was just . . . it was only . . ."

"Come here, wife," he murmured in that husky voice that never failed to turn her knees to pudding.

When she slid up to lie beside him, he kissed her hard, then placed her hand on his very reckless and impudent standard. And that led to his placing *his* hand inside *her* drawers, and before she knew it, she was lying on her back being made love to with great enthusiasm. What a delightful way to begin the day.

And once again, she marveled at how intimate, how *personal* it felt. How could men do this just for enjoyment? For that matter, how could women allow it? She couldn't imagine letting a man be inside her like this without . . . being in love with him.

Later, as they lay gasping on the bed, he said, "How do I compare to Rockton in the bedchamber?"

She shifted to her side to stare at him. His hair was endearingly mussed, and his cheeks flushed from exertion. He looked adorable. She could still hardly believe he was hers. "What do you mean?" she asked coyly.

"You always describe him as a consummate lover. Did I meet your expectations?"

"You mean, given that I was a virgin and had no more idea of what a consummate lover is than I knew how a spy worked?" At his cocked eyebrow, she laughed. "You know perfectly well that I did. Surely you could tell."

"I can never be sure of anything with you. And you did have some idea about what to expect, as I recall. You mentioned kissing other men."

She propped her head up on one hand. "That's hardly the same."

He held her gaze a long moment. "You never answered my question during our 'interview' about how many men you'd kissed."

"How many women have you bedded?" she countered. At his look of chagrin, she said, "You see? Not an easy question, is it?" When he threw his head back against the pillow with a curse, she said, "But if you must know, I kissed very few." She threw a sop to his male pride. "None who were as good at it as you were, to be sure. After our kiss in the alley, I was spoiled for anyone else."

"Really?" He stared up at the ceiling. "It seemed to make you angry more than anything else."

"Not the kiss itself. Just what came after."

A muscle ticked in his jaw. "That's one thing I've never understood about that night. I know I was rather harsh with you—"

"You were downright cruel."

His sideways glance showed clear remorse. "That's because I knew I couldn't act on any attraction between us, and I thought it best to make that clear."

"You made it clear, all right. You said I looked like a tart and acted like a doxy, remember?"

He winced. "I may have overdone it a bit."

"You made me feel cheap and tawdry and foolish."

Shifting to face her, he murmured, "I'm sorry. But that's what I'm trying to understand. I realize you were angry—you had every reason to be. Still, you wrote your first book years after that night. Was your pride still so wounded after all that time? Did you really feel justified in discussing matters that I expressly asked you not to speak of to anyone?"

It wasn't just that my pride was wounded, you dolt. You broke my heart!

She nearly said it aloud. But he'd had no idea back then how she felt about him, just as he had no idea now how deeply she was coming to feel for him. And telling him might send him into a male panic again.

Besides, it would give him the upper hand, since *he* didn't have such an intensity of feeling for her. And she didn't like the idea of Giles having the upper hand and being too sure of her. He was just the sort of fellow to take advantage of that.

"I merely thought that the incident made a good story," she said lightly. "And what writer can resist using such fodder?"

When he got an odd look of alarm on his face, she felt a twinge of guilt, then squelched it. If he refused to tell her anything about his life, then perhaps he deserved to worry about what she might put in her books.

"But you're not planning to put the theft—"

"No, Giles," she said. "I told you before—I don't want to see my husband arrested for stealing. I'm no fool."

She left the bed. They were married, for goodness sake. Did he really think she would risk his career?

Honestly, he was taking this far too seriously. No one had noticed that the character was him. She doubted anyone ever would.

Oliver recognized the masquerade party. And he could one day realize that Rockton isn't him at all, but Giles.

She shook off that concern. That seemed extremely unlikely.

"Are we going to eat anything?" she asked. "I swear, I'm famished."

"I'll call for a servant," he said, leaving the bed. "What do you want?"

After that, they were a bit less awkward together, but only a bit. Even as they ate breakfast and went out to tour Calais, she sensed that something was still wrong between them. She couldn't put her finger on it, but Giles seemed preoccupied, worried even.

What could he be worried about here, on their wedding trip? She couldn't think of anything. Yet as they strolled the ramparts with its pretty gardens and walked to the end of the pier to watch the swimmers, he seemed to take little pleasure in their ramblings.

"Are you all right?" she finally asked after they'd climbed to the top of the Tour de Guet and were looking across the Channel at the cliffs of Dover.

He stiffened. "I'm fine. Why?"

"You're the one who wanted to come to Calais, but you don't seem to be enjoying it."

He forced a smile. "I'm just tired. A certain someone woke me early to have her wicked way with me."

"Early!" She laughed. "You have no idea what early is, sir. Just be glad I didn't get up in the middle of the night and light a candle so I could jot down notes for a book."

"Do you do that?"

"Sometimes." She stared pensively across the Channel. "I really ought to be making more notes if I'm going to use this trip as part of Rockton's spying adventures."

Giles groaned. "I still don't see why you had to make him a spy for the French."

"He's a villain. He couldn't be a spy for the English."

"But why a spy? Bad enough you made him a reckless gambler and a seducer of women."

"That description fits half the men in the ton, including my brothers and you. Rockton had to be something more . . . fearsome."

He got very quiet. "I *am* a patriot, you know."

"Of course you are." She squeezed his arm. "Do try to

remember that Rockton is fictional. He may have started out as you, but he became something else once he came to life on the page. He's a figment of my imagination more than anything."

"So you say," he grumbled.

"Look, if his very existence annoys you, I shall just kill him off."

She expected the same protest he'd made on their wedding day, so she was surprised when he said, "Perhaps that would be best." Then he cast her an uncertain smile. "Don't mind me. I'm just out of sorts. Do what you think best with the character."

He changed the subject, but she couldn't get his reaction out of her mind. He really had taken it to heart how she'd portrayed him. She ought to feel guilty for that, but she couldn't. He would never have come back into her life if she hadn't created Rockton.

They spent the next hour visiting the Notre Dame church, a pretty building. It was very Catholic, with a plethora of candles and an impressive altar of Italian marble bedecked by eighteen statues. There were little silver charms stuck to the statues, representing eyes, ears, hands, and the like. When they asked about it, they were told that the charms were offerings to whatever saint was believed to have cured the body part.

She raised an eyebrow at that, but wrote it in her notebook. And they both admired the painting over the altar, which was purportedly a Van Dyck.

By the time they returned to the hotel, Giles seemed more himself. Until he discovered there was a message waiting for him. When he didn't explain what it was for, just shoved the paper in his pocket, she asked about it. His comment that it was a note from the packet captain reminding them of the departure time for the next morning didn't ring true. Why would the captain go to such trouble?

Then again, whom else could Giles possibly receive a message from in Calais? He knew no one here, and no one in England had known they were going to be here.

Really, she was seeing problems where there were none. Perhaps the packet captain had worried about them because they were newly wedded. That was probably all it was.

They had a lovely dinner and retired to bed, where Giles made love to her with such care and sweetness that she felt guilty for doubting his truthfulness. She lay in his arms a long while afterward, chiding herself for her suspicious nature.

She was just dropping off to sleep when he murmured, "I'm going downstairs to the common room for a glass of wine."

Drowsily, she watched as he left the bed. "I thought you were tired."

He dressed with his back to her. "I'm tired but not sleepy, if that makes any sense. I'm hoping the wine will help."

Of course it made sense. It happened to her all the time. Still, something in his manner—the way he didn't look at her, the care he took in dressing—gave her pause.

After he left she tried to go back to sleep, but sleep eluded her. She started imagining all the reasons he might really have for going down to the common room.

After tossing for half an hour, she grew annoyed with herself. She was becoming exactly the kind of shrewish wife she never wanted to be, the kind that a man like Giles would never tolerate. If she stewed in her thoughts any longer, she would have him consorting with whores in her mind, and she would accuse him of all sorts of ridiculous things when he came back upstairs.

Perhaps she should just go downstairs and set her mind to

rest. She would tell him she couldn't sleep without him, and he would be flattered, and it would be fine. Then they'd have a glass of wine together. Why not?

She took her time dressing, hoping he would come back up before she even left the room. When he didn't, she tried not to let it bother her. She sauntered very casually down the stairs.

The common room was filled with travelers, mostly men, in various stages of intoxication. When a few eyed her with interest, it occurred to her that perhaps she shouldn't have come down here so late alone. Especially since she couldn't find Giles.

That she hadn't expected. The worst she'd feared was to find him flirting with some French maid. To find him absent entirely was terribly upsetting.

She sought out the owner, a squat little Frenchman who'd been solicitous of their comfort and who was presently serving wine to a couple of laborers. "Have you seen my husband, sir?" she asked in French.

"*Non, madame.* He eez gone upstairs, eez he not?"

The sudden hollow feeling in the pit of her stomach made her dizzy, but she managed a smile. "He must have gone to take the air," she said in French.

The innkeeper nodded and returned to pouring wine.

Perhaps Giles really *was* taking the air. That's what she would do at home if she couldn't sleep.

But she wasn't at home, and neither was he. Would he really have left her alone in an inn in a strange country, even to take a walk down the street?

She glanced out the front door, half hoping she would see him doing just that, but all she saw was a pair of drunkards stumbling home. Her heart lurched in her chest as she returned to their room. She was probably making too much of this, seeing shadows where there were none. She ought to go to bed and go to sleep.

But sleep wasn't a choice until she knew if he was safe. So she hunted up the book she'd brought, climbed back into the bed, and settled down to wait.

GILES SPENT SEVERAL moments outside the Quilliacq, the French hotel where Newmarsh was staying. Giles had sent a message to the man shortly after their arrival, arranging a meeting and instructing him to send his answer to the British consul, who'd already been made aware that Giles was expecting a message to come for him there. Then the consul had sent the note on to Giles's hotel.

He hadn't wanted Newmarsh anywhere near his wife, and he certainly hadn't wanted him to know where they were staying. No telling what the baron had up his sleeve.

So Giles took his usual precautions for any meeting with a suspicious character. He determined where the two hotel exits were, which apparently led into parallel streets. He paid close attention to the lighting—a few oil lanterns, badly trimmed. Though he didn't expect an ambush, it never hurt to be prepared.

Then he entered and surveyed the hotel. The downstairs was shaped in a square, with hotel offices all around; sandwiched between two of those was a modest dining room, where he was supposed to meet Newmarsh.

He surveyed the lobby but could see no one about. A glance at his watch told him he was a little early. He and Newmarsh were supposed to meet at eleven P.M.

So he went into the dining room and did a quick assessment. Other than a sleepy couple in one corner eating a late dinner and the servant who attended them, the place was quiet. This being a family hotel, there was no rabble drinking until all hours. Their conversation would be private, thank God.

He took a seat in the corner, keeping his back to the wall and his hand on his pistol. He'd had a little difficulty slipping his pistol into his coat pocket while Minerva had been watching, but her sleepiness had worked to his benefit. With any luck, she would sleep until his return.

And if she didn't?

He gritted his teeth. He'd cross that bridge when he came to it. Bad enough that he'd lied to her twice today already, but if she were to suspect that he'd left the hotel . . .

An image of her in bed assailed him. In her nightdress, she'd look sweet and fetching . . . and trusting. He didn't like abusing that trust. But he couldn't let her know secrets that might ruin him if she said something heedless.

Or if she wrote about them in a book. *I just thought that the entire incident made a good story. And what writer can resist using such fodder?* She would certainly find *this* worthy of putting in a book.

A motion in the doorway arrested him, and he turned to see a man making his slow way across the room. Newmarsh? Surely not. Newmarsh wasn't even fifty. How could this gray-haired, thin, and stooped creature possibly be the hearty lord Giles had once known as a casual acquaintance?

But when Giles saw the man's face, he dragged in a breath. It *was* Newmarsh, for God's sake! What on earth had happened to him?

Giles rose to pull out a chair for the fellow, too flabbergasted to do anything else. At least he needn't worry about Newmarsh trying to murder him.

The baron settled into the chair with ill grace. "You think I'm decrepit now, I suppose."

"Certainly not," Giles lied blandly as he took his seat.

Newmarsh summoned the servant and ordered a bottle of wine. "The doctors say I have a cancer in my liver. They do not expect me to live out the year."

The news shocked Giles. There'd been no word in Newmarsh's letter of being ill.

"Of course, who can believe these French doctors, eh?" Newmarsh settled back against his chair to cast Giles a long, piercing glance. "That's why I had Ravenswood send you here. I want to return to England to consult with doctors there. And I want to see my mother—she's too old to make the journey to France. I need you to convince Ravenswood and his superiors to allow me to go home."

That Giles hadn't expected. "Why me?"

Newmarsh eyed him askance. "Let's not dance around the truth, shall we? We both know that you're the one who stole those financial documents from my desk and brought them to the government. You're the 'concerned citizen' who turned them over, and you alone are responsible for my present state of exile."

Giles fought to keep his features unreadable. "What makes you think that?"

"You're here, aren't you?" At Giles's scowl, he said, "I've known it was you for a long time, Masters. I daresay you lifted those documents during that ill-conceived masquerade party I held."

Giles tensed. "I was out of town for that."

"Were you?" The servant brought the wine and poured two glasses. After he left, Newmarsh took a sip, then said, "That's not what your brother told me."

A chill swept down Giles's spine. "My brother."

"Didn't he mention running into me in Paris eight years ago, while on his honeymoon?"

"No," Giles said, his mind reeling.

"He was here with his first wife. Sarah, right?" At Giles's wooden nod, he said, "I always suspected that the documents were stolen by someone Sully had bilked, or one of their relations, but that encompassed a large number of suspects. Still, your father's suicide made you two the most likely candidates. Except that you were both supposedly in Berkshire at the time."

Giles remained silent, astonished that the baron knew so much, and by such a strange means, too.

"When I ran into Kirkwood in Paris, I decided to see what I could learn. Within moments I realized he hadn't engineered my ruin. He seemed surprised to hear that I was living out my days in France. Then I asked about you. I told him that the last time I'd seen you was at my masquerade party, the one he'd missed."

With a curse, Giles downed some of his wine.

Newmarsh settled back with a cold smile. "He said, 'Aha, so *that's* where he ran off to.' It seems you'd left Berkshire early, telling your mother you had to return to town for a trial. Kirkwood had always assumed you'd gone back to town early to cavort with the demi-reps."

A churning began in Giles's stomach that even the wine wouldn't quell.

"I daresay I could find out for certain if you were there," Newmarsh went on. "Someone is bound to have seen you in town or at the party. Not that it would matter. The minute I mention that papers were stolen from my study that implicated me in a crime, everyone will be eager to figure out who did it. Someone is sure to know something."

Or to remember reading about such a masquerade party in his own wife's book.

Giles gritted his teeth. "Expose me, and you expose yourself as well. Until now, with no one knowing of your perfidy, you've been free to live off your family's money and keep company with your countrymen in Paris without fear of scandal. That would end."

"Ah, but I don't care about my place in society anymore." Newmarsh's gaze hardened. "I want to go home to die. And if you don't convince Ravenswood and his superiors to allow it, I will reveal the true state of affairs behind Sully's trial. I daresay it won't help your reputation to be branded a thief publicly. Some of your lofty friends might not be so friendly anymore."

The old anger rose up in Giles's throat to choke him. "You have the audacity to blackmail me after what you did to my father—"

"Your father did it to himself. He should have been more careful. But he never could resist a risky investment, could he?"

Giles seethed. That was true. Though Newmarsh had brought his father into the risky scheme that Sully had concocted, Father had made the choice to invest.

"I don't know if I can convince Ravenswood to allow it," Giles said truthfully. "And even if he agrees, his superiors might not. The British government has a strict policy of never giving in to blackmail."

Newmarsh's lips thinned into a cruel line. "Then you'd better hope they bend that policy for you. Because if they don't, every newspaper in London will have the real story of what happened with Sir John Sully. And I don't think you want that."

Giles stared coldly at the man.

Newmarsh continued, "You will arrange it because you have a future that you want to secure. I, on the other hand, have no future. And what I ask is a small inconvenience compared to what you did to me."

"What *I* did? You mean, keeping you from ruining anyone else in your eagerness to gain a cut of Sir John's fraudulent profits?" His voice rose with anger. "Making sure that the son of a bitch was hanged for bilking hundreds of people out of their money? He would never have been brought to justice without those documents, and you certainly weren't going to turn on him."

Newmarsh showed no trace of remorse. "True. And my only regret is that I didn't hide them well enough from the likes of you." He leaned back. "Tell me, how do you think the bar will respond to accusations that one of their attorneys helped the government make a case by illegally obtaining evidence?"

Sickened by the very thought, Giles rose. "I'll do what I can. That's all I can promise."

When he turned to leave, Newmarsh said, "I understand you have a new wife."

An icy chill swept down Giles's neck. Slowly he faced Newmarsh. "She has nothing to do with this."

"I daresay she'll feel otherwise if her husband's past actions are dragged through the papers."

Newmarsh was right. How would Minerva handle watching her husband's reputation held up to scrutiny, his trials questioned, his every move examined and reexamined by the press? She'd lived through one such scandal in her life. He could never ask her to endure another.

In a voice less shaky than he felt, he said, "You've made your point, Newmarsh. I'll take care of it."

But as he left, he realized how precarious his position was. He'd stolen those papers before he'd started informing for the Home Office. Burning with the need for vengeance— and a way to make up for his own wasted life—he'd acted precipitously. The ends had justified the means for him.

Unfortunately, others might not view it that way. He hadn't lied about the government's policy concerning blackmail—they were *not* going to want to give in to Newmarsh's demands. So Giles would have to offer them something they wanted in order to gain their compliance.

And they wanted only one thing from him—his continued work as an operative.

He swore foully as he strode back to the hotel. He didn't want to return to that, damn it. He wanted his life back. He wanted a future.

If Minerva found out that the risks he'd taken nine years ago had come back to ruin both their lives, she would lose all the faith she'd put in him. So would his family. So would everyone. He would return to being the failure, the waste of a second son. He refused to do that. He'd worked too hard to leave that behind him.

He might get lucky and the government just might decide to bend their policy for him.

And if not?

Ravenswood had said they wanted him badly enough to offer him political favors. And he knew exactly what favor he wanted, even if it *did* mean giving in to Newmarsh's blackmail. And returning to working with Ravenswood.

Damn it all to hell!

Now fully in a temper, he entered the Hotel Bourbon, ignoring the owner, who tried to gain his attention as came in. After hurrying up the stairs, he slowed his steps to the whisper-soft ones he used when sneaking around trying to get information. It was a little harder to unlock the door silently, but he managed it.

So it came as a shock when he opened it to find Minerva sitting up in bed, reading. For half a breath, he hoped that she'd just been waiting for his return. But when she put the book down and cast him an anxious stare, he knew that was a futile hope.

"Where the devil did you go?" she asked, her eyes showing pure betrayal.

He was in big trouble.

Chapter Twenty

Minerva watched, her stomach sinking, as Giles removed his coat and turned away to hang it on the back of a chair. "Well? I went down to the common room looking for you, but you weren't there."

He paused in the act of unbuttoning his waistcoat. "Still don't trust me, I see."

"It had nothing to do with trust. I couldn't sleep either, so I thought we could have a glass of wine together." The half-truth caught in her throat. Forcing herself to go on, she tried not to sound like some accusing wife. "But you weren't in the hotel."

He removed his waistcoat and placed it with precise motions over the chair. "When the wine didn't help, I went for a walk."

His explanation was plausible, except for one thing. "The hotel owner said he hadn't seen you in the common room at all. He seemed to believe you were still upstairs." When Giles remained silent, she said in a low voice, "You promised not to lie to me."

"And I won't," he snapped. "Just don't ask me questions about things that don't concern you."

The knife went in so quickly that it took a moment for her to react. Then the hurt set in, bone deep. "I see," she choked out. Rolling over to put the book on the bedside table, she pulled the covers up to her chin.

Giles cursed under his breath and came toward the bed. "Damn it, Minerva, I'm sorry. I didn't mean that how it sounded."

"Then how *did* you mean it?" She fought to keep the quiver from her voice, but when he hesitated, that was impossible. She turned to stare at him, the knife twisting in her chest. "Were you . . . were you with a woman?"

"A woman!" he exclaimed with clear outrage on his face. "God, no. I would never do that to you."

The vehemence in his voice made her want to believe him.

Yet when he came to stand beside the bed, his eyes looked lost. "I had to take care of a matter of business," he went on, "and I didn't want you thinking that this trip . . . that we came here—"

"For some reason other than a honeymoon?" she asked.

"Yes! Exactly." He hastily stripped off the rest of his clothes and got into bed beside her. "That's all it was. I swear."

Somehow she knew there was more to it than that. His nervousness earlier in the day, the look of pure shock on his face when he'd come through the door to find her still up— everything said that this was more than a matter of business.

For one thing, there was no reason he couldn't have told her that in the first place. For another, who did business in the dead of night? And why wouldn't he look at her?

"So what was this matter of business?" she asked, watching his face.

His expression went cold. Still not looking at her, he leaned over to blow out the candle. "As I said, nothing to do with you."

The knife slid deeper. "Do you know what?" she said,

fighting for some semblance of equilibrium, "I think you're right—not asking you questions at all probably *is* the safest course of action. At least then I don't have to hear you lie to me."

"Darling, please," he began, sliding his arms about her waist.

"Don't," she whispered. "Not now."

Wisely, he retreated.

She turned her back to him once more, struggling not to cry. They lay there in the dark, both silent. She could feel his breathing on her neck, feel his eyes boring into her, but she refused to acknowledge him.

What had she been thinking, to believe that Giles might change for her? He was going to be exactly like all those men who told their wives only what they wanted to hear. Who lived separate lives. He would keep his secrets and add new ones, while she was expected to go on in her own sphere, entirely apart from him.

At least he was allowing her to write her books. It was probably more than she could have hoped for from any husband.

Except that she *had* hoped for more from him. She'd let herself be lulled into believing they could have a real marriage, that in time he would grow to trust her enough to tell her what was important to him. The loss of that hope was almost too much to bear.

She lay there, her stomach churning and her eyes stinging with unshed tears. She hoped he really hadn't been with a woman—that would destroy her. It did seem a bit too blatant for their wedding trip, even for him. Plus, he didn't smell of French perfume. That tiny realization reassured her somewhat. He smelled of wine, but that wasn't odd—if he'd really been doing business, a drink wasn't unusual.

But then, why couldn't he tell her about this "business"? It made no sense.

After a while she heard his breathing become even, and anger surged in her again. How could he sleep when there was this rift between them? Her heart was shattered, and he didn't care. But then when had Giles ever cared about breaking her heart?

She couldn't sleep—it was impossible. There was only one thing for it. Slipping from the bed, she lit a candle, then settled into the chair by the window.

She glanced over at him. He slept as innocent as a babe, his chest rising and falling in a soft rhythm that made her heart ache.

Such a handsome husband she'd got for herself. What was wrong with women that they let such things blind them? First, Mama, then her . . .

I'm not your father, Giles had claimed. But what if he was exactly her father? What would she do?

There was naught she *could* do. That was the trouble with marriage—once you were in it, you were trapped forever.

But how was she to go on with him when she felt this rip in the fabric of her soul?

She would simply have to find a way to go on. She couldn't let him keep doing this to her. The trouble was that she had already let him get too far under her skin. She'd given up her freedom, while he'd given up nothing. So she must retreat, must find a way to protect herself.

There was only one thing that worked for that, only one thing that had sustained her through her parents' deaths, through the weeks after Giles had first broken her heart, through the long, hard years of enduring public censure and gossip.

She took up her notebook and licked the tip of her pencil.

Words bounced around in her head, fragments falling into place—bits from the trial, images from her morning rambles with Giles, the feel of her heart breaking inside her . . .

Slowly she began to write.

DURING HIS FIRST two nights with Minerva Giles had slept like a man drugged. Drugged by the pleasure of her in his bed, the warmth of her in his arms, the contentment that came of knowing someone well enough to sleep comfortably beside them.

But not last night. He'd awakened near two A.M. to find a candle lit. Remembering what she'd said about sometimes getting up to write, he'd forced himself to stay quiet, listening to the scratch of her pencil.

Once, he'd stolen a glance at her. She was crying, yet it was as if she didn't *know* she was crying. She just kept scratching away, like an engraver with a hammer and graver, etching life into the inanimate.

Giles had burned to know what she was writing. Turning Rockton into an even worse villain, most likely.

It was probably what he deserved, yet he kept his silence. He was *not* going to drag her into this mess with Newmarsh, especially when the only way out of it might be to go back to living his double life. He couldn't tell her about that—she wouldn't approve when she realized what it would entail. Besides, he had a faint hope that Ravenswood and his superiors would agree to the blackmail without his having to give up his future for it.

For now, he could deal with her anger. She would get over it. She had to. They were married.

The next two times he awoke, she was still writing feverishly, but when he finally awoke again near dawn, he found her beside him in the bed, sleeping. For a moment, he just lay there, watching her. She was so beautiful. And too bloody smart and suspicious for her own good. He should have known he could never manage his meeting with Newmarsh without her catching on.

But devil take it, he was a man! He had a right to live his life without his wife nosing into his business. Father had never told Mother a damned thing about his financial affairs.

Yes, and that had certainly worked out well. Mother had been widowed at the age of fifty, forced into near poverty, and saved only by the sacrifice of her oldest son, who'd had to marry a deceitful bitch for money. But only after Giles had separated him from the love of his life, another heiress, who might have saved the family and herself if she'd married David, as everyone had expected.

Giles winced. He had a history of bungling things. Oh, sure, he'd done well by Ravenswood in his later years, and he was competent in the courtroom, but his early life kept coming back to haunt him. How could he endure the look on her face if she learned he'd done it again?

He couldn't. Besides, she had a habit of writing things down that she shouldn't. He turned over to stare at the notebook that lay on the table by the window. What had she written? Another scathing commentary on his life?

He glanced back to where Minerva still slept, then slipped from the bed. It wouldn't hurt to look. Just to make sure what she'd written. So he'd know how to act.

Stealthily he walked over to the table and opened the notebook. It took him a moment to decipher her appalling handwriting before he read, "Dear Reader, there are times in a woman's life when—"

"What are you doing?" snapped Minerva from the bed.

Damn, she was a light sleeper. He looked up to find her glaring at him. "I was just curious about—"

"Give me that!" She practically leaped from the bed and dashed to his side to snatch up her notebook, cradling it to her chest like a small child. "You have no right!"

"Why?" he growled. "What are you writing now?"

"Nothing to do with you, don't worry." She glared at him through red-rimmed eyes, and guilt stabbed him. "If you can keep secrets, so can I."

The words struck him like a blow to the chest. She was just giving tit for tat. That was to be expected. But it shocked him that it hurt so much. That the thought of her keeping secrets from *him* blasted a hole in his gut.

Well, he'd be damned if he let *her* know that. He schooled his expression to nonchalance. "I didn't mean to upset you. If you don't want me to read what you write, I won't."

His words came out more affronted than he would have liked, but she just sniffed and turned her back on him.

Her silence fell like a weight on his chest, and when she went behind the privacy screen to perform her ablutions and dress, he gritted his teeth. How long would she punish him? How long would he have to suffer her coolness?

It had better not be too bloody long. This wasn't how he'd expected their marriage to work. He jerked his clothes on, now fully in a temper, though he wasn't sure who he was angrier at—her or himself.

She came out from behind the screen wearing her shift, drawers, stockings, and untied corset. Pride made her chin stiffen as she stared at him. "Would you please help me with my corset? I think I can manage the gown myself."

With a terse nod he did as she asked, though being so near

when they were at odds was torture. He wanted to kiss her neck, to bury his face in her hair, to run his hands over the body he'd begun to know very well. He wanted to make love to her, even though he suspected that wasn't the way to handle this.

That was the trouble. For the first time in years, he didn't know *how* to behave. Should he try to jolly her out of her mood? Seduce her?

Given how she darted away from him when he was done with her corset, seduction wasn't going to work just now. He would bide his time and wait for her mood to change. She couldn't stay mad at him forever.

No? The last time you angered her, she kept you at arm's length for nine years.

He scowled. That was different. They hadn't shared a bed. She would get over this eventually. She had to.

They finished dressing in silence, both aware that they had to be on the steam packet in a short while. He itched to get back to London and find out what Ravenswood had to say about Newmarsh.

At least in London he wouldn't have to sneak around. He'd always incorporated his meetings with Ravenswood into his workday. He would send a note to Ravenswood tonight and meet the man early tomorrow.

Their ride on the steam packet seemed endless. He tried to take solace from the ebb and flow of the water, but he could only think of the woman beside him, so lovely and mute.

After hours of that, he could bear it no longer. As they neared the Thames estuary, he asked, "Are you never going to speak to me again?"

She cast him a long, shuttered glance. "Don't be absurd."

"I don't want to be at odds with you."

"Then don't."

Could it really be that easy? They'd just go on as if nothing had happened?

They were passing the Isle of Sheppey, so he tested his theory by telling her a story about him and his father taking a rowboat down the Thames to the isle to see an eccentric aunt of his who lived there. They'd found her digging for fossils in a marsh, wearing men's trousers and a large hat.

As he described his old aunt for Minerva in outrageous terms, he coaxed a smile from her, then a laugh.

Relief coursed through him. He'd been right. Minerva couldn't stay mad at him.

They got through the rest of the trip more easily, and by the time they reached home, she seemed more her usual self. So he decided to press his luck and take her to bed. To his immense satisfaction, she complied.

His satisfaction didn't last long, however. It wasn't that she didn't participate in the lovemaking. She wasn't cold to him or angry. And clearly she found her release at the end.

But something was missing. There was none of the exuberance she'd shown on their first two nights together, none of the closeness. And when it was over, she turned her back to him and fell asleep, as if she'd just finished with a duty and now was done with him.

He told himself that, too, would end eventually. In the days to come, she would get over her annoyance with him, and everything would go back to the way it was.

It had to. Because he didn't know how he'd bear it if it didn't.

Chapter Twenty-one

*I*n the next few days, however, things did *not* go back to the way they were, and it was driving Giles mad.

Ravenswood had been called to his estate to deal with an emergency there, so Giles couldn't reach him without leaving town, which his trials wouldn't allow. And he couldn't write to the man—Ravenswood had always been adamant about not communicating by the mails. So he had no choice but to wait until the viscount returned, chafing at having the matter left up in the air.

Nor did it help his mood that Minerva still kept him at a polite distance even when they were making love. Oh, she was cordial enough. She told him of her day and listened as he told her about his. She began to decorate the town house, turning it from a sterile building that smelled of linseed oil and sawdust into a home that smelled of flowers and lemons. In every way, she behaved like a wife.

Or rather, like the average man's image of a wife—one who would see to his needs and not bother him with anything of herself. If Giles asked about her book, she closed up, saying only that it was going well. She never told him how she felt— she was never playful *or* angry at him. She was just . . . there, like a doll he'd conjured up to share his bed.

It was making him insane. Every night he tried to crack her armor, to bring back the old Minerva, but though she shared his bed willingly and cried out her pleasure in his arms, she still kept him at a distance afterward.

He tried to convince himself that it didn't matter if she didn't blather on about feelings and such. He'd never wanted that. Things were as they should be. With her accepting her role as his wife, he had nothing to worry about.

Yet he worried all the same. The thought of continuing on in this formal sort of marriage made an odd panic seize his chest. Worse yet, though he tried not to let his rabid desire for her make him behave like an idiot, every time she was cool to him, it got more difficult to restrain himself. But he wasn't going to beg.

So by the time Ravenswood returned to town and arranged a meeting with him, he was in a foul humor.

The morning after he'd received the note from Ravenswood, Giles left the house before Minerva was awake. She wasn't always an early riser, given her habit of writing at odd hours.

Ravenswood was waiting for him at the boathouse in Hyde Park. Briefly Giles explained the situation with Newmarsh.

The viscount took notes, frowning here and there. "Had he guessed the other work you did for us?"

"No, I don't think so. He was very focused on his own troubles."

"Thank God for that." He sighed. "Still, he's put us in a devilish position."

"I realize that. And I regret that my rash actions nine years ago are the cause of it."

"If not for those rash actions, we would never have caught Sully. You may regret them, but I don't." Ravenswood searched his face. "You realize that the British government's policy is not to—"

"Give in to blackmail. Yes, I know."

"You wouldn't want us to, anyway, would you, after what he did?"

"I'd rather see the man rot than allow him back into England. If anyone deserves to die alone in France, it's Newmarsh." Giles glanced away. "Unfortunately, *not* giving in to his blackmail means the end of my future. Which is why . . ." He dragged in a hard breath. "I'm willing to return to working for you, if that's what it takes to get your superiors to comply with his blackmail."

He could feel Ravenswood's surprised gaze on him. "You're serious."

Giles nodded. "I don't see that I have much choice, if the government will not give in to his demand otherwise."

"That's not true. You have one other choice. You can call the bastard's bluff. Even if he does as he's threatened, I don't think the consequences will be as dire as he predicts. You were acting on your own. You were young and foolish. And you were on the side of right, whereas he was a villain. The public never sides with the villain."

"Perhaps. But I won't risk putting my family—and my wife—through another scandal. Besides, my career would be over—I'd certainly never be made King's Counsel."

"Ah, but you have friends in high places now," Ravenswood said. "We can do a great deal behind the scenes to bury the story and make sure Newmarsh doesn't get very far with it in the press."

"Even if you could manage that, you can't keep me from being disbarred."

"You'd be surprised what we can do." When Giles said nothing to that, Ravenswood eyed him closely. "Don't you trust me? Surely you don't think we'd leave you to fend for yourself after all you've done for your country."

Giles met his friend's gaze. "I know how the game of politics is played."

"That may be true, but no one will abandon you, I swear."

"I'd rather not stake my future and my career on that."

"And I'd rather not have an operative whose heart is no longer in it," Ravenswood retorted. "That does me no good."

"Damn it, Ravenswood, you owe me this!"

"No—as your friend, I owe you better than this. I'm not going to watch you go back to a way of life that no longer suits you, just because you think you can't trust anyone but yourself." Ravenswood shook his head. "You've been doing this work so long that you've forgotten how to trust your friends. Be careful with that. If you never put your life in someone else's hands, then you can't really expect them to put theirs in yours. In the long run, never trusting anyone is a hard way to live."

The statement took Giles by surprise. Had he really stopped trusting people? Was Ravenswood right?

He thought of Minerva, how she'd been so distant, so reserved. Was that how he appeared to *her*? Was that why she continued to be so vexed with him?

"I tell you what," Ravenswood went on. "I'll ask my superiors if they'd be willing to meet Newmarsh's demand. If they refuse, as I suspect they will, then we'll talk again, and you can tell me then what you want to do. That'll give you some time to think about it."

"Thank you," Giles said, though he'd made up his mind already. "I'd appreciate that."

He turned to go, but Ravenswood wasn't finished with him. "By the way, I found out some information concerning that map of Plumtree's."

Giles blinked. He'd forgotten all about the bastard. Perhaps this was something he could sink his teeth into while waiting for Ravenswood to give him an answer. It would certainly help him with Minerva. She would surely come around if he presented her with decent information about Plumtree's role in her parents' deaths.

"What did you learn?" he asked.

"It's a bit odd, actually. The map is a copy of one that's in the British Museum."

"What exactly is it supposed to show?"

"That's the interesting part." A gleam shone in Ravenswood's eyes. "You are *not* going to believe this . . ."

MINERVA SAT AT the desk in her study and tried to write, but it was no use. She'd been out of sorts since before dawn, when she'd felt Giles leave the bed. She'd considered asking him where he was going. He went early to work some days, but never that early.

But she hadn't asked. It was easier not to ask than to deal with his lying to her. Though she didn't think he'd done so since France, she no longer knew what to expect from him. And that was killing her.

She'd just decided to go for a walk to clear her head, when Mr. Finch appeared at the door.

"You have several visitors, madam—" he began, but before he could even introduce them, practically her entire family invaded the room—Oliver and Maria, Celia, Gabe, Jarret and Annabel, Gran, and even Freddy and his wife, Jane. The only one missing was Jarret's stepson, George, who was in Burton, visiting his other family.

She sprang up in delight. She hadn't realized just how much she'd wanted to see them until they'd appeared. "What are you doing here?" she exclaimed as she exchanged kisses and hugs with them.

Gran glanced around the room, eyebrows raised. "Celia told me you'd sent her a note saying that you and Mr. Masters hadn't gone to Bath after all, so we figured we'd come call on you. We thought it was about time we saw where you were living."

Celia grabbed her hands and leaned near to whisper, "You sounded a bit down to me, though I didn't tell *them* that."

Leave it to her sister to guess what she didn't dare say. Marriage to Giles wasn't turning out quite as she'd hoped. But she certainly didn't want her family to know that.

"No, I'm perfectly fine." She ignored the skeptical look Celia shot her. "Did you bring the map?"

Celia nodded and slipped it to her surreptitiously. Minerva shoved it in her apron pocket.

"And what is this room?" Gran demanded. "Looks like a library."

"It's the study Giles fitted out for me so I could write," Minerva said proudly. Even with things so strained between them, it touched her every time she thought of his considerate gift to her. "He had the bookshelves specially built and bought me that desk and couch and everything."

"How wonderful!" Annabel cast a knowing look at Jarret. "I told you he would take good care of her."

"He's not here, is he?" Jarret said.

"He had to work." Minerva scowled at her brother. "He has a very important position, you know."

"He could get away if he wanted to," Jarret countered. "He always managed to do so before, disappearing for days at a time with no explanation to anyone."

Yes, and she'd begun to wonder about those disappearances. They hadn't bothered her so much before, but after Calais . . .

"You have no right to criticize him for working all the time," Annabel told her husband. "*You* said you could only stop in here for a minute because you have a meeting with the cooper. Or had you forgotten?"

"Damnation!" Jarret cried. He bent to press a kiss to Minerva's cheek. "Sorry, sis, got to run." He started for the door, then stopped to glance at her. "He *is* treating you well, isn't he?"

She pasted a teasing smile to her lips. "Except for the nightly beatings. Those are growing rather vexing." At Jarret's raised eyebrow, she said, "Now go on, before you miss your meeting."

"He *beats* you?" Freddy said, wide-eyed.

"It was a joke, old boy," Oliver said, clapping his hand on Freddy's shoulder. "You know Minerva."

"Yes, dear, a joke," Freddy's wife said, though a moment before she'd looked as shocked as Freddy.

"Well?" Gran said. "Are you going to show us the rest of the house, girl?"

"As long as you realize it's a work in progress," Minerva said. "I still have much to do to get it how I'd like it."

Maria eyed her closely. "And Giles doesn't mind you taking that over?"

"If he does, he hasn't said a word."

"Then he's a more long-suffering husband than I gave him credit for," Oliver muttered.

They trooped about as Minerva gave them the grand tour, explaining what she intended to do with furnishings. They oohed and ahhed over the jasperware fireplace surround and anthemion moldings in the drawing room, the crystal chandelier in the large dining room, and the fine Chippendale dressing table in the master bedchamber.

"You don't have your own bedchamber?" Oliver asked as he spotted her notebook on one bedside table and Giles's law journal on the other. "Maria has her own—even if she never uses it." He and his wife exchanged a knowing glance that grated on Minerva's nerves.

"I don't want my own," Minerva retorted. "I'm perfectly happy to share Giles's."

"Besides, they'll need the rooms for their children," Gran said. "These town houses never have enough bedchambers."

The remark brought Minerva up short. How was she to bring children into a marriage where the parents were at odds? That was too much like her parents' marriage for her comfort.

No, she couldn't bear to think on it. "Come, let's go see the garden."

As if sensing her sudden dark mood, Oliver fell into step beside her. "He's not going out every night and leaving you here alone to brood, is he?"

She could feel her brother's searching gaze on her. "Of course not," she said brightly.

"Not even to his club?" Oliver asked in surprise.

"He comes straight home and dines with me," she told him. "So you had nothing to worry about."

"I'm glad to hear it," he said, though he still looked unconvinced.

"Even Oliver goes to his club occasionally." Maria cast a shy smile up at her husband. "But he never stays out late."

"No reason to," Oliver said, patting her hand. "I have all the entertainment I want at home."

Gabe and Celia snorted at that, but Minerva felt a stab of despair. Did Giles feel the same way as Oliver—that he would rather be at home with her than at his club? Or was he just keeping up appearances in these initial days? Would he soon be trotting off every night to find more amusing entertainment?

She wanted to think that her marriage would become like

her brother's in time, but Oliver and Maria were in love. Giles was not.

Still, he'd promised to be faithful. He'd also promised not to lie to her, though, and he'd broken that promise within days after their wedding.

"What's in here?" Gabe asked as they passed a closed door on their way out to the garden.

"Giles's study."

Gabe opened the door and went inside.

Giles had never said she couldn't enter it, but he'd never invited her in, either. The first time she'd breezed in, shortly after their return from Calais, he'd jolted up in his chair, shoved something into a desk drawer, then asked in a rather terse voice if there was something she'd wanted.

Later, too curious to resist, she'd gone to see what he'd been so eager to hide, but every drawer in his desk had been locked. It had reminded her with painful clarity that she wasn't privy to everything in his life. After that, she'd left it alone.

That was probably why, as her family crowded inside now, she felt uneasy. Which was absurd. It wasn't as if Giles were Bluebeard or something, hiding dead wives in his closet.

"Good God," Gabe exclaimed. "Look at this place. He's as bad as you."

Minerva blinked, then looked around at the shelves full of books organized first by category, then alphabetically by author. On his desk, the inkwell sat in a precise line with the quill holder and the wax seals. She'd thought nothing of it when she first saw it, but now she burst into laughter. It was exactly like the items on her own desk. They both preferred to keep their surroundings under strict control.

Celia chuckled. "Gabe can't imagine anyone preferring order to the chaos that is *his* desk."

Gabe scowled. "I don't like things hidden away where I can't find them."

"Which means that you think they should be strewn across every available surface," Celia shot back. She smiled at Minerva. "Personally, I find it rather sweet that you both keep your studies so tidy."

"Thank you." A pity that they kept their marriage so messy.

"Makes you wonder what you two are like in the bedroom together," Gabe muttered. "You probably make love with your eyes shut." When everyone gasped, Gabe said, "What? You know you were all thinking it."

"*I* wasn't," Freddy retorted. "I was thinking that Masters has a damned fine desk. I shall ask my father-in-law for one like that in my office. Do you know where he got it?"

Minerva wanted to kiss Freddy for changing the subject. She did *not* want to talk with her brothers about Giles's bedroom prowess, of all things.

But as she answered Freddy's question and ushered them out of Giles's office and down to the garden, she couldn't help thinking that Gabe wasn't far wrong. Giles *was* a bit too controlled in bed.

Not that he didn't give her pleasure. He knew exactly where to touch her, how to touch her, how to enthrall her, even when she didn't want to be enthralled.

Unfortunately, he did so with a curious lack of feeling, as if he were trying to win a competition. She'd kept herself aloof in an attempt to provoke him into showing some deep emotion, but it hadn't worked. It was killing her.

After her family left, promising to have her and Giles out to dinner at Halstead Hall soon, she wandered back into her husband's study. The place really did remind her of how buttoned-up and restrained he could be. Not cold or stiff, just . . . curiously unengaged.

She'd tried to wall up her own heart against him, but that hadn't worked, either. Something about the intimacy of sharing a bed with a man night after night made it difficult to keep him at arm's length.

So where did that leave her? She ran her fingers over the surface of his desk, with its locked drawers. How was she to make a man like him fall in love with her? Was that even possible?

"Madam, you have another caller."

Wondering if one of the family had returned to speak to her privately, she glanced up to see the butler, Mr. Finch, standing in the doorway with Mr. Pinter at his side.

Relief swamped her. Now she might learn enough about her recalcitrant husband to figure out a way into his heart.

With a nod at Mr. Finch, she rose. "Mr. Pinter, how good to see you. Do come in."

When Mr. Finch frowned, she gave him a frosty glance. She was married now, and there was nothing improper about her entertaining a male friend of the family in her own home, no matter what Giles's stodgy new butler might think.

"Forgive me for intruding, Mrs. Masters," Mr. Pinter said, with a furtive glance at the butler, who positively radiated disapproval. "I had thought your husband might be home. I could return later . . ."

"Nonsense. He'll be here soon." That was a blatant lie, but at least Mr. Finch didn't know it. Giles had already told her he might not be home until quite late, because of one of his trials. "Do take a seat. Mr. Finch, if you'd be so kind as to send a maid up with some tea?"

Mr. Finch seemed less disturbed, now that he'd been made to believe that Mr. Pinter wasn't calling on *her*, alone.

As soon as the butler hurried off, Minerva grabbed Mr. Pinter's arm and made him sit beside her on the settee. "Thank goodness you've come. So tell me, what exactly has my husband been up to?"

Chapter Twenty-two

Half an hour later, Minerva sat on the settee, her mind whirling with everything Mr. Pinter had told her concerning the Baron Newmarsh, a man named Sir John Sully, and the two men's connection to her husband.

"There's something else you should know," Mr. Pinter added.

She blinked. What he'd found out had already roused a million questions in her head. "Oh?"

"I've been following your husband for the past few days, wanting to see if he did anything that might explain those mysterious disappearances that your brothers were always mentioning."

"And did he?" she asked shakily.

"I'm not sure. This morning he met with Lord Ravenswood, the undersecretary of—"

"I know who he is," she said, letting out a breath. "They're friends from school."

"School friends don't meet in boathouses in Hyde Park at dawn. They don't arrive separately and part separately. They don't take great care to avoid being seen together."

She sucked in a breath. That *was* a shock. Why would they avoid being seen together when they'd been perfectly amiable at the wedding? What did it mean? "Did you happen to hear—"

"What the bloody hell are you doing here with my wife, Pinter?" growled a familiar voice from the doorway.

Both she and Mr. Pinter jerked up straight. With her heart in her throat, she looked up to find Giles standing in the doorway, glowering. Only then did she realize how it must look, the two of them seated close on the settee, whispering together, as if sharing confidences.

Then she squelched the niggle of guilt. She'd done nothing wrong. She had a right to consult with Mr. Pinter on anything she pleased. Anyway, it wasn't as if Giles really cared what she did.

Though he certainly looked as if he cared. He looked fit to be tied.

Mr. Pinter stood abruptly. "I thought I'd pay a call on the newlyweds," he lied with ease. "But you weren't here when I arrived."

Giles's anger didn't seem to diminish one jot. "So you thought that my absence gave you leave to get cozy with my wife in my own study?"

"Giles!" Minerva jumped to her feet. "Stop being rude!"

Her husband approached, his eyes narrowing to slits. "I'll be whatever I want. This is *my* house and *my* study, and you're *my* wife."

"This is *our* house," she said stoutly. "Or so I assumed when you married me."

"I . . . um . . . should go," Mr. Pinter said, edging toward the door.

"Good idea," Giles ground out, still glaring at her. Just as Mr. Pinter started to pass him, however, Giles turned and growled, "If I ever catch you alone with my wife again, I will beat you within an inch of your life, do you understand?"

"Oh, I understand you very clearly, sir," Mr. Pinter said. But as he turned to head for the door, Minerva caught a glint of amusement in his eyes.

Of course he was amused. Men always found such possessive posturing amusing in other men. Still, although she'd always thought jealousy a boorish emotion, she found it rather exciting in Giles. It was the first sign that she might mean more to him than just a convenience.

Not that she meant to let him get away with it. As soon as she heard the door close downstairs, she said, "You're being ridiculous, you know. What are you doing home so early? It's barely three o'clock."

That only seemed to anger him further. "The trial ended midday, and fool that I was, I thought I'd come spend time with my wife. Little did I know she had other plans."

"I do hope you're not implying that I was doing anything wrong."

"He was practically in your lap!"

"Nonsense. And I can scarcely believe you're jealous of Mr. Pinter."

"I'm not jealous," Giles said stubbornly.

"Then what do you call this display of masculine temper?"

Giles advanced on her with a brooding gaze, forcing her to back up. "I call it asserting my rights as a husband. You have to admit that you and he were very chummy when I came in."

"He's a friend of the family," she pointed out, not sure whether to be angry or delighted by Giles's behavior. "We've always been cordial."

"Cordial! Is that what you call it when a man is sitting far too close, whispering in your ear, nearly on the verge of pressing a kiss to your lips?"

She burst into laughter at that outrageous image of the straitlaced Mr. Pinter. "You have quite lost your mind."

"Have I?" He backed her against his bookshelves with a feverish look on his face. "You were far more friendly with him than you've been with *me* these past few days." Planting his hands on either side of her shoulders, he leaned in close. "With him you're easy and comfortable; with me you're a cool goddess, warning me to keep my distance."

Her amusement fled. "Is that so? And what about *you,* pray tell? All you do is keep your distance. So don't accuse *me* of—"

A squeak from the doorway alerted them to someone's presence. Giles pushed away from the wall and glowered at the maid, who stood mumbling apologies.

"Ah, good," Minerva said blithely. "There's the tea."

"Leave it and go, Mary," Giles ordered. "And close that damned door. We don't want to be disturbed."

"Y-yes, sir." Mary darted in to set the tray down on the desk, then fled, shutting the door behind her.

"Speak for yourself." Minerva glared at Giles. "I am perfectly happy to be disturbed when you're behaving irrationally."

"You haven't begun to see me behave irrationally, Minerva."

With a sniff, she edged past him for the door, but he blocked her path with a scowl. "I want to know what Pinter was saying to you so confidentially. How long have you been meeting secretly? Exactly how cordial *are* you two?"

She figured this wasn't the moment to reveal that she'd hired Mr. Pinter to find out his secrets. Or that she had hundreds of questions for him. Best to wait for that until he'd calmed down.

She cast him a lowering stare. "I haven't seen Mr. Pinter since the wedding, you dolt. There is certainly nothing going on between us, which you'd realize if you could ever see fit to trust me."

The words seemed to shake him. "I do trust you."

"Yes, I see how much you trust me. You think I'm having an affair with Mr. Pinter, of all people. Less than a week after our wedding. In *your* study."

He had the good sense to look uneasy. "You have to admit that the two of you appeared very—"

"Cozy? Yes, you said that. And *you* have to admit that I'd be a fool indeed to carry on a flirtation with the door open for all the servants to see. You're letting jealousy blind you to the facts."

"It's not jealousy," he protested. "I merely don't want people thinking that my wife might be . . ."

As he trailed off, she eyed him coldly. "Yes? Might be *what*? Visiting with a family friend? You have the audacity to worry about *my* actions when less than a week ago, you left me alone in a hotel to do God knows what, with little explanation?"

She pushed past him, now fully in a temper. But he grabbed her by the waist from behind and pulled her up against him to hiss in her ear, "If I ever really thought you were dallying with Pinter, I'd do more to the man than beat him up."

She hated herself for it, but the possessive edge in his voice thrilled her. "Does that mean you *don't* really think I'm dallying with Pinter?" At his hesitation, she snapped, "Well?"

His arm tightened about her waist. "All I know is that when I saw him sitting so close to you on that settee, I wanted to lay him out cold."

"You were jealous," she prodded. When he stiffened, she added, "For once in your life, be honest with yourself and me, Giles. You were jealous. Admit it."

He muttered a foul curse. "All right. I was jealous." He pressed his mouth against her ear. "I would never let another man have you. You know that, don't you?"

She hadn't known it. But she was certainly glad to know it now. "And I would never let another woman have you, so we're even on that score."

"Is that why you've been making me insane these past few days? Holding me at arm's length? Because you really thought I was with another woman in France?"

"Have I been making you insane?" she countered.

"You know you have," he ground out.

"You deserve it."

"Perhaps I do," he said in a low, husky voice, "but not for the reasons you think. I want only you, Minerva. Never believe otherwise."

"I don't know *what* to believe with you."

"Believe that I want you."

"My body, you mean."

"Not just that. All of you." Moving his hand up, he fisted it against her chest, and his voice grew ragged. "Your heart. Your mind. I want the woman you've denied me ever since France. The woman who laughs with me, who opens herself to me."

She could feel him hardening against her bottom, and it aroused her. He was different from before, more . . . impassioned. As if he really *felt* something for her. "You already have that woman, and you don't even know what to do with her."

"I know what I want to do with her right now." He flattened his hand over her breast and lowered his voice to a thick growl. "I want to take her to bed."

"No," she whispered, just to see what he would do.

"Don't deny me, love," he said in a choked voice. "Not today."

The word *love* drove her over the edge. Remembering how he'd claimed that she would never be able to "drag him about by his arousal," she said, "Very well. But only if we do it my way."

"Your way?" he echoed.

"You have to take me here. Now."

"In my *study*?" he said, clearly flummoxed by the idea.

He'd never tried to seduce her anywhere but in the bedchamber, as if keeping her there somehow kept her out of the rest of his life. Well, she was putting an end to that.

"Yes. Oh, yes." She rubbed herself against him, delighted to see that her suggestion had excited him even more. She wanted to see him lose control for once. She wanted to see *him* enthralled. "Take me like an animal, right here in your study."

"If I were to take you like an animal, darling," he rasped against her ear, "I'd bend you over my desk and take you from behind."

The minute Giles said the words, he regretted them. What was he thinking, to propose such an outrageous thing to his *wife*? She wasn't some whore, for God's sake.

So he was shocked to hear her say, "Yes. Do *that*."

His cock gave an instant response. It didn't have any problem whatsoever with the idea. "It's not . . . A man doesn't . . . not with his wife."

"Why not? Is there a separate set of rules for wives than for loose women?" She moved her bottom along his rigid flesh, and he thought he'd go out of his mind. "It's here and now, like that, or nothing. I'll sleep alone tonight if I must."

"The hell you will." So that's what she wanted, did she? Him behaving like a beast?

Then he would damned well give it to her. He tugged her over to his desk. "Why do you want to do this?" he bit out as he urged her forward until she was bent over it with her hands resting atop it.

"You said you don't want me keeping you at a distance," she whispered as he lifted her skirts. "Well, I want all of you, too. I want you as you are, not the small part of yourself you offer when you come to me in our bed. I want your heart and mind and even your soul. I want your trust."

Never trusting anyone is a hard way to live.

Damn Ravenswood for putting that thought into his head. "You want to twist me about your finger," he growled.

"Yes," she admitted without a trace of remorse.

"Bloody temptress," he muttered. Yet at the moment he didn't care. He was so hungry for her, for the *real* her, not the version she'd been giving him, that he could hardly think straight.

He fumbled to open his trousers, frantic with his need for her. The sight of her with her tender parts exposed to the air, exposed to *him,* was fueling his lust beyond endurance.

He didn't like being at her bidding, yet he did her bidding anyway. "Demanding wench. You won't rest until you have me panting at your feet like a lapdog."

Though she trembled a little in his arms, she managed a chuckle. "Somehow I can't imagine you as a lapdog. I imagine you more as a slave to my feminine charms."

At this moment, that's what he was. He spread her legs with his knee, more roughly than he should. "Given your present position, I'd say you're the one who's the slave."

He slid his fingers inside her drawers to fondle her. When he found her hot and moist and ready for him, he nearly spent his seed right there. "My God, you feel so good . . . I don't know how long I can wait to be inside you."

"Remind me again, who's the slave here?" she taunted.

"Damn you," he hissed as he jerked down her drawers, then rubbed his hard flesh against her. "You enjoy torturing me, don't you?"

"No more than . . . you enjoy torturing me." She let out a gasp when he slid into her without warning. "Night after night . . . lingering over me . . . never losing control . . ."

"I'm bloody well . . . losing control now," he rasped as he began to thrust hard, his breathing heavy and thick.

"Good," she whispered.

Teasing wench. Maddening seductress. She wanted him at her mercy, and God knows she was getting him there with this little stunt.

But he wasn't going to be alone in all this wanting. He reached under her to cup her breast, kneading it through her clothes. His other hand found her pleasure spot and worked it feverishly.

"You won't be so pleased . . . if I finish too quickly." His voice grew hoarse as he pumped into her, unable to restrain himself. "God help me, I haven't even . . . kissed you . . . sucked your lovely breasts . . ."

"I don't care! Take me quickly. Show me what you want."

"What I want is you, darling . . . so badly . . . you have no idea." The words boiled out of him, unthinking truths he couldn't help admitting. "All I think about is you. Having you. Being with you the way you were before. When you were truly mine."

"Oh, Giles," she breathed. "I've always been truly yours."

The words made him exult and panic at the same time. He couldn't stop pounding into her, holding her hips steady so he could slam into her over and over, rough and fast. His untrammeled need was apparently arousing her, for she squirmed and shimmied beneath him, her breath quickening, her body shaking.

"Forgive me, darling," he choked out, "I can't . . . I have to . . . I can't wait . . ."

He drove into her deeply, triggering her own climax, which she confirmed with her scream of pleasure. And as he poured his seed into her, his hands gripping her hips hard, he reveled at having finally broken through to the real Minerva. The one he wanted beyond all reason.

Afterward they stood there breathing heavily, like thoroughbreds after crossing the finish line. For a moment, he relished the feel of her against him, her beautiful bottom and thighs so soft that he wanted to stay cradled in them forever.

But his body was already softening. He withdrew from her, scarcely able to believe that he'd just taken his wife over his desk. It was so intensely erotic that he knew he'd be dreaming of it for nights to come.

He hoped she would be, too. "Are you all right?" he asked.

"I'm far better than all right," she murmured.

Pleased by that, he drew up her drawers, lowered her skirts, then pulled her around into his arms so he could kiss her. God, how he'd missed having her like this, eager in his arms, meeting him kiss for kiss with wild abandon.

When he drew back, the softness in her expression was a punch to his gut. "No more walls between us, all right?" he whispered.

She nodded. "No more walls." She cupped his face, pressed a kiss to his mouth, then drew back from him. "That's why it's time you tell me about Newmarsh and Sir John Sully, and what really happened that night you were gone in Calais."

Chapter Twenty-three

Minerva could tell Giles hadn't been expecting that. He stood frozen. "What . . . how did you . . ." Then understanding came over his face, and he released a bitter oath. "That's why Pinter was here. You had him investigate me."

She nodded, bracing herself for his anger.

"You told him about the theft of those papers, I suppose," he ground out, moving away from her to button up his drawers and trousers. "You risked my career and our future—"

"It wasn't a risk. He's very discreet, and I made it clear that if he ever told another soul about it, I would have his head on a platter. But I had to do something. You were never going to tell me the truth. And I had to know."

"Why?" he snapped. "Why the hell is it so important that you know everything about my life?"

"Because you know everything about mine."

A stunned look crossed his face.

"You've known it all for some time," she went on. "What you haven't learned from my family or me directly, you've deduced from my novels. Who I am. What matters to me." Her eyes filled with tears. "Yet I know nothing except the tiny bits you deign to let me see."

He dragged his fingers through his hair, clearly uncomfortable, and she pressed on. "Don't you understand? How can I be a wife to you when you keep so much of yourself secret from me? When you won't even trust me? Here you were, stealing papers to avenge your father, and you let me think—"

"Pinter told you that?" he interrupted hoarsely. "That I stole those papers because of my father?"

"Mr. Pinter said that what you stole was instrumental in bringing Sir John Sully to justice. And that your father had lost money in an investment with the man. He said that was the real reason your father killed himself."

Giles fixed her with a dark glance. "How the bloody hell did he find all that out?"

"I don't know." She met his gaze warily. "He merely said he had it on very good authority. I gathered that his informant was someone high in government. Although the man knew the role of the papers, he didn't know where they'd come from. But Mr. Pinter put it together after having heard my part of the story."

When Giles muttered a curse and glanced away from her, she went on hastily, "What you did is nothing to be ashamed of. Who could blame you for avenging your father's death? Surely you didn't think I would."

"You might," he said in a dull voice. "If you knew what the result could be."

She sucked in a breath. "You mean, because of whatever happened in Calais."

He swung a startled gaze back to her.

"Come now, Giles, I know that *something* occurred in Calais to upset you. We were having a lovely honeymoon until that last night. And Mr. Pinter told me that the government used those papers to make Newmarsh help them send Sir John to the gallows. That in exchange for his help, Newmarsh was pardoned but exiled from England and is now living in France. It can't be a coincidence that you wanted us to travel there."

Despite his curse, she pressed on. "You saw Newmarsh in Calais, didn't you? And he told you something alarming." She prayed that she'd guessed right, because if that hadn't been why Giles had insisted on hiding his actions that night, she would have to consider more upsetting possibilities.

Giles stared at her a long moment. "I should have known you'd never stay out of it. It's not in your nature to let a man be, to let him keep his failures to himself—"

"You have no failures," she protested. "I know you well enough for that."

"Then you don't know me at all." He strode to the window and stood looking out. "Newmarsh figured out that I was the one who stole the papers."

Her heart leapt into her throat. "Please tell me it wasn't what I wrote that gave it away."

"No, not that. I doubt he's ever read anything more than a racing list, much less your novels." He took a long breath. "My brother gave him a suspicion of the truth, quite by accident. And now Newmarsh is threatening to go to the press if I don't convince the government to allow him back into England."

Her stomach knotted. "Oh, Lord. How are you supposed to manage that?"

Giles was silent a long moment. "I . . . have connections that Newmarsh is hoping I'll use on his behalf."

She thought through everything Mr. Pinter had told her. "You mean Lord Ravenswood, I suppose. Is that why you met with him early this morning?"

Giles whirled away from the window. "Bloody hell, how did you know that?"

"Mr. Pinter followed you."

"Wonderful," Giles snapped. "Clearly I am slipping. I didn't even notice that the bastard was around." He cast her a look of betrayal. "Why the hell would you have Pinter do that? Bad enough that your grandmother set him on me, but to hear that my own wife has had him investigating me for God knows how long—"

"It's only been since the wedding, and I didn't tell him to follow you. He just thought he might find out for me why you're always disappearing so mysteriously." When Giles stiffened, she added hastily, "Anyway, is that why you were meeting with Lord Ravenswood secretly? You were discussing the Newmarsh problem?"

Giles hesitated, then gave a terse nod. "Ravenswood is the one who engineered the prosecution of Sully. He did it as a favor to me. And to gain justice for all those people whom Sully bilked out of their fortunes."

"Will his lordship do what you asked?" she whispered. "Will he let Newmarsh have what he wants?"

"He's going to let me know after he speaks to his superiors." Giles snorted. "But the government has a strict policy about blackmail. They don't give in to it without good reason."

"Still, judging from what Mr. Pinter told me, Lord Newmarsh is a thorough villain. Surely even if he goes to the press, people will give no credence to what he says."

"You sound just like Ravenswood," Giles snarled. "Both of you are so sure that right will win out. I have less faith in that than you. I've seen too many criminals go free for no other reason than a lack of evidence."

"Is that what worries you about Newmarsh? That he will ruin you somehow?"

"If it comes out that I stole those papers, I'll be disbarred," he bit out. "Lawyers don't look kindly on other lawyers who make cases by stealing evidence. It's illegal and arguably even punishable by death."

"Giles!"

"Oh, don't worry, they won't hang me. They'll brush it under the rug as much as they can, but disbarment is still a distinct possibility." He waved his hand about him. "This house, these furnishings . . . all of it would instantly become beyond our means. My brother will give us as large an allowance as he can afford, but we'll have to live on his largesse for the rest of our lives. If Ravenswood can't convince them to let Newmarsh return and I can't work it out otherwise, your life will be vastly different than the one I promised to you."

Understanding finally dawned. "Is that why you didn't tell me about meeting with him in Calais? Why you lied to me about where you were? Because you were worried about how I would take this news?"

"I didn't lie," he said stubbornly. "It *was* a matter of business. And yes, that's why I didn't reveal the truth. How was I supposed to tell you that our lives might be over? That your husband might be dragged through a scandal that could have you and your family once again in the papers?"

"I don't care about that!" she cried. "I only care about you."

He gave a bitter laugh. "Mere weeks ago, you called me a scoundrel and a rogue. It took me a great deal of effort to convince you otherwise. So forgive me if I didn't think you'd be thrilled to hear that I'd turned out to be the failure you already thought I was."

"I never thought you a failure," she said softly. "I just thought you reckless and heedless. Like my brothers."

"Which is exactly what this mess with Newmarsh proves me to be," he countered.

"That's not true."

He glanced away, pain slashing over his face. "I knew the law, but it didn't matter to me. I did what I pleased, for the fleeting satisfaction of gaining vengeance."

"That's not the only reason you did it, was it?" she pointed out. "You wanted to stop Sir John and Newmarsh before they could hurt others."

"But if I'd been less impetuous, I would have found a legal way to catch them. Then I would have gained a justice that was built on the law, unshakable and fair. Not a justice that was built on sand and has now come back to ruin me."

She began to see why this bothered him so. "Did Ravenswood know that you'd stolen the papers?"

His gaze slid back to her. "Yes. Why?"

"*He* has always been considered a careful man, full of good judgment. Yet he took the risk of using information illegally obtained. Because he knew that sometimes the end justifies the means."

That seemed to give him pause. "He did it because he was my friend and because—"

"It was the right thing to do." Though Giles's expression grew shuttered, she pressed on. "That's why no one used the documents in court, isn't it? So that the prosecution would be legal. Mr. Pinter said they just used the papers to force Newmarsh's hand and gain his cooperation with sending Sir John to jail. So justice *wasn't* built on sand."

"Yes, but—"

"Do you regret what you did?"

He blinked at her. "What do you mean?"

"It sounds as if you regret sending Sir John Sully to jail."

His gaze locked with hers. "I regret not doing it properly. I regret being such a thoughtless scapegrace that I didn't even attempt legal avenues. I regret thinking myself above the law. Most of all, I regret risking my entire future just to avenge a man who—"

He broke off with a curse.

"A man who didn't even care enough to stay around and take care of his own mess," she said softly. What had Giles said the day of Gabe's race? *I knew my father's faults as well as I know my own.*

Giles looked lost now. "I was like him for so many years—selfish, heedless of the cost. My brother wasn't. He knew Father would ruin us all. He watched Father making ever more reckless investments and warned me that one day we'd have to pick up the pieces."

He paced the floor. "And what was my reaction? I laughed and told him he was mad. I went on my merry way, gambling and whoring through London. I barely exerted myself in my studies—it's a miracle I was even called to the bar. The law meant little to me until the day Father . . ."

His expression chilled. "After he died and left us nearly destitute, I wanted to make up for those years, for the waste that had been my life. Newmarsh had been a friend of my father's. He convinced many of his friends to invest in Sully's scheme in exchange for part of the profits. I'd already figured that out when Newmarsh invited me to his party."

"I'm surprised that he even invited you," she put in.

A harsh laugh escaped him. "He believed me to be more concerned with pleasure than with reclaiming the family honor. He didn't think he had anything to worry about." His voice hardened. "He was wrong. I decided that his party was my chance to beat him, and I took it. Then I brought the papers to Ravenswood, and he said he would pursue justice if I'd only agree to—"

He halted, a look of chagrin crossing his face.

"If you'd only agree to what?" she prodded.

Scrubbing his hands over his face, he let out a curse.

"Giles, what did Ravenswood ask you to do?"

"I suppose there's no point in your not knowing now." He met her gaze steadily. "Ravenswood asked me to keep my eyes and ears open in society and . . . elsewhere. To give him information from time to time. To inform upon my peers." He drew in a ragged breath. "You asked about my 'mysterious disappearances'? That's what they were about."

She stared at him in shock. "You're a spy? For Ravenswood?"

"More like an informant. For the Home Office."

She just gaped at him, hardly able to believe it. All this time she'd told herself that such an idea was ludicrous. Leave it to Giles to thwart every one of her opinions about him. "For . . . for all these years? Ever since that night at the party?"

"I quit when I heard I had a chance at being King's Counsel. I thought I was done with it all until Newmarsh asked Ravenswood to have me meet with him in Calais."

"Oh, my word." The pieces fell into place at last. "That's why you could pick locks and lie so convincingly at the inn. Why you could seem like a scoundrel one moment and a responsible citizen the next."

He shrugged. "People say things to a scoundrel that they'd never say to a responsible citizen."

"So you've been acting the scoundrel to hide your *spying.*" She'd been so wrong about his true character. "Do my brothers know?"

"No one knows," he said in a warning tone. "If I'd had my way, *you* would never have known."

That wounded her. "Why not?"

"For one thing, it was in the past, and I was hoping to put

it behind me. For another, I'm not really supposed to discuss it."

"Not even with your wife?" she asked, unable to keep the hurt out of her voice.

Suddenly she remembered what he'd told her that day at the pond. *There are things in my past that I can't talk about with you. Things I've done. Things I've been. And I'll be damned if I lay them all out for you just so you won't worry that I'm like your father.*

"Especially with my wife," he said defensively. "Who has a tendency to put things about me in her novels."

"Only because I didn't know the significance of what you were doing! If I'd realized it was so important, not only to you but to the country, I would never—"

"I *told* you it was important," he snapped. "I asked you not to reveal it to anyone, and you did so anyway, all because I hurt your pride."

"It wasn't my pride you hurt," she blurted out. "I was in love with you, you dolt!"

When the words made the blood drain from his face, she cursed herself for letting him see her vulnerability. But there was no going back now.

"I was in love with you, and you broke my heart. *That* was why I wrote about you in my books."

Chapter Twenty-four

*G*iles stared at Minerva in disbelief. She'd been in love with him? "But . . . but you were only nineteen."

"Good Lord, Giles, by the time we had that kiss, I'd been in love with you for years. Ever since you were so kind to me at Mama and Papa's funeral."

"That's infatuation, not love," he protested.

"Don't tell me what love is," she said softly. "I know whether I was in love or not."

And that's when it hit him. She'd said "I *was* in love with you." Not "I *am* in love with you."

Bloody hell, why did that matter? He didn't want her to be in love with him. Did he?

She turned away from him and went over to pour herself some tea, though it had to be stone cold by now. Her hands shook as she lifted the cup to her lips. She barely took a sip before replacing the cup in its saucer.

When she spoke again, it was in a low, halting voice. "I'd practically worshipped you for half my life. I used to watch you with my brothers and pray that one day you would notice me, see me as a woman."

He'd had no idea. He tried to dredge up memories from those years, but all he could remember was how he'd wasted his life on drink and women and cards. It had been one long bacchanalia after his father had killed himself.

Her voice grew bitter. "But you never saw me as anything but the silly sister of your friends. Until that night." She faced him, tears sparkling in her eyes, and he felt something twist in his chest. "I was so happy to see you at that party. That's why I'd gone there—hoping that you would be there. I thought perhaps if you saw me in that low-cut gown, you'd desire me and fall madly in love."

"I *did* desire you in that gown," he said, wanting desperately to soothe her hurt. "You were a revelation."

She arched one eyebrow. "Just not the sort of revelation you wanted."

"Not then, no. My life was in a shambles. My father had just killed himself, and I was seeking justice for him. I'd begun to realize that I couldn't go on in my same hapless manner, but I wasn't sure how to change my path. Adding a woman to that mess would have been unconscionable."

"Then you should have said *that* to me, instead of . . ." She waved her hand. "Oh, it doesn't matter anymore. It's long in the past."

"I can tell from your face that it does matter." When she said nothing, he said, "I didn't mean to hurt you. Then or now."

"I still don't see why you couldn't have faith in my ability to keep your secrets. I understand why you didn't before, but after we were married—"

"It's hard for me to have faith in anyone," he admitted. "Ravenswood says it's because I've spent so many years playing both sides of the fence, hiding my true self from everyone, that it's become second nature to be secretive."

"That's not why," she said.

He eyed her warily. "What do you mean?"

A pitying expression crossed her face. "You don't have faith in other people because you don't have faith in yourself."

He dragged in a heavy breath. "I have faith in myself."

"If you did, you wouldn't be chastising yourself for what you did years ago. You wouldn't be calling yourself a failure for something that's out of your control now."

"It's not entirely out of my control," he bit out. He drew in a deep breath. Time to tell her the worst of it. "It's possible I could get out of this by agreeing to go on working as an informant. The government doesn't want me to quit, so if I agree to continue, they might give in to Newmarsh's demand."

"Is that what you want?"

"No, damn it! But I can't see any other way through. If I don't do it, Newmarsh may very well ruin me. Ruin *us*."

"And what does Lord Ravenswood say to that?"

Giles shook his head. "The bloody fool says that I should call Newmarsh's bluff, and trust him and his superiors to make sure nothing comes of his threats."

"Then perhaps you should listen to him." She stepped forward to cup his cheek. "I know you must have done a great deal of good for them since that night years ago. And I've seen firsthand what good you've done in the courtroom. Surely that will count for more than you think."

"Will it? I know how easily such things can all be wiped away because of politics," he said hoarsely.

"I believe we reap what we sow, and you've sown loyalty and honor and justice for many years. It's time for you to reap that harvest." She caressed his cheek. "Ravenswood clearly trusts you, and his superiors probably do as well. *I* certainly trust you. So perhaps you should consider trusting *us*, at least a little. We're not your father. We won't abandon you in your time of need, I promise."

A lump caught in his throat. "I may hold you to that promise, if I'm booted out of the legal profession and can't support you."

"I have a sizable inheritance coming to me, assuming Gabe and Celia marry. And there's my dowry—"

"I don't want your family's money," he ground out. "Not after everything they've said about my motives for marrying you."

"Well then, there's always my books," she said with a saucy smile. "Between that income and your brother's money, we can survive." Her eyes sparkled up at him. "Perhaps I'll have Rockton do something truly spectacular that will make him all the rage in literary circles."

He managed a smile, touched deeply by her willingness to do whatever it took to save him. "So that's why you made me a villain in your books? Because I broke your heart?"

She nodded.

Had her heart mended? Did she still love him? He was afraid to ask, afraid of what her answer might be. Afraid of what he *wanted* her answer to be.

Instead, he said, "And it wasn't as you told me in Calais, that you wrote about that night because you thought it would make a good story?"

"It did make a good story," she teased. "But no, that wasn't the reason. Mostly I did it to vent my anger and my hurt. I do that sometimes. It's as you said that day at the lodge—it gives me a feeling of power over what happened, even when I know I have no power."

"You had more power than you realize that night," he said softly. "I never forgot that kiss."

She dropped her hand from his face. "Don't patronize me," she whispered.

"I mean it. I still remember your gold satin gown—with something making it stick out on the sides—"

"Panniers," she said in a small voice. "They're called panniers."

"Your bosom was half bare, and you wore a blue cameo of a lady nestled between your beautiful breasts."

Her gaze shot to him. "I can't believe you remember that."

The hopeful look in her eyes fairly slayed him. "Oh, I remember it very well. I ached to put my mouth right where that cameo rested." He pulled her into his arms. "I've always noticed what you wear. At the Valentine's Day ball, you wore a pink evening gown with puffy sleeves. And I already told you how well I remember the sausage curl lying on your bosom at our house party in Berkshire."

"The party where you went off with a sultry widow, you mean?" she said tartly.

He brushed a kiss to her hair. "That was something I did for Ravenswood. He wanted me to learn what she knew about an agitator in the Commons. And I found it out for him."

"In her bed, most likely," she said with a sniff.

"I would rather have been in *your* bed," he countered, since he couldn't deny the accusation. "I wasn't lying when I told you that I imagined pulling that curl and watching your hair tumble down about your waist." He reached up to thread his fingers through her hair to tug it loose of its pins. "Like this."

He kissed her, suddenly needing to reassure himself that she'd forgiven him for that long-ago night. That she might be able to fall in love with him again. He might even want that, selfish devil that he was.

But just as he was considering laying her down on the settee, a knock came at the door to his study.

He tore his lips from hers with a low curse. "I said I wasn't to be disturbed!" he barked.

"Yes, sir," Finch said. "But this fellow from the Black Bull in Turnham insists upon seeing you."

As Giles sucked in a breath, Minerva exclaimed, "Your trap has sprung! Desmond took the bait!"

"Looks that way." And damn the bloody man for his bad timing.

Still, it would take his mind off what to do about Ravenswood and Newmarsh.

Hurrying to the door, Giles swung it open to find Finch standing there with the groom Giles had paid to keep him apprised of Desmond's actions. "Thank you, Finch," Giles said. "Saddle a horse for me. I'm riding over to Turnham."

"And one for me, too," Minerva said, struggling to pin her hair back up.

Giles scowled at her but didn't countermand the order. He wanted to hear what the groom had to say first. After Finch left, he asked, "I assume Plumtree is at the inn?"

"Aye, sir," the groom answered. "But he left almost as soon as he got there. Said he was going out to do some target shooting."

"A little late in the day to be shooting, isn't it?"

"I told him as much, sir. Plus, I didn't see him take a gun with him. Seemed right peculiar to me."

Remembering what Ravenswood had said about the map, Giles asked, "Did he by any chance take a shovel?"

The groom's eyes widened. "Aye, sir. How did you know?"

"Lucky guess. Did he have his son with him?"

"His son came in with him, but I didn't see him go out with him."

"Thank you for the information." Giles reached into his

pocket, pulled out a sovereign, and pressed it into the man's hand. "And if anyone asks—"

"I'm silent as the grave, guv'nor," the groom said. "Don't you worry none about that."

As the man left, Giles stalked over to his desk.

"What was all that about a shovel?" Minerva asked.

Giles unlocked a drawer and took out the map he'd re-created from memory. "Ravenswood found out what the map is of."

"Oh?" she asked, excitement in her voice.

"Turns out it's a copy of one in the British Museum that was found among papers belonging to Henry Mainwaring."

"The admiral?"

"And buccaneer. Some claim that it shows where he buried his treasure."

"Good Lord, it's a treasure map!" She pulled a sheet of paper out of her apron pocket and laid it beside the map he'd set on the desk.

"What's that?" he asked.

"The current map of the estate. Celia brought it to me this morning when the family came to visit." She gave him a sly smile. "I've had a busy day, between that and my wild affair with Mr. Pinter."

"Watch it, minx, I'm still chafing over that little incident."

She laughed, then turned to examining the two maps together. "I don't see how Desmond could think this a treasure map. It does have a strange marking in the center, but if I'm reading it right and it really is our estate, the marking falls in the middle of what is now the pond. If Mainwaring buried treasure there, Desmond will never find it."

Giles snorted. "I doubt there *is* any treasure. Your cousin is a fool." He unlocked another drawer.

"That's certainly true. And didn't Admiral Mainwaring die in poverty, anyway?"

"Yes." Giles pulled out the case for his dueling pistols. "But there's more to that story. After Mainwaring was pardoned by the king for his pirating and became vice admiral, there were rumors that he had a secret stash of jewels from his days as a buccaneer. Unfortunately for him, when Cromwell was on the march, Mainwaring threw in his lot with the king and was forced to flee to France once Cromwell won. He died there, which is supposedly why he never got back to England to retrieve his ill-gotten gains."

Giles removed both pistols and the bag containing shot, gunpowder, and the other necessary items. "Plumtree is mad if he thinks to find them on your family estate. Mainwaring lived in Dover. Why would he hide jewels near Halstead Hall?"

"Perhaps because he stayed there on his way out of the country," Minerva said as she ran her fingers down a line on each map.

Giles jerked his gaze up to meet hers. "What?"

"Don't you remember Gran mentioning it? He was the vice admiral who was visiting our family when he got word that Cromwell wanted his head. He went straight to the docks in London and hid on a ship captained by a friend, who slipped him out of the country. He got no chance to go home."

A chill ran down Giles's spine. Perhaps Plumtree wasn't mad. What if Mainwaring *had* buried treasure on the grounds of the estate?

No, that was absurd. "Why would Mainwaring have been carrying around a fortune in jewels while visiting friends? And even if he had, why not take it with him to France?"

"I have no idea. I'm just telling you that he did stay at Halstead Hall. I've never heard anything about any jewels."

Now Giles wished he'd followed Plumtree that day to determine exactly where the man was looking for this treasure. Because if Plumtree *was* fool enough to think that treasure was buried on the Sharpe estate, and was hunting for it on the day the Sharpes were killed . . .

Giles began to load the pistols.

"What are you doing?" Minerva asked.

"I'm not going after your cousin without weapons," he told her. "Even if he *did* only take a shovel with him."

"Do you really think that's where he's headed—to look for treasure on our estate?"

"Why not? It's the middle of summer—he's got several hours before sundown. And if I can catch him at it, I might get some answers out of him."

Folding up the two maps, she tucked them into her apron pocket. "I'm going with you."

"The hell you are." He shoved a pistol into each coat pocket and headed for the door. "Once I get to the estate, I'll fetch your brothers to help me."

"They're not at home. The whole family is spending the rest of the day in town shopping and going to the theater. No one is at Halstead Hall but the servants. You don't want to involve them and risk a lot of wild gossip being thrown about until you're certain it's necessary. You don't even know for sure that Plumtree is on the estate."

He glowered at her. "If he is, I can take care of him alone."

"Wait here one minute! Just let me change into my half-boots."

When she flew off up the stairs, he stood there debating. He didn't want her anywhere near Plumtree, especially if the man had killed the Sharpes.

He headed off toward the front door, but she caught up

to him just as he was striding down the steps to his waiting mount.

"I'm ready," she said, all out of breath as she hurried after him.

"You're not going with me."

"Oh, yes, I am."

He halted on the steps to stare at her. "Now see here, darling—"

"Don't you dare use that placating tone with *me*, Giles Masters. It never worked for my brothers, and it won't work for you. Take me with you, and I promise to do whatever you tell me." Her voice grew choked. "But I am *not* letting you go off alone to confront my cousin while I sit here for the next few hours wondering if you're dead or alive."

The worry in her face made his chest ache. "I can handle myself, love." He cupped her chin in his hand. "I've been in far more dangerous situations."

"But you don't *have* to face it alone this time." She covered his hand with her own. "Let me go. I want to help."

"If something happened to you—"

"It's Desmond, for heaven's sake—he's not exactly a criminal mastermind. And I'll stay well out of your way. Better yet, once we figure out for sure that he's on the estate and where he is exactly, then I'll go fetch you assistance."

That gave him pause.

"Please, Giles," she said, her heart in her eyes. "It's time you started trusting me, don't you think? You let me go with you when we followed Desmond and Ned to the inn, and everything turned out fine. I was even a help, wasn't I?"

"Yes, but—"

"This is no different. If anything, it's safer—you're armed this time. And if Ned happens to be with him, you won't be able to handle them both. You'll need me to go fetch someone."

"I wish I hadn't tossed Pinter out so hastily," he muttered.

"But you did, and there's no time to go after him. You don't know how long Desmond will be out there. We *have* to catch him in the act if we're to get the truth out of him."

When he still hesitated, she added, "Besides, if you don't let me go with you, I'll just follow behind."

He eyed her askance. "All right, but you do whatever I say, do you hear?"

"Yes, Giles," she said in a uncharacteristically obedient tone that he didn't trust for one second.

With a sigh, he helped her mount her horse, then sprang onto his own. "I *mean* it, Minerva." He flicked the reins to set off.

"Trust me, I won't do anything to put myself in harm's way."

Trust her? That was bloody difficult. Ravenswood might think that never trusting people was a hard way to live, but trusting them was harder. Especially when the person he was trusting was also the person he cared most about.

They rode swiftly through the streets. When they got out onto the country road leading to Ealing, they increased their pace even more. Bent on making good time, they rode in silence.

As they approached the estate, Giles slowed and began scanning the road for signs of Plumtree's gig.

"I don't see anything," Minerva said. "I do hope he hasn't left already."

Giles looked up at the sun. "I doubt it. Plenty of light left. He probably wouldn't leave his rig out where anyone could come along and spot it." He turned onto the long pathway leading to the hunting lodge. When they got within sight of the path to the pond, he saw a horse tied to a tree.

He moved his horse close enough to Minerva's to nudge her

knee and, when she glanced at him, pointed to the horse. She nodded. He pulled up, and so did she.

They both dismounted. "I'm going looking for him," he murmured. "Looks like he's alone, so I can handle him. You take the horses and go up to the hall."

"What if you need one of them here?"

"I won't. His is here, and if I happen to miss him because he's gone a different direction, I don't want him seeing a horse and realizing that someone has guessed his game. We might never have another chance to catch him doing whatever it is he's up to."

Worry showed in her face. "I hate to leave you here without a means of escape."

He smiled. "If you knew how many times I've extricated myself from dicey situations, minx, you wouldn't be so concerned."

"Still, I'll fetch a couple of brawny servants and bring them back in case Desmond proves stubborn, all right?"

Chucking her under the chin, he said, "Good girl."

He turned to leave, and she caught his arm. When he cast her a quizzical glance, she stretched up on tiptoe and kissed his mouth. "For good luck," she whispered.

Her anxious expression touched something long buried inside him. And it dawned on him that when a man didn't trust others to help him, he never got the chance to see them show concern for him, either.

His blood pounding, he gazed into her lovely face. "Answer one question for me, darling."

"Yes?"

"You said you were in love with me until I broke your heart. Since then, have you . . . That is, do you think you might someday . . ." He was a fool for asking. This wasn't the time, and no matter what she answered, it would take his focus from what he had to do. "Never mind."

But as he turned away, she whispered behind him, "Yes, I'm still in love with you. I've always been in love with you."

He froze, then kept moving, his mind awhirl. Minerva loved him. Was *in* love with him. And he realized he'd been waiting to hear those words all his life. Waiting for someone to see that he was *not* just the rascal second son, *not* only a failure who'd once ruined his brother's life and made a slew of stupid choices in his youth.

The fact that it was Minerva who saw him that way made his heart exult.

Plumtree's horse whinnied, jerking him back to the present. He had to keep his wits about him.

He searched for signs of a path into the woods other than the one to the pond, since he hadn't seen any signs of digging near there the day he and Minerva had taken their swim.

But before he even found the break in the underbrush, he heard the unmistakable sound of a shovel hitting rocky ground.

He slid his hand into his coat pocket and closed it around the handle of one pistol. Time to find out once and for all what Desmond Plumtree knew about the Sharpes' deaths.

MINERVA DIDN'T HEAD for Halstead Hall right away. For one thing, she wanted to make sure she knew exactly where Giles entered the woods, so she could find him when she returned. For another, she wondered about his reaction to what she'd said.

She knew he'd heard her. That one heart-stopping moment when he'd halted had told her that. She even understood why he might not have said anything in response. It wasn't exactly the time or place for a confession of love.

Indeed, she wasn't sure why she'd blurted it out, except that when he'd asked her about how she'd once felt, he'd looked so tense, almost doubtful of her answer. At that moment, she would have done anything to erase that look from his face.

And now he was going off to fight with Desmond, and she might never know if he felt the same.

She stiffened. No, she wouldn't think that way. He was *not* going to be hurt. He could take care of himself. He was a spy, after all.

Her husband, a secret operative for the Home Office. It boggled the mind.

Taking note of where he'd walked into the woods, she put her foot in the stirrup to mount her horse, then froze as a familiar voice said, "Well, if it isn't my dear cousin Minerva."

The bottom dropped out of her stomach as she took her foot out of the stirrup and turned to find Ned standing there, eyeing her with rank suspicion. Beyond them, a short distance back, was *his* horse. He must have spotted her and dismounted so he wouldn't alert her to his presence. That wasn't good.

"Ned!" she exclaimed, trying to sound pleased. "How lovely to see you. What are you doing here?"

"I was wondering the same thing." His gaze flicked over the horses. "Aren't you married and living in a big house in London now?"

"Can't I come home to visit?"

He narrowed his eyes on her. "This is a bit far afield, seems to me. And where's your husband gone off to?"

Did he know Giles was here, headed toward Desmond? If she lied and said that she was here with someone else, and he'd *seen* Giles, then he would know something was up.

Best not to take the chance. "He went off to find a good location for our picnic while I hold the horses. He said there's a pond near here."

"That's true. But you don't have a picnic basket."

She thought quickly. "He's got the basket with him."

"Now, why would he carry the basket when he could just leave it with you? And even if he did, why were you getting ready to mount your horse and ride off when I walked up?"

Unable to refute that, she went on the offensive. "Why are you asking all these rude questions?" she countered in the loftiest voice she could muster. "This is my home, and I can come here whenever I please, to do whatever I want. So if you'll excuse me, I'm going to see where Giles has disappeared to."

Before she could even round the horse, though, Ned stepped up to press a knife to her side. "I don't think so, cuz."

Her stomach clenched into a knot. "Ned," she said firmly, "what on earth are you doing? Put that knife away! I'm your cousin, for goodness sake!"

"Yes, and a fat lot of good that's done me. Father and I have a chance to pull the mill out of the fire, and I won't let you ruin it."

"I have no intention of ruining anything," she breathed. She couldn't fight him; he had a weapon and she didn't. He could have her gutted before she even screamed. "I don't care why you're here. You can do whatever you like, if you'll just let me go find my husband."

"We're going to go find him, all right. He could have been to the pond and back twice by now. So I expect he's not at the pond. And I expect you know that."

Oh no. Lord only knew how Giles would react to seeing Ned holding a knife on her. "We don't want any trouble. Just let me take the horses and—"

"Keep quiet, damn you! And start walking." He urged her into the woods, keeping the knife pressed in the small of her back. She considered stumbling but was afraid she might stumble the wrong way and get stabbed. Besides, a scuffle with Ned could distract Giles while he dealt with Desmond.

Ahead of her, she could hear the sound of a shovel hitting something. Desmond was probably digging, which meant Giles hadn't reached him yet. She had to give Giles time. The only way they'd both get out of this safely was if Giles took care of Desmond before she and Ned could reach them.

She walked as slowly as she could, dragging her feet, pretending to have trouble getting over the logs and rocks. "I don't know what's wrong with you. You're being ridiculous, and this is—"

"I said shut up!" he hissed. To her horror, he caught her about the waist and placed the knife to her throat. He kept whispering in her ear as he pushed her along. "You always were a meddler. Just had to shame the family with those wretched books. And Aunt Hetty doesn't even care—she still gives everything to you lot, while we don't get a damned thing."

She refrained from pointing out that his father had inherited the mill from Gran's brother. He just hadn't done as well with it as Gran had done with the brewery. "I'm sure Gran has put your family in the will for a tidy sum."

He snorted. "Not with all of you getting married and having brats. She won't leave anything for us now. We *deserve* the treasure. You've got everything else—I won't let you have that, too, you hear me? Not after how hard we've worked looking for it."

"Treasure? What are you talking about?" she said, trying to hide her terror at the thought of the knife at her throat—one slip and she could die.

"Shh," he whispered. "The digging has stopped."

It had. Did that mean Giles had heard them? That he'd found Desmond? Or was Desmond just resting?

Moments later, they emerged into a clearing to find Giles standing beside Desmond, holding a pistol to the man's head. Her cousin was sweating heavily, and the shovel lay at his feet.

As soon as Giles saw her and Ned, the blood drained from his face. His gaze met hers, bleak with worry, but when it shifted back to Ned it held deadly intent. "I see you're aiming to die, Ned," he ground out. "Or at the very least, get your father killed."

"You wouldn't dare!" Ned cried. "If you do, I'll . . . I'll slit Minerva's throat, I swear I will!"

"Then you and your father will both die." Giles drew his other pistol out of his pocket to aim it at Ned's head. "That treasure won't do you much good then, will it?"

"Stop being an idiot, son!" Desmond said hoarsely, his eyes looking stark and wild. "Let her go! She's your cousin, for God's sake!"

The knife wavered at her throat. "She gets everything," Ned said plaintively. "They all do. It's not fair!"

Giles just stared him down. "You've got no good way out of this, man. You might as well accept it and let her go."

"So you can have me and Father arrested for trespassing, or some other trumped-up charge? I saw your friends at the wedding—all those important gentlemen. You'll make sure that Father and I are ruined."

"He won't do anything to you, I promise," Minerva coaxed. "I won't let him. You're family, after all."

"That's what you say now," Ned retorted, "but as soon as I let you go, you'll have us both locked up."

"You don't think they'll lock you up for killing her, you

idiot?" Desmond cried. "They'll hang you! Stop being a fool and think, for once in your life."

At his father's insults, Ned stiffened. "Just for that, I'll take her off with me and leave you here with Masters. Let him kill you—what do I care?" He tightened his arm around her waist and began trying to urge her back the way they'd come.

"Wait!" Giles cried. "What if we agree not to turn you over to the authorities? And help you find the treasure."

"We've got a better map of the estate," Minerva said, playing on Giles's ploy. "It's in my apron pocket." If she could just get Ned to move that knife from her throat . . . "Compare it to your map, and you'll see exactly where the treasure is buried."

"How did you know about our map?" Desmond rasped.

"I've got my sources," Giles said. "And they tell me that you've got a map that leads to where Mainwaring buried some jewels."

Desmond shook his head. "Not jewels—Spanish gold, worth a fortune."

"Well, you're not going to see an ounce of it if you don't get your bloody son there to let my wife go!" Giles growled.

"Ned, please!" Desmond cried.

"That other map of yours," Ned said into her ear. "You really think you could find the gold with it?"

"I've already put them against each other to compare," she said. "It looks to me like that gold is buried right next to the pond. If you get the map out of my apron pocket, I can show you."

Ned hesitated, but greed won out. He slid his hand down to her apron pocket, letting out a grunt when he patted the outside and heard the crackle of paper. And as he slipped one hand inside the pocket, groping for the map, his other hand moved the knife away from her throat, just as she'd hoped.

In that instant, she brought the heel of her half-boot down on his instep as hard as she could and dropped to the ground.

Giles fired, the bullet whistling over her head. And Ned went down.

Chapter Twenty-five

As smoke clouded the clearing, Giles tossed his spent pistol aside and rushed over to Minerva. He'd seen the glint in her eyes moments before she'd stomped Ned's foot and had prepared himself for anything. Now his heart was about to pound right out of his chest at the thought that he might have hit her, even though Ned was the one writhing on the ground, screaming about his shoulder.

The first thing he saw when he reached her was the blood splattered all over her pretty gown. "Oh, God, Minerva!" he cried as he knelt beside her.

"I'm fine," she said. "It's all his, my love. It's not mine."

He found Ned's knife and threw it into the woods, then shoved his other pistol into his pocket so he could clutch her to him. What would he have done if he'd lost her? He wouldn't have survived it.

Suddenly she stiffened and hissed, "Giles, behind you! Desmond—"

He rolled away with her in his arms, reaching for his pistol as the shovel came down a few inches from his head. Before Desmond could lift it again, Giles pointed the pistol at him. "I swear I'll kill you," he said, letting anger take him over. "You and that damned son of yours both."

With an oath, Desmond lowered the shovel.

Giles rose, his pistol never wavering from the man.

Behind him, Ned groaned, "I'm dying, I tell you! You can't let me die!"

"You're not dying, Ned," Giles heard Minerva say. "It looks like the bullet went clean through your shoulder. You'll live."

"More's the pity," Giles bit out.

"Now hold still and let me bind it before you lose any more blood, will you?" Minerva said.

"You can let him bleed to death for all I care," Giles growled.

"He's still my cousin," she said. "And you don't need a death on your hands. Especially when you're about to become a K.C."

"She's right, Masters," Desmond said, backing away from him. "There's no reason to let any of this become public. You keep quiet about Ned's bumbling, and I'll keep quiet about your shooting him. We'll even give you some of the treasure. How's fifty percent, no, sixty percent of whatever gold we find?"

Now was his chance to figure out how this treasure hunt connected to the murders. Pretending to consider Desmond's offer, Giles said, "How can you even be sure there's any gold out here? Considering that you've been looking for it nearly twenty years—"

"No, I just started looking a few months ago. I mean, when Ned was seven and told me about finding some in the dirt, I did bring him out here to show me where, but he couldn't remember where it was, save that it was by the pond."

Giles's eyes narrowed. "Ned actually found gold out here?" Since Ned was Gabe's age, that would have been around the time of the murders.

"Yes!" Desmond cried. "It's here, I tell you. I looked for it a bit myself back then, but I never found any more so I gave it up as pointless. Then after I saw that map in the museum a few months ago, I knew Ned must have stumbled across Mainwaring's treasure."

"That's absurd," Giles said. "For one thing, Mainwaring's treasure was supposedly in jewels."

"They're wrong about that," Desmond said. "Mainwaring was a buccaneer—they all took Spanish gold. And you must admit that the map looks like this estate."

"It looks like a lot of estates."

"It's this one, damn it. I know it is!"

Suddenly they heard sounds of thrashing through the woods behind them. "What's going on here?" Stoneville cried as he burst into the clearing.

"Damn it all to hell," Desmond muttered, obviously realizing that his chance to keep the matter from being "public" had just gone up in smoke.

"Oliver!" Minerva cried. "I thought you were in town!"

Jarret rushed into the clearing, followed swiftly by Gabe. "The wives were tired, so we decided to come home. We were just heading up the drive when we heard a gunshot, and a few moments later two horses came bolting from this direction." Jarret glanced around. "Who the devil shot Ned?"

"I did," Giles answered. "He had a knife to Minerva's throat."

Stoneville lunged for the man, but Minerva held him off. "Leave him be. He's wounded."

"He'll be dead by the time we get through with him," Gabe put in.

"I wholeheartedly agree with *that* plan," Giles snapped.

"None of you are going to kill him," Minerva said. "He's simply laboring under a gross misunderstanding."

"What sort of misunderstanding?" Stoneville demanded.

Giles nodded at Desmond. "He and his father have some notion that there's a fortune in Spanish gold buried hereabouts."

As Stoneville groaned, Jarret said, "Oh, God, Ned. Tell me you're not that stupid."

"I saw the gold! Don't lie and say I didn't!" Ned cried as he struggled to a stand.

"Oh, for pity's sake, you're making it bleed more!" Minerva stood and leveled a hard glance on her brothers. "Could we continue this conversation elsewhere? Ned needs a doctor."

"He needs more than that if he thinks there's gold out here," Jarret said.

Annoyed that his wife was looking after Ned as if he were some wounded puppy, Giles gestured to Desmond to follow them.

"What does he mean about your being stupid, Ned?" Desmond asked as they trooped back through the woods. "You said there was gold here. You gave me several pieces of it."

"Then he *stole* pieces of it to give you," Gabe snapped.

"You mean from the treasure buried here—"

"There's no treasure buried here, Desmond," Stoneville said with a sigh. "There never was. The Christmas before our parents died, Father gave each of us pieces of eight from some old Spanish gold he'd won in a card game."

"I remember that!" Minerva said. "We all got ten pieces."

"Then the Plumtrees came to visit," Jarret said, taking up the tale, "and Ned was being such a brat to Celia that we . . . er . . . played a trick on him."

"Good Lord," Minerva said. "What did you three do?"

Giles had already begun figuring out what they'd done. He'd

been part of too many such "tricks" that the Sharpe brothers played on their friends.

"A trick?" Ned said hoarsely. "No, I saw you get it from the ground. You said a pirate had buried the gold. I dug through the dirt with you myself!"

"We put it there, you fool!" Gabe said. "When some of it went missing afterward, Oliver was furious. He thought Jarret and I had lost it in the dirt. But you took it, didn't you?"

"It can't be," Desmond said, his face deathly pale. "It was old gold, centuries old."

"Yes," Stoneville said. "That's what Father won. He was in one of his extravagant moods and gave some of it to us. We can show you ours, if you want."

"I can't believe it," Desmond said. "All those hours digging . . . coming out here and looking and—"

"That's what you were doing the day Minerva's parents died, wasn't it?" Giles prodded. "Digging for gold."

Everyone fell quiet as the four men surrounded Desmond.

"What happened, Desmond?" Stoneville demanded. "Did they catch you digging for it? Were you afraid they'd take the gold from you, so you shot them?"

"No!" Desmond said, true shock spreading over his face. "I had nothing to do with killing them, for God's sake! How can you even think it?"

"It's a stone's throw away," Jarret pointed out, "and we both know you were here that day. I saw you in the woods."

"And a groom at the Black Bull swore that he cleaned blood off your stirrup that very night," Giles added.

Desmond paled. "Oh God oh God oh God . . ."

"What happened, Desmond?" Stoneville growled. "If we prosecute Ned, he'll hang for stealing that much gold. Not to mention his attempt on Minerva's life. So Ned is going to the gallows if you don't tell us the truth now. How did the blood get on your stirrup?"

"I found them dead, all right?" Desmond cried. "I found Pru and Lewis after they were shot."

"You found them," Jarret repeated skeptically.

"I was out here looking for the gold when I heard the shots," Desmond babbled. "I went running to see what had happened, and I noticed that the door to the hunting lodge was ajar. So I . . . went in and saw the blood and fled."

"A likely tale," Gabe snapped.

"If I'd shot them for catching me digging, don't you think I would have shot them in the woods?" Desmond cried. "Why would I have done it over there in the hunting lodge?"

He had a point. And Giles had always thought it rather far-fetched that a milksop like Desmond would have committed cold-blooded murder.

"Besides," Desmond went on, "at that point I wasn't even sure there *was* any gold. All I had was my seven-year-old son's tales of it, and no evidence beyond what he'd claimed to have found. I certainly wouldn't have been mad enough to shoot someone over *that*." He glanced around at his cousins' murderous expressions, and cried, "I swear it! I had nothing to do with it!"

"Did you see who *did* shoot them?" Stoneville asked.

Desmond shook his head.

Giles brandished the gun at him. "You're lying." He'd spent too many years sifting lies from truth in people's tales not to recognize a lie when he heard one. "Who did you see?"

Desmond's gaze dropped to the pistol. "I swear, all I saw was someone on a horse."

"Describe who you saw," Giles prodded.

"I . . . I . . . can't be sure . . . it was dusk . . ."

"If you want me to keep your son from hanging, Desmond . . ." Giles began.

"Whoever it was wore a cloak!" he said, his voice desperate. "I-I couldn't even tell if it was a man or a woman."

"Describe the cloak then," Giles demanded.

"I-it was black and had a hood. Or perhaps dark blue. I'm not sure. It was getting too dark to see by that time."

"And the horse?" Giles asked.

Desmond glanced around at the four men. "A black Arabian with a blaze face. And one white stocking on the left hind leg."

Stoneville glared at him. "All these years, and you never told anyone about this. We could have been looking for their murderer, for God's sake!"

"No!" Desmond protested. "You don't understand. The one I saw on the horse was riding *toward* the lodge."

That stymied them all. "Toward?" Giles asked.

"Yes. I was in the drawing room when I heard a horse approaching. I looked out the window and saw the rider heading toward the lodge. So I went out the back and got right out of there. Didn't want whoever was coming to think I'd killed them, you see."

"Could it have been you, Oliver?" Jarret asked. "You were the one to find them."

"No, I was with Gran," Oliver reminded him. "And we came at night. Desmond just said he heard the shots right before dusk."

"All I know is that the horse was from *your* stables," Desmond said. "That much I remember."

"He's right," Gabe said grimly. "We had a horse just like that."

"If someone came upon them right after they died, why didn't the person say anything?" Stoneville said.

"For the same reason as Desmond, probably," Minerva said. She stood outside the circle, still supporting Ned, who was looking decidedly peaked. "For fear they might be accused of their deaths."

"Whoever it was must have been going there for a reason, though," Jarret pointed out. "He might have known why Mother and Father were there—might even have been going to join them. We should find out who it was."

"That won't be easy," Giles said. "Any of the guests at the house party could have taken that horse out of the stables."

"Not just guests," Minerva pointed out. "With so many people on the estate, a complete stranger could probably have taken a horse, and the grooms might not have realized he wasn't with the guests."

"Or she," Jarret said. "Let's not rule out a woman. So now we're back to needing to question the grooms. Assuming Pinter can track them all down."

Ned moaned, and Minerva said, "We can talk about this more later. We've got to get Ned back to the house and fetch a doctor. I don't want my husband having to endure a trial for murder, even if he *was* defending me."

That galvanized her brothers into action. They hoisted Ned onto Desmond's horse, and Stoneville led it toward the mansion. Giles kept his pistol trained on Desmond as the brothers continued to pepper him with questions about what he'd seen in the hunting lodge.

Regrettably, he hadn't seen enough to be useful. So Minerva mentioned Giles's visit there, and despite the grumbling from Stoneville about her meddling, Giles laid out everything he'd noticed. That sparked more discussion about their parents' deaths.

Stoneville promised to have Pinter out to Halstead Hall first thing the next morning so they could give the runner the new information and see what more he could learn.

They'd finally reached the house, where two very anxious wives and Minerva's grandmother came running out to learn what had happened.

While Minerva sent a servant off to fetch a doctor for Ned, Hetty Plumtree demanded to hear the whole story. Once they were done telling her everything, she rounded on Desmond with the fury of a lioness protecting her cubs. "How dare you come onto my grandson's property and try to steal what wasn't yours!"

"There wasn't anything to steal!" Desmond cried. "They told you—it was a misunderstanding."

"The only misunderstanding was in their not coming to me first, to let me know what they suspected of you. If I'd heard any of this, I would have demanded answers of you. Hell, I would have had your head!"

"You were ill, Mrs. Plumtree," Giles put in. "Your grandsons didn't want to worry you."

She shot him a dark glance. "And *you,* young man, helping them keep all this from me! I thought you were on my side!"

"I am," Giles said. When Minerva raised an eyebrow at him, he added, "Sort of."

"Then call me Gran like the rest of them," she said with a sniff. "You're part of the family now." Then she marched over to where Ned had been laid on a settee to await the doctor. "But *you,* my own great-nephew. How dare you pull a knife on your own cousin!"

"I had to!" he protested. "She was going to ruin everything, she and that damned husband of hers."

"Stop cursing! And stop your whining, too. I have done everything I could to help your father, and he repays me by filling your ears with poison and teaching you to hate your cousins. He started out in this world with plenty of advantages: my brother left him a perfectly good cotton mill. It is not anyone else's fault that Desmond has frittered it all away with bad management. For God's sake, he even hires children to run his mills!"

"It's the only way I can make it pay," Desmond complained.

"Nonsense. I make the brewery pay, and there are no children working there," she snapped. She leveled a hard glance at both of the Plumtrees. "So what am I to do with you two? I cannot have you continuing this sort of nonsense simply because you resent your cousins."

"You could hand them over to the authorities," Oliver drawled. "I'd be all for that."

"So would I," Giles added.

She shot them a quelling glance. "And have everyone talking about us in the papers again? Not on your life. I am finally getting your names out of the gossip rags, and I mean to keep them out."

"Besides, prosecuting them would make Cousin Bertha and the other children suffer, too," Minerva pointed out, "which hardly seems fair, since they didn't do anything. If you ask me, you should let Ned and Desmond both go home."

At the storm of protest that rose around her, she cried, "Let me finish! What if we agree not to prosecute them in exchange for Desmond agreeing to stop using children to run his mill?"

That gave everyone pause. Personally, Giles would rather have watched Ned hang, but he knew his tenderhearted wife would never stand for it. And he was beginning to think she had a better instinct about these things than he did.

"That sounds like a fine proposal to me," Gran said.

"Now see here," Desmond complained. "How can I run my mill without workers?"

"Try hiring workers of a respectable age and paying them a decent wage," Jarret drawled. "It works rather well for the brewery." A cold smile touched Jarret's lips. "In fact, I am willing to agree to the arrangement Minerva proposes, providing that I get to oversee its implementation. Doesn't that sound enjoyable, Desmond? Me and you and young Ned working together in Rochester to help your mill run more successfully?"

Jarret's expression of ruthless intent made Giles stifle a laugh. Jarret might help the mill in the end, but he would make Desmond's life a living hell first.

Desmond looked as if he might protest again. Then he glanced around at the men gathered there and drew himself up stiffly. "That would be fine, cousin."

Apparently Desmond had some brains after all. He knew when he was being handed a reprieve he didn't deserve.

Just then, the doctor arrived from Ealing. After examining Ned, he confirmed that the injury wasn't too severe. He treated the wound and pronounced Ned capable of being taken back to the inn in Turnham; he promised to look in on him there.

Once a coach had been dispatched to return the Plumtrees to Turnham so they could pack up and leave for Rochester, Gran announced that it was well past time for dinner.

As they all settled around the table, Jarret glanced over at Minerva. "How did you and Giles even know that Desmond and Ned were here? Or where to find them?"

Minerva launched into an explanation, but when she got to the part about Ned holding a knife on her, Stoneville scowled. "You shouldn't have let her come with you, Masters."

"Have any of you ever successfully said no to Minerva?" Giles drawled.

Though a profound silence was his answer, he had to agree with his brother-in-law. He'd never been so terrified in all his life as when he'd seen her come through the woods in Ned's power.

"I only agreed to let her come when she threatened to follow me," Giles went on. "Besides, she promised to do as I ordered. Sadly, I believed her."

"I *did* do as you ordered!" Minerva protested. "I was just mounting the horse to leave when Ned surprised me."

"I don't know, Masters," Jarret said, "seems to me that you may not be the man for Minerva after all. She's a lot for any man to handle, and if you can't keep her safe . . ."

Despite knowing that Jarret was joking, Giles bristled. "I'd like to see how well *you* handle the woman you love when she insists upon—"

"Giles!" Minerva cried.

"What?" he snapped. He glanced at her to find her gazing at him with a sweet softness in her eyes, and it dawned on him what he'd just said. *The woman you love.*

Well, of course he loved her. He'd known that the moment he'd seen Ned with the knife to her throat. How could he not? She was his other half. The woman who could follow him into danger and still keep her wits about her, who could shock him by proposing an outrageous sexual encounter, and warm his heart with her generosity to a cousin who didn't deserve it.

Yes, loving her was risky as hell. But since he'd spent the last nine years taking risks for Ravenswood, perhaps it was time to take one big risk for himself.

He looked over to see Oliver watching him with an eyebrow

raised. "And another one falls," Oliver said softly. "She's got you now, man."

Giles smiled at Minerva, putting all the love he felt for her into his gaze. "Yes, I believe she does."

When she beamed at him, he let the warmth of it steal into his heart and heat the parts that he'd hidden away from the sun for so long.

"Well, all I can say is thank God Giles managed to hit something for once with that pistol of his," Gabe said. "Didn't know you had it in you, old chap. You've never been that good with firearms."

"He's better than you think, Gabe," Minerva said hotly as she served herself some trout. "He's just been trying not to show you three up all these years, so you'd agree to let him court me."

As her brothers laughed, she met Giles's bemused gaze with a smile that showed she understood how hard it had been for him, pretending to be incompetent, playing the fool, never seeming to care. And now he wondered why he'd taken so long to let her see the real him. There was something incredibly satisfying about being recognized for who he truly was by the person who had his heart.

He didn't want to give that up. He *wouldn't* give it up. To hell with Newmarsh. It was time he had his own life, even if he lived it in a garret. As long as he had Minerva, that was all he needed. Today had shown him that life was too short not to take personal risks once in a while. The kind that meant putting one's faith in the people one trusted and loved.

Much later, he and Minerva left beneath a bright moon, having refused everyone's urging that they stay at Halstead Hall for the night. He wanted to be at home in his own bed, making love to his wife.

As they set off down the drive, Minerva glanced over at him. "Did you mean it?"

He didn't have to ask what she was talking about. "Do you think I'd lie about something like that in front of your brothers?" he countered.

"Giles! I want an answer, not another question."

"Of course I meant it. I love you, Minerva. I love that you believe in me no matter what. I love how you take whatever you see and distill it into your books. I love your clever mind and your generous heart and every inch of your beautiful body. I love you even when you give me heart failure by risking your life before my very eyes." He smiled tenderly. "I only hope that in time I can prove worthy of your love."

"You saved my life. That already qualifies you as 'worthy' of my love."

He remained silent a long moment, thinking through what to say. "Minerva, I've decided that if Ravenswood's superiors refuse to give in to Newmarsh's demand, I'll abide by their decision and take my lumps, whatever they might be. No more spying for me."

"Good," she said stoutly, to his surprise.

"You do realize that I'm risking the possibility of losing everything by doing so."

"You risk losing everything by *not* doing so," she pointed out. "Because if you keep on having a secret other life, you give no one the chance to really know your true character. I think that would be very lonely, don't you?"

"I think I have a very wise wife," he answered with a smile.

"Well, of course. Isn't that why you married me?"

"No. I married you because you looked so fetching in your wet shift that day at the pond that I momentarily lost my mind."

She laughed, then cast him a sly glance. "You know, that pond isn't terribly far away. What do you say to having a swim in the moonlight?"

His blood ran high at the thought. "Naked?"

"Why, Mr. Masters, what a wicked and perfectly delicious idea."

He glanced at the dark woods, then grinned. "I'll race you there."

Chapter Twenty-six

Minerva and Giles waited for Lord Ravenswood inside the Hyde Park boathouse a week after their confrontation with Desmond and Ned. She was nervous, but apparently he was not.

Giles was full of surprises like that. Though he couldn't tell her much of what he'd done for the Home Office, he'd been able to tell her some of *how* he'd done it, and his ingenuity and sheer brashness never ceased to amaze her. Not to mention, entertain her. Indeed, their shared knowledge of that part of his life had become their private joke. Whenever someone asked her how it felt to be married to such a notorious scoundrel, she told the truth—it felt marvelous. The way he'd announced his love for her in front of her whole family still warmed her heart.

She was rapidly discovering that the only place her husband was really a scoundrel was in the bedchamber. He worked hard at being a barrister. He kept meticulous records and read huge tomes with titles like *A Complete Collection of State Trials and Proceedings for High Treason and Other Crimes and Misdemeanors from the Earliest Period to the Year 1783* that came in twenty-one-volume sets. He spent long hours poring over precedents and evidence. That was fine with her, since she needed those hours to write.

But occasionally, she thought him a bit *too* diligent. This meeting was clear evidence of that. He'd driven her mad with all his preparations to make sure they weren't followed. No doubt he was still chafing over the fact that Pinter had shadowed him twice without his knowing.

"Giles?" she asked, when the silence became unbearable.

"Yes, love?"

"You really have no idea why Lord Ravenswood wants this meeting?"

"None. Last week, when he met me to tell me what his superiors had decided, he gave no indication that he'd want to meet again."

"And you're sure he said they wouldn't do as Newmarsh asked?"

"Yes."

"But there hasn't been even a whisper in the papers about you. Is it possible they changed their minds?"

"No. They probably just haven't told Newmarsh yet."

She sighed. "Right. I suppose the mails to France aren't swift." She gazed at his dear face. "You know, if you really *want* to keep on working for Lord Ravenswood, I'll understand."

He fixed her with a piercing glance. "So you'd be fine with my spending nights at the gaming tables, dandling taproom maids on my knee, and pretending to spend huge sums of money all over town, so I can coax some suspicious character into spilling his secrets."

"Well, no, but I don't want to see you suffer in the papers, either. Or be disbarred. I know how you love the law."

"Do you know what I love?" he said, taking her hands in his. "You. And our life together. I won't trade that for anything." He chucked her under the chin. "And didn't you say it was time I trust someone other than myself? That's what I'm doing—trusting Ravenswood. Just be aware that it might be something of a bumpy ride."

"I knew I was in for a bumpy ride the day I married you," she told him.

He kissed her, and that's how Lord Ravenswood found them when he entered.

She pulled away from her husband, blushing furiously. Lord Ravenswood looked equally discomfited. She wondered if Giles had even told the undersecretary she was coming to their meeting.

"You remember my wife, Minerva, don't you, Ravenswood?" Giles said, calm as ever, while his lordship continued to stare at her in surprise.

The viscount smoothed his features into solemnity. "Of course." He bowed slightly. "How are you this morning, Mrs. Masters?"

"Anxious about my husband's future," she said, slipping her hand into the crook of Giles's elbow. "I do hope you and your superiors have considered how hard he's worked through the years and what he's gone through."

"So you decided to tell her about all that, did you?" Lord Ravenswood said to Giles.

"Only in the briefest terms."

"He's very discreet," she put in. "It took him years to tell me about Lord Newmarsh, even though I saw Giles take his papers."

That so startled Lord Ravenswood that she glanced at Giles, worried even though they'd agreed beforehand to her revealing it. Giles patted her hand reassuringly.

"So you *are* Rockton!" Lord Ravenswood exclaimed.

Giles winced. "Don't remind me."

"Oh no!" Minerva cried. "You guessed?"

"Only because I knew the details of the theft," Lord Ravenswood said. "But if I were you, Mrs. Masters, I'd reconsider using your husband's past as fodder for your fiction."

"Duly noted, sir," she said, a little mortified that he'd caught on to her game. She would have much preferred that Rockton remain a private joke between her and Giles.

"Well then, I won't keep you in suspense," Lord Ravenswood said. "I thought you'd like to know that you needn't worry about Newmarsh anymore."

Giles's arm tensed beneath her hand. "Oh?"

"I paid him a visit in France. I pointed out that if he exposed everything concerning him and Sully, then he would force the government's hand and we would have to revoke his pardon. I offered instead to allow him to come to the Isle of Man."

"The Isle of Man?" Minerva asked.

Giles's face lit up. "Technically, it's not British. It's an English Dependency, not the same thing. He wouldn't be returning to England. He'd still be fulfilling the terms of his pardon, and the government would not be giving in to blackmail."

"His mother lives outside Liverpool," Lord Ravenswood continued, "which is a short steam packet ride from the Isle of Man. He agreed that she would be able to manage that trip despite her age. I told him it was the closest he'd get to being home, and I pointed out that pursuing a vendetta against you would devastate his mother, perhaps even hasten her death. That all he would accomplish was to vent his spleen." Lord Ravenswood smiled. "He saw the wisdom of that advice, and agreed to my offer."

"You called his bluff," Giles said.

"In a fashion."

Minerva glanced up at Giles to see his eyes misting over.

Only then did she realize how deeply he'd feared the outcome of Newmarsh's threats. He had never let on. But then, that was Giles.

"Thank you," he said in a choked voice as he seized Lord Ravenswood's hand and pumped it furiously. "You don't know what you've done."

"Oh, I think I do," Lord Ravenswood said. "I've just ensured that the Crown has an excellent King's Counsel on the bench. At least that's how my superiors look at it."

As soon as he was gone, Giles lifted her in the air and swung her around. "We're free, darling! The past is really in the past this time."

She laughed giddily as he lowered her to the ground. "You see what happens when you trust people? Sometimes they come through."

"I have you to thank for this," he said.

"In what way?"

"You made me want to change my life so badly, I was willing to take a chance. And as a result, I got everything I wanted."

Looping her arms about his neck, she smiled up at him. "Well, that's only fair, since I got everything *I* wanted."

"You mean being forced into marriage to a scoundrel, thus losing your opportunity to thumb your nose at your grandmother's demands?"

She thrust out her chin. "I was *not* forced into marriage, I'll have you know. I wanted to marry you from the time I was nine. It just took me a while to get there."

"About that," he said, a sudden gleam in his eye. "I've been thinking about you and the novels, and it's occurred to me that perhaps you didn't just write them because you were angry at me. Perhaps, deep down, you were hoping I'd read them and behave exactly as I did."

She searched her heart and realized he was probably right. The books with Rockton in them had almost certainly been her cry to him—*see me, notice me, love me.* "So you've uncovered my dastardly plan. Oh dear."

He drew her into his arms. "But perhaps there was even more to it than that. Perhaps I didn't tell you the truth that night because I *wanted* you to wonder about it and keep me in your mind all those years. Perhaps it was all just part of *my* dastardly plan to woo a most reluctant lady."

"My, my," she said with a grin, "that really *is* a convoluted plot. You should be an author."

"No thank you. I'm perfectly content to be married to one." He shot her a teasing look. "But you may use it in a book sometime, if you want."

And as he took her in his arms and kissed her oh so sweetly, she smiled to herself, partly in joy, and partly with pleasure at what he would never know.

She would be using all of this in a book. He wouldn't recognize it, nor would anyone else. Sometimes she wouldn't even recognize it herself. But it would be there—the danger, the fights, her mad family . . . the love. Because the best things in life always deserved celebrating.

And how better to celebrate them than in a book?

Epilogue

Two weeks had passed since Lord Ravenswood had told Minerva and Giles the good news. It was Gabe's birthday, so Minerva had dragged Giles out to Halstead Hall for a weekend visit. But Giles suspected she had an ulterior motive.

And he was right. Her book was finished. And now she had forced him *and* Maria, the biggest supporter of her novels, to sit in separate rooms reading her only two copies of it at one sitting. She'd practically locked them in, begging them to tell her what they honestly thought once they were done.

He supposed he couldn't blame her. Ever since he'd been made a King's Counsel, time was something he could ill afford. But reading her latest made him nervous—if he hated it, how was he to tell her?

The further he read, the more nervous he got. After reading a few hours, he poked his head out of the door of Oliver's study to find Minerva sitting in a chair reading someone else's novel as she waited for their verdicts.

She glanced up in surprise. "You're done already?"

"Halfway through. I thought you were going to kill Rockton off. It's looking more and more like he's the hero of this particular book."

"He is."

"But do you think it's wise to—"

"Keep reading."

With a shrug, he went back into the study and closed the door. It was a good book, but he couldn't believe what she was doing with Rockton. He kept waiting for her story to head in another direction, but it soon became clear that she was doing the unthinkable.

It was nearly evening when he finished, and when he came out into the hall he got right to the point. "I can't believe you didn't kill him. I kept waiting for the ax to fall, and it never came!"

She watched him warily. "I never said for sure I was going to kill him."

"So you married him off instead?" He shook the manuscript at her. "To a woman named *Miranda*? Don't you think people will notice how close the name 'Miranda' is to 'Minerva'?"

Before she could answer, Maria came running up. "This is so *sweet* of you!" She hugged Minerva. "You gave Rockton a wife just like *me*!"

Minerva smirked at Giles over her shoulder, but all he could do was gape at Maria. Couldn't she see that it was about him and Minerva? It was so obvious!

Maria drew back, wiping tears from her eyes. "Oliver will be so touched that you reformed him."

"I seriously doubt that," Giles muttered.

"Oh, but he will! He's always been a little hurt that Minerva would portray him as such a rank villain. And now he gets to be the hero! It's truly delicious, Minerva." She smiled shyly. "I like to think that I played a small part in your decision to reform him in the book."

"Absolutely," Minerva said, casting Giles a minxish glance. He snorted.

"It's hard not to notice that the heroine is short and plump—just like me," Maria said. "And that *is* why you named his heroine Miranda, isn't it? Because I like Shakespeare? And for the *M* in my name, too, of course."

"Of course," she said cheerily.

The little liar.

Clutching the manuscript to her chest, Maria gave a sad sigh. "But I suppose this means there will be no more Rockton in the books."

"I'm afraid not." Minerva glanced at Giles, eyes gleaming. "Reformed villains don't have the same oomph, you know. I'll have to find a new favorite villain." As Giles raised his eyes heavenward she added, "Originally, I considered just killing him off—"

"Oh, no! That would have been awful. Your readers would never have stood for that." Maria patted the manuscript. "But they'll love this. It's truly wonderful. And parts of it were so poignant, even poetic. Some of your best writing ever."

"Thank you," Minerva said, glowing beneath the compliments.

Pressing a kiss to Minerva's cheek, Maria said, "I have to go tell Oliver. He'll want to read it, too."

And off she went.

As soon as she left, Giles approached his wife with a dark scowl. "You *knew* she would react that way."

The chit had the audacity to laugh. "I had some idea, yes."

"And I suppose your other readers will do the same. Everyone will say it's about Oliver and how his new wife reformed him. Rockton will forever become your brother in readers' minds."

Her eyes twinkled at him. "Probably."

"They're not going to guess that it's you and me at all, are they?"

"Probably not."

"So why didn't you warn me before I read it?" He tossed the manuscript onto a hall table. "I lost half a lifetime when I saw you'd named his heroine Miranda. Clearly you're trying to give me heart failure so you can run off with Pinter."

Her running off with Pinter had become their little joke, though Giles still bristled a bit whenever he saw the fellow.

"But tell me honestly—what did you think of the book?" she asked.

"Well, you gave Rockton far too little to do for my taste, and his heroine should have been taller, but all in all . . ." He paused just to torture her, then laughed when she made a face. "It was a splendid novel."

"So you liked it?" she pressed him.

"Of course I liked it. You wrote it."

Cocking her head to one side, she eyed him with suspicion. "You're not just saying that to be nice, are you?"

"Darling, if I've learned anything in the past few months, it's that lying to a woman as clever as you is just asking for trouble."

"Because you end up as a villain in my books?" she teased.

"Because I break your heart. There was one scene that I know was drawn from life—the one where Rockton lies to Miranda and hurts her deeply. I even know when you wrote it. In Calais, right?"

"Giles—"

"It's all right. I understand." He drew her into his arms. "But I want you to know I will never again give you cause to write a scene like that. You'll have to find something else for your inspiration. I may annoy you or frustrate you or make you want to scream—but I will never break your heart again. That's a solemn promise."

Her eyes bright with tears, she looped her arms about his neck. "I know. I trust you."

He kissed her thoroughly, wondering how he'd been so lucky as to snag this woman, whom he loved more than life, who made his days sparkle and his nights soar.

When he drew back, heat shone in her face, and her eyes held a mischievous glint. "Now, about your making me want to scream—"

He burst into laughter. Then he took her upstairs to their bedchamber and did precisely that.

The Hellions of Halstead Hall . . .

See how it all began

with

The Truth About Lord Stoneville

and

A Hellion in Her Bed

by *New York Times* bestselling author

Sabrina Jeffries

Now available from Pocket Books

The Truth About Lord Stoneville

A sudden cry of "Stop! Thief! Stop him!" from inside the house jerked Maria up short. Oh no, surely Freddy had not . . . he wouldn't have . . .

But of course he would have. Freddy didn't think.

Racing up the steps with sword in hand, she hurtled inside just in time to see a man block Freddy's path on a staircase as Freddy clasped the satchel to his chest like a shield.

"We've got you now, thief," said the man.

Her heart plummeted into her stomach.

Several steps above Freddy stood their quarry, red-faced and half-dressed, and behind him other men crowded around the stairs to see what was happening. Meanwhile, women in various stages of undress emerged into the hall.

"Polly, go fetch the constable," the man called to one of the women.

Oh no! This was a disaster!

The two men closed in on Freddy, with him stammering that he just "wanted a look at it, is all."

Hefting Freddy's sword, she brandished it at the nearest fellow. "Let him go! Or I swear I'll spit you like an orange!"

To her right, a voice drawled, "An *orange*? That's your dire threat, my dear?"

Panic seized her as she caught sight of the tall man who'd emerged from the front room. He wore no coat, waistcoat, or cravat and his shirt was opened down to the middle of his chest, but his commanding air said he would be in control of any situation, regardless of his attire. And he stood much too close.

"Stay back!" She swung the sword at him, praying she could actually use the curst thing. She hadn't realized that swords were so heavy. "I merely want my cousin, sir, and then we'll leave."

"Her 'cousin' tried to steal my satchel, my lord," cried their quarry.

My lord? Her pulse faltered. The tall fellow didn't *look* like the elegant men she'd imagined from Miss Sharpe's novels, though he did seem to possess their arrogance. But his skin was darker than she would expect, and his eyes bore a deadly glint that shot a chill down her spine. If he was a lord, then she and Freddy were in even bigger trouble.

"You take the woman, Lord Stoneville," said the other fellow, "and we'll seize the man. We'll hold the thieves until the constable arrives."

"We're not thieves!" She swung the sword between the two men, her arm aching from its weight as she glared at the man at the top of the stairs. "You're the thief, sir. That satchel belongs to my fiancé. Doesn't it, Freddy?"

"I'm not sure," Freddy squeaked. "I had to bring it into the hall to get a look at it. Then this fellow started shouting, and I didn't know what to do but run."

"A likely tale," their quarry sneered.

"I tell you what, Tate," Lord Stoneville said, "if Miss . . ."

When he arched one raven eyebrow at her, she answered without thinking, "Butterfield. Maria Butterfield."

"If Miss Butterfield will hand me the sword, I promise to arbitrate this little dispute to everyone's satisfaction."

As if she could trust a half-dressed lord in a brothel to arbitrate anything fairly. The English lords in books fell into two categories—honorable gentlemen and debauched villains. This man seemed more of the villain variety, and she wasn't fool enough to put herself into that sort of man's power.

"I have a better plan." With her heart thundering in her chest, she darted forward to thrust the point of the sword at Lord Stoneville's neck. "Either you tell them to let my cousin go, or you'll be wearing this sword in your throat."

He didn't even flinch. An unholy amusement lit his face as he closed his hand around the blade. "There's no chance of that, my dear."

She froze, afraid to move for fear of slicing his fingers.

"Listen well, Miss Butterfield," he went on in a voice of frightening calm. "You're already guilty of attempted theft, not to mention assaulting a peer. Both crimes are punishable by hanging. I'm willing to be reasonable about the assault, but only if you release the sword. In exchange, I'll let you argue for yourself and your 'cousin' concerning the theft." He said the word "cousin" with skeptical sarcasm. "We'll sort this out, and if I'm satisfied you're blameless of theft, you and your companion will be free to go. Understand?"

He had her now, and clearly he knew it. If she hurt him, her life would be worth nothing among this crowd.

Trying not to let her fear show, she said, "Do you swear on your honor as a gentleman to let us go if we explain everything?" If he agreed to be reasonable, then perhaps he wasn't a villain. Besides, he gave her little choice.

A faint smile quirked up his lips. "I swear it. On my honor as a gentleman."

She glanced to Freddy, who looked as if he might faint. Then she met Lord Stoneville's gaze. "Very well. We have an agreement."

"Excellent," Oliver said, releasing a breath. Until that moment, he hadn't been sure he would prevail. Any woman brave enough to thrust a blade at him was unpredictable at best, and dangerous at worst. "On the count of three, we both release the sword. All right?"

She nodded, her blue gaze dipping to where her hand gripped the hilt.

"One. Two. Three," he counted.

The sword clattered to the floor.

Instantly, Porter and Tate seized the stripling she'd called Freddy. When the chap let out a cry, she whirled toward them in alarm. Oliver bent to retrieve the sword, then handed it off to Polly, the brothel owner, who carried it to safety.

"Bring him in here," Oliver ordered, nodding toward the parlor as he caught hold of Miss Butterfield's arm and urged her in that direction.

"You needn't manhandle me," she hissed, though she didn't fight him.

"Trust me, Miss Butterfield, you'll know when I'm manhandling you." He stopped before a chair. "Sit," he commanded, pushing her into it. "And try to restrain your urge to attack people for half a moment, will you?"

"I was not—"

"As for you," he growled at her companion, "give me the satchel that caused all this furor."

"Yes, sir . . . I mean, my lord."

Oliver took the satchel from the young man, whose face was drained of all color. Clearly, he lacked his companion's fierceness.

The satchel appeared ordinary—made of decent leather, with the usual brass fittings. Though it contained a number of banknotes, that didn't necessarily mean the lad had been trying to steal it. Most thieves would have removed the money and left the satchel, if only to keep from alerting anyone.

"Where did you get this, Tate?" Oliver asked.

"At the pawnshop round the corner. I bought it months ago."

When Miss Butterfield snorted, Oliver shot her a dark glance. "You claim that it belongs to your fiancé?"

"If you'll check the lettering," she said loftily, "I daresay you'll find his initials, 'NJH,' stamped on one side, and the words 'New Bedford Ships' on the other. I had it specially made for him myself."

"Did you now?" Though she was right about the lettering, it didn't prove much. A couple of clever Newgate birds would have scouted the item before attempting to steal it. They would already know what was engraved on it.

Still, this pair didn't seem like Newgate birds. They dressed too well for that, in what looked like deep mourning. New Bedford was in America, and they were definitely American, judging from their accents.

That might account for the chit's boldness. He'd always heard that American women were saucy. But saucy was one thing; bold enough to brave a brothel and put a blade to a man's throat was quite another. They might merely be a higher class of thief. If so, wearing black was a nice touch. Who would suspect a woman in mourning of anything criminal?

Especially one who was so very pretty. Tendrils of strawberry-blond hair framed her lovely face beneath her bonnet of raven silk and crepe. She had a pert nose, freckled cheeks, and a mouth made for seduction. He skimmed his gaze down her form with the expert eye of a man long used to undressing women. Beneath the heavy fabric of her redingote, she clearly had a body made for seduction, too, with lush hips and lusher breasts. Exactly his sort.

Hmmm . . .

Perhaps he could use this situation to his advantage. He'd had little luck this week in finding a whore acceptable enough to further his plan.

He turned to Porter and Tate. "Release the lad, and leave us."

"Now see here, my lord, I don't think—" Porter began.

"They'll get their just deserts," Oliver asserted. "You won't have cause for complaint."

"And what about my satchel?" Tate pressed.

"*Your* satchel!" Miss Butterfield shot to her feet. "How dare—"

"Sit down, Miss Butterfield," Oliver ordered with a stern glance. "If I were you, I'd hold my tongue just now."

She colored, but did as he commanded.

Oliver tossed the satchel to Tate. "Take it and go. I'll let you know my decision about these two shortly."

Out of the corner of his eye, he could see the American woman bristle, but she remained silent until the two men had gone, closing the door behind them.

Then she exploded out of the chair to glare at him. "That satchel belongs to my fiancé, and you know it! Mr. Tate clearly stole—"

"I've been acquainted with Tate for years, madam. He has his faults, but he's no thief. If he said he bought it at a pawnshop, odds are that he did."

"You would take his word over the word of a lady?"

"A *lady*. Is that what you are?" He cast her a dismissive glance as he buttoned up his shirt. "You vault into a brothel with only this unlicked cub for a protector. You hold a sword to my throat and attempt to extract him from the place by force. And you expect me to accept your word about the situation simply because you're female?" He gestured at the hapless Freddy, who stood frozen in terror. "You must think me as stupid as your 'cousin' there."

She marched up to him, hands on her hips. "Stop sneering the word 'cousin.' Freddy is not some accomplice in crime."

"Then why is *he* with you, instead of your supposed fiancé?"

"My fiancé is missing!" She took a steadying breath. "His name is Nathan Hyatt, and he's my father's business partner. We came to London to find him. Papa died after Nathan left, so he needs to return home and run New Bedford Ships. I wrote him several letters, but he hasn't answered in months. I recognized his satchel when I saw your friend carrying it near where Nathan was last seen, and we followed him, hoping he might lead us to Nathan."

"Ah." He strolled to where his cravat lay draped over a chair, then knotted it about his neck. "And I'm supposed to believe this Banbury tale because . . ."

"Because it's true! Ask the people at London Maritime! Nathan came here four months ago to negotiate with them for some ships, but they said that after negotiations fell through within a month, he left there and hasn't been seen since. They assumed he'd gone back to America. And the owner of the boardinghouse where he'd been staying said much the same."

She paced the room in clear agitation. "But there's no

record of him traveling on a company ship. Worse yet, the boardinghouse owner still has all my letters—unopened."

Whirling around, she cast him a concerned glance. "Something dreadful has happened to him, and your friend likely knows it. Nathan would never pawn that satchel. I gave it to him for Christmas—he wouldn't have parted with it!"

Her distress was quite convincing. He'd lived in or near London all his life and had seen sharpers and schemers by the score. They could never quite hide the hardness beneath the smooth surface of their roles. Whereas she . . .

His gaze took in her agitated breaths, her worried expression. She seemed an innocent in every sense of the word. One advantage to having a black heart was that he could spot an innocent from a hundred feet off.

She was probably telling the truth. Indeed, it would be pointless for her to lie, since he could always hold her here while he confirmed her story. But he didn't intend to do that. Her tale of woe made her even more perfect for his plan.

Still, before he proposed his unorthodox arrangement, he should find out exactly what he might be getting into. "How old are you?"

She blinked. "I'm twenty-six. What has that got to do with anything?"

So, she was an innocent but not a child, thank God. Gran would be suspicious if he brought home some chit fresh from the schoolroom.

"And your father owns a ship company," he said as he donned his waistcoat. A rich man had connections. That could be a problem.

"Owned. Yes." She thrust out her chin. "His name is Adam Butterfield. Ask anyone in the shipping industry about him—they all knew him."

"But do they know *you* is the question, my dear."

"What's that supposed to mean?"

"So far you've given me no evidence that you're his daughter." He buttoned up his waistcoat. "Have you letters of introduction to smooth your way here?"

She thrust out her chin with a mutinous air. "I didn't expect to need such a thing. I expected to find Nathan at London Maritime."

"You can ask at the shipping office," the stripling put in helpfully. "They'll tell you what ship we came here on."

"They'll tell me what ship Miss Butterfield and Mister Frederick came on," Oliver interjected as he slid into his coat. "But unless the captain introduced you to them as such, that isn't much evidence."

"You think we're lying?" she said, outrage flaring in her face.

No, but he'd gain nothing by letting her realize it. "I'm merely pointing out that you've given me no reason to believe you. I imagine that America is little different from England in certain respects: ship company owners have a station to uphold. And since I assume that your father was wealthy—"

"Oh, yes," Freddy put in. "Uncle Adam had pots and pots of money."

"Yet his daughter could not send someone to find her fiancé, like any respectable female would do?"

"I was worried about him!" she cried. "And . . . well, right now Papa's money is all tied up in the estate, which can't be settled without Nathan."

Ah. Better and better. "So you're here virtually alone, with no money, despite your claim to have a rich father and a certain station in society." He fished for more information. "You expect me to believe that the daughter of a wealthy ship company owner—who would be taught to keep quiet, do as she is told, and respect the proprieties—would go sailing across the ocean in search of her fiancé, looking for him in a brothel, attacking the first gentleman who dares to question—"

"Oh, for pity's sake," she snapped. "I told you why I did all that."

"Besides," her companion put in, "Uncle Adam isn't . . . *wasn't* like other rich gentlemen. He started out a soldier in the Marine Corps. He never put on airs. Always said he was born the poor bastard of a servant, and he'd die the rich bastard of a servant, and that was better than being a rich ass."

She groaned. "Freddy, please, you're not helping."

"So you see, sir," Freddy went on, to Oliver's vast amusement, "Mop— Maria isn't like other women. She's like her father. She doesn't listen to those who tell her to sit still and keep quiet. Never has."

"I noticed," Oliver said dryly. It was a point in her favor. "And what of her mother? Did she not teach your cousin to behave?"

"I'll have you know, sir—" Miss Butterfield began.

"Oh, she died in childbirth," young Freddy explained. "And anyway, she was only a shopkeeper's daughter herself, like Ma, her sister. Uncle Adam took us in after Pa died, so Ma could raise Maria. That's why I came here with her." He puffed out his chest. "To protect her."

"You're doing a fine job, too," Oliver said sarcastically.

"Leave him be," Miss Butterfield said, her eyes alight. "Can't you tell he wasn't trying to steal anything? He went in for *me*, to check the satchel and see if it had the right lettering on it— that's all."

"And was caught running out of the place with it. That's why those men out there want him hanged."

"Then they're fools. Anyone can tell that Freddy is no thief."

"She's right about that," the dull-witted Freddy put in helpfully. "I've got two left feet—can't go anywhere without running into something. That's probably why they caught me."

"Ah, but in cases like this, the fools generally prevail. Those fellows out there don't care about the truth. They just want your cousin's blood."

Panic showed in her face. "You mustn't let them have it!"

He stifled a smile. "I *could* put in a good word for him, soothe their tempers and get you two out of this with your necks attached. If . . ."

She instantly stiffened. "If what?"

"If you accept my proposition."

A fetching blush spread over her pretty cheeks. "I shan't give up my virtue, even to save my neck."

"Did I say anything about giving up your virtue?"

She blinked. "Well . . . no. But given the kind of man you are—"

"And what kind is that?" This should be amusing.

"You know." She tipped up her chin. "The kind who spends his time in brothels. I've heard all about you English lords and your debauchery."

"I don't want your virtue, my dear." He flicked his glance down her delectable body and suppressed a sigh. "Not that I don't find the idea tempting, but right now I have more urgent concerns."

And no man of rank was fool enough to seduce a virgin—that was the surest way to end up leg-shackled to a schemer. Besides, he preferred experienced women. They knew how to pleasure a man without plaguing him about his feelings.

"This may surprise you," he went on, "but I rarely have

trouble finding women to join me willingly in bed. I've no need to force a pretty thief there."

"I'm not a thief!"

"Frankly, I don't care if you are. The important thing is that you suit my purpose perfectly."

She had the same brash temperament as his sisters, which Gran had always deplored. She had the sort of upbringing that Americans seemed to prize and Englishmen to despise. A mother who'd been a shop-keeper's daughter, and a father who'd been an illegitimate American of no consequence? Who'd fought in the very revolution that had cost Gran her only son? He couldn't ask for better.

Best of all, the chit was in trouble—which meant she wouldn't cost him a small fortune, unlike the whore he'd planned to hire. But since he'd met her in a brothel, he could still use that to thwart Gran.

He strode up to her. "You see, my grandmother and I are engaged in a battle that I intend to win. You can help me. So in exchange for my extracting you and Freddy from this delicate situation, I'll require that you do something for me."

A wary expression crossed her face. "What?"

He smiled at the thought of Gran's reaction when he brought her home. "Pretend to be my fiancée."

A Hellion in Her Bed

Jarret cast the man a sharp glance to find him eyeing Annabel with a more than neighborly interest. The alien feeling of possessiveness that welled up in him shook him. So did the sudden murderous rage he felt when Allsopp ran his gaze down her body.

The man had a wife, damn it! He shouldn't be looking at Annabel like that. *No* one should be looking at her like that. Only with great effort did he squelch the warning that sprang to his lips. Instead he said, "It's rather surprising that she's never married."

Allsopp downed his punch. "It's not for lack of proposals. I understand she's turned down two or three men who offered marriage."

That flummoxed him. Apparently he wasn't the only man who didn't meet Annabel's lofty standards. While that should have soothed his pride, it raised more questions, instead. Why would a woman so obviously sensual and capable of a deep love for children avoid marriage?

"Perhaps she stays at home to care for her brother," Jarret ventured.

"Well, he needs looking after, to be sure."

Something in the snide way Allsopp said it raised Jarret's suspicious. "You mean, because of his illness."

Allsopp laughed. "Is that what they're calling it these days?"

Jarret went still. Forcing himself to sound nonchalant, he said, "No, I suppose not." He held his breath, hoping the man would go on. If he asked him point-blank what he meant, Allsopp was liable to close up.

"Of course, we don't tolerate drunkenness the way you lords do. There's nothing wrong with having a tipple from time to time, but when a man neglects his business because he's drowning himself in a bottle, we can't overlook that."

A lead ball dropped into the pit of Jarret's stomach. Was *that* what Annabel had been hiding all this time?

But perhaps he shouldn't trust the word of a competitor who might have sniffed out Jarret's real reason for coming here. "I didn't realize my friend's problem had become so pronounced," he said smoothly. "The ladies said he was ill, and I assumed that was the reason for his negligence of late."

"Well, of course they aren't going to tell *you* the truth. It would be embarrassing. They've tried to hide it from everyone." Allsopp snorted. "As if that will work in a town as small as this. People talk. Servants talk. Does the man look ill to you?"

He nodded toward the dance floor, where Lake was dancing a reel quite competently for someone who'd supposedly been under the influence of laudanum only hours ago.

Then again, Lake *had* been asleep in the middle of the day. Who but an ill man did that?

A man who's been up drinking all night.

Confound it all to hell. Now other pieces fell into place—George's discomfort at the subject of his father's illness. Annabel's alarm when he'd said he was traveling to Burton to look at the company. Mrs. Lake's nervousness. He'd known all along they were hiding *something*. And clearly it wasn't that Mr. Lake was mortally ill.

He should have guessed. This wasn't London, and men in the provinces didn't abandon one of their own simply because he was ill. They made allowances, attempted to help the man's family, showed a neighborly concern for his condition.

But a drunk garnered no such sympathy—especially in the more conservative circles of tradesmen. He was seen as weak and unstable, which of course he was. His family was pitied, or worse, ostracized.

Anger swelled in his chest. A mortal illness could have been handled. It would have been problematic but manageable. But this was far more dicey. If Lake had lost the confidence of his fellow brewers due to a character flaw, how the hell was Jarret supposed to convince the East India captains to place orders for his pale ale?

If Lake had been on the edge of death, Jarret could have convinced the man to put Annabel in charge. Geordie would have inherited, and Annabel could have managed Geordie. But a drunk was unpredictable and untrustworthy. And anyone getting into bed with him would be deemed untrustworthy, too, or a fool.

Either way, it would be a disastrous association. Plumtree was already struggling—teaming up with a company on the brink of disaster could very well push it off the cliff. How could he have been so stupid? He'd let Annabel's talk of a quick solution to the bad market seduce him into taking a foolish risk.

No, he'd let the thought of having her in his bed seduce him. And now the company would suffer, because he could never pass up a good wager. Because he had wanted her.

Still wanted her, damn it all to hell. "How long has Lake been neglecting his company?" he bit out.

"A year, at least. From what I hear, he started drinking

heavily after the Russian tariffs began to affect business. He began showing losses, and he couldn't handle the pressure. Or so I assume. Since then, only the efforts of Miss Lake and his brewery manager have kept the place together. Granted, Miss Lake will do just about anything to save her father's brewery, but she's a woman, after all, and she—"

"—can't effectively run a brewery that she doesn't own, can she?" said a stricken female voice behind them.

They turned to find Annabel standing there, ashen-faced, acute shame showing in every line of those beautiful features. When she glanced to him, guilt flashed in her eyes.

And he knew for sure then that everything Allsopp said was true.

A cold fury seized him, turning his heart to ice. She'd lied to him, knowing full well how it would affect his interest in the project. She'd used his sympathy for an ill man against him. For all he knew, even her kisses had been feigned to make him go along with her brother's scheme. *Her* scheme.

Miss Lake will do just about anything to save her father's brewery.

And he'd followed her lead blindly, like some besotted idiot. When was he going to learn? Caring about someone was the surest way to pain and loss. And the loss of the Annabel he'd thought he could trust was the cruelest blow yet.

"Miss Lake," Allsopp said after a moment's horrible silence, "I'm so sorry. I did not see you there."

"Clearly," she choked out.

Despite everything, her devastated expression tugged at his sympathies. He tamped that impulse down ruthlessly. She was a lying schemer, and he wanted no part of her.

But when he turned to walk away, she stepped forward to lay a hand on his arm. "I came to fetch his lordship for the waltz," she told Allsopp, her hand digging into Jarret's arm in a silent plea. "He asked me earlier to save it for him."

It was a bold move, and one that showed her resourcefulness, since he most decidedly had *not* asked her to dance, knowing that it would only heighten his urge to carry her off and swive her senseless.

For half a second, he considered calling her a liar to her face. But he couldn't put aside years of good breeding that easily, even for a lady who'd turned out to be a schemer. Especially when those damned soft eyes of hers quietly beseeched him.

Lying eyes, he reminded himself. She'd known all along that he was taking a great risk, and had willfully hidden the truth from him. She'd called *him* irresponsible? She'd railed against *him* for being a gambler? She had some nerve.

Very well. They would dance. And he would make it clear that he was done with her and Lake Ale, wager or no wager. He'd not agreed to *this*.

They walked to the dance floor in silence, both aware that others were nearby. Only when the music started and he had her in his arms did she venture to speak.

"I suppose you want the truth now."

"What a novel idea," he said coldly. "Yes, let's do have the truth. If you even know what such a thing is."

"Jarret, please don't be angry."

"All this time, you've played me for a fool—"

"No! I believed—I still believe—that investing in pale ale will save the brewery. But I knew you'd never consider helping us if you thought—"

"That your brother was incompetent? That he'd destroyed his own company by drinking himself into a stupor every day?" He cast her an icy glance, not caring one whit that half of the dancers in the assembly room were straining to see what was going on between them. "You're damned right I wouldn't have considered it."

He swung her into a turn so swiftly that she nearly stumbled, and he had to force himself to pay attention to the music, to keep his fury in check. It felt like a herculean task, which was astonishing. He'd always prided himself on being able to control his temper.

When he could speak again, he hissed, "Plumtree Brewery depends on me *not* to take unnecessary risks and *not* to drag it into the same pit your brother has dragged his company into. If you think I'll go along with your idiocy now that you've lured me up here with your sad tale of a sick brother, you're out of your mind."

"Lured you here!" Her eyes flashed at him. "*You're* the one who suggested that wager. The wager you lost. The wager you've apparently decided to renege on."

His temper ratcheted higher. "That wager was based on false pretenses, as you well know. As far as I'm concerned, that makes the whole bloody thing null and void."

They danced in silence for several moments, him going through the motions and her fixing her gaze beyond his head as they stepped and swirled and whirled in time, like two automatons turned by metal gears.

Then she shifted her gaze to lock with his. "What if we were to make the wager again—only this time, without the false pretenses?"

The steely glint in her eyes told him she was serious. And the instant response of his pulse told him he was just as swayed by the idea as he had been last time.

Angry at the way his body betrayed him, he opened his mouth to tell her to go to hell. Instead he said, "What do you mean?"

But he knew what she meant. Why was he letting her think he'd even consider it?

Because after everything, he still wanted her in his bed. And he deserved to have her, too! She'd lied to him and manipulated him. He at least ought to get something out of this damned mess.

"The exact same wager," she replied. "If I win our card game, you help Lake Ale with the East India Company. If you win, I . . ." She cast a furtive glance around them.

He bent close to whisper, "Share my bed for a night. Say it."

She turned her head the half inch it took to whisper, "I'll share your bed for a night. Same terms as before."

He drew back to stare at her. Her cheeks were pink, but that stubborn chin of hers was set defiantly. His temper flared again at the realization of how much she was willing to sacrifice for a brewery.

But it's no more than Gran was willing to sacrifice. Annabel has a family to save, too.

When that thought roused unwanted sympathy, he scowled. She wouldn't give up her innocence to a *scapegrace* like him without being sure of getting something for it. This had to be some new scheme. . . .

"An excellent plan, my dear. Either way, you get what you want. If you win, you gain my help with the brewery. And if I win, you go running to your brother about how I've ruined you, and next thing I know I'm wearing a leg shackle, and I'll have you and your brother's brewery on my hands for good."

She gaped at him. "What a horrible thing to say! I would never—"

"No? And why should I believe that, pray tell?"

Her gaze dropped to his cravat, the color of her cheeks

deepening. "Because it's impossible to ruin what is already ruined."

She'd said it so softly he wasn't sure he'd heard her right. "What?"

"Don't make me repeat it," she told him, sotto voce. "I had a fiancé, remember? We were young and impetuous and in love. You can guess the rest." She brought her gaze up to his. "Why do you think I've never married? Because no man wants an unchaste bride."

He searched her face, but the very fact that she was telling him this lent it truth. And she'd been far too comfortable with their intimacies, too knowledgeable about things no virgin should know.

"So," he said, trying to take it in, "more lies are unmasked."

Her eyes flashed fire. "I never lied to you about that. You never asked. You merely assumed that I was . . . what you thought."

The words made him grit his teeth, but she was right. She'd never once claimed to be an innocent. And even if she had, he could hardly blame her. That wasn't something a woman revealed about herself to just anyone.

"Does your brother know?" he asked.

"Yes."

"How could he—"

"I've said all I'm going to say on that subject." Her blush had spread to the tops of her breasts—her quite exposed breasts, which he suddenly realized he could plunder to his heart's content if he accepted her proposal. *And* won the card game.

Damn, how could he be considering this? Making foolish wagers with her had already landed him in trouble once.

And yet . . .

This was his chance to extract payment for her lying to him, for scheming to bring him here in the first place. And it wasn't really a risk this time, because he would make sure the odds were stacked in his favor.

"So are you willing?" she whispered.

"I have some conditions."

Her eyes widened.

"This time we play piquet."

"Why?"

"That should be obvious. It relies far more on skill than chance." And piquet was *his* game. His eyes narrowed on her. "Do you know how to play?"

"I do," she said, but her voice quavered.

Good. It was about bloody time he got some advantage.

He tightened his grip on her waist. There was no way in hell he would lose *this* game. There'd be no distractions, no Masters and Gabe making remarks that tore his attention from the cards.

"And we play one game only," he went on. "Winner takes all. I've already wasted enough time on this scheme of yours as it is."

She lifted her chin. "All right."

There it was again—the understated "all right" that never failed to turn his blood to fire. "You agree to both conditions?"

She nodded.

They took another turn about the floor as he weighed his choices. He could throw her proposal in her face, walk out of here tonight, and not look back. But when he won, he'd finally have some compensation for her deception. And he wanted that compensation. *Christ*, how he wanted it.

What's more, he deserved it, for all the times she'd kissed him and let him caress her without its meaning *anything* to her. She'd made it quite clear he wasn't acceptable as a husband, yet she'd refused to let them continue as lovers. And with no reason, given she was unchaste. So she'd probably been trying to reel him in, to get him so besotted with her that he wouldn't care what lies she'd told him. And that possibility infuriated him.

"I do have one request before you give me your answer."

"You don't get a request," he clipped out.

"The only time that Rupert and I . . . Well, he took . . . precautions against certain eventualities. If you win the wager, I would ask that you do the same."

"I can do that," he said.

She swallowed. "Does that mean you accept the wager?"

He paused, but it was a sure thing. And he'd never been one to pass up a sure thing.

"Yes." The waltz was coming to an end, and they probably would not get another chance to speak privately. "Where and when will this game take place?"

"One A.M. at the office in the brewery. We had to let our evening staff go, so Lake Ale will be closed, but I have a key." The music stopped and they stepped back, her to curtsy, him to bow. "I'll wait for you inside."

As he took her arm to lead her from the floor, she murmured, "And I would appreciate it if you could try not to be seen on your way there."

"Don't worry. No one will ever learn of this from me."

"Thank you. I'm still considered respectable by my neighbors here."

Her tone pricked his conscience, but he frowned it away. As far as he was concerned, she'd made her bed. And now that she'd done so, *he* damned well was going to lie in it.

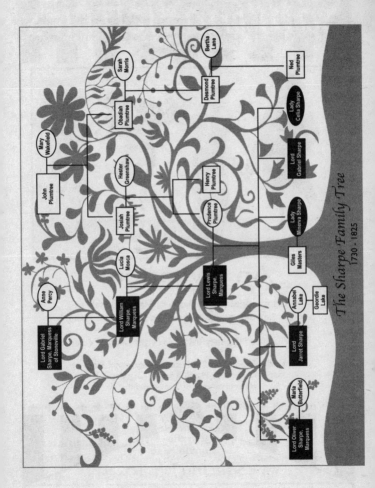

The Sharpe Family Tree
1730 - 1825